A Timeless Tapestry

KRISTEN SCHULTE

Copyright © 2023 Kristen Schulte

All rights reserved.

Printed in the United States of America.

No part of this book may be used or reproduced in any form whatsoever without written permissions of the copyright owner, except in the case of brief quotations in critical articles or reviews.

A Timeless Tapestry is a work of fiction. Any references to movies, names, characters, businesses, organizations, places, events and incidents either are the product of the author's imagination or are used fictitiously. Any resemblance to actual persons, living or dead, events or locales is entirely coincidental.

Independently published.

Cover design by Avery Daisy Book Design

ISBN: (paperback) 979-8-3303-3607-4

DEDICATION

Dedicated to the resilient spirits who find strength in the stories and joy in the dance of words.

In loving memory of my grandparents, Betty and Roy, whose timeless love and legacy will always stay with me.

A Timeless Tapestry

ALSO BY KRISTEN SCHULTE

THE LA VIE EN ROSE SERIES:
La Vie En Rose
City of Roses

1
ROGER
LOCATION: DECATUR, IL
YEAR: 1948

Love has a way of conquering all, of showing us a light at the end of the tunnel. It is beautiful, tragic, magical, and confusing. We love hard because we know that the one thing we can always find, no matter what, at the end of the day, is that love brings us together.

It was 1948, I had never seen someone so beautiful and elegant. I knew at that moment she was the one. Her name was Birdie Godwin.

She was walking across campus, and I couldn't take my eyes off of her. She swiftly made her way to the grand oak doors.

She was on a mission, but I knew I had to talk to her first. First semester of Sophomore year at Millikin University was coming to an end, as students hustled their way in between classes, and whispers of going home for the holidays. My curiosity was piqued about Birdie's plans.

She was a sorority girl, and I was there on a football scholarship.

Maybe it was fate. Maybe I knew it didn't matter what happened next—she was going to be mine, one way or another. I knew I had to play my cards right. I couldn't walk up to her. I had to plan it right. I had to make sure she noticed me in the best way.

Birdie wasn't any kind of lady. Her beauty came from her heart and soul. My goodness, she was so captivating. We had spoken only a few times whenever my fraternity, Sigma Alpha Epsilon and her sorority, Zeta Tau Alpha, got together. She was a cheerleader—every football game we'd get together. On Friday nights, we'd gather at a local diner. I'd watch her in a booth, sipping on a chocolate milkshake. She'd smile and laugh, and I swear her eyes would light up.

Birdie has this ability to elevate herself with both her kindness, her attitude, and the way she loves with complete strength.

She was astonishing in every way possible. I had never met anyone like her. Birdie had this amazing ability to show nothing short of grace towards everyone around her. She was easy to talk to and fun to be around.

I remember the first night I talked to her and how it changed my life for the better. It was during her sorority's house party. I noticed her walking from room to room, making conversation with everyone.

I believe there is beauty in being a good listener, and Birdie knew how to make connections. She found joy in everything and was able to see things from a new perspective. Her eyes made everyone feel safe.

I was outside on the deck with some buddies when she walked out and walked right up to me. She caught me off guard, boldly saying, "I know you've been watching me, Roger. When are you going to take me on a proper date?"

I stood there speechless. She stole more than my plan; she stole my heart, and I didn't mind, it was the best kind of thief.

I admired her boldness and set my beer down on the wooden fence. With a grin, I said, "How does Saturday night at 18:00 sound?"

Military time clung to my thoughts like a shadow that never left, shaping how I saw the hours. Birdie, insightful as ever, understood its language. With a Marine for a father, she moved through 18:00 as effortlessly as turning a page in a well-read book.

"Well, Roger, it's about time. I'll be ready by six on Saturday evening. Will you come by to pick me up?" Birdie responded.

"Ms. Godwin, you can count on me to be at your doorstep at 18:00 sharp. Prepare yourself for an unforgettable evening," I said, taking a sip of my beer.

She smiled back at me, grabbed my beer right out of my hand and said, "It's a date. But you should stop drinking if you're going to be well enough to take me out."

Birdie was a flower, every petal, bright and beautiful. I couldn't let her slip away from me. Some might see the signs plain as day, but for me, it was something much deeper.

She wore red lipstick, her auburn hair was curled, and I was the lucky one. I knew then, I would never be the same.

Lord, she had my heart. She had all of me. I believe meeting someone is a divine pleasure. Regardless of where this may lead, I am ready for the dance of my life. I am ready to know who Birdie Godwin is. I want to know so much about her but I plan to take my time. I'm trying my best not to form any opinion of her. I'm going to let her develop like an old polaroid photograph, nice and slow. Maybe she's the love of my life, a lifelong friend, the most nurturing and warm person. Either way, I am grateful for the day I met Birdie Godwin.

2
BIRDIE

The first glimpse of Roger Scott struck me like a whisper of curiosity, a gentle stirring that hinted at the potential for something more.

We were in college and it was the place where my love story with Roger took flight, quite literally for him. As I pursued my passion for English, dreaming of a future in the world of publishing, Roger was charting his course as a pilot. Our paths collided in the cozy corners of the university library, where pages turned and dreams unfolded. I noticed Roger, he was immersed in aeronautical charts, his eyes reflecting the vastness of the skies he aspired to conquer.

Intrigued by his determination and drawn to the adventure in his soul, I tried to muster up the courage to strike up a conversation but decided against. But that's the funny thing about fate. It will throw you into the Lion's den whether you like it or not. And each day after the library moment, Roger and I were always somehow in the same place at the same time.

It wasn't until Zeta Tau Alpha's party I finally became brave. Little did I know our first real conversation would set the stage for a love story that spanned the pages of books and the heights of the atmosphere.

He was the most handsome man I had ever seen. His blond slicked back hair, he looked like James Dean, standing there in his white t-shirt. I was mesmerized by his ocean eyes. I thought for a moment I was daydreaming. But there he stood on the deck of my sorority house. It would be untrue to say it was a crush. I believe if any one juncture in time anchored our souls, creating a tether to this plane of reality, it would be the moment I fell in love with Roger. I am in love with all that he is.

The truth is, I have heard fancier words. I have beheld more gracious faces. I have been offered fine gifts of gold. But it was Roger who was always real. He didn't need to give me gifts or buy me anything. He was the real deal. He was my real thing, the one who I loved without measure. He gave even when it was prudent to keep more in reserve. And I believe, in this carnival of life, you are not the carousel of painted horses or Ferris wheels that spin. We come as the rock beneath the frantic feet of the revelers.

Meeting Roger was providence. It was truly the first

time in my life I felt I was someone and I could be someone. He was my soul elevator. And all I could hope for was that I was the same to him.

I recollect that day vividly. I marched right up to him, looked him square in the eye, and told him to quit looking at me unless he intended to ask me out properly. I knew if I didn't speak up, he would simply keep watching me from afar, and as a lady, I couldn't stand idly by and let that happen. I wanted him to be bold, but I suppose I'll have to make the first move. He was a catch, but I knew I was even better. Together, we could make something remarkable.

We were right out of central casting—him, the handsome jock, and me, the cheerleader. We were perfect for each other—on paper.

But I had to know if our love story could be more than fiction. It wasn't about our status—no, it was something deeper than that. Because Roger had something special. I could see it in his eyes. I observed Roger's smile, noting how it widened effortlessly, like a sunbeam breaking through clouds after a storm. Whether he was conversing with a professor or exchanging pleasantries with the janitor sweeping the floors, Roger's approach was consistently genuine and respectful. His eyes sparkled with interest as he leaned in, hanging onto every word spoken as if it held the key to a hidden treasure.

In those fleeting moments of connection, it wasn't the recipient who felt valued; it was as if Roger possessed a unique gift for making everyone in his orbit feel truly seen and appreciated. For a brief moment, I felt like the belle of the ball, with all eyes on me. That's the effect he had on me. And that's why I couldn't pass up the opportunity—I needed to ensure he took me out properly. I had to know if these feelings were genuine. If not, I'd turn the page and forget about him. But for the present, I had to see if it was more than a fleeting fancy.

Roger arrived precisely at six o'clock, as he promised. It was the final week before Thanksgiving break, and I was leaving the following day to visit my family upstate in New York. He had arranged a picnic in the park—simple and charming, especially for a first date. We laid down the picnic blanket. He had sparkling cider, and we cheered as if we had been toasting for forty years. Amid the autumnal browns seemed to calm both our spirits, he was the warmth. I didn't feel the cold Illinois wind, or notice the fine mist, or the students wandering past. Truthfully, I was blind to life beyond the trees that formed the wall of the park. You could say I was smitten, and I wondered if he could love as deeply as I.

But I don't dare speak of love. It's the thing neither of us could speak, especially so early on. But it was in our laughter, in the soft way we touched, in the gaze that lingered when we parted. Roger was the one. He always was.

As we packed up the remnants of our picnic, the sky turned a dusky pink, signaling the approach of evening. I felt a pang of sadness knowing I would be leaving the next day, but also a thrill at the thought of what might come. Roger walked me back to the sorority house, our fingers brushing occasionally, each touch a promise of what could be. When we said our goodbyes on the steps of the house, there was a lingering hesitation, a silent acknowledgment that something had begun that night—something both exciting and uncertain.

I lay in my room that night, with the memory of our time together replaying in my mind. The warmth of the cider and the gentleness of Roger's presence were like a comforting blanket against the chill of separation. I closed my eyes, hoping this feeling was the beginning, that what we had shared in that moment would be the foundation of something enduring. As I lay there, the warmth of his kiss lingering in my thoughts, I couldn't help but imagine the chapters of our story yet to be written.

Each moment with Roger felt like a promise of more—of shared dreams, of overcoming trials, and of building a life together. With a hopeful heart, I drifted off to sleep, eager for the future and what it might hold for us. The night seemed to hum with possibilities, as if the stars themselves were whispering tales of our burgeoning romance. In the quiet solitude of my room, I embraced the serenity of the night, comforted by the thought our love, though young, was poised to be as resilient and steadfast as the dawn that would greet us.

3
ROGER

The first day with Birdie was a real dazzler. Had me all caught up in the moment, as if I was floating on air. But even with all the excitement, I had to stop and wonder if maybe I was getting ahead of myself. I quickly brushed off any slight hesitation. I had been admiring Birdie for a while and this was finally the moment.

I appeared on her doorstep, and when she opened the door, I stood there for a moment, at a loss for words. I was in awe of her. Any previous doubts floated away. Anticipation was bubbling within me like a fizzy pop on the verge of overflowing. My heart raced with a mix of excitement and nerves as I waited for her to appear. She had a way of combining simplicity with dignity, a vision of effortless grace that left me breathless.

A TIMELESS TAPESTRY

Her hair, delicately curled and pinned back with a simple clip, framed her face like a work of art. The muted light of the evening sun kissed her cheeks, highlighting the subtle flush that adorned them, and brought a warm radiance to her chestnut locks, revealing hidden shades of auburn as they caught the light. Her lips were painted crimson red, and I was utterly infatuated. She was a delicate dream. Her eyes sparkled with a mixture of eagerness and jitters, mirroring my own emotions. As she stepped forward to greet me, her movements were graceful and poised, like a dancer gliding across the stage. "Hello, Roger," she said, her voice soft and warm, sending a shiver down my spine. "I'm all set when you are."

I couldn't help but smile, captivated by her presence. "You look absolutely stunning, Birdie," I replied, my words laced with sincerity.

Her cheeks flushed a deeper shade of pink, and she gave a shy smile in return. "That's kind of you, Roger. You clean up pretty nicely yourself."

With a gentle laugh, I offered her my arm, feeling a rush of excitement as she linked hers with mine. As we set off towards our destination, I couldn't shake the feeling this was the beginning of something truly astonishing.

We ordered Italian to-go and found a quiet spot in the park. As I poured the cider into our glasses, I felt her eyes trained on me like a hawk. It made my heart race, but I managed to keep my composure. I had to mask my nervousness. A swirl of emotions churned inside me. For the first time, I wondered if this was the real McCoy.

Birdie must have noticed my nervousness, for she

placed her hand gently on my wrist, holding her glass in the other. Looking me straight in the eye, she said, "Here's to a delightful evening with the most charming gentleman. Here's to an autumn day full of nuances and beauty. Amid the holiday bustle, there is light. To us and to new beginnings!"

We clinked our glasses together and we each take a sip. Silence fell between us. The wind was picking up, and we watched the leaves flutter in the distance. I knew I couldn't stay quiet for long and had to say something, but I feared if I opened my mouth I would say something ridiculous, and she would laugh. Then I remembered her laugh was soothing and kind.

"Birdie, I've been meaning to ask you out for some time," I began. "It feels rather unconventional that you made the first move. But honestly, I can't think of a more perfect way to spend this autumn evening than with you."

As I gazed into her eyes, a pleasant sensation spread throughout my body. Her gentle expression and the way she drew near to me made me feel like the most fortunate person on earth to spend time in her company. The initiator of our plans was of no consequence, for what matters most was the present moment and the chance to appreciate each other's presence.

With a gleaming smile, Birdie responded, "I wholeheartedly mirror your sentiment. Being in your presence is absolutely delightful, and I cannot envision a more fulfilling way to utilize my time. Let us ensure every moment is fully savored."

I enthusiastically concurred with her perspective, and I

eagerly looked forward to making the most of our time together.

The delightful picnic afforded me the opportunity to fully relish the beauty of the autumn day. As I reclined on the blanket with the grass beneath us, I couldn't help but marvel at the playful light filtering through the trees, casting dancing shadows around us. There was a sweet fragrance of pine trees mingling with the crisp, cool air, and the golden leaves rustled ever so gently in the breeze. It was an elongated moment of sheer bliss, and I was immensely grateful for being able to savor it.

During our initial rendezvous, Birdie and I established a strong connection. Our exchange of ideas was fluid, and we discovered we had many things in common. The true realization of our love transpired a few weeks later. Though we both sensed the depth of our feelings, neither of us dared to voice them yet. It took time, but eventually, we broke through our emotional barriers and bared our hearts. The moment was truly enchanting and will forever be etched in my memory.

As the sun began to set, we packed up what was left of our picnic. We took the long way home sharing our favorite Thanksgiving traditions with our respective families. Birdie talked about a pumpkin pie recipe her grandmother made every year and it was the one thing she could not wait to devour. I described memories playing football in the park with my brother, uncle, and father while my sister stayed home with my mother, aunt, and nana. As they prepared the feast, they always wanted the men out of the house.

Birdie chuckled at the thought of them shooing us men away. It was as if time had stopped and all I could see was her face and hear her voice. Truth be told, I'd crossed paths with a few ladies in my time, but none had ever held my gaze as firmly as Birdie. She was like a rare gem outshining all the others, turning my head in a way no one else ever had. We reached her door and said goodnight. I thanked her for a winsome evening and expressed my hope to see her again after the holiday break.

When Birdie kissed me on the cheek, I refrained from asking for more. The gentle brush of her lips set my heart racing like a fluttering butterfly, but I kept my poise. Once I was back at the fraternity house, I noticed a red lipstick mark on my left cheek. I didn't want to rinse it off, so I went to bed with Birdie Godwin's lips imprinted on my cheek.

***

DATE: NOVEMBER 1948

Two days after my date with Birdie, I found myself back in New York with my family for Thanksgiving. As I sat at the kitchen table, my thoughts were entirely consumed by her. I couldn't help but wonder how her holiday was taking shape. Was she in the kitchen assisting her grandmother with her renowned pumpkin pie? Was she enjoying a warm conversation with her mother? I found myself yearning to hear all about her experiences. It seemed rather foolish, given we had only been on one date, yet she occupied my every thought. My reverie was interrupted by the sound of my mother's voice.

"Roger, dear. Your father's asking if you're ready to head to the park?"

I stood, clearing my throat, "Yes, ma'am."

I walked over to her and kissed her on the cheek, before grabbing my coat and heading to the door to meet my father, brother, and uncle outside. "Try not to burn the house down, mother," I teased.

I loved my mother, but she wasn't always the greatest cook. She was a bit of a scatterbrain. When she focused, everything was delicious. But if there was the slightest interruption, everything would go up in smoke—literally. One year, our turkey caught fire. With no time to prepare a new one, we ended up having smoked trout instead.

On any other evening, I might have enjoyed that fine. But Thanksgiving was a time for us to relish the traditional turkey feast. Anticipation can breed disappointment when expectations aren't met. In essence, Thanksgiving revolves around gratitude for the people in your life, your wellbeing, and your blessings. It's not solely about the food.

This year, it was colder than I remembered. The park, and its little patch of grass, had transformed into a sacred area for our annual tradition. Leaves crunched beneath our feet as we took up our positions. The air was filled with the familiar banter and playful taunts; it was a friendly yet fiercely competitive match. My brother, Alton, and my father, Edward, played against my uncle, Stefan, and I. Before the first kick, we engaged in a nostalgic warmup, reminiscing of years past.

My father had a way of imparting his wisdom to Alton

and me, and my uncle Stefan shared tales of his glory days, which created a tapestry of family history plaited into the foundation of our game. Laughter echoed as memories were relived, and the ball started its journey, passing from hand to hand in a ritualistic passing of the torch. This year was different. An inescapable knot of tension twisted in my stomach as I watched my brother from across the field. I was determined to beat him this year. The strained atmosphere on the field was palpable, thick enough to slice through the football Alton was wielding.

As we were face to face, I stared him down, football touching the ground, preparing to hand it off to Stefan. "Easy there, brother," Alton said, attempting to keep his tone light despite the undercurrent of animosity between us.

I shot him a sharp glance. His jaw clenched. "I can't wait to give you a good drubbing today," I retorted, my voice terse.

Alton sighed inwardly, knowing any attempt to diffuse the situation would likely be futile. I had hoped this Thanksgiving dinner would be an opportunity to show my brother I was as good at football as he and my dad were. I was a star quarterback, after all. Maybe this was our chance to mind the rift that had grown between us since the previous year. But it seemed old wounds ran deep, and the scars were far from healed. As the game unfolded with a unique blend of styles, the intergenerational playbook was fused with both the skills of youth and the wisdom of experience. Alton showcased agility and speed, and I secretly despised him for it. My father exhibited strategic prowess—it was admirable. And my uncle Stefan brought a touch of finesse from days of old.

We moved in harmony with an accord of familial bonds and shared a love for the beautiful game. Amidst what I believed to be a friendly competition, the park rang with cheers and jeers as goals were scored and celebrated. Each goal was a moment frozen in time, a snapshot of family unity and the simple joy of playing together. I knew I needed to be the bigger person and move on from the competitiveness growing within me. Alton and I always felt as if we needed to one up each other. He was the oldest, and it always seemed the oldest would always have the upper hand. I wanted to show I was more than his younger brother. I was good enough to beat him at this year's annual football tradition. The match was marked not only by the score but the shared glances, high-fives, and embraces which defined the true essence of the Thanksgiving kick-about. Before we knew it, my mother had sent my sister, Jane, to fetch us. With an invisible whistle, we all came together for a post-game feast, the taste of victory and defeat lingering on our lips.

As we gathered around the table, we left behind a trail of memories on the field that would be cherished for years to come. This was what I loved about Thanksgiving. It's a time to cherish our family tradition that transcends time and celebrates our bond of love, laughter, and football.

The dining room was adorned with the warm glow of candlelight, and the aroma of the Thanksgiving feast filled the air.

But it was a fragile façade, masking the tension simmering beneath the surface. Despite the laughter and chatter, an underlying unease lingered, waiting to erupt. This year, Stefan and I had emerged victorious in the annual Thanksgiving football game, and I couldn't resist rubbing it in Alton's face. As we settled into our seats around the table laden with dishes of turkey, stuffing, and all the festive trimmings, I couldn't contain my grin. "Ah, another year, another victory," I proclaimed, lifting my glass of wine in mock toast.

Alton shot me a glare. His jaw clenched. "Don't get too brash, Roger," he muttered, his voice laced with thinly veiled resentment.

"Oh, come on, Alton, don't be such a poor sport. Remember last year when you won, and I had to let it go," I teased, taking a hearty bite of turkey. "But you know, I'm the king of football around here. Maybe next year you'll dethrone me once again."

Alton's fists clenched under the table, his face flushing with frustration. "We'll see about that. I always end up coming on top," he retorted through gritted teeth. I chuckled, thoroughly enjoying getting under his skin. "In your dreams, big brother," I replied smugly, savoring both the taste of victory and the sweet satisfaction of teasing Alton mercilessly. After all, what's Thanksgiving without a little friendly sibling rivalry?

I looked across the table at my mother as she shifted uncomfortably in her seat. Her fingers toyed with the linen napkin in her lap, twisting and turning the fabric in restless movements. My father raised his glass to toast. With an attempt to change the subject before my brother and I got into it any further. "Here's to another year of gratitude, love, and a perfectly cooked turkey. Cheers, everyone!"

Glasses clinked, and smiles were exchanged around the table. My brother was digging into the mashed potatoes. "These are amazing, Ma. What's the secret ingredient?"

My mother, with a playful grin, said, "Well, a pinch of love, of course. But don't go blabbing about it." Laughter erupted as Uncle Stefan joined the conversation. Nodding approvingly, he said, "And I must say, the turkey is cooked to perfection. You've outdone yourself, Claude."

My mother blushed. "Oh stop it, you. It's a team effort." She looked at her mother adoringly.

Looking around at the spread on the table, my father said, "Speaking of teamwork, I wish you all could have seen our football game earlier."

"Yeah, it was quite the match!" Alton chimed in. "I scored a touchdown in the second half."

Uncle Stefan chimed in, "Ah, the beautiful game. I remember playing with your father when we were your age. Those were the days."

My father grinned and nodded. "The Thanksgiving kickabout is shaping up to be quite the tradition."

"Absolutely. It wouldn't feel like Thanksgiving without it," I added.

The mention of the football game seemed to hit a nerve again. Sensing tension rising, my mother swiftly intervened, determined not to let Thanksgiving be spoiled by another showdown between my brother and me over who ruled the field. She gracefully steered the conversation elsewhere, preserving the peace. We all took a moment of quiet, savoring the meal in front of us, letting the flavors of Thanksgiving settle in.

My mother looked at me. "Roger, how's school treating you? Any exciting stories to share?"

I leaned back in my chair, weighing my words carefully. "Oh, you know how it is, school's school. I've met a few interesting people, but mostly, I'm keeping up with the books. Still, nothing beats coming home for Thanksgiving."

My father raised an eyebrow, a playful gleam in his eye. "Interesting people, you say? Would that happen to include a certain someone?"

Grinning, I replied, "Well, if you must know, yes. I'm quite taken."

Eyes widened with curiosity as everyone exchanged playful glances.

My mother was glowing. "Do share more, darling," she said.

"Well, there isn't much to share. We've only been on one date. Her name is Birdie Godwin, and she's part of Zeta Tao Alpha sorority and a cheerleader."

My news hung in the air as laughter and conversation continued, filling the dining room with the warmth of our family bond and the joy of the holiday—removing any tension my brother and I had over football.

After Thanksgiving break, Birdie and I went on our

second date. We headed to the local drive-in theater to watch, *It's a Wonderful Life*. The crisp evening air carried the scent of popcorn as we pulled up to the lot, finding a cozy spot beneath the glow of the large screen. As the film started, we settled into the car, sharing a blanket and letting the warmth of the holiday classic envelop us. Birdie's laughter was music to my ears, her hand resting gently in mine, making the moment feel timeless.

The flickering images on the screen illuminated her face, capturing the magic of the night and the growing connection between us. I made a conscious effort to take things slowly, gently placing my arm around her. As we left the drive-in, Birdie had a different idea. Instead of driving her straight home, she asked if I'd return the car to the fraternity first. "I'd much prefer a walk," she said with a playful smile. So, after parking back at the house, I walked her to The Zetas—what she fondly called her sorority. Her hand in mine, we strolled under the moonlit sky, savoring the sweetness of the evening, taking our time with each step. I felt a flutter in my stomach, amazed at how deeply I was falling for her. Birdie had an indescribable effect on me, pulling me closer with every glance and word.

Over the next few weeks, we spent more and more time together—lingering in the library, celebrating after football games, and walking each other to our classes. Time seemed to both stretch and vanish, and before we knew it, Christmas break was upon us. Soon, we'd be parting ways to visit our respective families. A few days before our departure, we took a final stroll around Birdie's block, neither wanting to say goodbye. As we rounded the corner, I pulled Birdie close and kissed her, stopping all her anxious thoughts in their tracks. In that moment, it was like catching lightning in a bottle—something rare and electrifying, like it was meant to happen.

With the kiss lingering in the crisp night air, a hush fell between us. The streetlights cast a soft, amber glow on the pavement, their flicker reminiscent of a bygone era. We walked a few more steps, the silence between us filled with unspoken words. It was as if the night itself held its breath, offering us a final, serene moment before our inevitable parting. As we reached Birdie's doorstep, the reality of our impending separation settled in. She turned to face me, her eyes reflecting a blend of wistfulness and hope. "I suppose it's time," she said, her voice a tender murmur.

The weight of her words hung between us. I took her hands in mine, feeling their warmth against the chill of the evening. "I'll miss you more than words can express," I said earnestly. "But remember, this isn't goodbye—it's a brief interlude. We'll see each other again soon."

Birdie's eyes shimmered with unshed tears as she nodded. "I wish I could tuck you away like a cherished keepsake and take you with me," she said softly. She then let out a light, melodious laugh. "It might sound foolish, Roger, but it feels like I've known you forever."

Her laughter, though soft, was sweet. A comforting sound that eased any tension between us. I couldn't help but smile at her whimsical comment, the warmth of her presence still vivid despite the approaching farewell. "I don't think it's silly at all," I said gently. "Sometimes, it feels like we're connected in ways that go beyond time and distance."

The thing about Birdie—time seemed to lose its meaning around her. It was as though we'd been intertwined for far longer than the few short weeks we'd spent together. Our bond felt ancient, like an old tune we both knew by heart, yet had only begun to hum. Even the looming separation, a mere holiday break, felt like a chasm we weren't prepared to cross.

The evening clung to us as we stood there, wrapped in the delicate silence of the moment. I leaned in, and our lips met once more—softly, tenderly—as if we were sealing a promise only the stars above could understand. When we parted, her smile was like the flicker of a candle in the wind—brief, but it lit something eternal within me.

She slipped inside, the door closing with a whisper. Leaving me alone on the porch, the warmth of her touch still lingering in the air. As I made my way back through the quiet streets, every step felt like it carried a fragment of her. The night, cool and still, seemed to murmur faintly of what was to come. A promise, not yet spoken, but already written in the stars. The streetlights, casting long shadows on the pavement echoed the distance that would soon lie between us. But in my heart I knew it was only temporary. We were not bound by the passing days but by something far more enduring—something that felt like destiny, even if it was wrapped in the ordinary moments of everyday life.

4
BIRDIE
DATE: NOVEMBER–DECEMBER 1948

Sitting here enjoying the brisk evening, I couldn't help but be captivated by Roger's voice, savoring every word he spoke. The alluring fragrance of his cologne paired with the mellifluous tones of his voice and eloquent choice of words had me enamored.

He exuded a natural charisma that eased my nerves and made me feel at home in his presence. Each second spent with him felt like a surreal experience, one I would forever hold dear in my heart.

However, the most unsettling part was the uncertainty that clung to me, like a shadow I couldn't shake. At times, I found myself questioning my judgment when it came to him, as though my heart was leading me astray. Roger seemed to possess all the qualities I had ever dreamed of in a partner, yet doubt lingered like a quiet whisper in the back of my mind—was I merely weaving a fantasy from threads of desire, imagining a connection that didn't truly exist? Was Roger's affection sincere, or a carefully played hand to win me over? These questions swirled around me like a restless breeze, refusing to settle, and left me adrift in their ceaseless current.

While I dedicated myself to my studies, striving tirelessly to achieve my ambitions in the publishing industry, I couldn't shake worrying Roger didn't share my passion for academia. He possessed intelligence aplenty, and I couldn't help but believe if he applied himself with even half the diligence I did, his potential would be boundless. But then here in this moment, as I walked home with him, I couldn't help but notice the genuine joy coming from Roger's every move. His smile, a crescent of light amidst the shadows, seemed to dispel darkness with each curve. It danced across his face, casting a gentle glow that softened the edges of the world. As he spoke, his words wove a cadence of melodies, each syllable a note in a symphony only I could hear. I found myself leaning closer, caught in the rhythm of his voice, the tempo of his speech a soothing balm to my restless mind. And when he drew near, his touch lingered like a whisper, a silent promise of a connection beyond words.

Nevertheless, as the Thanksgiving break approached, I was overcome by a sense of uneasiness creeping back into my mind. What if he changed his mind about me? But then again, if he did, then perhaps he wasn't the man I thought he was. How foolish would I be to let a guy change the course of my life? I clung to the hope when we returned to school he might ask me to go steady. In my eyes, Roger Scott was the epitome of chivalry, and I couldn't imagine a more perfect man. If perfection existed.

Upon arriving at my doorstep, I summoned the courage to take a bold action. Without hesitation, I leaned in and placed a gentle kiss on his cheek, leaving behind a faint trace of my lipstick. Yet, my intention was not merely to leave a physical mark, but to imprint a lasting memory on his heart. I yearned for him to remember me long after our parting, thus, I bestowed upon him a kiss that would never be forgotten.

Spending Thanksgiving with my family was a mix of emotions for me. On one hand, I was grateful to be reunited with my loved ones after being away at school. On the other hand, I couldn't help but feel a sense of longing for the people I had left behind. And then there was Roger. I hoped to leave a lasting impression on him, but realized he had already left an indelible mark on my heart.

Each passing day without him felt like an eternity, and I found myself constantly wondering how he was faring during the holiday. Were they already gathered for the traditional football game? Or were they seated at the dinner table, giving thanks for all their blessings? Did he think of me as much as I thought of him? As tempted as I was to reach out to him, I ultimately decided against it. It was time for him to step up and prove he was worthy of my love. As a lady, I deserved nothing less than a partner who cherished and respected me. I had an absolutely lovely time during Thanksgiving break with my family. The aroma of cinnamon and pumpkin spice wafted through the kitchen, filling me with joy. My grandma's famous pumpkin pie was a hit, receiving praise from all corners of the room. I couldn't resist sneaking a second slice when no one was paying attention. The sweet, rich flavor was divine, and I found myself wishing my dear Roger was there to sample it as well.

The thought of introducing him to my family and spending holidays together filled me with warmth. I could picture him chatting with my loved ones while I busied myself in the kitchen, and it was a beautiful image. Though it was early days, considering we'd only been on one date, I had a feeling Roger and I were meant to be. I couldn't help but dream of our future together and hoped it became a reality. The dining table was adorned with a simple elegance, and the air was filled with the comforting aroma of a home-cooked meal. My family had gathered, eager to catch up on each other's lives. With a sparkle in my eyes, I shared about my recent experiences with Roger.

"You won't believe what happened to me before the break," I exclaimed with excitement. "I met someone truly special."

"Really? Do tell us more, Birdie," my mother, Marjorie, encouraged, her voice laced with curiosity.

Beaming, I replied, "His name's Roger, and he's simply wonderful. We're at the same school, and we met at a party my sorority was hosting. He's in a fraternity—Sigma Alpha Epsilon—and plays quarterback for the football team. We seemed to click."

My father, Clark, raised an eyebrow. "A sorority party, you say? Is that one of those fortuitous meetings?"

"You didn't happen to get knocked over by a football while cheering at a game, did you?" my brother Dean teased.

"Not quite," I laughed. "But we did connect over our shared love for the game."

My mother leaned in with interest. "Do go on, dear. What's he like?"

"Well, he's on a football scholarship, but he's got a great passion for aviation. He's incredibly curious about the world. We had this wonderful conversation about life, dreams, and everything in between."

"And what sort of father would I be if I didn't voice my concerns?" my father affirmed with a solemn nod, his concern etched in the furrow of his brow. "You know the importance of focusing on your education and securing your future. While he might seem like a catch, it's wise to approach this with caution."

"Is he ready to face the ultimate test—meeting the family?" Dean said, smirking.

I couldn't help but blush. Noting what my father said. The words haunted my mind, as I had been having doubts about Roger myself. My goals would always be my top priority. But was it possible to have both? I wanted to give into Roger but I also didn't want to give up on my dreams.

"That's precisely why I wanted to bring this up," I said.

"If things continue to progress favorably, I was considering inviting him over for Christmas."

My mother clapped her hands together with enthusiasm. "Oh, that would be simply delightful! We'd be so pleased to meet him."

My father arched an eyebrow. "Is he ready for the barrage of family inquiries and our good-natured ribbing?"

Giggling, I replied, "I'm confident he can manage. Besides, I want him to meet the wonderful people who brought me up."

Dean flashed a grin. "If he can endure our family game nights, he's certainly a keeper."

I looked at Dean with a playful glint in my eye. "That's the spirit! But seriously, if he agrees to join us for Christmas, I hope you all make him feel right at home."

My mother nodded with a warm smile. "Absolutely, dear. We'd be delighted to meet this Roger and see the joy he's brought to you."

The dinner table echoed with laughter and affection as we shared stories, looking forward to the new experiences Roger might bring into my life.

The emotion of love is a multifaceted and compelling force that holds the power to significantly impact our lives. Its effects can be both uplifting and devastating, often contingent on the specific circumstances involved. At times, it appears love takes on a life of its own, and we become helpless to resist its magnetic pull. We may find ourselves engaging in actions we never thought possible, all in the name of love. Despite this, we cannot help but question if our feelings are reciprocated.

The fear of unrequited love is daunting and can be paralyzing. The paradox of love is that it holds the potential to bring us immense happiness and unbearable pain simultaneously. Yet, despite these uncertainties, I found solace in the certainty of my connection with Roger. Ever since we first met, we were inseparable. I vividly remember the rush of excitement I felt while cheering for him on the football field, and the quiet moments we shared studying together in the library. These moments, both exhilarating and serene, became my refuge from the fears and doubts that love often brings.

After Thanksgiving, our bond grew stronger with each passing day, and we found ourselves spending every available moment enjoying each other's company. From relaxing picnics in the park to savoring milkshakes at our favorite diner, everything felt perfect. As the Christmas holiday season approached, I found myself hesitant to leave Roger behind. The thought of asking him to join me for Christmas crossed my mind, and after all, I had told my family I would invite him. But in the weeks following Thanksgiving, I knew deep down it was too soon for us to take that step. I knew my family would be disappointed, so I wrote them a letter to inform them I'd decided to wait before introducing them to Roger. I didn't have the heart to tell them I was having cold feet about bringing him, so I said it was important for him to spend Christmas with his family and we would have a proper introduction to each of our families later on.

We spent a charming evening meandering through my neighborhood, savoring each other's company. It was in that gentle twilight that Roger leaned in and bestowed a kiss upon me, and all my anxieties seemed to dissolve into the night. It felt like a true testament to our genuine connection.

Of course, we were well aware our relationship would not be without its trials. We understood that a lengthy and arduous journey lay before us, fraught with numerous obstacles. Yet, we were resolute in our determination to confront these challenges together, fortified by an unwavering affection and steadfast support for one another.

5
ROGER

During the holiday break, we exchanged promises of correspondence—me to write to Birdie, and she to do the same. Each letter she sent carried with it a warmth which bridged the distance between us, allowing me to deeply empathize with her sentiments and recognize their sincerity.

It dawned on me the true value of an action often lay not in its grandeur or the eloquence of the words, but in the thoughtfulness and intent behind them. The small gestures and heartfelt letters spoke volumes, revealing the depth of our connection and the earnest care we held for one another. Composing a handwritten letter was an exquisite way to articulate one's thoughts and feelings. It has the potential to leave an indelible mark on the recipient. I had hoped my letters were leaving a mark on Birdie's heart. I was always elated to hear from Birdie, to know the letters she received resonated with her and liberated her spirits. I believed sharing such experiences served as a reminder of the potency of human bonds and the significance of demonstrating affection and concern towards others. While I sat there reading the letters Birdie had sent, one in particular made my heart soar.

My dearest Roger,
I hope this letter finds you in the best of health and spirits. As we approach the holidays, I want to express my heartfelt sentiments and convey how much you mean to me. The holiday season is always a special time for us all, and it brings back memories of all the delightful moments we have shared together but also new memories I look forward to us making. From picnics in the parks and afternoon strolls to enjoying cozy evenings by the fire, every moment spent with you is a true blessing. Though we may not be able to celebrate together in person this year, please know you are always in my thoughts and close to my heart. I am grateful for your unwavering love and support, and I eagerly anticipate creating many more cherished memories in the future. May this festive season be filled with an abundance of love, laughter, and all your heart's desires. Wishing you a joyous and blessed holiday season.
With sincere love and gratitude,
Birdie

The mere idea of spending each and every holiday with Birdie filled my heart with joy and wonder. At times, I found myself lost in contemplation about our relationship, and have to remind myself to snap back to reality. It was truly astonishing to realize I had developed such strong feelings for someone in such a short time. The period we spent apart was incredibly challenging, but the handwritten letters Birdie sent me proved to be a lifeline that kept our love aflame. I had an unwavering belief in our relationship, and I was confident we would stand the test of time. The extended holiday hiatus seemed like an interminable period, but before I knew it, it had drawn to a close. I was overjoyed to be back on the Millikin campus and eagerly anticipated reuniting with Birdie. I couldn't help but ponder whether she had undergone any changes since our last encounter. Would she recollect my presence in the base of her memory? I had included a polaroid of myself in one of my letters, so she would remember me. Birdie had an uncanny ability to transport me back to my childhood, and she was undoubtedly the high point of my day.

In our last letters to each other, we remarked on the first day back we would meet on campus under our favorite tree. There, we always found ourselves in a peaceful oasis, basking in the warm rays of the sun filtering through the leaves overhead. The gentle rustling of branches in the breeze was like a calming melody, lulling our senses into a state of serenity. Every time I sat under this tree, I'd inhale deeply, the fresh scent of the outdoors filling my lungs, and I always felt any anxiety dissipate. The distant chirping of birds and the softness of the grass beneath us were all part of this idyllic scene. It was always a moment of pure tranquility, far removed from the bustling activities of campus life.

Sometimes I'd find myself gazing up at the towering tree, struck by its magnificence and majesty. It was a poignant reminder that nature had a way of putting things into perspective and that taking a moment to appreciate it could be a healing balm for the soul. As I sat there, nestled under the shade of the tree, eagerly anticipating Birdie's arrival, my heart began to beat faster than normal. The excitement and nervous energy coursing through me was palpable as I anxiously awaited the moment to see her. I couldn't help but feel a mix of emotions. A heady combination of joy, anticipation, and trepidation. Seated there in deep thought, I wondered what would be the most appropriate way to greet her. Should I offer a hug or a kiss? Would she be at ease with either gesture? My musings were abruptly interrupted when I finally noticed her approaching, having been so absorbed in my reflections that I nearly missed her presence.

"Are you dreaming of me?" she asked.

My thoughts, momentarily adrift, my gaze fixed upon her, and my lips curled into an immediate smile. "Always," I responded, my voice filled with affection.

Without a moment of hesitation, I drew her close and pressed my lips to hers. It was a gentle, tender kiss that conveyed all the love I held for her. Our lips remained entwined for a fleeting moment, and in that instant I knew how fortunate I was to have her in my life.

As our lips lingered, the world around us seemed to fall away, leaving only the serene hush of our secluded sanctuary beneath the tree. The soft rustling of leaves and the distant hum of campus life created a gentle backdrop, amplifying the quiet intimacy we shared. I marveled at how this simple, natural setting could make our reunion feel so profound, as if the universe itself had conspired to offer us this perfect moment of closeness.

Birdie pulled back slightly, her eyes glistening with a mix of happiness and relief. "I've missed you so much," she whispered, her voice a soothing balm to my eager heart. I could see the warmth of her smile reflected in the dappled sunlight filtering through the branches above. Every nuance of her expression seemed to tell a story of longing and joy, each detail accentuated by the gentle play of light and shadow. We settled ourselves comfortably beneath the tree, our hands intertwined as we began to share stories of our holiday experiences. The conversation flowed easily, punctuated by laughter and affectionate glances. With each word exchanged, the anticipation and excitement which had been building during our time apart seemed to dissolve, replaced by a deep sense of contentment. In that moment, it was clear no matter the time or distance between us, our bond remained steadfast and unbreakable.

As the afternoon waned and the shadows grew longer, we reluctantly acknowledged it was time to part ways once more. We stood up, brushing off the remnants of our peaceful repose, and with a final, lingering embrace, we bit each other farewell. As I set off, my heart overflowed with a beautiful blend of warmth and optimism, fully aware that this marked the beginning of another captivating chapter in the ever-unfolding story we were weaving together.

6
BIRDIE

With the sun sinking below the skyline, casting a warm golden glow across the campus, I found myself lost in the labyrinth of my own thoughts. The past few weeks had been a whirlwind of emotions since I crossed paths with Roger, a charming stranger who seemed to have stepped out of a dream.

Our connection had deepened with each passing day, and tonight, we found ourselves on the rooftop of Roger's fraternity house with a breathtaking view of campus. The iconic clock tower stood tall in the distance, and the lush greenery of the quad below added a touch of serenity to the scene.

Leaning against the ledge, I couldn't help but steal glances at Roger. His eyes sparkled with a mixture of excitement and vulnerability, mirroring my own feelings.

The soft breeze carried the scent of pine, adding a touch of magic to the moment and reminding me of Christmastime. It left me pondering what Christmases might hold with Roger by my side. A lingering question gnawed at me—could this truly be the enduring love I had yearned for, or was I, in my youthful naivety, yet to discern the full measure of such a deep connection?

"Tell me, Birdie," Roger began, breaking the comfortable silence between us, "what's your favorite memory on campus?"

I paused, my gaze wandering over the illuminated campus buildings. "I believe it's a moment yet to bloom," I said with a soft smile. "But if I had to choose, it would be this moment right now, overlooking Millikin."

Roger's eyes met mine, and a warm understanding passed between us. "Me too," he confessed, a playful grin tugging at the corners of his lips.

As we shared stories from our days on campus, dreams for the future, and the intricacies of our favorite classes, the bond between us deepened. Time lost its significance as we reveled in the joy of each other's company. The night unfolded like a symphony with our laughter and whispered confessions composing the sweetest melodies. We talked about the stars above and the stories etched in the constellations, while the campus embraced us with its timeless charm.

Lost in the serenity of the night, Roger leaned in, his gaze meeting mine. Without a word, our hearts spoke in a language only we could decipher. As our lips met in a tender kiss, it felt like the world around us vanished. In that transient pause between dusk and dawn, on the roof-top under the night sky, Roger and I discovered sometimes the most beautiful moments of a love story are written in the quiet whispers of the heart, amidst the storied halls and timeless beauty of Millikin University.

The days that followed were filled with my nose buried in books, but I made every effort to spend as much quality time with Roger as possible. The week after our beautiful moment on the rooftop led us to our favorite diner, where the soft hum of conversations and the clinking of cutlery created a lively backdrop. The scent of freshly brewed coffee enveloped us, adding a cozy warmth to our continued journey together.

Diners have a unique charm, a blend of nostalgia and simplicity that mirror the essence of our connection. It was in a booth like this one where I was sipping on a chocolate milkshake and first noticed Roger watching me. Time moved swiftly to our first date—a picnic on the campus lawn—and then to our first meal together. Those early awkward exchanges soon gave way to something far more meaningful, setting the stage for a journey that felt like the beginning of something truly special.

Roger looked up from his menu, his eyes meeting mine with that familiar sparkle. There's a sense of comfort in these moments, surrounded by the familiar sights and sounds of our shared experiences. We ordered our usual, a stack of pancakes for me and a hearty omelet for Roger, I couldn't help but reflect on the countless conversations that have unfolded in this booth. From late-night discussions about dreams and ambitions to lighthearted banter over the silliest of topics, this diner has been the witness to the concert of our words.

Our relationship is like the warm cup of coffee in front of me—rich, comforting, and something I can't imagine my life without. Roger is my steady anchor, and this diner is the stage where our story continues to unfold.

The waitress, a familiar face who has seen us through many meals, placed our orders with a knowing smile. She has become a silent observer of our relationship, witnessing the highs and lows as we navigate the menu of life.

With our meals nearly demolished, the atmosphere became a sonnet, narrating our shared moments. Laughter mingled with the chatter of other diner, creating a melody that felt uniquely ours. Roger's laughter, deep and genuine, was the sweetest note in this sonata. In between bites of pancakes and sips of coffee, we shared updates on our lives. There was a comfort in the routine of this diner. A familiarity that spoke of the depth of our connection. The clinking of forks against plates was a percussion to our conversation, and I found myself lost in the melody of Roger's voice. It was in these simple moments, surrounded by the hustle and bustle of the diner, I realized how extraordinary our love story was.

As we finished our meal, I caught Roger's gaze, and we shared a silent understanding. The diner may be a backdrop, but the memories we've created here are the heartstrings of our relationship. With a satisfied sigh, we left the booth, hand in hand, ready to embrace the next phase of

A TIMELESS TAPESTRY

our love story—one diner conversation at a time.

7
ROGER
YEAR: 1949

Birdie and I decided to step back in time, heading to a local dance hall which still had the charm of the 1940s, with its checkered floors and big band music filling the air. The moment we stepped inside, we were greeted by the lively sound of a swing band playing a lively tune of "Sing, Sing, Sing" by Benny Goodman. The energy in the room was contagious, with couples twirling and gliding across the dance floor, their laughter echoing off the walls.

Birdie's eyes sparkled with excitement as she looked around. "I haven't been dancing in ages," she confessed, her smile infectious.

"Well, then it's time to change that," I replied, taking her hand and leading her to the dance floor. The band struck up a familiar tune, and before we knew it, we were caught up in the rhythm. Our feet moving in sync as we danced the night away.

The room seemed to blur around us as we focused on each other, the music guiding our every step. Birdie's laughter was the sweetest melody, her joy radiating as she spun in my arms. Her red polka dot dress swirling around her like a blossoming flower. We didn't need words; the dance spoke for us, a conversation in movement, where every turn, dip, and sway brought us closer together.

After what felt like hours of nonstop dancing, the band finally slowed down with a tender ballad. I recognized the melody, as my mother used to play it. "Moonlight Serenade" by Glenn Miller, filled the room. I pulled Birdie close, feeling the warmth of her body against mine as we swayed gently to the music. The world outside the dance hall faded away, leaving only the subdued lights and the gentle hum of the music surrounding us.

"This reminds me of an old movie," Birdie whispered, her head resting against my chest.

"It's better than any movie," I murmured, feeling the truth of those words as I held her close, her heart beating in time with mine.

There was something about her that left me completely spellbound. Birdie was like a ripe Georgia peach on a dewy spring morning—fresh, sweet, and utterly irresistible. When the music finally ended, we lingered on the dance floor, neither of us wanting the night to end. We stepped outside into the cool night air, our breaths visible in the chilly breeze. The street was quiet, the glow of the streetlights casting long shadows as we walked hand in hand. Then, on a whim, I stopped under one of those lights and turned to Birdie. "One last dance?" I asked, the mischievous grin on my face making her laugh. "Here?" she asked, raising an eyebrow, though her smile gave her away.

"Why not?" I shrugged, taking her hand and spinning her around.

The empty streets became our private dance floor, the soft hum of the distant city our only accompaniment. We moved slowly, savoring the moment, and when I dipped her low, her laughter filled the air, a sound I knew I'd remember forever. When I brought her back up, our faces inches apart, I couldn't resist stealing a kiss. As I leaned in, capturing Birdie's gaze.

Without words, our hearts engaged in a silent dialogue known only to us. With our lips locked in a tender embrace, the world around us blurred into insignificance, leaving behind only the reverberations of our love story inscribed in the stars above. When we finally parted, we stood there for a moment, basking in the afterglow of our impromptu dance.

"I'll remember this night forever," Birdie whispered, her hand still entwined with mine as we started our walk back.

"Me too," I replied, knowing this simple night out had turned into something extraordinary, a memory lingering in our hearts for years to come.

★ ★ ★

DATE: FEBRUARY 1950

As the months swept past in a blur, there were days when the calendar's pages seemed irrelevant, lost in the timeless orbit of my thoughts consumed by Birdie. In the kaleidoscope of moments, she wasn't only the apple of my eye but the constancy that painted my world with vibrant hues and made every passing day a chapter in our shared narrative. In the embrace of February, the month where love unfurled its tender wings or so the world whimsically agreed and I couldn't escape the imminent arrival of Valentine's Day.

As the day drew nearer, her excitement bubbled over with each passing day. She adorned the sorority house with red hearts and romantic trinkets, her anticipation infectious. Meanwhile, I couldn't shake my distaste for the holiday. It felt commercialized and forced, but my feelings for Birdie were anything but manufactured.

Her love for this holiday was a masterpiece, and every note and gesture resonated with the passion she poured into making sure I felt the heartbeat of her affection echoing through the days of love.

So, despite my reservations, I began secretly planning something special. I knew how much this day meant to her, and seeing her happiness was worth every effort. Deep down, I realized that while Valentine's Day might not be my cup of tea, Birdie was the person who made every day brighter. For her, I wanted to show how much she meant to me, even if it meant stepping outside of my comfort zone.

The crisp February air whispered tales of romance as I set out to weave a tapestry of memories for Birdie. Our love story was etched in the bricks and pathways of the campus, and I aimed to guide her through the milestones of our journey. The morning came as if even the clouds had an inner grin. As I handed a note to one of Birdie's sorority sisters. "Follow your heart," it read, a key to unlocking the scavenger hunt of our shared history. The first stop was the local diner where our eyes first met. A jukebox played 50s melodies as Birdie discovered a small envelope tucked under the sugar dispenser. Inside, a Polaroid of that booth captured the moment our story began.

Next, we strolled through the campus park, the spot where we shared our first date. A hint hidden beneath the bench led her to a faded love letter, the ink still holding the remnants of our whispered promises. The aroma of pastries and coffee guided us to our favorite café, where the barista handed her a cup inscribed with the date of our first coffee date. As she sipped the rich brew, I imagined the sounds of our laughter from those early days. Afterwards, I told Birdie I needed to stop by my fraternity and that I would meet her back at her the ZTA house.

I quickly changed into a navy-blue suit. I knew I didn't have to dress all fancy, but I would do anything for Birdie and she loved this suit. As I followed the trail of memories through the chill of February, the snow-laden branches of the trees whispered secrets in the quiet air. The sorority house stood tall against the backdrop of a gray sky, its brick façade weathered by the winter's frost. With a single red rose clutched in my hand, I stood beneath the archway, my breath forming clouds in the cold. Birdie's approach broke the stillness, her laughter ringing out like a melody in the frosty air. Her cheeks flushed with excitement and her eyes sparkled like icicles catching the sunlight. Each step brought her closer, marking the culmination of our scavenger hunt, a quest through the winter landscape of our memories.

As she reached me, I extended the rose, its petals kissed by the frost yet still vibrant against the white backdrop. She took it in her hands, her touch warm against the cold, her smile thawing the winter around us. In that moment, amidst the snow-covered courtyard, the beauty of our journey together unfolded like a delicate snowflake drifting to the ground.

In the soft glow of the winter twilight, we stood together surrounded by the hushed whispers of snowflakes and the promise of new beginnings. The rose spoke volumes in the silent landscape, its scarlet hue a sign of hope and love.

And as we exchanged glances, I knew that our journey was only beginning, each step forward a testament to the enduring warmth of our connection.

8
BIRDIE
DATE: FEBRUARY 1950

Valentine's Day was more than a date on the calendar for me; it was a celebration intricately stitched into the core of my heart. From the first rays of February sun to the twinkling stars that adorned the night, the anticipation of this special day filled me with a unique kind of joy.

As the month unfolded, each day seemed to carry a touch of magic. I reveled in the simple pleasures of crafting handmade cards, choosing the perfect shade of red for decorations, and envisioning the joy that would light up Roger's eyes as he unwound the surprises, including the meticulously selected vintage watch that I couldn't wait to present as a symbol of timeless love.

The scent of roses and the melodies of classic love songs became my companions, weaving together into a harmonious blend that resonated with the romantic spirit of the season. I couldn't help but smile as I walked through the campus, the air alive with the promise of love. Valentine's Day, to me, was a canvas where I could paint my affection in vibrant hues.

It wasn't about grand gestures or extravagant gifts, but the joy of expressing love in the simplest, yet most heartfelt, ways.

Handwritten notes, carefully selected tokens of affection, and the anticipation of seeing Roger's eyes light up with every surprise were the moments that fueled my love for the day. The excitement reached its peak as I received a note from one of my sorority sisters, setting in motion a scavenger hunt Roger had crafted. Each clue was a step deeper into our shared history, a journey through the moments that had defined us. With the trail unfolding before me, my heart danced with every memory. From the diner where we first met to our first date's location, and the café where our laughter waltzed through the air. Each stop was a part of our love story, and I couldn't wait to give Roger the watch. After the café, he returned to his fraternity but promised to meet up soon, so I took my sweet time walking back to the house. Today I felt immersed in the tangible traces of our affection. I believe it is a day of celebration; a testament to the depth of our connection, a love story that was unfolding with every beat of our hearts.

The heavy wooden door to the sorority house courtyard creaked open, revealing Roger standing there, holding a single, vibrant red rose that seemed to glow in the moonlight. The air was thick with the sweet scent of roses, and my heart skipped a beat as I realized what a wonderful surprise he had in store for me.

"Roger," I said, my voice filled with delight and surprise. "Happy Valentine's Day."

"Happy Valentine's Day, Birdie," he replied, his eyes twinkling in the moonlight.

I stepped closer. "Today has been a journey through our shared history, Rog. From the diner where we first met and locked eyes, to the park where we had our first date, and the cozy café where we laughed together for hours. And now here at my sorority house, reliving the night we decided to jump headfirst into our first date, which ultimately catapulted our relationship. It is as though we have been rediscovering the magic of our love story all over again."

He took my hand, and I felt a warm and comforting connection. "Every moment with you is a celebration, Birdie. I wanted today to be a beautiful reflection of our shared history, a melody of the love we've built together."

Meeting his gaze, I smiled at the soft glow of the moonlight that illuminated his face. "And this vintage watch," I added, unable to contain my excitement, "is a timeless token, like the love that has grown between us."

Roger's eyes widened with surprise and gratitude as I presented him with the vintage watch, carefully wrapped in a box adorned with a red ribbon.

"I wanted to give you something special, something that signifies the time we've shared and the moments yet to come."

He took a moment to absorb the gesture, then looked

at me with genuine appreciation. "Thank you, Birdie. It's not just a watch; it's a treasure that I'll carry with me, a constant reminder of the beautiful moments we're creating together."

He took the watch out of the box and slipped it on, and the intricate details of the timepiece seemed to mirror the delicate moments we've woven into the fabric of our relationship. The ticking of the watch echoed the rhythm of our shared experiences, and as he fastened it around his wrist, it became a symbol of the enduring love we cherished.

He chuckled, his laughter carrying warmth and love. "I'm thrilled that you liked my scavenger hunt, and I'm truly grateful for this beautiful watch. Time might pass, but my affection for you only deepens with every passing moment."

When he handed me the red rose, the night seemed to embrace us with its quiet beauty. "For you, my love."

Cradling the rose in my hands, I felt a surge of gratitude and affection. "Thank you, Roger. Today has surpassed all expectations."

Leaning in, he pressed a gentle kiss to my forehead, and my heart swelled with love and happiness.

"The pleasure was all mine, Birdie."

Beneath the moonlit sky, surrounded by the echoes of our unique love story, I couldn't help but feel that this Valentine's Day hadn't been merely a celebration; it had been a promise, a glimpse into what lay ahead. Our hearts were entwined in the dance of everlasting love.

Later that evening, as I laid in bed, the overwhelming feeling took over. Today was magical so why was I feeling scared? It wasn't like me to jump headfirst into anything. I was the kind of girl who took calculated risks. I made plans, and I never dared to draw outside the lines. But with Roger, I always felt as if I could do anything. And that scared me. I was always waiting for the other shoe to drop. I didn't want to tell him for fear of losing him. I think Roger may love me more than I love him. And I'm not sure if that's a good thing. Shouldn't our love for each other be equal? I couldn't talk to anyone about this and I certainly couldn't tell Roger.

The only logical thing seemed to play the dutiful girlfriend. But was playing a part really me? I know deep down Roger is everything I could ever dream of and that's what makes this so scary. One look from him and I'm hypnotized. I love him—I really do. But is love enough to go the distance with someone.

9
ROGER
YEAR: 1950

Ah, Birdie, she's the bee's knees, the one who makes my heart do the jitterbug. From the moment I laid eyes on her, it was like stepping into a scene from a technicolor dream. She's got that charm, that 1950s grace that takes me back to sock hops and jukebox melodies.

When she walks into the room, it's like the whole place lights up, and suddenly, I'm spinning her around a dance floor that exists only in our imagination. Her laughter, oh, it's the sweetest melody. Like the crackle of a vinyl record playing our favorite tune on a lazy Sunday afternoon. It's the kind of laughter that lifts the weight off my shoulders and makes me forget about the troubles of the world.

Birdie's got those poodle skirts and saddle shoes, a

style that's straight out of a rock 'n' roll ballad. She's a vision in polka dots and pastels, and every time I see her, it's like a page out of a Norman Rockwell painting. But love in the 50s ain't all milkshakes and drive-ins. We've had our share of heartaches and doo-wop dramas. The jitterbug of emotions, you could say. Yet, in the end, we always found our way back to each other. It was the kind of love that weathered the storms, like an old convertible cruising through a summer rain.

I courter her with handwritten letters and passed notes in class, the kind of sweet gestures that seem straight out of a coming-of-age flick. And when we slow danced to the tunes of Sinatra or Elvis, it was like time stands still, and it was me and Birdie in our own little soda shop paradise. Here I am, a fella, head over heels for Birdie. She's my jitterbug partner, my poodle skirt sweetheart, and together we're dancing through the nostalgia of a bygone era. The truth is college was a whole new world opening up before me and as I walked around campus, feeling the rhythm of rock 'n' roll in the air, my mind went to Birdie. All I could picture are her curls that could rival the stars, standing out like a beacon in the crowd.

While we didn't attend the same high school, there's a whimsical nostalgia in our college rendezvous, like a sweet echo of what could have been our shared high school experience, complete with milkshakes at the local diner. I thought about seeing her under the bright lights of college life. All I know is the moment our eyes met it was like the universe began playing on a love song that's been playing ever since.

***

DATE: MARCH 1950

As the days unfolded, I found myself falling deeper in love with Birdie. Each shared moment, every laugh, and every glance exchanged between us felt like a cherished note in the melody of our blossoming romance. One vibrant spring afternoon, I decided to surprise her with a picnic in the heart of the sprawling campus. I wanted to remind her of our first date and how much I have adored her ever since. Choosing a picturesque spot beneath the blooming cherry blossom trees, their petals drifting like delicate confetti in the breeze, I aimed to make this moment as enchanting as the season itself. I planned every detail meticulously from the array of fresh fruits to the soft blanket spread beneath the cherry blossom canopy. As Birdie's eyes sparkled with delight, I reached into the picnic basket and produced a small velvet box.

The anticipation in her gaze fueled my excitement as I opened it to reveal a delicate silver bracelet, adorned with a small charm shaped like the campus clock tower.

"For all the moments we've shared on this campus and the countless ones yet to come," I said, my voice carrying the weight of a commitment that went beyond words.

As we sat side by side beneath the trees, the campus bathed in the warm glow of the spring sun, I couldn't help but reflect on the significance of this moment. The bracelet shimmered in the soft light, a testament to our love story intertwined with the freshness and renewal of the season. In that moment, as the petals fell like a gentle rain around us and the air filled with the sweet scent of spring, I marveled at the depth of my feelings for Birdie. The commitment I felt was not only to a person but to a shared future, to the countless chapters yet to be written in the story of our love at Millikin. Hours slipped away unnoticed, the sun's gentle warmth giving way to the cool embrace of the evening.

As twilight descended, we found ourselves still lost in conversation, our laughter mingling with the soft chirping of crickets in the cool evening air. The transition from day to night seemed almost seamless, the fading light replaced by a canopy of twinkling stars above. And in that moment, as Birdie and I sat beneath the night sky, I realized that our afternoon picnic had evolved into a timeless journey, marked by the exchange of a simple bracelet. A prelude to the unity of love and companionship that awaited us in the years ahead.

10

BIRDIE
FIRST SEMESTER OF SENIOR YEAR
YEAR: 1950

Navigating the challenges of college life together deepened our connection. The excitement of graduation loomed, and with it the realization that our dreams might take us in different directions. Still, love blossomed, resilient and unwavering.

I've always had a knack for words. Whether it was crafting eloquent essays in high school or jotting down my thoughts in a worn-out journal, words were my sanctuary. Setting forth on my path, I quickly discovered an avenue that would not only nurture my love for writing but also shape the course of my future.

It all began when I was, a wide-eyed freshman in college with dreams as vast as the Illinois sky, stumbled upon the bustling office of the university's student newspaper, *The Decatur Chronicle*. Intrigued and drawn to the energy radiating from the room, I decided to join as a volunteer writer. In the beginning, my contributions were modest, capturing snippets of campus events and student life. Yet, with every keystroke and printed word, I felt an undeniable thrill, a sense of purpose that grew with each passing article. The newsroom became my haven, a space where ideas flowed like an unbridled river, and the possibilities seemed endless. When I delved deeper into my role, I found myself tackling more substantial assignments.

Feature stories, interviews with faculty members, and investigative pieces became my forte. The campus began to take notice of my byline, and my articles resonated with readers, sparking conversations and inspiring change.

One fateful day, I was given the opportunity to cover a prominent author's visit to the university. As I engaged in a thoughtful conversation with the writer, I felt an invisible bridge connecting my passion for words with the world of publishing. The realization hit me like a revelation and I wanted to spend my future immersed in the world of writing and publishing.

Fueling my newfound ambition, I started seeking internships with publishing houses, attending writing workshops, and building a portfolio that reflected my diverse range of skills. The student newspaper, once a stepping stone, had become the launchpad for my aspirations. Every interview, every article, and every late-night editing session was a building block toward my dream. My dedication did not go unnoticed. Professors and mentors took note of my exceptional writing prowess, guiding me toward opportunities that would refine my craft. The more I explored the realms of publishing, the more I became captivated by the art of storytelling whether it was through investigative journalism, creative writing, or editing manuscripts.

With graduation looming in our future, I felt excitement and apprehension. Armed with a rich tapestry of experiences from my time at the student newspaper, I was ready to embrace the next chapter of my life. The world of publishing awaited, and I was determined to make my mark, spending all my future days doing what I loved most: writing and shaping stories that would resonate with readers for years to come.

Roger was more than a boyfriend; he was my greatest cheerleader. Every article I penned, he devoured with an unwavering enthusiasm, preserving each one in a collection of carefully kept newspapers. His constant encouragement ringing in my ears, urging me to pursue my dreams relentlessly. We'd playfully jest about the prospect of me becoming the CEO of my own publishing house, a whimsical dream, or so I thought. I harbored reservations about placing all my aspirations into a single basket. The fear of being pigeonholed as someone who only excelled in one area loomed over me. Yet, Roger, through his own pursuits, taught me a valuable lesson. I witnessed him passionately chasing after his dreams while simultaneously expanding his frame of reference with new endeavors. It dawned on me that there was wisdom in embracing diverse interests; after all, that's what hobbies are for. I grappled with the idea that I didn't have to stretch myself thin to maintain my authenticity.

Roger's steadfast support became a guiding light. With every stroke of the pen on paper, the notion of evolving into a future publisher became increasingly tangible. Roger's influence went beyond his love; it was his dependable support that became the anchor for my aspirations. I cherished him for countless reasons, but above all, for being the staunch pillar propelling me toward my dreams.

11
ROGER

The realization came to me one crisp morning as I watched a solitary plane dance across the clear blue sky. It wasn't a fleeting fascination, but a calling that stirred something deep within me. Growing up, I'd watched my dad fly, and I wanted to follow in his footsteps.

By the time I was fifteen, I knew with certainty that I wanted to fly. I wanted to become a pilot. The decision to pursue this dream was a quiet whisper at first, a subtle shift in the currents of my aspirations. I started researching flight schools, reading about the mechanics of aircraft, and immersing myself in the world that had, until now, felt like a distant fantasy.

One day, when I had turned eighteen, I walked into the local flight school, a blend of eager anticipation and jittery energy buzzing through my veins. The instructor, a season pilot with a twinkle in his eye, greeted me warmly. "Looking to learn to fly?" he asked, as if sensing the unspoken dreams that brought me to his doorstep.

I nodded, a grin breaking across my face. "I want to become a pilot."

And so, the journey began. The first time I stepped into the cockpit, the hum of the engine and the array of controls felt like stepping into a different world. The instructor guided me through the basics, explaining the intricacies of navigation, the science of flight, and the art of handling the aircraft. The moment the plane taxied down the runway under my control, exhilaration surged through me. The ground gradually fell away, and I was suspended in the boundless expanse of the sky. It was an indescribable sensation, an intoxicating blend of freedom and responsibility.

Lesson after lesson, I learned to read the skies, to dance through clouds and tempests, and to place my trust in the wings that bore me. The hours in the air became a tapestry of my aspirations, each flight weaving new threads of knowledge into my soul. Every challenge was a trial by wind, and with every lesson, my passion for flight took stronger root within me, growing ever more fervent with the sky as my guiding compass. There were moments of doubt, of course.

Learning to fly demanded discipline, focus, and a willingness to confront the unexpected. But with each hurdle, I found a reservoir of determination within me that pushed me to persevere. Then came the solo flight—the defining moment when the instructor stepped out, leaving me alone in the cockpit. The responsibility was solely mine, and as I taxied onto the runway, I felt the weight of my dreams and the freedom of the skies converging. The plane lifted off, and I soared through the clouds, realizing that this was more than a skill, it was a part of who I was meant to be. The dream had transformed into a tangible reality, and as I guided the aircraft through the sky, I knew I was on the path to becoming the pilot I had always envisioned.

With each lesson, with each flight, I embraced not only the technicalities of aviation but the resonant bond between myself and the vast, limitless sky. The dream had taken flight, and I was determined to let it soar to new heights. I kept my ambitions for the future discreet at first, choosing to reveal little to Birdie in the beginning. All she knew was that I possessed a private pilot's license and harbored dreams of a career aloft.

Though dreams do evolve, this one remained steadfast. I was resolute—this vision of soaring through the skies was one I would never abandon.

Softly, I would retreat, grateful that she never pressed for answers. What we shared thrived on trust, and Birdie was never one to seek constant revelations. It wasn't about concealing anything; rather, I wished to accumulate enough insight and experience before sharing with her. I aimed to have a substantial foundation before revealing any exciting news to her.

One day, as I gently guided the plane through the skies, the wind whistling past the wings, I couldn't contain the excitement bubbling within me. The realization that I was fulfilling my dream as a pilot filled me with an electrifying energy. I imagined myself soaring through the clouds, pushing the boundaries of the sky, and discovering adventures only a pilot could know. The news of my next pursuit couldn't wait to be shared, and there was one person I was particularly eager to tell—Birdie. She, too, had been pursuing her dreams in the world of publishing, and I couldn't help but feel a sense of pride for both of us.

We were like two eagles, each soaring toward our aspirations, and I couldn't wait to share my sojourn with her. After landing, I rushed to the nearby pay-phone, eager to dial her number and share the exhilaration that was still coursing through my veins. As her familiar voice greeted me on the other end, I couldn't help but burst with enthusiasm.

"Birdie, you'll never guess what I've been up to!" I proclaimed, my words tumbling out like an excited child, brimming with the thrill of my latest adventure. "I've been advancing in my flying lessons, striving for my commercial license. Today, my instructor was silent, allowing me to take full command. Can you picture it? Me and the plane, cruising through the sky!"

There was a pause on the other end, and then I could hear the excitement in her voice. "Roger, that's amazing! I knew you had it in you. Flying? Really?"

I chuckled at her infectious enthusiasm. "Absolutely! It's like a dream come true. I've discovered this whole new world up there, and I can't wait to share it with you."

My words seemed to bridge the distance between us, and I felt her passion resonate through the phone as she recounted her triumphs and trials in the world of publishing.

Though our dreams had manifested in different ways, the essence remained constant: the pursuit of something greater than ourselves.

"Hey, Birdie," I said, my voice softening with affection. "I've been thinking. What if, when we both achieve our dreams, we take on the world together? You conquering the literary realm with your words, and me soaring through the skies as a pilot. Together, we can face anything."

After a thoughtful pause, her voice came through with heartfelt warmth. "Roger, I'm all in with that idea. We're like a team, supporting each other's dreams no matter how lofty they may be. I'm so proud of you for pursuing your passion, as you're proud of me."

In that moment, I felt a profound connection, not only to the vast, limitless sky above, but to the unwavering support and understanding that bound Birdie and me together. As we continued to share our dreams, I couldn't help but feel that together we were unstoppable, ready to conquer anything that lay ahead.

12
BIRDIE
YEAR: 1950-1951

The day Roger announced his choice to advance his flying lessons is etched in my memory like a vivid painting. I recall how, during his early training, he had called to tell me about his first flight, his excitement palpable through every word. He was so excited and started talking about our future and the adventures we'd go on. I told him how amazing the news was. And honest truth, I was excited for him.

But that small fear crept into my mind. I've heard stories of smaller planes crashing or people going missing. What if Roger wanted to be like Amelia Earhart and attempt to conquer flying around the world only for something to go terribly wrong? No one truly knows what happened in her disappearance but I wasn't about to send my boyfriend off into the world of flying to find out if he was about to succumb the same fate.

I know I should have told him I was scared for him but yet again, I bit my tongue. This was his dream and who was I to tell him not to chase his dream. And if it were me, I'd be furious if he told me to not chase mine.

I hurried through the hushed aisles of the library, my mind racing with excitement and anticipation. My fingertips brushed against the spines of countless books on my route to our usual meeting spot.

There, leaning against a bookshelf with his usual nonchalant demeanor, was Roger, engrossed in a paperback about aviation during the Civil War.

"Hey Roger!" I called out, my voice bubbling with enthusiasm.

Roger glanced up, a lazy grin spreading across his face as he spotted my approaching. "Hey, Birdie. What's the latest scoop?"

"I've been thinking about our weekend plans," I began eagerly, my heart pounding with anticipation. "There's this book festival in town, featuring local authors that will be on a panel. Along with a few publishing houses. I think it could help get my foot in the door."

Roger's smiled faltered for a moment, a flicker of uncertainty crossing his features. "Hmm, that sounds swell, Birdie, but I was thinking of doing something else this weekend."

My excitement waned, replaced by a sinking feeling of

disappointment. "Something else? Such as?"

Roger hesitated, his gaze shifting away momentarily before meeting mine again. "Well, there's this aviation expo happening, and I thought it was be a great opportunity to check out the planes and talk to seasoned pilots."

I felt a twinge of frustration rising within me. We had always supported each other's dreams, but sometimes Roger's passion for flying clouded his focus.

"But Roger, we talked about this. Is flying a job you want for the future? This could be an opportunity for you to see what I want to do with my future. We always do what you want to do but what about me?"

Roger shrugged, his casual demeanor masking the tension between us. "I know, Birdie. And I've always supported you in that. But flying is my passion. It's what I want to do with my life."

I struggled to contain my frustration, my thoughts battling each other. "I get that, Roger. But we're in college now, and we need to focus on building our futures. Writing is my passion, like flying is yours."

Roger's expression softened, his eyes searching mine for understanding. "I know we're different, Birdie. But isn't that what makes us work?"

I sighed, my resolve wavering as I searched for a compromise. "Maybe you're right, Roger. Maybe we can find a way to balance our passions without losing sight of our goals."

I told Roger, he should go to the expo and that I would attend the book festival with one of my sorority sisters, Blair. Roger decided he would ask one of his fraternity brothers to attend the aviation expo. As we walked out of the library, uncertainty lingered in the air. But beneath it all, I knew that as long as we faced our difference together, we could weather any storm that came our way.

SENIOR YEAR
SECOND SEMESTER
YEAR: 1951

Two weeks later, we were sitting on the porch of my sorority house, the warm breeze carrying the scent of blooming flowers. Roger's eyes sparkled with determination and excitement that I couldn't decipher. He took a deep breath, his gaze fixed on the distant horizon, as if the sky held the words he needed.

"Birdie," he began, his voice a blend of nervousness and anticipation, "there's something important I need to share with you."

I turned to face him, my heart picking up its pace. His hand found mine, fingers interlacing as if seeking comfort. The gravity of the moment hung in the air, and I held my breath, waiting for his revelation.

"As you know being a pilot is important to me. What I now need to share is that I've also decided to join the Air Force," he said, his eyes finally meeting mine.

Silence stretched between us, and my mind raced to process the weight of his words. The realization dawned, and a mixture of pride and concern washed over me. "Air

Force?" I finally whispered, my voice barely audible.

Roger nodded, his eyes searching mine for understanding. "It's been my dream for as long as I can remember, Birdie. My father was in the Air Force, and I want to continue that tradition. Flying is in my blood."

I felt a lump forming in my throat, the realization sinking in. The skies, once a distant canvas of dreams, were now calling him. "What does this mean for us?" I asked, my voice a whisper.

He squeezed my hand gently, his thumb tracing comforting circles. "I've thought about it, Birdie. I'll finish through to my senior year. The day after graduation, I'll leave for Air Force training. It won't be easy, but I want you to know you're my anchor. No matter where I am, you'll be in my heart."

Tears welled in my eyes, a mix of pride for the man I loved and the ache of the impending separation. As I spoke, my voice trembled with suppressed anger. "I believe in your dreams, Roger," I began, struggling to keep my tone steady. "But do you even realize what you're doing?" My words cracked with frustration. "You're chasing after something that's going to tear us apart!" I paused, trying to reign in my emotions, but they spilled out in a rush.

"We'll make the most of the time we have together before you set off, but damn it, Roger, why does it have to be like this?"

I rose abruptly, steadying myself against one of the elegant white pillars. "Roger, I don't understand," I began, my voice tinged with frustration. "I thought you would understand how I feel."

His expression pleaded for comprehension. "Birdie, I thought you would be happy for me?"

"I am happy for you, Roger," I replied, my tone softening slightly. "But it's not about your dreams. It's about us, too. I had plans for us this summer. We were supposed to meet each other's families. My birthday is in July and you're going to miss it."

As I spoke, a single tear slipped down my cheek, betraying the turmoil within me.

"I'm sorry, Birdie," Roger's voice softened, his words laced with sincerity. "But I can't put my dreams on hold to make you feel better. You may not understand or be thrilled about it, but I need you to respect my decision. Can you at least try to understand?

Roger stepped closer, reaching out for my hand, but I recoiled, a mixture of hurt and frustration swirling inside me. With trembling hands, I wiped away the tears that began to cascade down my cheeks, silently pleading for him to see the depth of my pain. I was upset, feeling the sting of disappointment, but amidst it all, I realized the last thing I wanted was for us to be consumed by anger and resentment. Despite the ache in my heart, I made a silent vow to myself: *I would try to understand. Our love deserved that much.*

The sun gradually descended, casting a warm, golden glow across the sky, painting it in a breathtaking blend of orange and pink hues. The decision had been made, and the road ahead seemed cloaked in a veil of uncertainty. Yet, our love stood as a steadfast beacon, illuminating our way through the trials that awaited. As Roger enfolded me in his embrace, I marveled at the man who dared to pursue his dreams with such fervor, even knowing that the day after graduation, he would embark on a new journey with the Air Force.

13
BIRDIE
DATE: MARCH 1951

The months stretched ahead like an uncharted flight path as Roger delved into the rigorous training required to advance in his pilot endeavors. The familiar porch of my sorority house became a silent witness to his relentless dedication and the transformation that unfolded.

Roger's study routine became a ritual, marked by the soft glow of lamplight filtering through the curtains. He immersed himself in aviation manuals, charts, and flight simulations. While I immersed myself in books about publishing. The distant hum of airplanes overhead seemed to synchronize with the cadence of his focused efforts. Each page turned, every equation mastered, brought him closer to the realization of his lifelong dream. There were nights when the weight of the responsibility he was undertaking mirrored the gravity of his decision. As I watched him pour over his notes, I could see the determination in his eyes, a reflection of the countless hours invested in understanding the intricacies of flight. I would sit by his side, offering encouragement and a comforting presence when fatigue threatened to overwhelm him.

Weekends were spent at the local airfield, where Roger took to the skies under the watchful eye of seasoned instructors. The roar of the engines and the crisp air against his face became familiar companions. I would stand by the runway, eyes fixed on the small plane as it taxied and soared into the open sky, disappearing into the clouds. The day Roger successfully completed his first solo flight was a moment of triumph. The sense of accomplishment radiated from him, and as he touched down with precision, a wave of applause and cheers erupted from the onlookers. I ran towards him, the pride in my heart echoing in every step. Roger emerged from the cockpit, a grin of pure exhilaration on his face.

"I did it, Birdie!" he exclaimed, the joy in his voice resonating with the achievement.

We embraced, surrounded by the backdrop of aircraft and the camaraderie of fellow aviators. It was a milestone etched not only in logbooks but in the shared story of our flight through life.

The days turned into weeks, and Roger continued to navigate the complexities of flight training. I witnessed his growth not only as a pilot, but as a man fueled by passion and resilience. Late nights turned into early mornings, and the anticipation of the looming pilot's license exam hung in the air.

Finally, the day arrived when Roger emerged from the examination room, a gleam of accomplishment in his eyes. He held the coveted pilot's license in his hands, a testament to the countless hours of study, practice, and unwavering determination. As I congratulated him, I knew that this milestone marked the beginning of a new chapter. A chapter that would propel him into the boundless skies he had always yearned to conquer.

* * *

```
DATE: JUNE 1951
AGE: TWENTY-ONE
```

The day of graduation dawned with a mix of celebration and bittersweet anticipation. It was the middle of June; the campus buzzed with excitement, and the air was filled with a sense of accomplishment.

As I stood among the sea of caps and gowns, my eyes searched for Roger in the crowd. Spotting him, I couldn't help but marvel at the journey we had undertaken together. It had been two years of Roger and I dating and here we were about to leave one chapter behind to embrace another.

The struggles, the late-night study sessions, and the moments of doubt had all led us to this pivotal day. While most of us were in caps and gowns, Roger was in his crisp Air Force uniform, standing tall and proud. The distinct wings pinned to his chest symbolized not only his achievement but also the commitment he was about to make.

The commencement ceremony passed in a haze of speeches, applause, and the soft swish of graduation gowns. As the names were called one by one, Roger's turn drew closer. My heart swelled with pride as he walked across the stage to receive his diploma, a testament to his academic prowess and dedication. The moment wasn't about academic achievement; it also marked the bridge between the familiar grounds of university life and the uncharted territories awaiting him in the Air Force.

The dean's words echoed through the auditorium, emphasizing the significance of stepping into the future with courage and fortitude. After the ceremony, we gathered with friends and family, exchanging hugs and congratulations. The atmosphere was filled with joy, but an underlying current of somberness lingered. Roger's departure loomed, and the reality of our separation settled in.

Amid the festivities, Roger took me aside, his eyes searching mine for reassurance. "Birdie," he said, his voice carrying a mix of excitement and apprehension, "this is it. The day has come, and tomorrow I begin a new chapter in the Air Force. I wish you could be there with me, but you'll be in my thoughts every step of the way."

I nodded, my eyes brimming with both joy and sadness. "I'll be cheering you on from here, Roger. Go and conquer those skies, and know that I'll be waiting for you when you return."

While the fiery orb gradually made its descent, enveloping the campus with its warm and radiant glow, we found ourselves standing in a serene corner, captivated by the beauty of the moment.

"I never imagined graduation day would feel like this," I admitted, a tear escaping my eye.

Roger held me close, his gaze fixed on the distant skyline, mirroring the determination I had seen on that porch months ago. "Birdie, our journey doesn't end here. It's just taking a different route. No matter where the Air Force takes me, you'll be my anchor, and our love will be the constant that guides me."

With those words, we embraced, holding onto each other as if time itself was reluctant to let us go. The chapter of university life was closing, but a new one was unfolding—Roger's service to his country, with all the challenges and adventures awaiting him in the vast skies. As we parted ways that evening, the promise of reunion felt euphoric. With a final glance back at the campus, we stepped into the unknown, hand in hand.

14
ROGER

I can still remember the moment I first took the controls of a small plane—a wave of excitement came over me, accompanied by a flutter of unease. Having a pilot's license was a dream that had lingered in my mind since childhood, fueled by my father's tales of adventure in the sky.

Now, as I taxied down the runway, I could hardly believe that the day of working towards getting my commercial license had finally arrived.

The cockpit enveloped me, the smell of aviation fuel and the hum of the engine creating a sensory experience. I glanced at the Certified Flight Instructor, also known as CFI, sitting beside me, his experience evident in the way he effortlessly adjusted the controls. I had flown hundreds of times before, each flight a stepping stone towards my ultimate goal. Today, every maneuver, every navigation checkpoint, every adjustment of the controls carried the weight of my aspirations. He must have sense my anticipation, because he turned and grinned, his eyes reflecting the thrill of flight.

"Alright, Roger," he said, his voice steady and reassuring. "You're in control. Take us up."

I gripped the yoke, the weight of responsibility settling in. I gazed down the endless runway, took a deep breath, and pushed the throttle forward. The plane's engine roared to life, and I felt the powerful acceleration as the wheels began to roll. I increased the throttle, and the plane lifted off the ground, soaring into the sky. As we ascended, the world below transformed into a patchwork of field and roads. The CFI guided me through the basics—turns, climbs, descents. Each moment of the controls was a dance between precision and instinct. The sky, once a distant dream, became my playground.

"Feel the aircraft," the instructor advised, his words a mantra. "You're not flying it; you're part of it."

And I did. The subtle shifts in the air, the way the plane responded to my touch. It was an intimate connection that went beyond the mechanical. It was a dance with the clouds, a flirtation with the stratosphere. Hours passed, and with each maneuver, my confidence grew.

The instructor nodded approvingly, offering guidance when needed but giving me the space to truly take command. This wasn't my first rodeo—I had been around planes my whole life. During my childhood, I would sit in the passenger seat of the plane, my small hands gripping the edge of the seat in excitement as my father took to the skies. I watched in awe as he guided the aircraft with dexterity and grit, each movement a testament to his ability to command the skies. And here I was now, the one in control with my instructor seated beside me. We climbed to higher altitudes, the landscape below shrinking into miniature.

I had been training with the CFI for the last few months. Each day seemed to carry the weight of countless hours spent studying flight manuals, mastering the intricacies of navigation, and honing my skills in the cockpit. With the end in sight, the final phase of my training loomed large.

Every flight no longer a lesson but a test to my readiness to take the skies with confidence and competence befitting of a commercial pilot. The thrill of soaring through the clouds were tempered by the gravity of the responsibility I was about to undertake. As I prepared for the last series of evaluations, nerves danced like flickering flames in my chest. Yet, amidst my anxiety, there was a steely determination, a resolve forged through the countless hours of dedication and sacrifice. And the moment I had been eagerly anticipating had finally arrived—my last solo flight. Left alone in the cockpit, the realization hit me that it was me and the plane, suspended in the boundless sky.

Taxiing onto the runway, a mix of exhilaration and nerves coursed through me. The engine roared, and I lifted off. I soared through the sky with the wind whispering its secrets, and for that moment, I was untethered—a pilot with the world at his feet. Touching down after that solo flight, I couldn't help but grin. The journey to earn my commercial pilot's license had been challenging, but every lesson, every correction, and every moment into the sky had shaped me into a pilot. I carried that license, not only as a piece of paper, but as a symbol of dreams fulfilled and boundaries transcended.

The sky, once a distant realm seen through the lens of childhood wonder, was now my domain. Guiding the aircraft toward the hangar, I sensed that the adventures awaiting above were only beginning. As I taxied back, the sun started its descent, casting a warm glow across the airfield. My heart was still racing from the exhilaration of the final solo flight as I shut off the engine. The propellers slowed to a gentle spin, and I took a moment to savor the quiet hum that replaced the road of the engine.

The instructor approached with a congratulatory smile. His words broke the silence, proclaiming the culmination of my efforts and the attainment of a lifelong ambition. "Well done, Roger! You handled that final solo flight like a seasoned pro."

"Thanks," I replied, still riding the high of the experience. "It's incredible up there. I can't believe I get to do this."

He clapped me on the back. "Your earned it, and you'll only get better with each flight. Remember, this is the beginning of your next adventure."

I followed him back to the flight school building.

As I walked, the gravity of what I had accomplished sank in. With a mixture of relief and euphoria, I knew that I had finally earned my wings. I was ready to embark on my next adventure where the sky was no longer a limit, but a boundless expanse of possibilities. I had transformed from a dreamer with my head in the clouds to a Commercial Pilot (CPL). The sense of achievement was both humbling and empowering. In the coming weeks, I continued to hone my skills.

The skies became my classroom, and every flight brought new challenges and lessons. I delved into navigation, reading weather patterns and practicing emergency procedures. Each experience was a building block, strengthening the foundation of my newfound passion.

One day, as I prepped the plane for another flight, a fellow pilot approached. "Hey, Roger, mind if I join you? I could use a wingman for some formation flying practice."

Excitement surged through me. Formation flying was a whole new level of skill and coordination. I nodded, and soon we were soaring together, side by side. The synchronicity required was demanding, but the thrill of flying in harmony with another plane was unmatched.

The days turned into weeks and the weeks into months, I ventured into uncharted territories. I flew to neighboring airports, embraced the challenges of cross-country navigations, and experienced the beauty of sunrises and sunsets from the cockpit. The sky, vast and ever-changing, became my second home.

One evening, after a rewarding day of flying, I sat by the hangar, gazing at the stars beginning to twinkle above. The instructor, who had become both mentor and friend, joined me.

"Roger," he said, his eyes reflecting the same passion

that had ignited mine, "you've come a long way. But remember, the sky has endless lessons to teach. Keep learning, keep exploring. Your journey is only beginning."

I looked up at the canvas of stars and knew he was right. The adventures that awaited me in the boundless sky were infinite, and my story as a pilot was only beginning.

★ ★ ★

DATE: JUNE 1951
AGE: TWENTY-ONE

The day of my college graduation arrived, and I stood tall in my Air Force uniform, the wings proudly pinned to my chest, signifying a commitment to something greater than myself.

As my fellow graduates donned caps and gowns, I felt a unique weight on my shoulders—the weight of honor, duty, and sacrifice.

The military attire marked not merely the end of my academic days but the start of a journey steeped in purpose. Family and friends gathered around, their proud smiles and hearty congratulations reflecting the steadfast support that had been with me throughout my studies. The uniform was more than garb; it symbolized a commitment to serve and protect.

The commencement speaker's remarks underscored the importance of embracing change and facing the future with courage. At that moment, the wings on my chest felt weighty, signifying my pledge to serve my country. The turning of the tassel represented not only the conclusion of my academic career but the beginning of a path dedicated to something greater than personal ambition. The celebration was a blend of joy and solemnity, shared with classmates who had become comrades in both study and service.

In the days following, I adjusted from student to Air Force officer, seeking to blend my academic training with the dedication demanded by military life. My flying continued, now with renewed purpose. As twilight settled on my return to base, I reflected on the paths that led me here. The Air Force uniform was a profound symbol of commitment, merging academic achievements with aviation dreams. The next chapter, with its promise of challenges and successes, beckoned with a sense of duty and pride. The journey, like the dusk sky, was just beginning, and I stood ready—not only as Roger Scott but as an officer with wings, poised to serve my country.

15
BIRDIE
DATE: JUNE 1951

The days leading up to Roger's departure were a whirlwind of emotions. We spent every waking moment together, cherishing each memory we created as if we could hold onto them for the days to come. Sunsets felt more precious than ever, and every shared glance seemed to carry the weight of everything left unsaid.

Then, the day after graduation arrived. The campus buzzed with the energy of new beginnings as families gathered to celebrate their graduates. Amidst the sea of people, Roger and I sought solace in a quiet corner, holding onto those final moments before the unknown stretched out before us. His duffel bag stood by his side, a tangible reminder of the imminent separation. Roger looked at me, his eyes reflecting a mixture of curiosity and wariness.

"Birdie," he said, pulling me into a tight embrace, "this is it."

We stood there, holding onto each other as if time could stand still. The familiar scent of his cologne lingered, and I tried to memorize every detail of the moment. The reality of his departure lingered like a shadow, but we held fast to the present, savoring the closeness of our last moments together before the unknown took him away.

In the grip of his hands, I felt something steady, something that kept me from unraveling; a quiet strength that seemed to whisper everything I couldn't put into words. This, I realized, was love.

Love, like cosmic stardust, binds the senses; as it coalesces into the vast universe, a newborn star emerges, wielding its gravitational pull and casting its brilliance across the cosmos.

The sound of a distant airplane engine roared in the sky, a haunting whisper of our farewell.

Roger gently pulled away, cupping my face in his hands. "I'll come back, Birdie. I promise."

A bittersweet smile played on my lips as I nodded, understanding the duty that called him. "I'll be waiting, Roger. Always."

With a final lingering kiss, Roger picked up his duffel bag, and we walked, our hands clasped tightly, towards the waiting military transport. When we reached the entrance, he turned to me, his eyes filled with gratitude. "Thank you for believing in me, Birdie. I love you."

"I love you too," I whispered, watching him board the bus that would take him to his next destination.

I envisioned him later stepping onto the plane that would carry him into the unknown skies. The roar of the engine would swallow every unspoken word, leaving only the silence of what was left behind. With a heavy heart, I watched the bus drive away, taking Roger from the familiar into a world of duty and honor.

When the bus faded into the endless horizon, I felt a blend of pride and sorrow. Our love, strong and unwavering, would bridge the distance, sustained by the promise of a future reunion. The porch of my sorority house felt emptier, but the memories of Roger's resolve and the gleam in his eyes lingered, a testament to a love that soared beyond the edge of the world.

In the months that followed, I immersed myself in the routines of everyday life, trying to fill the void left by Roger's absence. Each letter sent from him became a cherished lifeline, connecting us across the miles.

His words were a source of comfort, and I clung to them like a sailor to a lighthouse in a storm. I devoted my time to pursuits that would make him proud, channeling the strength of our love into my endeavors.

The sorority porch, once a witness to our farewells, became a place of solace and reflection. Thoughts of our laughter lingered, a reminder of the joy that had once filled those moments. With the changing seasons came a transformation in the landscape of our lives. Friends came and went, but the memory of Roger remained a constant.

The porch, adorned with flickering candles during our shared evenings, became a shrine of sorts—a place where love and longing converged. In the quiet hours of the night, I would sit on that porch, gazing at the stars, wondering if Roger was looking at the same sky. Our love, like those distant constellations, persisted beyond the constraints of time and space. I learned to navigate the complexities of a love tested by distance, drawing strength from the memories we created. The scent of his cologne, though absent in the physical realm, lingered in the corners of my heart, a comforting presence in moments of solitude. And life moved forward, a journey marked by the letters that bridged the gap between us.

I knew my time at Zeta Tau Alpha had reached its conclusion. The cherished memories of sisterhood and my flourishing relationship with Roger would forever be engraved in my mind and heart. As the years advance, we face choices—some lead to grand opportunities, while others offer life's valuable lessons. Yet, it seems that the path we choose matters less than the journey itself, for life is a grand adventure, ever filled with lessons to be learned.

16
```
ROGER
DATE: JUNE 1951-MARCH
        1952
```

The morning sun bathed the airfield in warm hues, casting a golden glow on the sleek fighter jet that stood before me. Clad in my Air Force uniform, a legacy passed down from my father, I felt a surge of pride and nostalgia. My thoughts drifted back to the day I boarded that bus and said goodbye to Birdie.

Her eyes were a mix of pride and concern, and her whispered encouragement, *Your father would be so proud*, lingered in my mind. I had only returned briefly before being deployed on my first mission. Now, as I prepared to leave for six months, the weight of departure felt heavier. The embroidered patches on my uniform told stories of service and sacrifice. As I promised Birdie, "I'll make him proud, and I'll come back to you," the bus pulled away, taking me to the unknown.

THREE MONTHS LATER
DATE: SEPTEMBER 1951

The initial period of my deployment was intense. The first three months were consumed by training and acclimation to the new environment. The days were filled with rigorous exercises and strategic briefings. I found solace in the letters from Birdie, each one a reminder of home.

SIX MONTHS LATER
DATE: MARCH 1952

As the final days of my six-month deployment in Novaria drew near, I reflected on the journey that had led me here. In the cockpit, I thought about the generations before me who had soared through the clouds, leaving a legacy that now rested on my shoulders.

The aircraft ascended, and as I entered the vast expanse of the sky, I carried with me the weight of duty and the promises I had made to Birdie. The altimeter climbed steadily, marking our ascent into the boundless blue. The cockpit was an orchestration of dials and controls, a familiar dance I had perfected during training. Below, the patchwork of fields and rivers seemed almost surreal. The words Birdie had spoken to me echoed in my mind, her encouragement mingling with the hum of the jet engines.

I glanced at the photograph of my father stowed in the dashboard. His steely gaze seemed to urge me onward. The radio crackled to life, guiding me through the airspace.

As the mission details unfolded in crisp instructions, I had set aside thoughts of political complexities and focused on the task at hand.

My deployment involved aerial support for ground troops, transporting humanitarian aid, and conducting reconnaissance missions in Novaria.

The diverse landscapes and vibrant communities provided both challenges and opportunities. Despite the obstacles—from logistical issues to unexpected developments—my team and I remained committed to our mission of maintaining peace and stability. Navigating rugged terrain and engaging with local communities, I found myself immersed in Novarian culture. The mission remained our primary focus, guiding our actions and decisions. My training kicked in, and muscle memory guided my hands over the controls. The sun cast its warmth on us, and my thoughts drifted to Birdie, holding out hope for my return. I The mission unfolded with tension and focus. Hours passed quickly, and as the sun began to set, I thought about the homestretch. The familiar sight of the airfield from thousands of feet above now felt distant as I landed in Novaria. Throughout my deployment, I had witnessed the resilience of the Novarian people, and their commitment to building a better future resonated deeply with me.

After my six-month mission neared its end, I received a letter from Birdie, short and sweet: "My darling Roger, you're almost home. Come back to me." I was eager to return to her. As I approached the base, I asked her to meet me there, where other airmen and their families would be waiting.

Upon landing, I taxied toward the hangar, excitement building. he cockpit opened, and I descended from the jet, feeling my father's legacy shift from a burden to a source of strength. I rushed to where Birdie was standing, and we embraced amidst the hum of aircraft engines—a reunion marked by fulfilled promises and a continuation of our tradition in the skies.

In the early morning, beneath a sky adorned with stars fading into dawn, Birdie and I stood together. Her gaze held a mixture of relief and apprehension. "You made it back, like you promised," she said, her voice tinged with emotion.

"I did," I replied, though the words felt hollow. "But things have changed, Birdie. I've changed."

Her brow furrowed in confusion. "What do you mean?" she asked softly.

I hesitated, struggling to articulate the complexities of my experience. "The mission in Novaria… it wasn't what I expected," I admitted.

Birdie's expression softened, and she reached out to

grasp my hand. "You don't have to tell me everything now," she said gently. "But whatever you're going through, I'm here for you, Roger. Always."

Her words offered a lifeline amidst my uncertainty. Yet, beneath the surface, unspoken fears and doubts lingered, casting a shadow over our reunion. As we walked toward the hangar, the fighter jet's silhouette stood tall against the clouds, embodying the stories of countless missions.

Inside the hangar, a small gathering of airmen and their loved ones awaited. Their expressions were a mix of camaraderie and respect. As I observed the scene, a sense of detachment washed over me. Despite the celebration, I felt adrift, caught between who I once was and who I had become.

The squadron commander approached, extending a firm handshake. "Officer Scott, you handled the mission with precision and skill. Your father would be proud."

The words validated my efforts, but my internal struggle remained. The mission had forced me to confront moral dilemmas and ethical quandaries, leaving me altered in ways I struggled to express. The life I had known now seemed distant, and I faced the challenge of reconciling my experiences with my past. As I stood amidst the celebration, the weight of my journey pressed heavily on me. Being a peacekeeper had drained me, and the true test of my resolve lay ahead. Glancing at Birdie, her eyes filled with concern, I knew our future would be fraught with challenges greater than any I had faced before.

The following day at dawn, I took to the sky again. It

was the only time I felt I could breathe, perhaps the key to rediscovering myself. The plane ascended, and the promise I made before the mission resounded in my mind—a guiding force as I soared into the limitless expanse, embracing the unknown with determination and a heart full of love.

17
BIRDIE
LOCATION: NEW YORK
YEARS: 1951-1952

After graduation, I found myself once again in my parents' upstate New York home, where the intoxicating aroma of freshly printed books filled the air, each page whispering of dreams. I stepped into the world of publishing at a renowned city firm, as if walking into a long-awaited destiny. Meanwhile, Roger soared through the clouds.

The day after graduation, he left for training and was gone for three months. He returned for two days before being sent on his first mission. He couldn't share a lot of details, all I knew was he was going to Novaria. Something about keeping the peace. He would be deployed for anything six months. The distance between us bridged by handwritten letters and late night calls.

In the vivid landscape of my imagination, the conclusion of Roger's deployment marked the beginning of a beautiful chapter. Envisioning his return to New York, I pictured us artfully crafting our dreams into the vibrant mosaic of the city's heart.

Together, we aimed to paint a life filled with shared aspirations, skillfully intertwining our stories with the pulsating energy of the urban dreams.

My career flourished as I discovered the magic of words to transport readers to new worlds. Roger sent postcards from some exotic location—Novaria, his messages carrying the thrill with a hint of importance of his adventure. Despite Roger being in another country half way across the world, the miles stretched out between us, we remained each other's biggest supporters. Through the last six months, we learned that love could thrive even when rooted in separate aspirations. As I penned enchanting tales within the walls of my publishing office and Roger charted his course among the clouds, our love story continued to unfold—a narrative of passion, support, and the unwavering belief that two dreams could coexist harmoniously in the vast tapestry of life.

I prayed that Roger would return to me. The turning point in our intertwined stories came when Roger's deployment on his recent mission was about to conclude. Half a year later, and his letters had taken on a different tone, filled with anticipation and a hint of something unspoken. The prospect of his return bubbled within me like a well-kept secret, the excitement building with each passing day. The day he was to return, the sky was crystal blue.

I stood on the base anxiously waiting for him to step off the airplane. The distant hum of jet engines blended with the chatter of his fellow airmen's' loved ones, creating a chorus of anticipation. My heart raced with a combination of nervousness and pure joy. I watched the plane coming in, as it landed and came to a stop, I couldn't help but scan the faces of the disembarking airmen. Then, I saw him, Roger, wearing his Air Force uniform with a confident stride, a hint of fatigue in his eyes, but a smile that lit up the entire base. My heart leaped as our eyes met, and I dashed toward him without a second thought.

Time seemed to slow as we closed the distance, and the moment our arms embraced, the world around us faded away.

"Roger!" I exclaimed; my voice filled with genuine happiness.

"Hey, Birdie," he replied, his warm embrace reassuring me that this was not a dream.

The scent of aviation fuel clung to him, blending with the familiar fragrance of his cologne. As we pulled away from our embrace, Roger's eyes sparkled with a mixture of emotions, I searched his face for the answer.

"I missed you," he confessed, and I could see the sincerity in his gaze.

"I missed you too," I replied, a wide grin spreading across my face.

It felt surreal to have him standing there in front of me, no longer confined to letters. Six lunar cycles of distance that once felt like an insurmountable chasm had evaporated into the past.

Internally, I marveled at how his presence seemed to fill the void that the miles had created. This reunion wasn't about the physical closeness; it was about the shared heartbeat, the rhythm that only the two of us knew.

I was happy to have Roger back but there was something different about his demeanor. A thickness hung in the air, and when Roger told me he wasn't the same person, a little part of my fell apart. I wanted to scream, I can fix you, no really, I can. My soul left my body, but I knew I needed to be there for Roger. I shared in my support—I didn't push for him to divulge what happened in Novaria. But I did let him know I would be here when he was ready to talk.

The next day, we spent the evening catching up on lost time, sharing stories of our respective journeys over a candlelit dinner. Roger regaled me with tales of his adventures, at least the details he was allowed to share. He talked about the camaraderie with his fellow wingmen, and the breathtaking landscapes he witnessed from high above.

A glint of moonlight caught my eye, revealing a small pendant around Roger's neck, a symbolic token we had chosen together nine months ago, before he left for training. Its gentle sway mirrored the undulating waves of our relationship, a silent testament to the enduring strength of our love. I, in turn, spoke animatedly about the world of books, the enchanting narratives I had been a part of, and the characters who had become my companions. The city lights twinkled outside the window as we laughed, reminisced, and allowed the rhythm of our conversation to rekindle the familiarity we had built.

The clinking of silverware and the distant murmur of other diners became a background melody for our reunion. It was a reunion that surpassed all expectations. In that moment, as Roger reached across the table to hold my hand, I knew our love story was entering a new chapter, one where the pages were filled with shared dreams of a future no longer confined by the miles that once kept us apart. And as I gazed into Roger's eyes, I couldn't help but marvel at the journey we had undertaken, the challenges we had faced, and the growth we had experienced individually.

A fleeting flashback brought forth a cherished memory of a quiet night under the sky filled with stars, a memory that anchored us in the foundation of our love. The reunion marked not only the end of a chapter, but the beginning of a new one filled with promise and the unwritten adventures that awaited us.

As we left the restaurant, the night air embraced us with its cool breeze, carrying a sense of anticipation. The city, with its myriad lights, stretched out before us—a metaphor for the countless possibilities awaiting our next steps. Although Roger had only been away for a total of nine months, it seemed like an eternity. In the throes of youth and love, one often finds themselves doing foolish things, unable to bear the separation from someone they hold dear. Imagining life without Roger was a daunting task, but now that he was back, that worry dissolved, and the future looked brighter than ever.

The months had passed us by. It was a balmy day in June, and the sun was casting its warm embrace upon Roger and me. The days stretched out before us, promising endless possibilities. Our summer unfolded harmoniously, each moment resonating with laughter, shared dreams, and the thrill of adventure.

We visited Coney Island—the scent of cotton candy hung in the air, and the lively melodies of carnival music dazzling around us. We indulged in the vibrant colors and laughter that painted the atmosphere. We kept our summer alive with enchanting ferry rides, the wind tousling our hair as we marveled at the cityscape. The rhythmic hum of the boat's engine blended with the laughter of fellow passengers. Central Park became our sanctuary where we took leisurely strolls beneath the green canopy. The fragrance of blooming flowers mingled with the distant chatter of fellow parkgoers. Each step brought us closer, physically and emotionally, as we discovered hidden gems around every bend.

Our summer was not only about us, but the blending of families. Gatherings with both Roger's and my families became cherished moments. Barbecues in the backyard brought the tantalizing aroma of grilled delicacies, and homemade dinner carried the warmth of shared stories and laughter. Roger, with his infectious enthusiasm, infused every outing with life. As the summer stretched out, I started to see the same excitement I grew to love, come back into his eyes. I remembered the day he returned from his Peacekeeping mission; he had changed. But here he was months later, on a summer day, with a flicker of hope. I could see the man I fell in love with, once again.

We lounged in the backyard at Roger's parents' house, enveloped in the comforting embrace of a lazy summer afternoon. The sun emanated a pleasant warmth over the scene, dappling the grass with golden light. The tantalizing aroma of barbecue wafted through the air, teasing our sense and stirring anticipation in our bellies.

Roger's father tended to the grill with practiced ease, the flames dancing eagerly beneath the sizzling meat. Each flip of the spatula sent sparks dancing into the air, while tendrils of smoke curled lazily upwards, carrying with them the promise of savory delights to come. As we waited, the sounds of laughter and conversation filled the air, mingling with the occasional chirp of a nearby bird or the gentle rustle of leaves in the breeze. It was a scene of simple contentment, a moment to savor among the hustle and bustle of everyday life.

But then, tension crackled between Roger and me. He leaned in, a playful glint in his eye. "You know, Birdie, you ought to let me teach you how to grill. Might save us another burnt steak fiasco."

My smile faltered; a flash of annoyance crossed my features. Roger's mother was a better cook than I would ever be—despite the stories he'd shared of her many cooking mishaps. I felt embarrassed to be the kind of woman that barely could make tea. "I told you; I like my steak well-done," I retorted, my tone sharper than intended.

Roger raised an eyebrow, his smirk widening. "Well

done? More like well ruined."

My cheeks flushed with frustration. "Can you drop it, Roger?" I snapped, my patience wearing thin.

Roger chuckled, oblivious to my growing irritation. "Hey, I'm trying to help you broaden your culinary perspectives."

I had had enough. With a frustrated sigh, I pulled myself up from the lawn chair and stormed off, leaving Roger to watch me go with a mix of confusion and remorse. I got into my car and drove off; I couldn't shake the feeling of unease that lingered in the pit of my stomach. I didn't say goodbye to anyone—not to Rogers parents, who had always been kind to me, nor to Roger himself. I felt a pang of guilt for leaving abruptly, but I couldn't ignore the way Roger had put me in such an uncomfortable position.

The miles stretched out before me, I cranked up the radio, as *Foolish Heart* by Mindy Carson blazed through the rusty speakers of my baby blue Ford Customline. I replayed the scene in my mind, wondering if I had overreacted. But with each passing moment, my resolve only strengthened. Maybe Roger was a changed man? I wondered. I refused to tolerate being belittled or ridiculed, even if it meant walking away from a family gathering. Deep down, I knew that Roger's family would understand. They knew him better than anyone and would surely recognize his tendency to push boundaries. And if Roger wanted to salvage our relationship, he would need to learn to treat me with the respect and consideration I deserved.

I drove into the sunset, a sense of empowerment washed over me. I may have left without saying goodbye, but I had taken a stand for myself, a small act of defiance that spoke volumes. As I left the chaos of Roger's family behind me, I felt a newfound sense of freedom and independence. Whatever lay ahead, I knew I was strong enough to face it on my own terms.

18
ROGER
DATE: SUMMER 1952

On my return to my New York haven, an unmistakable sense of excitement welled up within me. The anticipation of stepping back into my own space, paired with the joy of reuniting with Birdie after months apart, filled me with pure elation.

I was no longer the same person, perhaps my new reputation would precede me. Amidst this change there was animation and a sober awareness of the challenges ahead accompanied by me. The perpetual vigilance ingrained during my Air Force tenure lingered, creating a subtle resistance to fully relax and let go.

Nevertheless, the prospect of delegating authority, shaping future leaders, and aiding in their growth imbued me with a profound sense of purpose and motivation. Our training had endowed us with the ability to empower others and foster leadership qualities, and I was enthusiastic about applying these skills once more. As I reintegrated into my New York life, I acknowledged that the transition wouldn't be seamless. However, buoyed by the support of those around me and the eager anticipation of reuniting with Birdie, I was confident in my ability to surmount any challenges that might arise. The moment I reunited with Birdie; the air became electric with anticipation. It was a year since we'd last seen each other, but it felt like an eternity.

The mere thought of a life without Birdie was daunting, but with her back in my arms, worries dissipated, and the future seemed more promising than ever. We were young and in love, and every moment was filled with excitement and the anticipation of planning our future together.

During the summer days, every moment felt like a colorful brushstroke on a beautiful and ever-changing tableau. My favorite moments were going to Coney Island, which brought back memories as a child. The little boy in me folded with excitement over the whimsical carousel, rollercoaster rides, smell of cotton candy and freshly popped popcorn. Listening to nearby families and couples engaging in playful banter. Birdie and I reveled in the sheer joy of being together. In June, we took a ferry ride, as we sailed towards the iconic Statue of Liberty. With the cityscape as a setting, each moment became a snapshot of shared wonder and appreciation—I loved New York. How could anyone not love New York, I wondered?

I loved our days in Central Park, with its lush greenery and winding paths mirroring the twists and turns of our journey. Strolling beneath the leafy canopy, discovering hidden corners, our connection deepened with every shared dream and whispered confession. It was an afternoon, mid-June, when I invited Birdie to have a barbecue with my family. We had been getting together a lot lately bringing our families closer. This time, only Birdie would be joining. The air was filled with enticing aroma of grilled delights. I watched as Birdie's playing spirit reflected the joy we found in each other. We were sitting there, joking around when I made a remark about how bad of a cook Birdie was. I didn't mean anything by it. I pointed out the steak fiasco, chuckling over the memory. Birdie didn't think it was funny. I ignored her discomfort and continued to press on, oblivious to the tension building between us.

As Birdie stormed off, I watched her retreating figure with a mix of confusion and concern. "Birdie, wait!" I called out. I ran out the side gate to the front of the house, but she was already gone.

Turning back to the gathering, I found myself at a loss of words, unsure of how to explain Birdie's sudden departure to my family.

My mother approached me, a sympathetic look in her eyes. "Is everything alright, Roger?" she asked, her voice filled with genuine concern.

I sighed, running a hand through my hair in frustration. "I'm not sure. Birdie seemed upset all of a sudden. I don't know what happened."

My father, who had been manning the grill chimed in.

"Roger, take it from experience, never comment on another lady's cooking, no matter how bad it is."

My mother rolled her eyes. "Maybe you should go after her. Make sure she's okay."

I nodded, grateful for my mother's advice. "Yeah, you're right. But I think she already left."

I decided to get in the car, I don't know why I expected to find Birdie waiting down the street for me. But as I reached the empty driver's seat and scanned the surroundings, a sinking feeling settled in my stomach. She was gone. My heart raced as I realized the gravity of the situation. Birdie had left, and she wasn't coming back. Panic rising in my chest, I turned back to my family, my voice trembling as I struggled to find the right words. "She's gone," I muttered, my throat tight with emotion. "Birdie left."

Silence fell over the backyard as my family exchanged worried glances. Guilt washed over me as I realized the impact of my words. I had pushed Birdie too far, and now she was gone. As the reality of Birdie's departure sank in, I knew that I had to make things right. I couldn't let her leave like this. With determination fueling my every step, I sprinted back to the car, praying that I could catch up to her before it was too late. I was speeding down the streetway, searching for Birdie's car between the several headlights in front and next to me. I drove all the way to Birdie's house and when I didn't see her car in the driveway, another feeling of panic washed over me. Where could she have gone? I imagined her driving back to my parents and started to chuckle nervously. Not because I wasn't worried about her but because I imagined her being at my parents' house and here, I was at her house.

I pulled over and decided to wait. I was sitting there for what seemed like hours. I guess I had dozed off before being woken up by a knocking on my window. Startled, my eyes snapped open, and the sight that greeted me sent a chill down my spine. Standing before me, with his arms crossed and nostrils flared, was none other than Birdie's father. *Gulp*. The morning chill accentuated the intensity of his gaze, making his breath appear like wisps of smoke from a dragon. I knew I was clearly not in the man's good graces, especially not in this moment.

With a shaky breath, I stepped out of my vehicle. "Good morning, Mr. Godwin."

"Morning, Roger," came the curt reply. "What are you doing here?"

"I'm sorry, sir," I stammered, my voice betraying my nerves. "I guess I fell asleep while waiting for Birdie."

"And why were you waiting for her? Weren't you at a barbecue?" Mr. Godwin's tone was as cold as the morning air.

I felt as if I were under a heat lamp, sweat prickling across my forehead. "That's the funny thing… you see…"

"I'm not laughing, am I, Roger?" Mr. Godwin's gaze was stern, unwavering.

"No, sir. You're not."

"I'm going to ask you one more time, Roger. What are you doing here?"

Defeated, I hung my head low. "I'm here to apologize, sir."

Silence hung heavy in the air as Mr. Godwin regarded me with a steely gaze. Then, without a word, he turned and began walking back toward the house. I stood there, baffled, for a moment before he glanced over his shoulder and said, "Are you coming in or not?"

I sat on the porch swing, next to Birdie. She wasn't too keen on seeing me either but I had to apologize. It was a silly, stupid thing of me to say and if I could take it all back I would. *Note to self: never comment on a woman's cooking ability.*

Birdie stood at the edge of the porch. I stared up at the porch light still on and flickering as if it was about to burn out completely.

I was feeling like the porch light at this moment. We were outside, but it felt suffocatingly tense. Her arms were crossed tightly over her chest, and her posture radiated a sense of guardedness.

"My father said you were looking for me," Birdie's voice sliced through the air, sharp and cold like ice.

I drew a deep breath, gathering my thoughts before responding. "I did."

"Well, talk," Birdie demanded, her tone betraying a mix of anger and hurt.

"I wanted to apologize for yesterday. I was an idiot, Birdie. You know I was joking around," I began, my words carefully chosen but still tinged with uncertainty.

"Roger, if this is your apology then I don't want it," she retorted, her gaze unwavering.

"Okay. Well, what do you want from me? Because you

left without a word. Is that how this relationship works?" My voice cracked slightly, betraying the raw emotion beneath my calm façade.

"What are you saying?" her tone softened, a hint of vulnerability seeping through her defenses.

"I'm saying that when things got tough, you vanished. If me making a comment about a slight mishap with cooking could send you spiraling, then what else is going to happen when I say the wrong thing again?" My words hung in the air, heavy with unspoken fears.

"Don't say the wrong thing then," she shot back, her frustration palpable.

"Oh, come on, Birdie. That's not fair!" my voice rose, my frustration bubbling to the surface.

"What's not fair, Roger, is that I was excited about the barbecue and spending time with your family, and YOU embarrassed me," Birdie countered, her voice quivering with emotion.

"And you think I purposefully did that?" my eyebrows furrowed, a hint of hurt in my eyes.

"No…" She fell silent, her gaze dropping to the floor.

"But I do think sometimes you don't think before you speak. And besides, you're the one who said you changed after you came back from Novaria."

"Really, Birdie? You're going to use one remark that I made after being deployed for nine months. Yes, I have changed but my love and respect for you haven't changed," I responded, my voice laced with frustration.

"I love you, Roger, and it's ruining my life!" Birdie's voice cracked, tears welling up in her eyes.

"What do you mean, it's ruining your life? Are you unhappy?" My voice softened, concern replacing my frustration.

"No, Roger. I love you, and that's the problem. I love you so much that I'm willing to push aside the gnawing feeling of whatever it is you experienced while deployed. And you won't tell me a damn thing," Birdie confessed, her voice choked with emotion.

"It's not that simple, Birdie!" My voice trembled, my own emotions threatening to overwhelm me.

"Well, try. try to make it simple," Birdie pleaded, her voice barely above a whisper.

"You honestly think that my love for you has changed that much that you can't trust me? That you can't be happy with how things are now?" My voice cracked, hurt lacing my words.

"Roger, we are living in a God damn fairytale. If you think this is happily-ever-after, you are sorely mistaken," she retorted, her voice tinged with bitterness.

"For someone who reads fairytales, you should know this isn't a fairytale," I countered, my frustration boiling over.

"Don't do that. Do not turn all of this around me," she snapped, her patience wearing thin.

"Well, Birdie. What do you want from me then?" my voice softened, a hint of desperation creeping in.

"I want us to get back to who we once were. Is that really too much to ask, Roger?" her voice wavered, a note of longing in her tone.

"Birdie, part of life is growing and changing. I can't

undo the experiences I have had. They made me the man I am today," I replied, my voice tinged with resignation.

"The man that you are today is someone that belittles the one they love?" Birdie's voice cracked, tears streaming down her cheeks.

"No. I did not do that. Do not twist my words. I am trying here, and you're giving me nothing," I protested, my frustration evident.

Folding and unfolding her arms, Birdie walked over to the door and placed her hand on the knob. "I think you should leave, Roger. We're done here."

"Are you breaking up with me, Birdie?" my voice was barely above a whisper, my heart sinking.

"Yes, I am. Goodbye, Roger. I hope you find someone someday," Birdie replied, her voice trembling with emotion.

Before I could say another word, Birdie pushed the door open and disappeared inside, leaving me standing alone on the porch, the weight of her words hanging heavily in the air.

19
BIRDIE
DATE: JUNE 1952

I dashed upstairs, the echo of my footsteps reverberating through the house, and slammed my bedroom door shut, collapsing onto my bed with tears streaming down my face. Behind me, the door creaked open, and my mother's soft footsteps approached. She entered my room, her presence a comforting embrace.

Without a word, she gathered me into her arms, and I buried my face in her lap as she stroked my hair, each gentle touch a soothing balm to my turbulent emotions.

"Mother," I sobbed, my voice muffled against her skirt. "I lost him"

"Oh, my darling Birdie," she murmured, her voice a tender reassurance. "You didn't lose him."

"Yes, yes I did. I told him he was ruining my life," I

confessed, sniffling.

"You don't mean that, do you?" she queried, her voice filled with concern.

I sat up, accepting the tissue she offered, and she helped me wipe away my tears. "I don't know. I was angry."

"You have always been a headstrong lady, like your father," she said, her tone gentle yet firm.

"I love him, mother. What if I lost the love of my life?" I whispered, my voice trembling with uncertainty.

She was silent for a moment, choosing her words carefully. My mother loved Roger, but she also had her reservations about us.

"I broke up with him. He's gone," I insisted, my heart heavy with regret.

"There's still time, my darling Birdie," she said, her eyes filled with understanding. "My beautiful daughter don't cry. You're still young."

I stood abruptly, anger simmering beneath the surface. It all felt like white noise—whether I wanted to be with Roger, or not, it would be my choice.

"I have to get out of here," I declared, determination in my voice.

My mother stood as well; concern etched on her face. "Are you going to see Roger?"

"No," I replied, my words faltering. Suddenly, I missed him. Did I make a mistake in breaking things off? "I don't know…"

She softly smiled, a knowing glint in her eyes. She understood her daughter better than anyone. She had a feeling she knew where I'd end up.

"Will you be back for dinner later?" she asked, her tone hopeful.

"I'm not sure, Mother. But I need to do something," I replied, excusing myself as I disappeared into the bathroom. I splashed water on my face, the cool liquid soothing my flushed cheeks. With a trembling hand, I fixed my makeup, trying to conceal the evidence of my tears. But deep down, I knew I couldn't hide from my feelings any longer. Whether I wanted to admit it or not, my heart was leading me back to Roger.

I slid into the driver's seat, the weight of Roger's absence heavy on my mind. The engine roared to life as I pulled out of the driveway, aimlessly driving through the familiar streets that suddenly felt foreign. Without a destination in mind, I found myself at the train station, opting for the Metro North instead of braving the city traffic. Parking the car, I made my way to the platform, the rhythmic clack of the tracks a comforting backdrop to my swirling thoughts.

The train whisked me towards the heart of the city, soon I emerged from the depth of Grand Central Terminal, the bustling energy of Manhattan enveloping me. Navigating the maze of subway tunnels, I followed the signs for the 7 train, letting the steady stream of commuters guide me towards my destination. Emerging onto the streets of Midtown, I allowed the currents of pedestrians to guide me, my feet carrying me towards Central Park.

The park stretched out before me, a welcome oasis amidst the concrete jungle that surrounded it. Couples strolled hand in hand, children laughed and played, and families gathered for picnics under the shade of towering trees. But among the cheerful bustle, I felt alone, adrift in a sea of uncertainty. I found solace on a weathered bench, the wooden slats offering a fleeting sense of stability. I watched the world pass by, a silent observer in the midst of life's ebb and flow. With each breath, I felt the weight of my solitude pressing down upon me, the ache of loss gnawing at my heart.

But I couldn't stay rooted in that moment forever. With a steadying breath, I pushed myself to my feet and resumed my aimless wandering. I wandered the winding paths of the park, the cool breeze whispering secrets through the leaves overhead.

It was a late afternoon in August, I could feel the heat of the summer days beaming down on me. A memory of the time that Roger and I walked along this path crossed my mind and a tear sprinkled down my face. How can you go from talking about getting married to gone for good? I can't help but wonder who will be the one I run too. Roger took me to heaven and hell and back to heaven in one fell swoop. But I thought what we had forever would be legendary, was it momentary? Bringing myself back down to earth and shaking the thought of Roger, eventually, my steps led me to a quaint café nestled on the edge of the park. The aroma of freshly brewed coffee wafted through the air, inviting me inside. I ordered a cup and settled into a corner booth; the warmth of the mug cradled between my palms offering a fleeting sense of comfort.

Next door, a bookstore beckoned, its shelves lined with stories waiting to be discovered. I stepped inside, the scent of old paper and ink cocooning me like a familiar embrace. Lost amidst the rows of books, I felt a flicker of something akin to hope stirring within me. As I traced my fingers along the spines, I realized that amidst the uncertainty and pain, there was still beauty to be found. In the pages of a book, in the swirl of steam rising from a cup of coffee, in the quiet moments of reflection in the heart of the city, I found solace.

20
ROGER

I left Birdie's house feeling defeated. How could a silly joke turn into the end of us? I felt like an idiot. I still loved her. I fought with the nagging feeling of fighting for her. But she seemed clear in what she wanted on that porch. In the restless days that followed, I grappled with the urge to reach out to her, to knock on her door or dial her number. But hesitation held me back.

What if she wasn't there? What if her parents intercepted the message, leaving my words lost in the void? Or perhaps, I thought a letter would be better, more heartfelt, more sincere. Yet weeks slipped by, each day a silent battle between my longing and my fear of rejection.

Every night, I lay awake, haunted by the empty space beside me, yearning for her warmth, her presence. Like a desperate creature under a forlorn moon, I found myself howling into the darkness, a primal plea for Birdie to return to me. It was madness, I knew, but love has a way of driving a man to the brink of sanity. The ache in my chest grew unbearable, a constant reminder of what I had lost. Her name reverberated through my mind like a far-off tune, a song of love and longing. I had to do something, anything, to show her that she meant everything to me. But silence persisted. One agonizing month passed, each day heavier than the last. If she wouldn't reach out to me, then it had to be me. I needed closure, the truth, no matter how painful. I knew she had ended things, but hope flickered within me like a stubborn flame. Perhaps, I thought, she was waiting for me to fight for her, to prove that I was worthy of her love. And with trembling hands, I sat at my desk, the weight of uncertainty pressing down on me like a leaden cloak. I reached for an inked pen, its tip poised over a blank sheet of paper, ready to capture my heart's desperate plea.

Dearest Birdie,

I hope this letter finds you well, though my heart tells me otherwise. In the quiet solitude of this past month, your absence has weighed heavily on me, a burden too heavy to bear alone. I find myself haunted by the memories of our time together, moments of laughter and love that now seem like distant dreams. Each day without you feels like a lifetime, an eternity of longing and regret. I know I have made mistakes, said things I wish I could take back, done things now I realize were foolish and hurtful. But please believe me when I say that my love for you has never wavered, not for a single moment. I cannot bear the thought of losing you, of living in a world where your smile no longer lights up my days, where your laughter no longer fills the air way joy. You are everything to me, Birdie. My heart, my soul, my reason for being. I understand if you need time, if you need space to heal and to find your own path forward. But please know that I am here, waiting with open arms and an open heart, ready to fight for us, ready to prove to you that our love is worth fighting for. I long for the day when we can look back on this time as nothing more than a distant storm, a trial that only served to strengthen the bond between us. Until then, know that you are always in my thoughts, always in my heart.

With all my love,
Roger

I sealed up the letter and wrote her address on it, my hand trembling slightly as I pressed down on the envelope. Walking down to the nearby postal office to mail it felt like a solitary journey through a world emptied of color. Each step weighed heavy with the uncertainty of whether Birdie would ever return. With every passing car, I secretly hoped to catch a glimpse of her, imagined her changing her mind and coming back to me. But the street remained as quiet and deserted as my heart.

Days turned into weeks, and still, no word from Birdie. The silence between us stretched like an endless chasm, filled with unanswered questions and unspoken regrets. I tried to preoccupy my time by throwing myself into my work at the nearby airport. Becoming a Certified Flight Instructor (CFI) was both a distraction and a lifeline. Guiding others through the skies gave me a sense of purpose, a fleeting moment of control in a world spiraling out of grasp. But even as I taught others to fly, I couldn't shake the feeling of being grounded, tethered to the earth by the weight of my own uncertainty. The cockpit, once a sanctuary of solitude and control, now felt like a prison of memories and lost dreams. On the days when I wasn't training, I'd take to the sky alone, seeking solace in the roar of the engine and the vast expanse of the horizon. Each flight was a bittersweet reminder of what I had lost, yet also a testament to the resilience of the human spirit. As I soared through the clouds, I couldn't help but marvel at the beauty and fragility of life. In those fleeting moments of freedom, I found a glimmer of hope, a reason to believe someday, I would find peace in the vastness of the sky. But even as I reached for the heavens, my thoughts kept drifting back to Birdie, to the love we had shared and the promises we had made. I wondered if she ever thought of me, if she ever regretted leaving. And as the days turned into months, I realized maybe some loves were meant to soar, while others were destined to crash and burn. But no matter where life took me, one thing was certain, the sky would never abandon me, and neither would the memories of the woman I loved.

It was a crisp October, when I had finished a lesson and was heading home for the day. As I pulled up to the house and walked inside, I noticed my mother in the kitchen.

"Roger is that you?" she called out.

"Hi mother" I walked into the kitchen. Kissed her on the cheek before turning and grabbing a beer from the fridge. I cracked it open and took a sip.

"How was your day?" she asked.

"It was good. It's always a good day when I'm up in the sky."

She laughed at my remark. "It's pretty nice down here on the ground too, sweetie." She turned and patted my cheek.

Smiling, I said, "I suppose it can be."

"A letter came for you today." She said nonchalantly.

"Oh. Really?" My heart leaped out of my chest.

I stepped forward to the counter on the opposite side of the kitchen and picked up the mail. There it was right on top, addressed to me, from Birdie. I walked out to the backyard to open it in peace. I sat down on one of the lawn chairs, remembering the last time I was sitting in one of these—the day I lost Birdie. As my heart began to pound, I opened up the letter and stared down at the words that bled across the page. It was short and to the point.

Roger,

If you mean what you said in your letter. Please meet me at our favorite spot in Central Park. I'll be here, Friday, July 21st, at 2:00 p.m. I'll wait for you...don't be late.

With love,

Birdie

I read the letter about fifteen more times, each word etching itself deeper into my mind. Tomorrow was Friday, and I realized I had received it just in time. I had to go. I had to know if Birdie and I still had a chance or if this was truly the end of us.

"With love"…. The words replaying in my mind, stirring up a whirlwind of conflicting emotions. Did she still love me after all? Or was it a polite farewell, masking the truth of her departure? I folded the letter with trembling hands, the paper crinkling softly beneath my touch. Tucking it into the inner pocket of my jacket, I sat there, lost in thought, the weight of uncertainty pressing down on me like a heavy burden.

Finishing my beer, I glanced around the backyard, the faint chirps of nearby birds and town sirens in the distance. Tomorrow held the promise of answers, but tonight, I was alone with my thoughts, wrestling with the ghosts of our past and the uncertainty of our future. With a sigh, I pushed myself up from the lawn chair. It was time to face the truth, whatever it may be.

As I made my way back inside, I couldn't shake the feeling tomorrow would mark a turning point in my life, one way or another.

21

```
BIRDIE
ONE MONTH LATER
DATE: JULY 1952
```

Friday morning dawned, casting a pale light through the curtains as I reluctantly opened my eyes. Despite the anticipation of the day ahead, my heart felt heavy with unresolved emotions. Ever since receiving Roger's letter, my thoughts have been consumed by him, like a relentless tide pulling me back to shore.

One month had slipped by in silence, a chasm widening between us with each passing day. I longed to reach out, to bridge the gap between us with words of apology and longing. Yet, every attempt was thwarted by a fear gripped me like a vice. I had written countless letters, pouring my heart onto paper only to bury them in a box beneath my bed. Some were filled with anger, the bitterness of past wounds still fresh. Others were steeped in regret, a desperate plea for forgiveness and understanding, and then there were those who spoke of finality, of letting go, and moving on, even as my heart rebelled against the notion. Each day brought a new wave of emotions, crashing against the shores of my resolve. I clung to the fragile hope that silence would somehow preserve what remained our love, Roger would return to me, drawn by the unspoken bond that still tethered us together. But deep down, I knew hope alone was not enough. If I wanted Roger back, I had to be willing to fight for him, to confront the demons that haunted our past and pave a path toward reconciliation.

Today would be a leap of faith into the unknown. I was determined to seize the opportunity, to lay bare my heart and soul in the hopes of reclaiming what was lost. For Roger, for us, I would not falter. Standing in front of my floor-length mirror, I buttoned my dress and took in my reflection. I felt beautiful. If Roger didn't drop to one knee and ask me to marry him when I looked like this, I don't think he ever would. Fear crept into my mind—what if he didn't show?

Walking downstairs, the wooden steps creaked beneath my weight, announcing my descent to the living room below. The familiar scent of my mother's sewing basket mingled with the faint aroma of coffee, creating a comforting atmosphere belied the tension simmering beneath the surface. As I entered the living room, I found my father settled into his favorite armchair, his reading glasses perched on the bridge of his nose as he pored over the morning newspaper. Across from him, my mother sat in her own chair, the fabric of my father's shirt stretched taut between her nimble fingers as she deftly stitched a fallen button back into place.

My father's gaze lifted from the paper at the sound of my footsteps, his warm brown eyes crinkling at the corners as he took in my appearance. "You look nice, Birdie," he remarked, a hint of pride coloring his voice.

"Thank you, daddy," I replied, a nervous flutter dancing in the pit of my stomach. I couldn't help but twirl slightly in my dress, seeking reassurance in his approving smile.

"Where are you off to?" he inquired, his tone gentle but curious.

"Central Park," I answered hesitantly, my heart pounding in my chest as I debated whether to divulge my true destination.

Their disapproval hung heavy in the air, an unspoken barrier between us threatened to suffocate any semblance of honesty. My father and brother's silent vigilance spoke volumes, their protective instincts poised to defend me from any perceived threat. And my mother, ever the voice of reason, offered silent judgment veiled behind her busy needlework.

"I'm meeting Roger," I declared, steeling myself against their inevitable objections. "And before you add in your two cents, I am giving him another chance. I love him, and this is my choice."

A pregnant pause followed my proclamation, tension

crackling like static electricity between us. My mother tore her gaze from the needle to meet my eyes, her expression a mixture of concern and resignation.

"Okay," she acquiesced, the word heavy with unspoken reservation.

I crossed the room to stand before her, leaning down to press a kiss to her cheek before turning to face my father. He rose from his chair, hands finding purchase on my shoulders as he pulled me into a firm embrace.

"Make good choices," he murmured, his voice a gentle reminder of the weight of responsibility rested upon my shoulders.

I nodded in understanding, the gravity of his words settling like a stone in the pit of my stomach. Returning his kiss on the cheek, I lingered for a moment longer before extricating myself from his embrace and heading toward the door.

Leaving them to their silent contemplations, I stepped out into the crisp morning air, determination burning bright within me as I made my way into the city and the uncertain future awaited me there.

LOCATION: CENTRAL PARK

I sat down on our favorite bench looking out to the fountain. Sipping a cup of coffee, I waited patiently. Every person I saw walking down the nearby steps, my head would perk up hopeful it was Roger. What if he doesn't show up? I thought. Maybe I'm better off without him. If he doesn't show, then I'll know I am better off.

I looked down at the delicate watch on my wrist. It was 1:30 p.m. I continued to watch each person passing by. The ticking of the clock growing louder and louder with each tick closer to the meeting time. I looked down, and it was now 1:45 p.m. Where was he? It was 1:57 p.m. I was losing hope. I heard a nearby bell ring, looking down my watch said 2:00 p.m. No Roger in sight. I guess this was the end of us. I stood up from the bench, not willing to wait another minute. I started walking towards the steps, looking down at my feet, too ashamed to look at people. I thought if I stared someone in the eyes, then tears would roll down my cheeks. And I was not about to be known as the girl who cried in Central Park.

As I climbed the steps leading up from the bustling path, my heart pounded in rhythm with each footfall. The whisper of leaves rustling in the gentle breeze accompanied me, lending an air of anticipation to the already charged atmosphere. As I neared the top, a voice pierced the silence, a whisper carried on the breeze, faint yet unmistakable. Birdie.

I froze mid-step, my heart lurching in my chest. I scanned the surroundings, searching for the source of the voice. Was it merely a figment of my imagination, or had Roger's voice truly reached me amidst the verdant expanse of the park? A surge of uncertainty washed over me, tinged with a hint of apprehension. Maybe I'm losing my mind, I thought, my breath catching in my throat. But then, like a beacon in the darkness, the voice came again. This time clearer, cutting through the air like a knife.

"Birdie."

I spun on my heel, my entire body pivoting back toward the direction of the sound. And there, standing by the bench, bathed in the soft glow of the afternoon sun, was Roger. My pulse quickened, adrenaline coursing through my veins as I locked eyes with him. The world seemed to fall away, leaving only the two of us suspended in a moment of perfect clarity. There he was holding a bouquet of my favorite flowers, pink peonies, clad in a gray blazer that seemed to shimmer in the golden light. His presence filled the air with a palpable tension, drawing me toward him like a moth to a flame.

With each stride, I felt the weight of the past bearing down on me, the memories of our shared laughter and tears swirling around me like a whirlwind. But amidst the chaos, there was a glimmer of possibility, a chance to rewrite our story, to build something new from the ashes of our broken dreams. As I closed the distance between us, I knew that whatever lay ahead, I was ready to face it head-on. For in that fleeting moment in Central Park, amidst the whispers of the wind and the beating of my heart, I knew that love had brought us together one more, and it was up to us to decide our fate.

22
ROGER

It would be my luck that I'd get to the spot late. It was past 2 p.m. My heart sank into my chest. I saw a nearby trash bin, tempted to toss the bouquet of peonies I bought for Birdie. She wasn't there at the bench. I searched around, but she was nowhere to be seen. How could I miss her already? I thought.

But then I see her coppery waves blowing in the wind—she was wearing a black dress with tiny flowers printed on it. I called out her name, but she didn't turn around. I called her name again—she had to hear me. I watched as she paused on the steps, slowly shifting her body around. I called out her name, once more, and she turned.

Our eyes locked, and she came running down the steps like a lightning bolt. She thew her arms around my neck, our lips touched, and for a moment, the world around us disappeared. The scent of her perfume filled my senses, a delicate mix of jasmine and vanilla, heightening the intensity of the moment. I could feel the gentle warmth of her breath against my skin, sending shivers down my spine. As we finally pulled away, I felt a rush of warmth spread through my body, like a comforting embrace from within. In her eyes, I saw a reflection of my own longing, a silent promise of endless possibilities. And in that fleeting moment, amidst the chaos of the world, I knew with unwavering certainty that I never wanted to let her go.

"Birdie," I whispered, my voice trembling. "I…I'm sorry."

"Roger, please, it's not your fault," she murmured, her eyes glistening with unshed tears.

We paused, our eyes locked in a silent exchange, before we extended the bouquet of peonies towards her. "For you, my love."

Her fingers fluttered as she accepted the flowers, the breeze bringing up their delicate fragrance. With a tender smile, she brought the blooms to her nose. As she inhaled, the sweet, heady scent of the pink peonies enveloped her senses, carrying with it memories of springtime and new beginnings. The fragrance danced on the air, mingling with the earthy undertones of the garden, creating an orchestra of scents that transported her to a place of serenity and beauty.

We walked over to the bench, as Birdie set the bouquet down in between us. She shifted her body enough to face me and grabbed my hands. I played with the spaces between her fingers, memorizing every crease. Our hands fit perfectly intertwined. I considered getting down on one knee right then and there but I couldn't do it. Was I even ready for marriage? Birdie and I weren't perfect, and we clearly had some things to work out. But she was worth it. I would fight for Birdie and right here, I was ready for war.

"Birdie," I began, my voice faltering as she raised a hand to silence me, the chatter of distant birds and rustling leaves filling the air around us.

"Roger, I've had a lot of time to think," she said, her tone lacking its usual warmth, the distant honking of traffic a reminder of the city beyond the park's borders. My heart pounded in my chest, h the memories of our time apart flooding back. Had she called me here to end it? Was this the moment she'd tell me it was over for good? I fought the urge to beg, to plead for another chance.

"And?" I prodded, the word barely escaping my lips.

She sighed, each syllable heavy with uncertainty. "Roger Scott, you're a good man. A really good man."

I braced myself for the worst, the park bench beneath us feeling too hard, too unforgiving. I couldn't bear to lose her, not again. I'd spent two agonizing months without her, counting down the days until this moment.

"Birdie, break my heart or tell me you love me," I blurted out, desperation edging into my voice. "Because I can't go on like this."

"You're right. I've missed you, Roger. It's been agonizing not being with you, but I don't know if we can ever get back to who we were before…" Her voice faltered, trailing off into uncertainty.

"Birdie, let's start over," I suggested, hoping to mend what felt irreparably broken.

She looked at me, surprise and confusion flickering across her features. "What do you propose?" Curiosity painted her face, seeking answers amidst the tumult of emotions.

"I don't mean we should forget all that happened. But I think we need a fresh start. I want to take you on a date, remind us why we fell in love in the first place," I offered, hoping she would see the sincerity in my words.

"Hmm… Roger, I don't know," she replied, her hesitation hanging in the air like a delicate balance between hope and apprehension.

I watched her face, drawn to its delicate features—the graceful curve of her cheekbones, the softness of her lips, and above all, her piercing blue eyes. They seemed to hold a universe of secrets, each glance a window into depths unknown. With every blink, they sparkled like facets of a sapphire, capturing the light in a mesmerizing dance. Her gaze was both calming and invigorating, like the serene expanse of a tranquil sea and the electric charge of a summer storm, all at once. And in that swift moment, sitting on a park bench in Central Park, I saw a glimpse of Birdie painted in an entirely different light. The expression was once worn out on her face soften.

"Oh, Roger," she giggled, tucking a loose strand of her golden hair behind her ear. Her blue eyes sparkled with a mixture of uncertainty and hope. "I suppose we could give us another shot."

My heart skipped a beat at her words, memories of our past flooding back. I hesitated for a moment, then dropped to one knee not because I was going to propose, but because I needed to do something to seal this fragile moment. Birdie was my once more, but I knew the road ahead wouldn't be easy. I pulled out of my pocket a fake ring. The kind you win from a gumball machine. It was small, threaded with multi-colors twisting in opposite directions.

"Roger, what are you doing?" Birdie's voice expressed curiosity and amusement.

I filled my lungs with air, trying to steady my nerves. "Birdie Godwin, will you be my girlfriend... again?"

Birdie's laughter tinkled through the air, a sound I had missed dearly. She shook her head in acceptance, unable to find her words through the joy bubbling up inside her.

"I didn't hear you," I teased gently, my eyes dancing with affection. "Does this mean we're back together?"

"Roger, you are correct," Birdie finally managed to say, her smile radiant.

"This doesn't mean we're getting married, in case you get any ideas," I added playfully, a mischievous glint in my eye.

"Well, maybe you shouldn't make promises you can't keep," she teased back, a grin spreading across her face.

"I love you," I whispered, my voice filled with sincerity.

"I love you too, Roger," Birdie replied, her eyes softening.

"I think we need to celebrate," I suggested, rising from

my kneeling position and holding out my hand to Birdie.

"And where do you think we should go?" Birdie asked, her curiosity piqued.

"Somewhere new, Birdie. Somewhere new," I declared, a sense of adventure lighting up my features.

I was driving. Birdie sitting in my passenger seat. We arrived at the Brooklyn Botanic Garden. It was a place neither of us had ever been. As we pulled up to the garden, we were greeted by a serene oasis nestled within the bustling cityscape of New York. Lush greenery enveloped the entrance, hinting at the verdant wonders waiting beyond. Towering trees cast dappled shadows across meticulously landscaped paths, inviting visitors to wander and explore.

Entering the garden, Birdie and I found ourselves immersed in a patchwork of colors and scents. Vibrant blooms adorned every corner, their petals unfurling in a riot of hues, from fiery reds to cool blues. The air was alive with the chirping birds and buzzing insects, creating a harmonious backdrop. Strolling through the various themed gardens, we encountered a kaleidoscope of botanical marvels. We marveled at the delicate beauty of the Japanese garden, with its tranquil ponds and graceful bridges, while the fragrance of exotic blooms transported them to distant lands in the Fragrance Garden. As we meandered along the winding pathways, we discovered hidden alcoves and secluded benches, perfect for a quiet contemplation or intimate conversation. I grabbed Birdie's hand, pulling her closer in one of the hidden alcoves. Both our hearts beating fasting, I kissed her like I'd never kissed her before. Each turn revealed a new tableau of natural splendor, from the tranquil serenity of the Water Garden to the riotous energy of the Herb Garden. With every step, we felt a sense of awe and wonder, as if we had stumbled upon a secret paradise hidden within the heart of the city.

23
BIRDIE

The Brooklyn Botanic Garden was not a place of beauty, but a sanctuary for the soul, where the rhythms of nature danced in perfect harmony with the urban landscape. When we left Central Park, I found my heart bidding farewell to the old me, the old us. Here we were in an enchanting haven, and we'd carry these new memories with us. I could see them lingering long after we had left its verdant embrace.

"It's beautiful here," I breathed. Linking my arm with Rogers.

"You're beautiful." He said. Staring at me.

"Stop it, Roger. You can't sweet talk me."

"Why not?"

"You know why, Roger."

"No, I don't, Birdie. Please enlighten me." He teased.

"No." I had my reservations still but who am I to defy his charm. I love Roger. And I know he loves me.

As we wandered deeper into the hidden alcove, a flutter of anticipation danced in the air, wrapping us in a cocoon of youthful exuberance and unspoken longing. The garden seemed to whisper secrets of romance as we explored its winding paths, our hearts skipping in a rhythm to the melody of newfound love. Roger's eyes met mine, sparkling with a warmth ignited a familiar fire within my soul.

Without a word, he guided me to lean against the sturdy trunk of a rough bark against my back grounded me, while his hand found mine with a tender reassurance, fingers entwining in a silent pact of devotion.

In the tranquil stillness of the garden, our lips met in a soft, tender kiss, brimming with the sweetness of real love. Each brush of his lips against mine was a chorus of innocence and passion, a testament to the pure, unadulterated joy of being young and in love. Lost in the moment, we surrendered to the magic of the garden, our hearts soaring on the wings of affection. In a fleeting embrace, beneath the canopy of nature's sanctuary, we discovered the timeless beauty of young love.

I couldn't help but giggle as I pulled away from Roger's embrace, the warmth of his presence sending a thrill through me. "God help me when I tell everyone you're my man," I playfully ribbed, my eyes sparkling with mischief.

But Roger's next words caught me off guard. "Let's run away together?" he said abruptly, his tone tinged with desperation.

Startled by his suggestion, my laughter faded, replaced by a mixture of confusion and concern. "What?" I asked, barely a whisper escaping my lips.

"I mean it, Birdie. I can't live my life without you. No one understands us. Let's go somewhere where it's you and me," Roger pleaded, his eyes searching mine for validation.

My heart pounded in my chest as I tried to comprehend his words. I shifted my body away from the tree, creating a small distance between us. "Roger, don't be ridiculous," I said softly, my fingers tracing the edge of my dress.

"Oh, come on, Birdie. Don't you love me?" Roger's voice cracked with emotion, his vulnerability laid bare before me.

"Of course I do, Roger. But you don't run away," I replied, my voice laced with uncertainty.

Roger looked down at his shoes, the weight of his words hanging heavily between us. Silence fell like a curtain, enveloping us in its embrace.

"Oh, Roger. Where would we go?" I played along, my mind racing with a thousand questions and doubts.

His eyes lit up with hope as he lifted his head to meet mine. "California. We'll head west. We could buy a house, have a ton of kids," he said, his voice tinged with excitement.

"Roger, you are living in a fantasy," I said with a faint smile, though my heart ached at the impossibility of his dreams.

"Say you'll consider it, Birdie. Please?" Roger begged,

his desperation palpable.

I inhaled deeply, knowing there was no use in trying to change his mind. "Okay. I'll think about it," I conceded, my voice barely above a whisper.

I would be lying if I said I wasn't considering it. Roger's earnestness touched something deep within me, stirring a whirlwind of emotions I hadn't expected. I did love him, deeply. Maybe California was the fresh start we needed.

We were leaving the city behind. I had taken the train in earlier, my car was still at the station. Roger had offered to drive me back to pick it up. As we drove, I knew he was waiting for my response to his question from before. My gaze wandered over the familiar landscape, watching the trees blur past as we made our way upstate. The quaint houses, the bustling main street, the comforting embrace of familiarity. Leaving all of this behind felt like stepping into the unknown, a leap of faith into an uncertain future. But as I looked over at Roger in the driver's seat, I saw something in his eyes, filled with hope and longing, I realized maybe uncertainty was a small price to pay for the chance at something greater. We were young, full of dreams and aspirations. Perhaps it was time to chase those dreams, to carve out our own path in the world.

With a soft sigh, I reached out and took Roger's hand in mine, squeezing it gently. "Okay," I said, the word hanging in the air between us like a promise. "Let's do it. Let's go to California."

A smile spread across Roger's face, lighting up his features with joy and relief. He grabbed my hand, kissing it, gripping it close as if afraid I might disappear if he let go.

A TIMELESS TAPESTRY

And in that moment, as we sat in the car heading back home, I knew whatever lay ahead, we would face it together. I was ready to write our own story in the golden sands of California.

24
ROGER
ONE MONTH LATER
DATE: AUGUST 1952

We didn't go to California. I don't think Birdie was lying when she said she wanted to go. But as the days followed, I could sense something was gnawing at her. The sun beat down on the park, casting dappled shadows under the swaying branches of nearby trees.

We sat on the swings, the chains creaking softly as they moved back and forth. Despite the warmth of the day in May, a cool breeze rustled through the leaves, carrying the scent of freshly cut grass. I glanced at Birdie, noticing the furrow in her brow and the distant look in her eyes. I sensed her unease, the unspoken words hanging heavy between us like a storm cloud at the vanishing point.

"I was thinking, we could fly out to California next

month," I finally broke the silence, my words hesitant. "Take a look at neighborhoods. They have a few airports nearby I could work at. If we stay in Southern California, I could work at LAX or at one of the smaller airports…"

Birdie remained silent; her gaze fixed on the ground as she kicked at the dirt with the toe of her shoe. I could feel the tension building, the weight of her unspoken thoughts pressing against me.

"Birdie, what do you think?" I asked, trying to break through her wall of silence.

Startled, Birdie blinked, as if returning from a distant reverie. "Huh… Oh, I'm sorry, Roger."

I frowned, watching her closely. "What's on your mind, Birdie?"

Birdie hesitated, her fingers twisting nervously in her lap. "Nothing…" she began, but I could see the lie in her eyes. I knew her well enough to sense the turmoil churning beneath the surface.

"Birdie, come on…" I urged gently, reaching out to touch her hand.

"I love you, Roger. You know, right?" Birdie's voice was soft, almost hesitant.

"Yes, of course," I replied, my heart pounding in my chest. "But where are you going with this?"

Birdie took a deep breath, steeling herself for what she was about to say. "Roger, I don't want to go to California," she admitted, her voice barely above a whisper.

My heart sank, a knot forming in my stomach. "I see…"

"I don't want to be without you," Birdie rushed to reassure me. "But I'm not ready to leave New York."

I swallowed hard, trying to quell the rising tide of disappointment. "Does this have to do with your parents?"

"No," Birdie replied, her tone sharp. "Roger, this is my choice. Why do we have to move across the country to be together?"

I struggled to find the right words, my mind racing with conflicting emotions. "I guess it's not about being together. It's about a fresh start for us both."

"But we can have a fresh start without moving to another state," Birdie countered, her voice tinged with frustration.

I felt a pang of guilt, realizing how my eagerness to move had overshadowed Birdie's concerns. "That's it. You make all the decisions in this relationship, and I have to go along with it?" I asked, my voice tinged with bitterness.

"I'm not making all the decisions," Birdie protested. "You asked what I was thinking, and I shared my concerns."

"You weren't concerned when you said yes," I retorted, my frustration boiling over. "What's not fair is getting me excited and then changing the game plan."

"I'm not saying we'll never move to California," Birdie replied, her voice pleading. "But can we not rush it?"

I sighed. I didn't want to argue about California. Truth was, I would go anywhere with Birdie and if staying in New York for a little bit longer was the start, then I was willing to put aside California for Birdie.

"Okay." I folded. "We don't have to rush to California. But don't cross it off the map yet."

"Of course not. We're only twenty-two, Roger. My heart is reserved for you. Let's give New York a chance for us."

"What do you mean?" I asked.

"Well since you proposed California, I want to propose a new way for us to start fresh."

"What are you saying, Birdie?"

"Let's move in together!" she said eagerly. Her blue eyes were shimmering with the sun.

"Move in? hmm…" I pretended to think it through. I watched her eyes go wild waiting for my response.

"Alrighty, Birdie. Let's do it."

"Really? You mean it, Roger?"

"Of course I do. I want a future with you Birdie. If moving in together pushes us in that step than I'm ready. Let's do it!"

She jumped up from the swing and sat down on my lap. The swing creaked from the weight of us both and we giggled as if we were back in High School, sharing secrets, passing notes in the hall, sneaking out late, and falling in love—that first love kind of feeling.

"I love you very much, Roger. I'm ready for us."

"I love you, Birdie Godwin."

* * *

As the days unfurled, we delved into endless discussions, mapping out our dreams of a new home. Enthralled by the allure—the thrum of the subway, the rhythm of the streets alive with activity. For us, New York City beckoned as the quintessential destination for young romantics, a place where every corner held the promise of adventure and every skyline whispered tales of possibility.

I sat at the worn kitchen table, the morning sunlight filtering through the curtains, casting a warm glow on the faded linoleum floor. I flipped through the newspaper, the pages rustling softly as I scanned the classifieds section for apartment listings. My mother bustled around the small kitchen, the aroma of fresh coffee mingling with the scent of toast. She hummed a tune under her breath, her apron tied securely around her waist as she poured steaming coffee into mismatched mugs.

"Find anything promising?" she asked, glancing over my shoulder as she set a plate of toast on the table.

I shook my head, my brow furrowed in concentration. "Not yet. It seems like every place is either too expensive or too far from the subway."

She nodded. "I'm sure you and Birdie will find something soon. But if not, you're always welcome here, sweetie. You won't be homeless."

I chuckled, trying to lighten the mood. "I know I won't be homeless. We'll figure something out."

She smiled. My own worry lines around my eyes softening. "It's just.. I want our first apartment together to be perfect."

My mother sat down across from me, taking my hand in hers. "It will be, Roger. You have to have faith."

I continued my search, determined to find the perfect apartment that would become Birdie and I's home in the bustling streets of New York City.

25
BIRDIE

The day I told my parents I was moving in with Roger, they were speechless for the first time in their lives. I think they decided it was better for me to move in with him than to move halfway across the country.

My father was coming around again with Roger. He decided to trust his little girl, that's what he said he would do. He would trust me. My mother was still part of the skeptics. She continued to press we were too young. She insisted on me exploring my options and even tried to set me up with the son of someone in her church group.

I went on one date with him to please my mother, it was during the time Roger and I were broken up. I didn't hate it but all I did was compare him to Roger. His name was Howard. He was charming and reserved. All it did was make me think about Roger, who was chaos and revelry. I always felt a sense of safety and wild joy with Roger, all at the same time. Howard was polite. That was it. He was a nice boy. But I didn't want a nice boy, I wanted my Roger. Howard took me to see a film at the old theater downtown, the flickering light of the marquee casting a nostalgic glow over the bustling street. We stood in line, surrounded by the chatter of moviegoers and the tantalizing aroma of freshly popped popcorn. As we settled into our seats, the dimming lights of the theater enveloped us in a cocoon of anticipation. The film played on the silver screen, the score swelling with emotion as the story unfolded before us. I stole glances at Howard beside me, but his attention remained fixed on the screen, his expression unreadable in the darkness. After the credits rolled and the lights came up, we made our way to the nearby ice cream parlor. The tinkling bell above the door greeted us as we stepped inside, the scent of waffle cones wafting through the air. We sat at a small table by the window, the neon lights of the city outside casting colorful patterns on the pavement. I tried to strike up a conversation, eager to learn more about Howard beyond his studies, but his responses were polite yet distant. I studied his face as he spoke, searching for any flicker of emotion in his hazel eyes, but they remained as inscrutable as ever. It was like staring into a vast, black void, devoid of any warmth or passion.

"What made you decide to become a lawyer?" I asked, curious to uncover the motivations behind Howard's career choice.

"All the men in my family become lawyers," Howard replied, his tone matter-of-fact, but a hint of reluctance tinging his words.

"Oh. I'm sure there's some excitement in being one. Helping people get justice," I ventured, trying to draw him into a more engaging conversation.

"Not really. I'm simply good at what I do," Howard remarked, his voice devoid of enthusiasm, as if the passion for his profession had long since faded.

I struggled to find common ground, to bridge the gap between us. Howard's curt responses left me feeling adrift, like I was grasping at straws in a sea of indifference.

"You win a lot of cases?" I probed, hoping to elicit a more animated response. But deep down, I knew the answer already.

"Always. I never lose," Howard declared confidently, his tone bordering on arrogance, but beneath the bravado, I sensed a hint of insecurity.

As the conversation faltered, a palpable tension hung in the air, a silent barrier between us seemed impossible to breach. And in that moment, I was compelled to consider what lay hidden beneath Howard's veneer of success and self-assurance. My attempts at conversation with Howard felt like navigating a maze with no exit. Each question I posed was met with terse responses, leaving me grasping for something, anything, to keep the dialogue afloat. As Howard's monosyllabic replies bellowed in the air, I couldn't help but compare our interaction to conversating with a mime. At least with a mime, there's the anticipation of a gesture, a hint of expression, however subtle. But with Howard, it was as if I were speaking into a void, my words disappearing into the abyss of his indifference. Frustration gnawed at my insides, mingling with a sense of futility. How could I connect with someone closed off, unwilling to engage in anything beyond the superficial?

The evening wore on, and I couldn't shake the feeling of disappointment gnawing at my insides. Howard seemed to fit the mold of the stereotypical lawyer—reserved, stoic, and emotionally distant. And yet, I couldn't help but wonder what lay beneath the surface of his composed facade. After that night, Howard faded from my life like a distant memory. My mother, ever curious, kept asking about him, but I simply shrugged it off, telling her it wasn't meant to be. Then, a few days later, I received a letter from Roger, an unexpected surprise reignited a spark within me. Reaching out to Roger turned out to be the best decision I ever made. Now, we were on the verge of moving in together, but finding the perfect apartment in New York City proved to be a daunting task.

Roger and I took turns scouring the classifieds, determined to find a place that met both our needs. Our only criterion was to be in the heart of NYC, where the pulse of the city thrived. We compiled a list of must-haves, and for me, top of the list was a café within walking distance, my sanctuary for an essential morning cup of joe. Despite our efforts, months flew by with no success. What we thought would take a few weeks to a month stretched into August, leaving us empty-handed and disheartened. By September, anxiety crept in, and the prospect of remaining under my parents' roof felt suffocating. California began to look appealing, but even that felt like a distant dream. What guarantee did we have of finding a place there? We'd be back at square one. Yet, as I circled potential neighborhoods to explore, a glimmer of hope flickered within me. This was real, we were on the cusp of a new chapter, and I had to believe we would find our home soon.

26
ROGER

Our shared dreams unraveled like the pages of a storybook, and the future held the promise of more chapters written together. As August settled in, the summer warmth clung to our efforts to find the perfect apartment. Despite our best attempts, each viewing left us with a sense of disappointment, the ideal remaining out of reach.

With our anniversary approaching, the question of how to commemorate it lingered between us like a ghost of uncertainty. Should we cling to the nostalgia of our relationship's origins or embrace a new beginning? We tossed ideas back and forth, the weight of tradition clashing with the allure of spontaneity. In the end, we opted for whimsy, choosing a date on a whim—September 13th.

Laughter bubbled between us as we marked the calendar, the act itself a celebration of our shared journey. Who needed anniversaries measured in years when we could revel in the moments shared between us, each one a thread in the intricate design of our love? As the decision settled, a quiet certainty washed over me, a realization this woman beside me was my compass, guiding me toward a future filled with promise. Despite the fleeting doubts that sometimes crept in, I knew in my heart Birdie was my home, my anchor in a sea of vacillation.

The certainty she was the one hit me from the moment our eyes first met. I can't predict the future, but I was willing to give into fate. Birdie and I had been through so much. Now, as the time to propose to Birdie draws near, I found myself on a quest for the perfect ring. Financial constraints led me to a local pawn shop, where I believed an antique ring would capture Birdie's taste. And there, amidst the treasures, I discovered the ring that would symbolize our commitment. I stepped into the dimly lit pawn shop, the air thick with the scent of old leather and forgotten stories, my ears caught the faint creaking of the floorboards beneath me. The display cases whispered tales of forgotten romances, and the anticipation of finding the perfect ring heightened my senses.

Approaching the display case, my fingers tingled with anticipation as I reached out to touch the vintage yellow gold engagement ring from the 1920s. Its warm, honeyed glow seemed to invite a tactile exploration, promising a glimpse into a world of timeless romance. The cool touch of the antique ring against my skin sent shivers down my spine, connecting me to an era of elegance and sophistication. Captivated by the intricate details defined the ring's

Roaring Twenties charm, I marveled at the craftmanship.

The yellow gold band, rich and inviting, cradled a mesmerizing Old-European-cut diamond sparkled with the brilliance of that era. Delicate filigree work, intricate prong settings, and enchanting milgrain detailing adorned the ring with a touch of vintage elegance.

As I examined the ring closer, the smaller accent stones and intricate patterns on the band to tell their silent tales—forgotten romances, each facet carrying the weight of a love story from the past. The low-set design, a characteristic feature of Art déco rings, promised both comfort and style, reflecting the sensibilities of an era which celebrated tradition while embracing modernity. Amidst my exploration, my mind wandered to a specific memory with Birdie, the way her eyes sparkled when we first danced under the moonlight. It was in those moments the decision to propose felt more real, more profound. I left the dimly lit shop, surrounded by the whispers of decades. I thought to myself, is this the end of one era but the beginning of another?

✯ ✯ ✯

DATE: SEPTEMBER 1952

It came in one fell swoop; it was as if the God's were finally answering our prayers. One month later, Birdie and I were sitting in a local café, we split the newspaper, each checking the classifieds in hopes of finding our new home. There they were, we circled at least five places. We called the number at the bottom requesting to schedule a time where we can come by.

"This is happening, Roger," she beamed.

"I guess it is, Birdie."

"I'm not going to get my hopes up," she said, sipping her coffee.

"Fair enough. But I think we should still be excited."

"Even if we've found some and are looking at them doesn't mean it'll work out."

"Oh Birdie, can't you be spontaneous for once in your life."

She laughed. I know I had a tendency to play the Golden Retriever vibe, but I wasn't one to be cautious. Birdie and I balanced each other out. She was the cautious, list making, headstrong one, and I was a little bit of mayhem, it was an art.

"I think you play the spontaneous one enough for the both of us." She teased. She stretched her foot across the underneath of the table lightly kicking me.

Before she could do it again, I placed my hand on her knee, stopping her in her tracks. She grabbed my hand, as it brushed against her upper thigh letting it linger. I could sense the heat between us, her cheeks turning pink. It was soon after she brushed my hand away, shifting her body entirely.

"My mother would like for you to come to dinner tomorrow," she said. Changing the subject.

Okay. I'll play along. "That sounds lovely. What time should I be there?"

"5:00. And bring yourself, Roger." She knew me well enough to know that would be my following question.

"I'm bringing wine, no objections." I declared.

"Fine. But make sure it's a merlot. That's my mother's favorite."

"Ah. Taking notes."

We laughed, the full belly laugh. The few people in the café looked over at us. But I didn't care. In a perfect world, everyone would be in black and white, and Birdie and I would be in color. That's how I saw us. Bright and wonder eyed. A flicker of what life could be like, but it dissipates quickly. I went home that evening, excited for the next few days. We had a busy week. Tomorrow would be Sunday; I would go to church with Birdie and her family. Later on, I would come over for dinner. I needed to impress her parents. They were still hesitant about Birdie and me. I needed to show them I was here for the long run. It wasn't only Birdie I needed to prove this too, it was her family. I needed them to know I am the man for their daughter. I turned off the light, the room enveloped in darkness as I settled into my bed. Thoughts swirled in my mind like autumn leaves in a gusty wind. With a sigh, I closed my eyes, ready to embrace the sweet refuge of sleep, leaving behind the worries of the day.

27
BIRDIE

Dressed in our Sunday best, Roger and I joined my family at the local church. The sermon felt interminable, and I squirmed in my seat like a restless child. Finally, when the last song concluded, a momentary relief washed over me as we spilled out of the church doors.

Walking alongside Roger, my mother approached us.

"That was a lovely sermon, wasn't it?" she asked.

"It was indeed," Roger replied politely.

"Roger, would you mind stepping aside with me for a moment?" my mother requested.

I hoped their conversation would be brief and kind.

"Of course, Mrs. Godwin," Roger replied.

As they stepped away, I watched them, anxious about what was being discussed. My father approached, offering me reassurance.

"Don't worry, little bird," he said, squeezing my shoulder.

"But what do you think they're talking about?" I asked, unable to shake my concern.

"Your mother wants to ensure Roger is right for you," he explained, though his uncertainty lingered.

Frustrated, I stepped back from him. "But Daddy, I love him. Don't you believe he's good for me?"

"I had my doubts, but he seems like a standup guy," he admitted.

"It's my choice, Daddy. Why does mom keep trying to interfere?"

"She's looking out for you, pumpkin. Her hearts in the right place," he said, trying to calm me.

"But I'm tired of her meddling. Roger is the love of my life—I'll choose him," I asserted.

"Well, then he better be good at convincing your mother he's the right choice," my father remarked before we were interrupted by my mother's approached.

As she reached us, I noticed Roger standing a little apart. I moved toward him, eager for an explanation.

"Roger, what happened?" I asked, hoping for reassurance.

"Your mother cares about you, Birdie. She had some questions for me," he explained.

"And…?" I prompted.

"She wanted to know my intentions. She doesn't want anything to jeopardize your ambitions," he said earnestly.

"You've never stood in the way of my goals," I said, feeling defensive.

He took my hands in his, drawing me closer. "Of course not, Birdie."

Before we could continue, my father called my name. "I have to go, Roger. You're still coming to dinner, right?"

"Absolutely. It's another chance to prove to your parents I'm committed to you," he reassured me.

I smiled, grateful for his devotion. With Roger by my side, I felt confident in our love, regardless of my mother's reservations. Call me a rebel, but I was done letting others dictate what was best for me. I knew in my heart Roger was the one for me, and nothing would change that.

The clock ticked toward 5 p.m., each second stretching into an eternity. Roger would arrive soon, and a familiar blend of excitement and apprehension knotted my stomach. It was far from our first meeting, yet I was nervous like introducing a new flame to my parents. Roger had become an integral part of my life over the years, and I cherished his constant presence. Even when we were broken up for those longest two months of my life, he was still all I thought about. As I paced the room, memories of past encounters with my mother's skepticism flooded my mind. The subtle glances, the guarded conversations, they all betrayed her reservations about Roger.

Yet, despite her doubts, I remained resolute in my choice. I loved him, and that was nonnegotiable. Still, a small flicker of hope lingered within me, yearning for my mother's acceptance, even if it seemed improbable. With each passing moment, the tension in the air thickened, a silent testament to the unspoken battle between my heart and my family's expectations. Deep down, I wished for a day when my mother would welcome Roger with open arms, but until then, I stood firm in my decision, ready to face whatever judgements may come.

The doorbell rang, and I ran to open it. Standing there with his bedroom eyes was Roger. He held a bottle of Merlot, two bouquets of flowers and a case of beer.

I took the bouquets from him. "Roger!" I squealed.

Holding up the beer in one hand and the win in the other. "I brought reinforcements." He teased.

I gripped his wrist pulling him into the foyer and kissed him deeply.

"Well hello to you too." He replied.

"Hi…" Was the only words I could whisper. No one ever told me love could hurt and feel good all at once.

The soft hues of the setting sun painted the sky as my family gathered in our backyard nestled amidst the tranquility of upstate New York. Spring was in full bloom, the air carrying the sweet scent of newly blossomed flowers. My mother, ever the gracious hostess, had meticulously arranged the outdoor table, adorning it with a vibrant tablecloth and delicate floral centerpieces. She had also strategically placed heaters around the perimeter, a thoughtful gesture in anticipation of the chill often crept in with the nightfall. Anticipation coursed through me as I led Roger through the sliding glass doors, his presence adding an extra layer of warmth to the evening. I couldn't wait for him to meet my family, to share in this intimate gathering under the starlit sky.

As we stepped into the backyard, Dean, bounded over with his trademark grin. "Hey there, Roger! It's good to see you." Dean's voice carried the familiar cadence of Brooklyn, a reminder of his recent relocation to the bustling city.

"Dean, it's great to see you too," Roger replied, extending a hand in greeting. "How's Brooklyn treating you?"

"It's a whirlwind, but I'm loving every minute of it," Dean replied, his eyes alight with excitement. "I hear you and Birdie are thinking of making the move?"

Roger nodded, a hint of excitement mingled with nervousness dancing in his eyes. "Yeah, we are. It's a big step, but we're ready for the adventure."

Dean chuckled, clapping Roger on the back. "Make sure you take care of my little sister, alright?"

A nervous laugh escaped Roger's lips, but he met Dean's gaze with determination. "Always."

Only then, my father emerged from the shadows, his presence commanding attention as he strode over to greet Roger. A firm handshake was exchanged, accompanied by a warm smile of welcome. Roger handed him the case of beer he had brought, a gesture of gratitude my father accepted with a nod of thanks, already popping open a bottle.

"Thanks, Roger," my father said, his voice tinged with appreciation as he passed a bottle to Roger and Dean. "I'll get these chilled in no time."

My mother glided over, her presence exuding warmth

and hospitality as she enveloped Roger in a hug. "Thank you for joining us, Roger," she said, her eyes sparkling with genuine warmth as he handed her a bottle of wine and flowers.

"We're thrilled to have you here," she added, accepting the bottle and bouquet with a gracious smile.

With the pleasantries exchanged, my mother gestured towards the table, a spread of tantalizing dishes awaiting our eager appetites. "Shall we eat?"

"Yes, please," I chimed in eagerly.

After dinner, my father, Roger, and Dean wandered off to enjoy an evening cigar while my mother and I cleared the table.

"It was nice of Roger to bring you wine and flowers," I remarked, handing another plate to my mother as she stood over the sink, rinsing away any residue.

"He's trying, mother," I noted as I scraped leftovers from the plates into the trash.

She was quiet for a moment before nodding. "Birdie, I'm not the enemy here," she said sternly.

I paused, searching for the right words. Time seemed to pass slowly before I could respond. "I know," I said slowly.

"Birdie, I have my reservations. It's what a mother does."

"Are you always going to be reserved?"

"Until that boy puts a ring on your finger, I can't promise much."

"It's all about marriage?"

"It will always be about marriage. But I still think

you're too young to be making any final decisions."

She put down the dish towel and gestured to the table. We sat down across from each other as she poured us each a glass of wine.

Pushing my glass towards me, she asked, "If Roger proposed tonight, would you say yes, Birdie?"

Taking a sip from my glass, I pondered the question. Without hesitation, I quipped, "Yes, I would."

"Well then, Birdie, I will support you. I don't have to agree to be supportive."

"I know, mother. But it would be nice if you let your guard down a little bit."

"I will try if you promise not to give up your dreams for some boy."

"I promise." Rising from the table to join the men outside, I turned to her once more. "And for the record, Roger is a man, not a boy."

28
BIRDIE

Later in the evening, Dean left to drive back into the city and my parents went back into the house. I said goodnight to Roger and thanked him for the flowers. I watched him pull away from the house. As I walked back into the backyard, I could hear the crickets and the distant hum of the town. I shifted on the swing, feeling the cool breeze against my face.

What if we find more than an apartment tomorrow? I mused, the night offering no immediate answers. The journey ahead was a tapestry of uncertainties, and as I continued to gaze into the darkness, I found solace in the shared unknown with Roger, the stars above bearing witness to our whispered doubts and hopes.

The soft glow of a nearby streetlamp cast dancing shadows across the grass. A stray cat prowled along the fence, its eyes reflecting the same curiosity tugging at my heart. Tomorrow wasn't about securing a new living space; it was a symbolic step towards adulthood and a life entwined with Roger. I imagined us navigating the bustling city streets, hand in hand, our laughter echoing through the urban canyons. I let my mind wander, a memory resurfaced of our first date on the grassy field on campus, the warmth of Roger's hand, the excitement of discovering shared interests. The familiarity of our connection provided comfort amid the uncertainty. "Remember that night?" I whispered to the stars, as if seeking their cosmic affirmation. The swing rocked gently, and I contemplated the balance between the comfort of familiarity and the thrill of the unknown. The city awaited promising opportunities and challenges. What if this is the adventure we've been waiting for?

The question hangs in the air, a testament to the exhilaration and trepidation accompanied by stepping into the unknown. In the distance, a faint sound of music wafted through the air, a reminder life has its own inherent rhythm. The beat of our hearts, the tune of our shared laughter, and the blend of our dreams were interwoven with the city's nocturnal orchestra. Are we ready for this? I contemplated, realizing readiness was a subjective concept, shaped by the courage to embrace the unfolding chapters of our lives.

I glanced at the stars, now a comforting presence, and could almost envision them forming constellations telling the story of Roger and me. What if this is exactly where we're meant to be? I wondered. A newfound sense of reassurance settled within.

The backyard porch, bathed in moonlight, was a haven for introspection and anticipation. As the night progressed, I embraced the unknown, the fear of the unfamiliar transforming into excitement for the possibilities awaiting us. "What if this is our chance to create something extraordinary?" I whispered, not to the stars but to the universe which seemed to respond with a gentle, reassuring breeze. And so, with a heart full of dreams and uncertainties, I sat on the porch swing, ready to face the city's embrace with Roger by my side.

The night, once a realm of doubts, transcended the boundaries of the known and ventured into the magic of the uncharted.

★ ★ ★

When the morning sun painted the sky, a chorus of birdsong serenaded the awakening of the day. Blinking as I open my eyes, I found myself nestled on the gently swaying swing. The air, laden with the crisp essence of autumn, carried the tantalizing scent of waffles, eggs, and bacon wafting from inside the house.

Entering the kitchen, I discovered my mother orchestrating a breakfast masterpiece.

The sizzling sounds and fragrant aromas created a sensory feast, while my father, engrossed in the morning newspaper, sat at the table.

"Good morning, my little bird," my father greeted with a warm smile.

"Good morning!" I chirped, drawn in by the enticing aroma. "Mmm, smells amazing, Mother." Leaning my head on her shoulder, I peered over.

She patted my head. "Morning, darling, and thank you. I see you slept outside again."

Stealing a piece of bacon, I perched myself on the countertop and took a satisfying bite. "It's peaceful outside," I mused.

"You know, these late nights have me worrying about you," she expressed her concern.

"Mother, you have nothing to worry about. I can't sleep sometimes, and the fresh air feels nice."

"It's not normal to struggle with sleep. Maybe moving in with Roger isn't the best idea."

"Mother, please. We're adults, and I love him."

"Loving him doesn't mean you have to rush into living together. After all, I don't see a ring on your finger."

Taking another bite of bacon, I replied, "We're going to look at places. Doesn't mean anything."

"Oh, sweetie, it means everything. I'm your mother; I know these things."

"Well, I'm confident about Roger and our future together. I think we'll be fine."

Or so I told myself. Little did my mother know I had been up half the night wondering the same thing—was there a future for Roger and me? Shaking off the thought, I realized Roger would be here any minute. I kissed my mother on the cheek before sneaking another piece of bacon. Heading upstairs to my bedroom, I quickly changed. Seated on my bed, I picked up a book, intending to squeeze in some reading before Roger arrived. Lost in the narrative, I failed to hear Roger's arrival. Descending the stairs, I discovered him in the backyard with my father. While my mother sat at the kitchen table fixing a button on one of my father's dress shirts, I absorbed the details of the cozy kitchen, the sunlit backyard, and the comforting sounds of a home in motion.

"Mother, why didn't you tell me Roger was here?" I asked.

She hardly looked up, engrossed in her task. "Oh, I'm sorry; I guess I got sidetracked."

Seating myself beside her, I inquired, "What is Dad talking to Roger about?"

"Who knows, sweetie? Why don't you go out there and find out?"

Part of me wanted to, but the scene beyond the window suggested they didn't want to be interrupted. It wasn't long before the two of them returned, leaving me to ponder how long they had been immersed in conversation, a mystery. The day unfolded, I couldn't shake the nagging doubt about my future with Roger. The fragility of our plans lingered in the crisp air, and for the first time, the autumn morning felt as uncertain as my thoughts. As my father and Roger stepped inside, I rose from the table, eager to welcome Roger with a warm hug. "I'm so happy to see you!" I exclaimed as I embraced him, and he responded with a gentle kiss on the cheek.

"I'm thrilled to see you, too. Today is going to be amazing!" Roger declared.

After a brief exchange with my mother, doubts began

to gnaw at me. Roger sensed something was amiss, but I couldn't voice my concerns in the presence of my parents.

"What were you two discussing outside?" I inquired, trying to bring some levity into the atmosphere.

In that moment, Roger's usually composed face turned as pale as a ghost, an unusual sight, considering I hadn't seen him nervous since our first date. My father, opting for avoidance, sat down at the kitchen table to resume reading the newspaper, and an uneasy silence settled in.

"Did I not speak loud enough?" I pressed, attempting to break the tension.

"Birdie, sweetie, don't you and Roger have somewhere to be?" my father interjected. "You must get going before you hit all the traffic going into the city."

Recognizing my father's classic diversionary tactic, I chose not to press further. I bid my parents goodbye with kisses on their cheeks, and Roger and I made our way outside. The midday sun cast a lazy glow as we stepped away from the embrace of my childhood home. The atmosphere, previously fragrant with breakfast aromas, now contained a subtle tension—a residue of the morning's weighty conversation.

We strolled down the familiar path, the crisp crunch of fallen leaves beneath our feet provided a soundtrack to our conversation. Sunlight filtered through the trees, creating mottled patterns on the pavement. I inhaled slowly, gathering the courage to address the lingering unease.

"You want to tell me what all of that was about?" Roger asked, his fingers intertwining with mine.

"It's nothing," I replied, my gaze fixed on the uneven

path ahead.

"Well, it didn't seem like nothing. I'm confused, Birdie. Am I not allowed to have a conversation with your father?"

"Don't be silly, Roger. Of course you are. You were out there for a while, and then you come inside acting like you were holding the biggest secret in the world."

A subtle gulp escaped Roger as I mentioned the word "secret," intensifying my nervousness.

"You know, my mother doesn't think we should move in together. It's ridiculous. We're in love! Why wouldn't we want to live together?"

Roger, the perpetual optimist, reached for my hand. "Your parents care, Birdie. It's concern, nothing more."

A half smile played on my lips, but the doubts from earlier still lingered. "I know, but sometimes I wonder if we're moving too fast."

He squeezed my hand gently. "Birdie, we've been through so much together. Moving in feels like the next natural step. What's bothering you?"

As we continued our walk, I confessed, "You know, my mother ... she's concerned."

Roger's expression shifted, a blend of understanding and concern. "Birdie, we're not rushing. We're taking our time, figuring things out together."

We reached Roger's car, and he opened the passenger door for me. Unable to contain my thoughts, I sighed, the turmoil within me seeking an outlet. "It's not about living together. It's about our future, our plans. Are we on the same page, Roger?"

His gaze wandered into the distance, thoughts churning. "Birdie, I want us to have a future together. I've been thinking about it a lot, about where we're headed."

A moment of quiet reflection passed between us. The car seemed to hold its breath, waiting for the decisions that would shape our lives.

"I want us to be sure," I confessed, my voice a mere breath. "Not only about today, but about tomorrow and the days after. I don't want to lose what we have because we rushed into something we weren't ready for."

Roger nodded, his eyes meeting mine. "Birdie, I want what's best for us, too. Let's take the time we need. We can look at places, plan our future, but let's do it at our own pace."

He shut the car door and made his way to the driver's seat, and the weight on my shoulders lifted slightly. Roger's understanding and willingness to take things at a measured pace reassured me. Driving into the city, the uncertainty of the morning began to dissipate. Our journey ahead was still unclear, but one thing was evident: we were determined to navigate it together, step by deliberate step.

29
ROGER

I approached the Godwins' residence, a persistent unease settling over me like a heavy shroud. The rustle of leaves beneath my feet seemed to amplify the gnawing feeling in my gut. The need for a private conversation with Birdie's father weighed on me, an urgent yearning that grew with every step.

Surprisingly, upon reaching the door, I found Birdie still upstairs, providing an unexpected chance for an intimate conversation with her father.

The interior of the Godwin's home embraced me in warmth, a blend of comforting scents.

Hints of cinnamon and vanilla, perhaps Marjorie's signature touch. I exchanged pleasantries with Birdie's mother, whose eyes hinted at a latent curiosity. Then, with

Clark, we stepped into the backyard, where the brisk autumn air bit at our skin, contrasting with the warmth inside.

"It's great to see you, Roger," Clark's voice was resonant and welcoming, echoing in the crisp air.

"I feel the same way." Despite my usual ease with words, a lump lodged in my throat, a tangible testament to the weight of my intentions. My heart raced, a palpable rhythm that mirrored the urgency of my purpose.

"Why don't you cut to the chase, Roger, and tell me what it is you wanted to discuss?" Clark's straightforwardness mimicked the brisk wind, cutting through any pretense.

Realizing that further delay was untenable, especially with Birdie potentially descending at any moment, I took a deep breath and plunged into the revelation. "Well, sir, I love your daughter very much," I began, the words carrying a gravity hung in the air. "I see a future with her. While today is about finding a place to live, I have grander aspirations. I'm here to seek your blessing to marry Birdie."

Leaves rustled, a cacophony of nature's approval, and the distant chirping of birds served as an unintentional chorus to our unfolding drama. The silence between us became charged, each second pregnant with anticipation.

"Ah, you want to marry my daughter? My only daughter."

"Yes, sir."

"And how do you think you will provide for her?"

The wind carried my response. "Well, sir, I currently work as a flight instructor. It pays well enough. I'd love to work for an airline soon. I've arranged some prospective interviews."

"Is being a pilot truly your dream job?"

"Yes, sir."

"Do you see yourself living in the city forever?"

"I see myself being with Birdie. Wherever life takes us, I know we'll be fine."

"Do you have a ring?"

"I do." I retrieved the ring from my coat pocket, and its glint caught the autumn sunlight. The symbolic circle felt weighty in my hand, a promise and a plea.

He took the ring, turning it between his fingers, and admiration flickered in his eyes. "Well done, Roger. This is a beauty."

"Thank you, sir. I spotted it in a local pawnshop and knew it was calling Birdie's name."

A few more seconds of silence hung between us, pregnant with the unspoken. Any minute now, Birdie could appear. What was taking him so long to decide?

"Roger, I like you. I think you're good for my daughter, and I know you'll treat her right." His words carried a paternal warmth, a silent approval resonated deep within me. "You're young, but we all were once, and age shouldn't hinder you from planning your future. I know my wife may have some reservations. But I know you love Birdie, and that's why I'm giving you my blessing."

"Oh, sir, Clark, thank you. Thank you so much, Mr. Godwin." My excitement overflowed, and I repeated every name possible.

I extended my hand, and he shook it. "You're a good

man, Roger. I can't promise you she'll say yes. But I believe in you two and know you'll make each other happy."

"Thank you, sir."

"Now, put this somewhere safe." He handed me back the ring just in time for Birdie's arrival.

The moment hung in the air, charged with significance. It was time to head back inside, back to the warmth of the Godwins' home. As Mr. Godwin and I walked in, an overwhelming feeling engulfed me. I was about to propose to the woman I loved, and I prayed to God she would say yes. Mr. Godwin and I stepped inside Birdie's childhood home, my attention was drawn to her as she got up from the table with genuine excitement.

Her warm embrace welcomed me, and I responded with a gentle kiss on her cheek, savoring the connection we shared. The familiar scent of her family home enveloped us, creating a comfortable backdrop for what lay ahead.

"Roger, I'm so happy to see you!" Birdie exclaimed as she hugged me tightly.

"I'm thrilled to see you, too. Today is going to be amazing!" I declared, hoping to inject a sense of positivity into the moment.

After exchanging pleasantries with Birdie's mother, I sensed a subtle shift in the atmosphere. Doubts seemed to linger in Birdie's demeanor, but in the presence of her parents, she refrained from voicing her concerns. Her attempt to lighten the mood with a casual inquiry about our outdoor discussion met with a restrained tension. My usually composed demeanor faltered as Birdie pressed for details, and an awkward silence settled in. Mr. Godwin, opting for avoidance, immersed himself in the newspaper.

Mr. Godwin suggested we leave. We bid her parents goodbye and stepped outside into the midday sun. The leaves crunched underfoot while we wandered down the path. The air, once filled with the comforting scents of breakfast, now held the residue of unspoken worries. Reaching the car, I opened the passenger door for Birdie, and a subtle sigh escaped her, hinting at the turmoil within. As she settled into the seat, her movements were slower than usual, deliberate, as if she were carrying the weight of unspoken thoughts. Her hands, normally steady, lingered on the edge of the seat, tracing the upholstery as though searching for the right words to match the emotions stirring inside her.

I could sense her mind was elsewhere, tangled in the concerns that had surfaced after our recent visit with her mother. The lingering echo of her mother's cautious words had clearly planted seeds of doubt in Birdie, causing her to question the path we were on. She was trying to find her footing, to navigate the doubts that had quietly crept into our relationship.

As I moved around to the driver's side, I glanced at her, noticing the way her eyes remained fixed on the dashboard, lost in contemplation. Uncomfortable silence hung in the air, thick with the weight of her pending decisions. Her usual brightness was dimmed by the burden of needing reassurance, not only from me, but from the future we were stepping into together. I took my seat behind the wheel and paused, allowing the stillness to speak for us. The car's interior felt like a cocoon, insulating us from the world outside, yet amplifying the tension within. I didn't need her to say anything; her posture, the way she held herself, was enough to convey the depth of her uncertainty.

I reached for the steering wheel, but hesitated, turning toward her and placing a gentle hand on hers. The warmth of her skin contrasted with the cool metal beneath our fingers, and I felt a surge of protectiveness rise within me. I wanted to tell her it was okay to be uncertain, we didn't have to have all the answers right now. But more than that, I wanted her to feel that no matter what lay ahead, we would face it together. She looked at me then, her eyes softening as they met mine, and I could see the vulnerability she was trying to shield. In that moment, we didn't need words. I squeezed her hand lightly, offering silent reassurance, hoping she could feel the steadiness I wanted to give her. We sat there for a while, the hum of the engine the only sound between us, as if the car itself was waiting for us to decide our next move. The tension slowly eased, replaced by a quiet understanding. Birdie seemed to draw strength from the silence, her shoulders relaxing slightly as if the weight had been lifted, if only a little. Eventually, she released a breath, almost imperceptibly, and the corners of her lips curved into a small, grateful smile. I returned it, feeling a renewed sense of purpose. Whatever confusion we faced, I knew together we could navigate it, step by step, hand in hand.

With a final squeeze of her hand, I released it and

turned back to the road ahead. As I shifted the car into drive, the atmosphere shifted as well. The air between us was still thick with unresolved questions, but it was no longer oppressive. Instead, it felt like a space where we could grow, where we could find our way forward together. As I pulled away from the curb, the world seemed less daunting. The Godwin's home faded in the rearview mirror. The road stretched out before us, a path yet to be written.

30
BIRDIE

The crisp autumn air embraced Roger and me as we strolled through the bustling streets of New York City. The city's heartbeat reverberated in every corner, and the prospect of finding our dream apartment added an extra skip to our steps. I marveled at the towering skyscrapers which framed the cityscape, an overwhelming contrast to the small town we had left behind. The energy of the city was infectious, and we were determined to find the perfect nest amid the concrete jungle.

Our apartment hunting adventure began with a list of must-haves and nice-to-haves clutched in my hand. The items scrawled across it represented the dreams Roger and I shared. A cozy kitchen for his culinary experiments, a spacious living room for our shared movie nights, and, of course, enough natural light to nurture the plants I envisioned adorning our home. As we stepped into the first apartment, my eyes widened, taking in the exposed brick walls and large windows that allowed the city's heartbeat to echo within. The hardwood floors creaked beneath our feet, and as I wandered from room to room, the scent of fresh paint and the soft glow of sunlight painted vivid images of our future life together.

"This could be it, Roger," I whispered, my voice filled with a mix of excitement and wonder.

Roger nodded in agreement with a twinkle in his eyes. "It's got character. I can already imagine cooking up a storm in that kitchen."

We moved from one apartment to another, each offering a unique glimpse into the city's diverse housing landscape. Some were too small, others too noisy, but each one brought us a step closer to finding our perfect match. In the heart of Greenwich Village, we discovered a cozy apartment tucked away on a treelined street. The quaintness of the neighborhood contrasted with the city's hustle, creating a harmonious blend resonated with my soul.

"It's like our own little oasis amidst it all," Roger mused, gazing out of the window at the passing pedestrians below.

The apartment search became a journey of self-discovery for Roger and me. We learned to compromise and to dream bigger simultaneously.

The city, with its myriad options, challenged our perceptions and expanded our understandings. Through laughter and shared glances, we navigated the maze of possibilities, growing closer with each potential home. As the sun dipped below the skyline, casting a warm glow over the city, Roger and I found ourselves standing on the rooftop of a high-rise building. The panoramic view of the city lights sparkled below, and a sense of serenity settled over us.

"This is it, isn't it?" I murmured, leaning against Roger.

He wrapped his arm around me, a smile playing on his lips. "Our own piece of the sky."

And so, with the city as our witness, Roger and I took the plunge into a new chapter of our lives, submitting an application, ready to turn a New York apartment into a place we could proudly call home. we embraced our decision on which apartment we wanted, my mind raced with the images of lazy Sunday mornings in our cozy kitchen, the aroma of Roger's cooking filling the air. I imagined game nights in our spacious living room, the soft glow of the city outside serving as the perfect backdrop. The plants I envisioned dotted every corner, thriving in the ample natural light streaming through our windows.

Yet, amidst the excitement, a subtle undercurrent of uncertainty tugged at my thoughts. What challenges awaited us in this bustling city? Would the dreams we were weaving together withstand the tests of time? As I looked out over the city lights, a quiet determination settled within me, a commitment to face whatever lay ahead, with Roger by my side.

Reflecting on the journey, I marveled at the growth we had undergone. From the small town to the city lights, each step had shaped us, molding our relationship into something resilient and beautiful. Roger and I meticulously pored over every detail of the apartment application, ensuring we didn't miss a single field. We eagerly submitted it to the landlord and waited in nervous anticipation for their response. The mere possibility of living in New York City was a dream come true, and I couldn't help but feel a flutter of excitement every time I thought about it. The thought of leaving my hometown, where I had lived all my life, was daunting. But the idea of living with my boyfriend in a new city was thrilling. It was an opportunity to start fresh, to experience new things, and to grow together as a couple.

While I reflected on my experiences, I realized the only time I had ever lived away from home was when I went to college in a completely different state. However, the prospect of moving to New York City was vastly different. The city's vibrant energy, diverse culture, and endless possibilities were alluring. The idea of exploring new neighborhoods, trying new restaurants, and meeting new people was exhilarating. I couldn't wait to see what the future held. The mere thought of starting this new life with my partner made my heart skip a beat. I was eager to see what awaited us in New York City and how it would shape us, both individually and as a couple.

After a morning of navigating the bustling city streets, filled with towering buildings and the constant hum of urban life. Roger and I found ourselves winding down from the intensity of apartment hunting. The excitement of potential new beginnings was palpable, but an undercurrent of uncertainty lingered. The city had presented us with a myriad of options, each apartment boasting its unique character and charm. Though none felt like an immediate home, a particular unit had caught our attention. A cozy corner space with a panoramic view, seemingly embracing the city lights like a warm, inviting hug. While we couldn't put our finger on why this apartment felt different, the thought of settling down there sparked an ember of excitement within us. As we drove back, the anticipation of whether we would secure this space consumed our thoughts, casting a subtle spell over the afternoon.

Eager to escape the concrete jungle, Roger suggested a detour before heading back to my place. "How about we take a little break and clear our minds?" he proposed with a mischievous smile.

Always one for spontaneous adventures, I readily agreed. Both of us remained silent on the stroll back to the car, mostly looking around and taking in the uniqueness of the city.

As we drove away from the city's skyline, the landscape transformed from steel and glass to serene suburbs and open spaces. The car zipped through narrow roads lined with trees, their branches forming a natural canopy overhead. It was as if we were escaping the clutches of the urban chaos, seeking refuge in the tranquility of nature. Eventually, Roger turned onto a quiet road, and the car rumbled along until we reached a hidden gem—Blue Haven Pond. The name itself carried a sense of serenity and calm, and the sight unfolded before us affirmed it.

The pond, nestled in a secluded clearing surrounded by lush greenery, reflected the soft sunlight of the afternoon. Its surface shimmered with a gentle blue tint, creating an ethereal glow dancing with the soft ripples caused by a light breeze. A wooden dock extended gracefully into the water, inviting us to step into this tranquil oasis.

"We could use a moment of peace," Roger remarked, parking the car nearby.

With the city's chaos behind us, we stepped out onto the dock with the planks creaking beneath our feet. The air was crisp, carrying the fragrance of pine and earth.

We found a pair of weathered Adirondack chairs at the water's edge and settled into them, allowing the quietude to envelop us. The only sounds were the distant calls of birds and the soothing lull of the water against the shore. As the sky transformed from vibrant hues to the calming palette of afternoon, the city's hustle and bustle felt like a distant memory. Roger broke the silence. "You know, sometimes the best places are the ones you stumble upon unexpectedly."

I couldn't agree more. Blue Haven Pond, with its simple beauty and timeless charm, felt like a hidden sanctuary, a shelter away from the frenetic pace of city life. We sat there, savoring the peace, as the sunlight filtered through the leaves overhead. Like a distant promise, the city lights shined brightly against the darkening sky and in that moment we were offered hope and excitement holding onto us within its limits.

31
ROGER

The sun, a molten orb, painted the skyline with its golden brushstrokes as Birdie and I meandered through the outskirts of our town. We left the city behind and drank in the beauty of upstate. The peals of our laughter reverberated between us, guiding us to an undiscovered refuge—a pristine pond. Its surface was a liquid canvas reflecting the rich palette of the setting sun.

After a leisurely stroll, we found ourselves ensconced by the water's edge. The pond sprawled before us. My hands trembled as I kept them inside my coat pockets, the clamminess of my palms betraying my nervousness. I looked around the pond, shifting my gaze from the scene before us to Birdie. Her eyes, aglow with wonder, drank in the surroundings, oblivious to the butterflies fluttering within me. The tranquil waters of the pond mimicked the depth of my emotions, each stroke adding to the masterpiece of the impending proposal.

We exchanged few words. Blue Haven Pond, now transformed into a cosmic theater, awaited the revelation of emotions that could no longer be confined. As the last rays of daylight faded into the night, casting hues of amber and rose, I reached for Birdie's hand. Her fingers interlaced with mine, and the connection felt like a silent covenant. We sat there, bathed in the warm glow, the weight of the engagement ring in my pocket a tangible reminder of the chapter awaited. The first stars emerged in the darkening canvas of the sky, and I seized the moment to share the secrets of the celestial vault. Birdie listened with a mix of curiosity and enchantment, her eyes reflecting the cosmic wonder above.

Summoning courage, I turned to her, the pond now a shimmering reflection of the night sky, heightening the gravity of the moment. Locking eyes with Birdie, I poured my heart into words, expressing the profound depth of my love. In the serene beauty of the Blue Haven Pond, beneath the twinkling stars, I posed the question that would irrevocably alter the course of our story. "Birdie," I murmured, my voice both steady and laced with emotion, "will you marry me?"

Time seemed to suspend, and the world held its breath. The nearby glow of a park lamp lit up the pond where we stood. In the mirror of the pond, I glimpsed a luminous sheen in her eyes, and a radiant smile adorned her face. With tears of joy, she nodded, an exquisite affirmation marking the beginning of a new chapter, one imbued with the promise of a lifetime entwined. The night was tranquil, with the moon casting a pale glow over the landscape, and the stars twinkling like diamonds in the sky.

Birdie's whispered affirmation was like a gentle melody in the stillness of the night, resonating in the depths of my soul. A profound sense of liberation replaced the weight that had burdened my shoulders, and I could finally breathe again. An exhilarating feeling of lightness enveloped me, making my heart soar to the divine rhythm of newfound happiness. I felt like I was floating, my body weightless with the joy filling me. In that transformative moment, the pond became more than a backdrop. It was a sacred witness to our union, with nature itself blessing our commitment.

The stars seemed to dance in the sky, radiant and twinkling like cosmic confetti, commemorating the profound decision would shape the alchemy of our shared existence. My own tears, a testament to the overwhelming emotions coursing through me, mingled with the moonlit night. Delicately retrieving the ring from my pocket, the cool metal warmed by the love that had fueled my journey to this pivotal point, felt like a promise fulfilled. Slipping the ring onto Birdie's finger wasn't a symbolic gesture; it was a silent vow which reverberated with unspoken promises and future dreams. In the moonlit glow, our clasped hands reflected in the calm surface of the pond.

The celebration following our engagement was a joyous affair, with friends and family joining us to toast to

Birdie and I as the newly engaged couple. Well-wishes poured in from all corners. The engagement ring sparkled on Birdie's finger, a beacon of love and commitment.

In our journey to find a dream apartment in the heart of the city, we discovered the landlord was a friend of a friend, creating a sense of serendipity. Eagerly awaiting a response on our application , the prospect of a shared space in the bustling city added an extra layer of excitement to our plans.

The engagement ring, now a constant presence on Birdie's finger, became a conversation starter as we shared the news with friends and acquaintances. Each time we recounted the proposal under the stars, the magic of the night was relived in our conversations. As we walked through the city streets, the memories of our time at Millikin flooded back. Holding Birdie in my arms was no longer a distant dream, but a tangible reality. The winding paths and serendipitous moments had led us to this juncture felt like a series of interconnected dots, creating a beautiful mosaic of our shared history.

If someone had told me in late November 1948, I would fall deeply in love with Birdie and she would not only become my girlfriend but my fiancée, I would have thought they were crazy. But here we were, standing on the edge of something life-changing. The future was bright, and I couldn't wait to see what it had in store for us.

32
BIRDIE

The air, already charged with the weight of Roger's question, crackled with an energy that transcended the mere physical realm. My heart, having danced to the rhythm of anticipation, now pounded in a mélange of joy and love. The echo of his proposal lingered, and I felt the gravity of his words settle like stardust on my soul.

Tears welled up in my eyes, a testament to the overwhelming emotions surged within me. Roger's gaze, steady and filled with an earnest vulnerability, held mine as if seeking affirmation that rose above spoken words.

The warmth of his touch and the sheer beauty of the moment enveloped me like a protective cocoon. A smile, radiant and genuine, blossomed on my lips. I could feel the tears spill over, trailing down my cheeks like liquid diamonds. With a heart brimming with love, I nodded, the gesture both a response to his question and a silent pledge to the journey ahead.

"Yes, Roger," I whispered, my voice carrying the weight of a thousand promises. "Yes, a thousand times over."

As if breaking a spell, Roger's eyes lit up with an indescribable joy.

The pond, the stars, and the surrounding nature seemed to celebrate our union. Roger, overcome with emotion, reached into his pocket, retrieving the symbol of our commitment—a ring that sparkled with the same brilliance as the stars above.

As he delicately slid it onto my finger, the world seemed to hold its breath once more, capturing this exchange of vows in a timeless tableau. The stars seemed to shimmer with an added glow, as if celebrating the union of two souls beneath their watchful gaze.

I was ecstatic to show off my engagement ring to my family and friends. It was a symbol of my commitment to Roger, the man I loved and was going to marry. I couldn't wait to start my new life as his wife. As a little girl, I used to dream about the moment when I would get engaged, and now that moment had finally arrived. The ring was a beautiful old-European diamond, sparkling in the light and catching everyone's attention. I felt proud to wear it on my finger and show it to everyone.

As I looked at it, I couldn't help but wonder what my younger self would think of me now. Would she be proud of the woman I had become? I was filled with joy and excitement, knowing I was about to embark on a new chapter in my life with the man of my dreams.

A lump filled my lungs as I remembered each detail of the day by the pond. I hoped I'd never have to wonder what life would be like without Roger. It was a scary feeling.

Letting someone in, falling in love. Allowing them to see all your greatest, purest moments but hoping they'd love you still in your deepest, darkest moments. As I lay in bed that night, my eyes were fixated on my ring, shining in the faint moonlight. My thoughts drifted, and memories of when Roger was in Novaria and I was uncertain if he would ever return flooded my mind. When he left for Novaria to save the world, I would tell myself he was like a superhero, like Superman, flying around the world. But deep down, all I wanted was for him to come back home and save me from my loneliness. The mere thought of Roger's return was always more comforting than the reality of anyone else's company. I couldn't bear to love anyone else in the same way I loved him, for he was the one who had stolen my heart long ago.

33
ROGER

Birdie Godwin would soon be my wife. Things were moving at a fast pace, even though it felt as if time itself was slowing down. Part of me was grateful time seemed to move a little slower. The days that followed were of many wedding details. Birdie spent most of her time between work and wedding planning with her mom and grandmother.

I had my say in the parts that mattered to me, like choosing the cake, the song for our first dance, the color of my tux, and the food. But for most of the planning, I was happy to let Birdie take the lead. I knew how much these details meant to her, and I wanted to make sure she had everything she'd ever dreamed of.

While Birdie was wedding planning, I began moving

more items into our new apartment. We had slowly collected items and brought each one over to the apartment. Birdie and I would go to flea markets and thrift shops to find picture frames, a couch, and small items to make the place feel like home. Nestled on the fourth floor of a pre-war building on the Upper West Side, the apartment embodied the vibrant and eclectic charm of New York City. As I stepped into the cozy living space, the narrow entryway opened up to reveal a warm and inviting ambiance.

The filtered sunlight seeping through the timeworn curtains cast a patchwork of warm light across the hardwood floors, emanating an atmosphere of comfort and tranquility. The exposed brick walls, adorned with the scars of years past, whispered tales of the city's history. The vintage velvet couch, though worn at the edges, exuded timeless elegance, serving as the focal point of the room. A collection of mismatched throw pillows, scattered across the couch, hinted at Birdie's love for thrift-store finds and Sunday market treasures. The compact kitchen, with its freshly brewed coffee aroma mingling with the scent of well-loved cookbooks, was a delightful retreat. The small dining table, adorned with a vase of wildflowers, sat near the window, offering a modest view of the neighboring brownstones and the distant hum of city life.

In the snug bedroom, the crisp white linen on the bed invited us weary city dwellers to sink into its embrace after a long day navigating the bustling streets below. The gallery wall, adorned with black-and-white photographs capturing moments frozen in time, served as a visual ode to the city's ever-changing rhythm. I couldn't wait for our wedding day when we could place a photo of Birdie and I along this wall. The bathroom, with its vintage clawfoot tub, would become a sanctuary for late-night soaks and quiet contemplations as a counterpoint to the city that never slept. The flickering neon sign from a nearby jazz club cast a subtle glow, creating an ambiance which transcended the physical boundaries of the space.

As I settled into this urban cocoon, imagining the life Birdie and I were about to have, the ambient sounds of distant sirens and the muffled chatter of pedestrians below would become the lullaby of our nightly routine. The apartment, though modest, held the heartbeat of a city that embraced dreams, hardships, and the relentless pursuit of something more. In this quiet sanctuary, amidst the towering skyscrapers and the ceaseless symphony of NYC, the apartment became more than a dwelling; it was a character in its own right. It served as a refuge and witness to the unfolding narrative of urban life.

I walked inside the apartment, setting down a box of my things from my childhood home. As I looked around the room in awe. Birdie's mother wasn't too keen on us living together especially before marriage. I proposed a compromise. Birdie and I got the apartment, and we would be moving in under one condition. Birdie, herself, would not officially live here until we were married. It was a good thing neither of us wanted a long engagement. We would only be apart at night for a month, and I could live without Birdie living here if it meant we got to live together for the rest of our lives.

Entering the bedroom, I laid down on the bed. I didn't realize how exhausted I was. I had closed my eyes for a brief moment, only to be woken up by a familiar voice.

"Rog, honey, are you here?"

It was Birdie. I sprang off the bed and immediately went to the kitchen area, where she stood.

"Well, hello there, beautiful." I pulled her close and kissed her deeply. You could feel the love between us. A love I had never known before.

I'd already thought about this many times. When you asked yourself "what is true love," what was the answer? No one knew. But when I looked at Birdie, I saw true love. She was genuine and kind. No one stopped me the way Birdie did.

Genuine love acted as a shield, a steadfast ally, an unbreakable connection weaving its presence into every aspect of your life. It was unrefined, ready to unleash a powerful roar when needed. In moments of tranquility, it became your silent companion, providing solace and reassurance.

True love not only reveled in your joys, lifting you to new heights but also cradled your sorrows, gently kissing the scars you concealed. It was a rare treasure. Real love was, without a doubt, the most sublime blessing from the heavens. In the gentle embrace of Birdie's love, I found a sanctuary of emotions that transcended words. Birdie had become my unwavering ally, weaving an unbreakable connection through every shared moment. Her love was a resilient roar, a stalwart defender in the face of life's challenges, standing strong by my side. In the quietude of our togetherness, she transformed into my soothing refuge. Our triumphs were not only mine but shared celebrations, with her lifting me to heights I never thought possible. In moments of vulnerability and sorrow, her love was a gentle touch, tenderly tracing the unseen imprints I held close to my heart, hidden from the world. This bond we shared, Birdie and I, was a rare treasure in my life. Our love was a testament to the extraordinary beauty of a connection going beyond the ordinary, turning each day into a journey enriched by the exceptional presence of her genuine affection.

"Did you fall asleep?" she asked, gently pulling away from our embrace.

"Guilty," I confessed, raising my hands in surrender.

"Oh, Roger, I'm so sorry. We've both been tirelessly juggling wedding planning, settling into this new apartment, and our demanding day jobs. It's been exhausting, but I wouldn't trade it for anything."

"It's okay, Bird. I love you, and I can't wait for you to be my wife."

Birdie's cheeks flushed a slight rose-pink, revealing her excitement about our upcoming wedding.

"Speaking of our wedding, everything is pretty much planned. The only thing left is the cake testing, which I want us to do together."

"Cake? Count me in. That's my favorite part."

She looked at me with a playful smile.

"I mean, besides marrying you, how could you not be excited about cake?" I replied, grinning.

Her voice was filled with excitement as she looked at

me and said, "I can't wait to marry you, Roger Scott."

I felt a rush of happiness inside of me as she leaned in and kissed me on the cheek. As she began to turn away, I gently took her hand, pulling her back towards me, and kissed her with all the love I could muster, as though it might be our last kiss together.

"Now, let's go pick out our cake. We'll say, 'I do,' and I will finally get to call you Mrs. Birdie Scott," I said, smiling at her.

"Mmm, I already love the sound of that," she replied, her eyes sparkling with joy.

We left the apartment to head over to the bakery in the heart of the city where we would be cake testing. The anticipation hung in the air like the sweet aroma of freshly baked goods as we navigated through the bustling city streets. The skyscrapers loomed above us, casting shadows on the pavement, while the distant hum of traffic provided the backdrop to our excitement. The bakery, a hidden gem in the midst of the urban jungle, was renowned for its exquisite confections. Nestled between iconic buildings, its large display windows showcased a tantalizing array of cakes, capturing the essence of the vibrant city around us.

As we approached, the aroma of freshly brewed coffee intertwined with the tempting scent of sugar guided us through the bakery's doors. The cheerful chime of a bell welcomed us into a world of sugary delights as we stepped inside. The atmosphere was a delightful blend of New York's hustle and the comforting warmth of a neighborhood bakery. The city's energy filtered through the windows, infusing the bakery with a unique vibrancy. A friendly pastry chef, seemingly unfazed by the city's relentless pace, greeted us with a warm smile.

"Welcome! You must be Birdie and Roger. We've been eagerly awaiting your arrival," the chef said, leading us to a cozy corner adorned with a pristine white tablecloth.

As we took our seats, a menu with a list of delectable cake options awaited us. From classic New York cheesecake to innovative Manhattan skyline-inspired creations, the choice paid homage to the city's diverse culinary landscape. With eager nods, Birdie and I agreed to sample a trio of their signature cakes, ready to commence on a sweet adventure that mirrored the eclectic spirit of the city. The first forkful was a revelation, a combination of flavors resonating with the diverse cultural tapestry of New York. The pastry chef observed our expressions with a knowing smile, proud to represent their craft in a city that celebrated individuality and creativity. Amidst the lively chatter of the bakery and the distant sounds of the city outside, Birdie and I exchanged notes on each cake's unique character.

The sweet journey unfolded like a love letter to New York City and as we bid farewell to the bustling bakery, the city's skyline illuminated in the evening glow, Birdie and I carried the sweet memories of our cake testing adventure through the vibrant streets. The experience, flavored by the city's energy, had transformed a simple task into a celebration of the diverse and delightful world of desserts thriving in the heart of the Big Apple.

34
BIRDIE

As a young girl, I had a vivid imagination and a simple dream. Which was to become a wife and a mother. I spent countless hours playing house with my baby dolls and taking them for walks in their stroller. My imagination ran wild as I pretended to feed them and care for them, and my imaginary friends became my closest companions.

One day, while sitting in the backyard, I discovered a grand oak tree with a branch arching to the left side of the yard. On the other side stood another oak tree with a branch stretching to the right. I would stand under it and imagine my wedding day, carefully arranging my dolls and stuffed animals around the yard, as one of them would become my husband. I imagined the ceremony, the music, and the joy of starting a family. Looking back, it may seem silly, but to me, it was a highlight of my childhood. The innocence of my dreams and the joy of my imagination made me feel safe, happy, and loved. And now, here I was, about to embark on my real-life wedding with a man whom I loved more and more with each passing day. It was strange, really; we go through life dreaming of our wedding day and then poof! It had all happened fast. You met someone and time flies by, and the next thing you know, he's getting down on one knee and you're wearing his ring and everything feels magical! I felt like I was living a real-life fairytale. Mine and Roger's fairytale. I wanted to shout it from rooftops, "I, BIRDIE SCOTT, AM IN LOVE!"

As I giggled to myself, it felt like a weight had been lifted from my chest. I felt safe with Roger. He made me undeniably happy, and I couldn't imagine a life where Roger wasn't in it. Being a dreamer, I'd always found joy in the little things making life enchanting. As Roger and I waltzed through the intricate dance of wedding planning, every decision felt like weaving our fairytale. With invitations sent, flowers chosen (pink peonies), and the venue secured, the only remaining adventure was the delightful task of cake tasting. Upon arriving at the apartment, silence filled the air, and for a moment, I wasn't sure if Roger was even home. I couldn't think where he could be. I hadn't had time to call him earlier and figured he was still at the apartment, but my mind raced as we had an appointment with a bakery in the city to cake test for our wedding. It was an opportunity we couldn't miss out on. I called out for Roger. Nothing. But then I heard the bedsprings. He must be in the bedroom. I walked over to the kitchen counter and set my purse down. I could hear footsteps and Roger appeared in the kitchen. He looked tired. As he rubbed his eyes briefly, color lit up his face. I suppose everyone needed a good nap once in a while, and we had both been going a million miles an hour. No wonder he was exhausted.

"Did you fall asleep?" I asked.

Roger held up his hands in surrender. "Guilty," he said.

I didn't have much time to waste. I shared with Roger the only thing left to do was cake testing and we needed to get to the bakery now. Roger's eyes lit up at the thought of cake. He had a sweet tooth, and I did too. It was dangerous for the two of us being around desserts. But it was the last thing on my list of wedding planning and nothing felt more satisfying than to check off the final item. Plus, who doesn't love cake?

The bell above the bakery door tinkled as Roger and I stepped inside, greeted by the comforting scent of freshly baked delights. The pastry chef, adorned in a flour-dusted apron, welcomed us with a warm smile, his eyes sparkling with the promise of sweet magic.

"Welcome! You must be Birdie and Roger. We've been eagerly awaiting your arrival," he exclaimed. "Are you ready to savor the last sweet moment before your big day?"

We settled in a cozy corner, surrounded by a parade of wedding cakes whispering tales of love and celebration. The chef presented an array of cake samples, each a canvas of flavors and dreams.

"Let's start with the classic vanilla," he suggested, cutting a delicate slice for us.

As I savored the timeless taste, memories of childhood birthdays and joyous moments flooded my senses. "Oh, it's divine," I sighed with a content smile. "But I've always imagined something a bit more whimsical. Something capturing the essence of our love story." I looked over at Roger adoringly.

The chef nodded in understanding, ready to turn our visions into reality. From rich chocolate ganache to the burst of tangy raspberry fillings, each tasting felt like a step closer to the perfect creation. As we explored the possibilities, I couldn't help but feel a sense of wonder this cake, like my love for Roger, was a unique creation, a blend of flavors and imagination. We left the bakery with our hearts brimming with joy. The final piece of the wedding puzzle had fallen into place, and I couldn't wait to share the sweetness of our love through a cake that spoke our story. With every bite, our guests would taste not only delicious flavors but the magic of our journey together.

Roger and I left the bakery hand in hand, we walked along the treelined streets of NYC. We reminisced about the cake, how wonderful life had been, and how excited we were to get married.

I knew a wedding was something a girl dreamed about, but I could tell Roger had dreamt about this too. He'd grown up with the love of his parents, and when you surround yourself with that kind of love, how could you not want to experience that kind of love yourself? I swore if fate ever stepped in and forced us to say goodbye, I hoped

Roger remembered these little moments.

It was the little moments that became big moments in our lives. When I was with Roger, I felt unstoppable. It was me and him against the world. I would fight a dragon with him if he asked me to. That was what love did to you.

Roger and I decided to visit the local market near our apartment to pick up some groceries. As we walked down the streets, Roger held my hand tightly, making me feel safe and secure. He spun me around, and I couldn't help but laugh out loud. My laughter was uncontrollable I ended up snorting, and we both laughed even louder. Our laughter echoed through the busy streets, but we didn't care because we were caught up in the moment. Roger was always such a kind and gentle man who loved deeply. He wasn't afraid to express his feelings, which meant more to me than anything else in the world. I still remember the sensation of his warm hand wrapped around mine as he spun me around. It was a simple gesture, but it meant the world to me.

After we finished our grocery shopping, we headed back to our apartment, and Roger insisted on cooking us dinner. As he prepared the meal, I couldn't help but admire his cooking skills and the way he moved around the kitchen with such ease. I was curious to see what he was making, and to my delight, he was preparing his famous spaghetti bolognese. I felt lucky to have him in my life, and I knew he was my everything. I decided to help and made a simple salad with heirloom tomatoes. I picked up these gorgeous heirloom tomatoes while we were at the market, each one with its own personality. Slicing through them felt like unlocking a burst of flavors. In our cozy kitchen, I arranged the slices on a plate, adding crisp lettuce for texture. A drizzle of olive oil, a sprinkle of sea salt, a dash of black pepper, and the croutons it was simple yet perfect.

As Roger and I set the table, taking the first bite, the beauty of these tomatoes turned into a celebration on my plate. I took a forkful of spaghetti, it was a delightful blend of flavors and textures. The steam rising from the plate carried the rich aroma of the slow-cooked meat sauce, teasing my senses with the promise of a comforting meal. I glanced over at Roger as he twirled the fork, capturing a perfect amalgamation of al dente spaghetti strands and the hearty bolognese sauce. We both were left with a contented sigh after every delicious mouthful. I imagined nights like this with Roger, cooking together, enjoying a meal together, experimenting with different recipes. We'd sit down each night and share about our day. And one day, we'd have a family of our own, and we'd all gather around the table, experiencing the joy of something so simple as a meal.

As the delicious dinner came to an end, we got up from the table and proceeded to clear it. We worked together to wash the dishes, chatting about our day, and making each other laugh. As the night grew darker and the time ticked away, I realized I didn't want to leave yet. The thought of driving all the way back to my parent's house from the city seemed daunting. I decided to spend the night there. As I settled in for the night, I felt the warmth of the cozy blankets enveloping me. It was the first time I'd had a real glimpse of what it would be like to live with Roger.

35
BIRDIE
DATE: OCTOBER 1952

It was hard to believe a whole month had passed since the day Roger had proposed to me. And now, as I stood before the mirror, taking in the image of myself, a twenty-two-year-old woman, in my white gown, I knew this was the day I had been eagerly waiting for. Today, I was going to become Mrs. Roger Scott, and Roger would be my husband. The mere thought of it filled me with a sense of joy and excitement I had never experienced before. I felt like my heart was about to burst with happiness.

I had been dreaming of the day when I would walk down the aisle and look around at the people who had gathered to witness this momentous occasion. I felt overwhelmed with gratitude. It was as though the whole world was rejoicing with me on this special day. This was not a dream, but a beautiful reality I would cherish for the rest of my life.

As I stood in front of the mirror, I couldn't help but admire the beautiful dress I was wearing. It was a hand-me-down from my mother, and it had been passed down through generations of women in my family. The tradition was to wear the same dress, with a few alterations, on one's wedding day. The dress was a symbol of the love shared by all the women in our family, and it was a tradition I planned to keep. I remember seeing the dress for the first time when I was a little girl. It was stored in a chest in my mother's room, and I was always fascinated by it. One day, when my mother was downstairs cooking, I snuck into her room, opened the chest, and pulled out the gown. I slipped it on, even though it was way too big for me, and stood in front of the mirror and pretended it was my wedding day. It was a magical moment I never forgot. The dress was made of ivory silk and delicate lace, and it looked simply stunning. As I stood there, I felt the whispers of the past and the lingering essence of love dancing within its folds. It was a moment I cherished, and I felt proud to be a part of such a wonderful tradition.

When I finally saw my mother, she was beaming with pride. She looked at me with tears in her eyes, and I knew she was happy. On my wedding day, as I stood in her dress, I was no longer her little girl but a woman on the brink of marrying the love of my life. It was a beautiful moment we shared, and it was a memory I would always treasure.

I felt radiant in my wedding gown as I stood in front

of the vanity mirror, nervously fidgeting with my veil. My mother sat in a nearby chair holding a delicate bouquet of pink peonies.

"Birdie, my darling, you look absolutely breathtaking," she said softly.

Smiling, I responded, "Thank you, Mother. I can't believe today is finally here."

My mother approached me, gently adjusting the veil. She looked at my reflection. "You're all grown up now, my beautiful girl. It feels like yesterday you were playing make-believe in the backyard," she said, as I turned back to the mirror, a soft mist clouding my gaze.

I chuckled, the warmth of the moment lighting up my expression. "Time flies, doesn't it?"

My mother took a seat in a nearby chair, and I followed suit, sitting next to her. She took my hand, teary-eyed, "You know, Bird, I've been reminiscing about the day you were born. Holding you in my arms for the first time, I never imagined we'd be here today."

I squeezed my mother's hand as I looked into her eyes. "I wouldn't be here without you, Mama. You've been my guiding light through everything."

Smiling, my mother said, "And you've made me proud, little bird. Today, as your father walks you down the aisle, it will be a moment etched in our hearts forever."

I took a deep breath, fighting back tears. "I'm lucky to have both of you by my side. Your love and support mean the world to me."

She handed me the bouquet of pink peonies, a symbol of love and tradition, she whispered, "Your dad is waiting for you, and he's as excited as I am. Today is a celebration of love and family."

We shared a heartfelt moment, my mother and I both on the verge of tears. As I looked at myself in the mirror, I said, "I'm grateful for Dad. I can't wait to walk down the aisle with him."

My mother, teary-eyed once more, said, "He's ready and waiting to escort his beautiful daughter. Today is about honoring the past, cherishing the present, and embracing the future."

We shared a comforting silence, knowing this day marked a significant moment in all of our lives. Smiling through my tears, I said, "I love you, Mom."

She whispered, "I love you more than words can express, Birdie. Now, let's go make some beautiful memories."

I nodded, and together, we stood up, ready to face the path ahead. The room was filled with love, anticipation, and the promise of what was to come.

My bridesmaids, Dorothea Whitlock and Blair Lexington, were both friends I'd made at Millikin. We were not only on the cheer team together but also sorority sisters. Roger's sister, Jane, stood by my side as well. As the music started playing, signaling the beginning of my procession, my breath caught in my throat as I saw Roger standing there. While I walked down the aisle of St. Mary's Chapel, the creak of the wooden floor beneath my feet seemed to harmonize with the soft whispers of history clinging to its stone walls. Roger's eyes met mine, and in that moment, it felt like the essence of Pleasantville embraced the love that had brought us to this sacred place. The vows we exchanged at the altar resonated with the stories of countless unions unfolding within these chapel walls. Sunlight filtered through the stained-glass windows, casting a kaleidoscope of colors upon us. It was as if the town itself, with its timeless charm, was showering us with blessings on this special day.

Venturing out into the refreshing fall breeze, confetti and cheers rained down upon us in the town square. This town, with its picturesque streets and warm community, had become the perfect backdrop for the beginning of our forever. A short drive away from the church, the Serenity Grove, standing proud in Pleasantville, welcomed us into its embrace. The reception hall resonated with warmth and laughter, echoing the love surrounding us. Tables adorned with autumn blooms and candles set a scene of timeless romance. On the terrace, with the sun setting behind the skyline, Roger and I took the floor for our first dance. The music, a melodic ode to love, filled the air. Each step felt like a dance with the heartbeat of Pleasantville itself, a town witnessing countless love stories and now ours. The dance floor soon became a celebration of love, with friends and family joining us in joyous revelry. The night unfolded like a dream, with a feast of local delights and the sweet melodies of celebration. Our wedding cake, adorned with delicate flowers, stood as a centerpiece. The top tier, where we would cut into, featured rich Hazelnut Praline Chocolate, with decadent chocolate cake layers filled with hazelnut praline filling, offering a sumptuous start to the cake experience. Below it, the middle tier boasted Blackberry Lemon Thyme, where zesty lemon cake layers were paired with tangy blackberry compote and a hint of fragrant thyme-infused buttercream, creating a refreshing and sophisticated flavor combination. Finally, the bottom tier delighted with Coconut Pineapple Rum, featuring moist coconut cake layers infused with tropical pineapple compote and a touch of rum-infused buttercream, offering a taste of paradise and a perfect finale to the cake tasting experience. Together, they symbolized the sweetness the town had bestowed upon our journey.

Amidst the starlit sky, Roger and I stole away to the gardens, a quiet sanctuary nestled within the towns heart. The chapel stone and the autumn breeze became witnesses to our quiet vows and the future we dared to imagine. Underneath an arch of sparklers, surrounded by the love of those dearest to us, I couldn't help but feel the immense beauty of this day. A day celebrating not only our love but also the timeless charm of a town becoming the enchanting setting for our happily ever after.

36
ROGER

It's our wedding day, and I felt jittery. Maybe it was the many cups of coffee I'd drunk, or the small amount of scotch I added. My heart was racing. It wasn't the scary kind of racing, but the beautiful kind. The kind of racing when you were excited about something, like a little kid at an amusement park.

I recalled the day my mother took Alton and I to the town fair. I was excited, but as I was about to get on the rollercoaster, I stopped. I don't know why, but I couldn't move. All I could think about was what would happen if this rollercoaster ran off the tracks and we all were lost forever. But Alton was the brave one. He grabbed my hand and encouraged me to join him. I did, and we had the best day.

We rode the rollercoaster at least five times that day. I

guess you could say that's when I knew I loved heights. I loved the feeling of being up high enough to touch the sky. I remember seeing an airplane flying over us as we reached the top. And as we descended, I thought about what it would be like if I were flying. Now I was a pilot in the Air Force and about to step into something new. Marrying Birdie had to be one of the highlights of my entire life, next to that day at the fair.

I stood in front of the mirror, adjusting my tie for what seemed like the umpteenth time. A mix of nerves and excitement coursed through my veins, as today was the day I had been dreaming of since the moment I met Birdie, the love of my life. I couldn't help but flashback to that first time I saw her walking through campus. Back then, we were a couple of college kids enjoying life. And here we were, about to get married. Birdie had turned my world upside down and made me believe in the magic of love.

My groomsmen included my brother, Alton, as my best man; Peter Rusell, from my fraternity in college; Dutton Belmore, stationed with me during training for the Air Force; and Birdie's brother, Dean. They filled the room with laughter and joy, trying their best to distract me from the bundle of nerves threatening to take over. They exchanged stories, clinked glasses, and shared hearty laughs. But my mind was elsewhere, lost in a sea of thoughts and emotions that only intensified as the clock ticked toward the moment that would change my life forever.

Birdie and I had been through so much together, facing the highs and lows, the triumphs, and tribulations. I thought about the time I told her I was joining the Air

Force and leaving after graduation. I know she was proud of me, but I could see in her eyes she was scared. We wrote to each other but each passing day my love grew for her and I often wondered if she would she still be in love with me when I got back. You never knew how much you loved someone until you were away from them long enough to see what it would feel like to be away from them forever. Every obstacle that Birdie and I faced only strengthened our bond, and today we were about to embark on the greatest adventure of all which was marriage. I'd thought long and hard about sharing my life with her, waking up to her smile every morning, and facing the world hand in hand, it filled me with a warmth that surpassed any anxiety.

As I buttoned up my crisp white shirt, and wiggled my arms into my white suit jacket, I reflected on the journey that had brought us here. The countless dates, whispered confessions of love, shared dreams, and aspirations had all led to this moment. I guessed Alton could sense my mind was somewhere else, and while the others were joking around, he came over to me.

"Hey, Rog, you're about to be a married man!" He slapped me on the back.

"Yeah," I said nervously.

"You okay, brother?" he asked.

"Thinking about today …" I let my words falter.

"I know I'm not one to get sentimental. So, hear me when I tell you this. Today isn't merely about a ceremony or a celebration; it's a culmination of your love story with Birdie. It is a tale written in the stars of two souls brought together in a cosmic dance. When I tell you that you and Birdie belong together, believe it."

I knew my brother well enough to know he meant every word he said. And he was right. Our love was timeless. As I stood at the altar, my heart pounding with a mix of anticipation and joy that was palpable, as I waited for Birdie to make her entrance. Dressed in my best suit, I couldn't help but steal glances toward the entrance, waiting for the moment when my beautiful bride, Birdie, would make her grand entrance. My eyes glistened with pride, knowing that I was about to witness a milestone in both our lives. The venue was adorned with flowers, peonies, of course, because those were her favorites, and bathed in soft candlelight, creating an atmosphere of love and celebration. Family and friends filled the seats, their faces beaming with excitement. Yet, my focus remained fixed on the door, eagerly awaiting the sight of Birdie in her wedding gown.

As the music changed to a familiar melody, the room hushed in anticipation. My heart skipped a beat as the doors swung open, revealing the stunning vision of Birdie on the arm of her father. Time seemed to stand still as I laid eyes on my bride, who radiated elegance and beauty. Clark, his eyes filled with pride, handed Birdie over to me. I took a deep breath, overwhelmed with emotion. I couldn't believe how quickly the years had passed, bringing us to this significant moment. Birdie's eyes met mine, and a shared smile passed between us, a silent acknowledgment of the deep bond we were about to solidify. I couldn't help but reflect on the years leading up to this day. The laughter, the tears, and the countless moments that brought us to this pivotal moment. I listened intently to the vows we exchanged, my heart swelling with pride at the thought of spending the rest of my life with this incredible woman.

As the officiant declared us husband and wife, I turned to face the audience, locking eyes with Clark. The reception was a blur of laughter, toasts, and dancing. I couldn't resist holding Birdie close during our first dance as husband and wife. The music swirled around us as we moved together, lost in the moment. I whispered words of love and promises of a beautiful future into her ear. As the celebration continued, I couldn't help but smile, knowing that today marked the beginning of a beautiful journey for Birdie and me.

37
BIRDIE

They say time stops when you find the one you're meant to be with. That is how I'd felt every day since I'd met Roger. People often talk about weddings and vows, the kind that are etched on paper and shared in a crowded room filled with love and applauses. But for Roger and me, our wedding was much more. It was an unspoken promise that had lingered in the air from the first day we laid eyes on each other.

Roger and I had different recollections about when we first saw each other. He recalled the diner and football games and seeing me across campus and in the halls. Which was all true. But I recalled a moment before the sorority party, when I was in the local bookstore, the shelves lined with dreams bounded in hardcovers, and there he was, Roger, with eyes that mirrored the same passion I poured into my writings. It wasn't chance that brought us together; it felt more like destiny, a cosmic conspiracy written in the stars long before we ever met. Roger didn't see me that day in the bookstore or so I didn't think so. But to my dismay, Roger always noticed me. He may have been too shy to talk to me then, but he noticed me. And from that moment, we shared a connection that didn't always need words. It was like recognizing an old friend in a stranger's face, a familiarity that goes beyond the surface of things. When I first told Roger about seeing him in the bookstore, we laughed. From that moment on, we continued to laugh like we had known each other for a lifetime, and in a way, maybe we did. Our relationship unfolded effortlessly, guided by an unseen hand that seemed to orchestrate our steps.

Roger, navigating the skies with the grace of a seasoned pilot, discovered inspiration in the vast landscapes of my written words. In return, I witnessed my stories take flight through the lens of his eyes. Our connection was like a symphony in the clouds, a collaboration of dreams that soared beyond the limitations of earthly bonds. In the days that followed our wedding, I officially moved into our cozy apartment. Roger and I ate breakfast together every morning before I headed off to the office and he would head to the airport. Roger reveled in the freedom of flight; his passion evident in every lesson he shared about navigating the vast skies. Conversely, my comfort zone was firmly grounded. Yet I found solace in the ethereal realm of my own creations. Together, an unlikely duo, we formed an unbreakable team, our mutual support weaving a tapestry of shared dreams.

In our partnership, Roger not only thrived as a pilot but also embraced my world of written imagination. He eagerly delved into anything I penned, proving to be not just a supportive husband but a genuine enthusiast of my literary pursuits. Despite my professional role as an editor in a prestigious publishing house, I often grappled with a sense of detachment from my identity as a writer. The daily grind had its merits, the joy of uncovering new voices and stories but it also tethered me, leaving scant time for my personal creations.

Surrounded by the allure of bound pages and the intoxicating scent of ink, my own inspiration often waned amidst the demands of editing. There lingered a palpable fear that I was gradually losing the essence of my craft, destined to be remembered solely as the girl who molded others' words rather than crafting her own. The nagging worry persisted. Would I forever be consigned to the sidelines of literary creation, a mere spectator to the stories I yearned to write? Roger had a knack of seeing right through me. He could always tell when I had my head in the clouds, figuratively. One evening, Roger was out late for a flight lesson and I decided to cook for us. I wasn't nearly as great of a chef as Roger, but I could cook and I was quite proud of myself. As I placed our plates lined with meatloaf, mashed potatoes, and some roasted carrots and broccoli on the side, Roger immediately dug in. I guessed all that flying around really built up an appetite. I, on the other hand, couldn't shake this gnawing feeling.

"This is delicious, darling," Roger said with a mouthful.

"I'm glad you like it. I'm no chef, but I love this new recipe book my mother gave us."

"I can't wait for us to explore the many recipes in that book, Birdie. That was very kind of your mother to put together for us."

My mother had gathered up all the recipes in her family that had been passed down from generation to generation. She had even asked Roger's mother for recipes from their side of the family. Together, she bound them in a little book and wrapped it up for us. We'd been testing out recipes ever sense and even attempting to create our own recipes in hopes of adding to the book to pass down to our future kids.

"How was flying today? Is Judd, the student you've been teaching, getting better?" I asked.

"It was great. He has his check ride coming up and I think he has a real shot. It was a little bumpy in the beginning, but I think that's normal. No one is an expert at flying right away."

"Is he looking to become a commercial pilot?" I asked.

"Indeed," Roger answered with another mouthful. "How was your day at the office?"

"It was fine. We receive a lot of queries daily, so my pile of manuscripts to read through has expanded. But we have some very promising new authors."

"That's great, honey. I'm proud of you. You know that, right?"

"I sure do, Rog."

"Is something the matter?" He put down his fork to look at me.

Tears started to form in my eyes. I wasn't quite sure why I was getting so emotional about this. Roger scooted closer to me and placed his hand on my right hand. I had my fork in my left and placed it down.

"I love my job. I do. But I'm terrified that all I'll ever be known for is the girl who edited books but never got the chance to write one herself. Work has me reading thousands of manuscripts, editing nonstop, and by the time I get home, I'm exhausted. The thought of writing my own novel seems near impossible. I think my literary endeavors are becoming extinct."

"Oh, darling, I'm so sorry. I know I may not have the right words at this moment, but I don't think there's an end to any of this. I think it's just the beginning. You are so talented and I know one day, all those books on our shelves will say Birdie Scott. I believe in you."

He kissed me on the cheek and squeezed my hand three times. His words were like a warm embrace, enveloping me in reassurance. The kiss on my cheek felt like a gentle affirmation, and the three squeezes of his hand expressed a silent promise. In that moment, the weight of my insecurities began to lift, replaced by a glimmer of hope. As Roger continued to support me, I realized that the journey of self-expression was indeed ongoing. His encouragement became a beacon, guiding me through the doubts and fears that had clouded my creative aspirations. With renewed determination, I picked up my fork, not just to continue the meal but to savor the possibilities that lay ahead, embracing the belief that my literary dreams were far from extinction.

Marriage was a bond that went beyond just being in a relationship. It was about being there for each other through all the ups and downs of life. It was about being a constant support, a pillar of strength for your partner. You became each other's rock, the one person you could always rely on. It was about being a beacon of light for one another, shining a light on the path when the other was lost or uncertain. I believed that this was what Roger, and I had in our marriage, and I truly hoped that I could continue to be that unwavering support for him for the rest of our lives.

38
ROGER
YEAR: 1953

Months seemed to fly by and being married to Birdie was truly the highlight of my life. Before we knew it, we had been married for one year. Even as time passed by, I still remembered our wedding day, and I remembered the days before and after, falling deeper in love with Birdie.

I believe experiencing love is a sensation that is truly unparalleled. However, if you have never felt it before, it can be daunting. A new experience can be intimidating, and I remember feeling this way when I first met Birdie. Being loved is like embarking on a journey into the unknown, where everything feels different. The ground beneath you feels like it is made of a new material, the air you breathe in has a new aroma, and even the music you listen to changes. When Birdie expressed her love for me, I felt like I was soaring. Her love was pure and deep that it had the power to change me. It lifted me up and made me feel like I was on top of the world. Even though I often had my head in the clouds, Birdie's passion for me made me feel like I was always soaring higher and higher.

I spent most of my days up in the sky flying. And when I came back to the ground, Birdie was the one I ran to. She gave me purpose in life. But much like flying made sense to me, writing made sense to Birdie. She had a gift and I know it had been hard. She'd been feeling as if she was standing on a cliffside, watching as everyone else go to live out their dreams. I wanted her to experience living out her dreams. Every day, I encouraged her to write. I told her I'd leave the apartment and walk around the block if it meant she could have some alone time with her thoughts. She'd smile at me, hesitantly pacing the room before sitting down on the couch. She'd get up again and walk over to the small desk I set up for her with her typewriter.

"Alright, Bird, I'm going to head out for a bit. Happy writing." I'd give her a kiss and walk out the front door.

She was a writing whiz. I would be gone for maybe two hours and she would have six chapters written. As I strolled down the familiar city blocks, my mind couldn't help but wander back to Birdie, envisioning her hunched over the typewriter, fingers dancing across the keys like a maestro conducting a symphony of words. Her dedication to her craft was unwavering, a testament to the fiery passion that burned within her. I couldn't be prouder of the woman who, against all odds, pursued her dreams with an intensity that mirrored the intensity of her words on paper. I often found myself reflecting on the beauty of our symbiotic existence. The way her creativity fueled my flights, and my adventures inspired the narratives that flowed effortlessly from her fingertips. Birdie's writing was a force of nature, a cascade of emotions and imagination that painted vivid pictures in the minds of her readers.

One day, as I returned from the skies, I noticed a subtle change in the atmosphere of our humble abode. The air crackled with a newfound energy, and I could sense that Birdie had reached a breakthrough in her writing journey. The apartment, once a haven of quiet introspection, now echoed with the rhythmic clatter of the typewriter and the soft hum of inspiration. Birdie had become a literary sorceress, weaving spells with her words and crafting tales that transported readers to worlds unknown. Encouraging her became my daily ritual, a pilgrimage of love and support. I marveled at the resilience in her eyes, the determination that fueled her desire to share her stories with the world. Every departure from our shared space was a testament to my commitment to nurturing her creativity, allowing it to flourish like a garden in the sunlight.

And so, each time I left, it was not just a walk around the block; it was a pilgrimage to give Birdie the sacred space she needed to breathe life into her narratives. Our journey was a dance between the skies and the written word, a harmonious symphony that mirrored the melody of our shared dreams. As I meandered through the city streets, I found solace in knowing that, upon my return, I would witness the fruits of her literary endeavors. The pages adorned with inked tales, each word a testament to the dreams we dared to chase together.

One serene Sunday morning, the sun bathed the world in a soft glow, coaxing us out of slumber. Spontaneously, we decided to take a leisurely stroll towards Sweet Serendipity Bakery, our treasured spot nestled just around the corner. As we meandered down the charming streets, fingers interlaced, the aroma of freshly baked goods wafted through the air, a delightful overture from the heart of our favorite bakery.

Sweet Serendipity Bakery, adorned with ivy-clad walls and welcoming, weathered signage, drew us in with promises of aromatic delights. The friendly hum of baristas at work spilled out, a melodic backdrop to our footsteps. Each breath seemed to carry the intoxicating blend of roasted coffee and warm pastries, a sensory symphony that cocooned us in a world of culinary comfort. I We couldn't help but steal glances behind the counter, where skilled artisans crafted delicate pastries with a balletic grace. The bakers, their hands adorned with flour, transformed simple ingredients into works of edible art. Their camaraderie and shared passion for perfection added a sweet note to the air. Birdie and I found a cozy nook by the window, bathed in sunlight, and surrendered ourselves to the enchantment of our favorite spot. The rich aroma of brewing coffee, the gentle hum of conversations, and the occasional clink of porcelain against saucers merged into a sensory tapestry, painting our Sunday with the palette of contentment.

I couldn't help but inquire about Birdie's writing, knowing how much her creative pursuits meant to her. "How's writing going?" I asked, our hands still entwined as we shared this moment.

Birdie's gaze drifted toward the window, where a couple strolled by with their furry companion. Kids on bicycles added a lively backdrop to the scene. She turned back to me, a soft smile playing on her lips. "It's lovely, my dear. Your support means the world to me. Writing fills my heart with pure enjoyment. You are my muse."

I couldn't resist a playful tease. "Is that right? Should I be careful what I say or do, or I'll end up in your book as the villain?"

A genuine laugh escaped her lips. "Oh, stop it, Roger. You could never be the villain in my eyes."

"Everyone is a villain in someone's story. I just hope I'm never one in yours."

Birdie grinned mischievously. "Say yes to getting a puppy, and I would gladly promise to never make you my villain."

I sensed the familiar topic resurfacing, one that had become a constant in our discussions. The idea of a puppy had been lingering in the air for a while, but practicality often dimmed the initial excitement. "I would love for us to get a puppy, but it's just not a reasonable time. Do you honestly think with our jobs that we could handle a puppy right now?"

She took a sip of her coffee, her eyes reflecting a mixture of longing and understanding. "I know you're right, but that doesn't mean I don't think about it. Every time I see someone walking their dog, I instantly think how lovely it would be for us to take a stroll with a puppy of our own."

I sighed, torn between the desire to fulfill Birdie's dream and the practical considerations of our current lifestyle. "I think someday we'll have that. Just not right now."

Birdie nodded, her expression a blend of acceptance and optimism. The conversation lingered in the air like the rich aroma of coffee, leaving the promise of a future chapter where the pitter-patter of puppy paws might become the soundtrack to our shared moments.

39
BIRDIE

I still remember the day when Roger came home with a beaming smile on his face. My heart raced with anticipation as I hoped he might have brought home a delightful little puppy as a surprise. Although that wasn't the case, it was still an exceptional day. I was folding laundry in the bedroom when I heard his voice calling out, "Birdie! Are you home?"

I responded immediately, "Yes, I'm in the bedroom." But before I could even step out of the room, he suddenly burst into the bedroom, picked me up in his arms, and twirled me around.

And then he said with a grin on his face, "Bird, I have some exciting news. I found our dream home! It's absolutely breathtaking." I couldn't get a word in because he was so excited. Roger continued speaking, "You know how I went to visit my parents today? Well, on my way back to the city, I took a little detour. As I was driving along, I turned down a street and came across a cul-de-sac. At the end of the road, way off to the right, up a long, winding driveway, was this stunning one-story home. It had the most charming green shutters and a red door that perfectly complemented its white exterior."

My eyes widened with each detail, and my hands stilled in the midst of folding the blanket I had in my hand. "Sounds like quite the find, Roger. But you know, we can't just up and buy a house without seeing it first," I said with a touch of caution.

He nodded, understanding my practicality. "I know, Birdie. That's why I want you to come see it with me. It's everything we've ever talked about. It's the perfect home for us and that means we could get a puppy!"

I set the folded blanket down on the edge of the bed, a thoughtful expression crossing my face. "Well, I suppose I could take a look. Where is this place?"

Grinning from ear to ear, Roger grabbed a piece of paper and a pen, sketching a rough map to the hidden gem. As he handed it to me, he said, "It's just a short drive from here. You won't be disappointed, Birdie, I promise."

I studied the map, a smile playing on my lips. "Alright, Roger. Let's go see this dream house of yours."

I grabbed my coat and purse and followed Roger to the car, the anticipation building with each passing minute. Soon, we were in the car, navigating the streets towards the hidden sanctuary that held the promise of our future.

We turned the corner onto the cul-de-sac, and I could feel Roger's excitement building. At the end of the road, the dream house stood proudly, bathed in the soft glow of the setting sun. Roger parked the car, and with our fingers intertwined, we approached the charming home that seemed to beckon us closer. A "FOR SALE" sign perched in the yard added to the sense of possibility that lingered in the air. If this wasn't a sign, I'm not sure what else could be. Nestled atop a two-acre parcel, the house stood as a solitary sentinel, flanked only by a single neighbor to the right. Perched on the highest point of the cul-de-sac, its imposing elevation set it apart from the neighboring dwellings, each situated on gentler slopes. The steep driveway ascended boldly, carving a path through the terrain.

We approached the house, noticing the dense border of trees embracing it, standing sentinel and casting dappled shadows on the driveway below. The backyard, a sprawling expanse of green, stretched effortlessly into the untamed woods beyond, forming an oasis of tranquility. The rustle of leaves and the occasional trill of unseen birds filled the air, weaving together a symphony of nature that enveloped the secluded residence.

In the late afternoon, sunlight filtered through the thick foliage, casting a warm glow on the exterior of the house. The play of light and shadow created a mesmerizing dance on the wooden facade. The strategic placement of windows allowed glimpses of the picturesque surroundings from every room, inviting the beauty of the outdoors into the heart of the home. It was a haven perched at the edge of civilization, where the steep driveway acted as a natural barrier, providing both seclusion and a commanding view of the cul-de-sac below. The two acres of land were not just a property but an expansive canvas, showcasing the harmonious relationship between the carefully designed dwelling and the untamed beauty of the surrounding woods.

Together, we stood at the entrance, taking in the details that had captured Roger's heart. My eyes sparkled with a mix of curiosity and wonder. The dream house awaited our inspection.

Inside the home, it felt like we were trespassing on sacred ground. As we stepped further inside, the beauty of the home unfolded before us, more enchanting than I had ever imagined. The living room, adorned with large arched windows, allowed sunlight to dance through, illuminating the sweet toffee browns of the wooden floor beneath our feet. It felt as though the house itself was reaching out to embrace us, inviting us to become a part of its story. The wide hallway, with its old-fashioned parquet floor, led us further into the heart of the home. The walls, painted in a deep summer green, cradled memories of the family who had lived here before us. Photographs adorned the walls, capturing moments of joy and love. The white baseboard served as a timeless frame, grounding the lively greens and preserving the legacy of the home. Navigating down the hallway, we encountered the bedrooms, each door holding the promise of a private haven. It felt like we were exploring the intimate corners of the house, discovering the potential for peaceful nights and shared dreams that awaited us. At the center of it all stood the dining room, a symbol of connection and togetherness. It held the artifacts of laughter and camaraderie from those who had come before us, inviting Roger and me to continue the tradition of building a home filled with love and cherished memories.

Exploring the intricacies of the home, it became clear this was more than just a collection of rooms; it was a blank canvas, waiting for the brushstrokes of our shared experiences to bring it to life. The house whispered of love, dreams, and the comforting warmth of a sanctuary that could soon be ours.

40
ROGER

Stepping back outside, we left the house behind, and the crisp air carried the scent of fresh-cut grass and pine. The world seemed to slow, as if it, too, was holding its breath, waiting for what would come next.

"Tell me, Bird, do you love it?" I asked, my voice steady despite the flutter in my chest.

Birdie turned to me, her eyes bright in the late afternoon sun. "Oh, I do, Roger. I really do. I was skeptical at first, but seeing it in person, walking the halls, I can picture our life here." Her smile was radiant, a blend of relief and newfound hope.

Hearing her say that lifted a weight from my shoulders. I'd felt it the moment we arrived, but I needed her to feel it too. "I'm going to put an offer on the house."

"That sounds like a lovely idea." Birdie moved closer,

slipping her arm under mine—a gesture so familiar, yet it held the promise of all that was to come. "I could get used to a place like this. I've never seen anything more beautiful."

I took one last look around, the house standing proudly overlooking the trees. It wasn't just a place to live; it was where we'd build our future. "I couldn't agree more. It's the perfect spot. Close enough to the city but far enough to have some peace and quiet. We'll be closer to our families, too."

Birdie nodded, her gaze softening as if she were already seeing the life we'd create here. "We could start a family of our own here, Rog."

Her words struck a chord deep within me. This wasn't just about finding a house—it was about building a home, a life together. I didn't have the words to express what I was feeling, so I did the only thing that made sense. I kissed her. A kiss that spoke of all the dreams and promises we'd share, a kiss that marked the beginning of our new chapter. We walked back inside, and without a moment's hesitation, I turned to the realtor. "We'd like to place an offer on the house," I said, feeling a surge of excitement. The realtor nodded, assuring us she'd relay the offer to the owners as soon as possible. Birdie and I left the house, the door closing softly behind us as if it were saying, "See you soon." We didn't know if we'd ever return, but the hope that we would kept us warm as we drove away, leaving the house behind but carrying the vision of our future within us.

Back at the apartment, we both were anxious. Neither one of us could keep our minds off the house. It was all we spoke about on the drive home, at the dinner table, even right before we went to bed. We settled under the covers, and I turned off the light and leaned over to kiss Birdie goodnight. I let myself have one more thought about the house before closing my eyes. When the morning sun peeked into our bedroom window, I arose with this gnawing feeling. How was I ever going to go into work today when all I could think about was that house? Perhaps being up in the clouds was the perfect escape. I'd be so focused on flying that I wouldn't have time to wonder if the sellers accepted our offer.

"Roger, honey, your coffee is ready," I heard Birdie say just as I was finishing getting dressed for the day. I walked into the kitchen and she handed me my cup of coffee. I sat down on the couch and opened up the newspaper. I had a system. I would start with the news, updates on crime, job markets, and stocks. Then I would wander on over to the various items about the weather. And lastly, I always read the comic section. I wanted to end on a positive note.

Birdie sat down in the armchair with her cup of coffee and the latest book she was reading. As she flipped the pages of Jane Austen's *Persuasion*, I finished the last comic section. I folded the newspaper neatly and placed it on the coffee table.

"Are you enjoying your book, my dear?" I asked. I

knew better than to interrupt her when she was reading, but my mind was going crazy once more. I needed a safe space. Something to stop me from wondering if the realtor accidentally got our number wrong.

She was sitting there comfortably in the armchair with her coffee in one hand and the book in the other. I lounged on the sofa, curious about her enthusiasm for literature.

"It's wonderful. One of my favorites so far." She took a sip of her coffee before flipping to the next page. I suppose she could sense me watching her because she spoke again. "You know, Roger, there is something utterly captivating about this book. It's not just a love story; it's a masterpiece that delves into the complexity of human emotions."

I leaned forward. "Really? What makes it so special for you?"

Smiling, she replied, "First, the character of Anne Elliot. She's not your typical Austen heroine. She's older, wiser, and carries this quiet strength. I find her journey of self-discovery incredibly relatable. She's been persuaded by others in the past, but she learns to trust her own instincts."

"Sounds intriguing. What else?" I asked.

As Birdie leant in, she said, "Second, the social commentary is brilliant. Austen skillfully dissects the societal norms of her time, exposing the hypocrisy and superficiality. It's as if she's whispering timeless truths about love and class distinctions that still resonate today."

I raised an eyebrow before responding, "Interesting

perspective, my dear. And the romance?"

Birdie blushed. "Ah, and third, the romance! It's a slow burn, Roger, filled with rekindled emotions and unspoken sentiments. Austen captures the nuances of unrequited love and the bittersweet joy of second chances. The tension between Anne and Captain Wentworth is simply magnetic." She grinned with every word.

I took a sip of my coffee. "I see. So, it's more than just a love story; it's a commentary on life itself."

"Absolutely. *Persuasion* is like a mirror reflecting the complexities of human relationships and the resilience of the human spirit. Plus, Austen's wit and humor add that perfect touch."

"You've convinced me, Birdie. I'll have to give it a read," I said, smiling.

"I knew you'd come to appreciate the genius of Jane Austen. Prepare to be enchanted, my darling Rog," she teased.

We sat there until 8 am, divulging in conversation about novels. Her eyes lit up just with the word *books*, as much as if she were hanging a Christmas tree. The time flew, and I headed to the airport for another day of flying lessons, while Birdie set off for the office to immerse herself in more manuscripts. We had both found something we loved: me with flying and Birdie with books, and neither of us would ever ask the other to choose between the two. That was the beauty of Birdie and me. We both loved each other so, but we also loved our jobs and we wanted each other to thrive. By supporting each other in our endeavors, it allowed us to bloom in a way I didn't know was possible.

41
BIRDIE

The morning after visiting the house felt like a blur. Neither one of us stopped thinking about the house. But we also didn't want to talk about it nonstop; it was as if speaking about it out loud would run the risk of losing the house forever. We both desperately wanted the house to be ours. I prayed and prayed and prayed for the realtor to call. She said she probably wouldn't have an answer until this evening, just as Roger and I would be home from work. The anticipation was gnawing at both of us.

The aroma of freshly brewed coffee lingered in the air as we each sipped our respective cups in the quiet embrace of our living room. The morning sunlight streamed in, creating a warm ambience. Roger, engrossed in the daily newspaper, chuckled at the antics in the comics section.

His laughter, a familiar melody, evoked memories of

our shared past. I found solace in the worn armchair, book in hand. Jane Austen's *Persuasion* unfolded its enchanting narrative before me, each page drawing me deeper into the lives of Anne Elliot and Captain Frederick Wentworth. It was a world of subtleties and unspoken emotions, a world I relished escaping to.

It wasn't Roger's habit to take much interest in my literary pursuits. His hobbies varied from mine, and while he respected my love for books, romance novels weren't typically his cup of tea. Yet, on this particular morning, a sense of unspoken understanding filled the room, and he seemed to be intentionally avoiding any talk about the looming decision on the house.

As I lost myself in the words of Austen, Roger's gaze lifted from the newspaper. His eyes, softened by the morning light, met mine. With a sip of his coffee, he ventured into a territory rarely explored in our conversations. The tranquility of my reading was interrupted by Roger's unexpected inquiry. His interest in my book choice hinted at a shift in our routine, a change I welcomed with a small smile. He asked if I was enjoying the book, to which I shared my thoughts, momentarily closing the book. I remarked that Austen has this remarkable way of capturing the intricacies of human emotions and relationships; a true masterpiece.

Roger nodded, his brow furrowing thoughtfully, showing genuine curiosity. I seized the chance to share my passion with him, taking a moment to gather my thoughts. I explained to Roger that it wasn't just a love story but a journey of self-discovery. I described how Anne Elliot, the protagonist, differs from the typical Austen heroine. She's mature, resilient, and her path to happiness is paved with introspection and second chances. As I spoke, Roger leaned back on the sofa, absorbing every word. I continued, delving into the societal commentary, the subtle romance, and the timeless truths embedded in the pages of the novel. It felt liberating to bridge the gap between our interests and to invite him into a world that had captivated my heart. By the time I finished, the coffee cups were empty, and a newfound connection lingered in the air. Roger, now intrigued, expressed a willingness to explore the pages of Persuasion.

With a soft smile, I took a deep breath, knowing that the moment had come to share something deeply personal. "Roger," I began, my voice trembling slightly with both excitement and nerves, "there's something I need to tell you."

Roger looked up, his expression attentive and warm. I reached out and took his hand in mine. "I'm pregnant," I said, the words feeling both exhilarating and surreal.

The room seemed to hold its breath for a moment. Roger's eyes widened in surprise, and then a smile slowly spread across his face. He squeezed my hand gently, a mix of joy and disbelief dancing in his eyes. Our morning transformed into a delicate dance of shared emotions, the aroma of coffee mingling with the essence of new beginnings. The time seemed to fly by because before either one of us knew it, we each had to get the rest of our day going. Roger was headed to the airport for flying lessons, and I was making my way into the office. I had finally found the perfect balance to enjoy my love for writing and novels while also reading through thousands of manuscripts and editing. It was rough in the beginning, but I felt like I was finally getting the hang of it.

Amidst the hustle of the New York City publishing hub, my mind was aflutter with a whirlwind of emotions. Roger and I had fallen head over heels for this dream house, and our offer was hanging in the balance. To distract ourselves, both of us dove into our work—him soaring the skies as a pilot, me lost in the rhythmic dance of words at the publishing house. As the day unfolded, a sense of restlessness clung to every passing minute. But little did I know that the day, already pregnant with anticipation, would take an unexpected turn. Nervously, the editor-in-chief, Marcel, summoned me into their office, and the air crackled with an anxious energy that glittered like nervous sparks. In the sanctum of their domain, my boss revealed a twist of fate that caught me off guard. A promotion to senior editor at the London office. The news hung in the air, competing with the weight of the pending house offer and the life Roger and I had envisioned together. Caught between the thrill of professional advancement and the magnetic pull of our shared dreams, I hesitated. "Thank you for this incredible opportunity, Marcel," I stammered out, my mind racing. "But I need to speak with Roger before making such a life-altering decision."

Marcel nodded in understanding, releasing me back into the bustling rhythm of the New York office. The waiting game for the realtor's response had transformed into a labyrinth of choices. As I navigated the sea of desks, the uncertainty of our dream house intertwined with the unknown path that lay ahead echoed the profound decisions that awaited both in my professional and personal life.

I realized that it was best to roll with the punches. Life could be complex, unpredictable, and often nonlinear, resembling a tapestry woven with threads of joy and sorrow. When you weathered life's storms together, it was like two sailors braving the turbulent seas, their hands tightly clasped against the crashing waves. Open and honest communication became the anchor, grounding you amidst the chaos, while respect and kindness served as the sails, propelling you forward with grace. In these shared moments, when the tempest raged, the precious nature of true love revealed itself. It was a flame that flickered but never extinguished, casting a warm glow even in the darkest corners. Picture a couple standing hand in hand amidst the downpour, their love a steadfast umbrella shielding them from adversity. It was a testament to the enduring strength that lay within the core of genuine connection. As you navigated the ebb and flow of life's challenges, the realization of how enduring true love could be becomes a source of resilience. It was akin to a resilient tree bending but not breaking in the face of a mighty storm. When you emerged from the tempest, the sunshine seemed brighter, and your bond stood stronger than ever, much like a garden thriving after a nourishing rain. Life's storms could be inevitable, but with true love as your compass, you not only survived but flourished, each trial sculpting a more resilient and vibrant connection.

42
ROGER

As I started the engine on the Cessna Skyhawk, every inch of my body began to relax. I knew when I was up in the sky everything became calm for me. I wanted the house so badly, I believed it was ours. But that was the funny thing about life. Whenever you thought you deserved something or you went out of your way to get something, it all came crumbling down.

I'd like to believe I was an optimistic guy, but I didn't want to ever be blindsided. I didn't ever want to get myself into a trap. Waiting for the end of the day and praying the realtor called with positive news had really flipped my lid. I just wanted this beautiful life with Birdie and I wanted her to get everything she'd ever dreamed of.

Was that so wrong of me? I had to ask myself this because I wondered if I was doing too much or if I was not doing enough. It was scary. I wanted to be the man of the house, the one who could provide for this family that Birdie and I hoped to build together someday. If we didn't get this house, what would that mean for us? And what kind of provider was I?

I knew Birdie wasn't someone who cared much about materialistic things. But once you opened her eyes to something, it was hard for her to forget. It would be difficult if this didn't happen. When Birdie saw something she wanted, she went after it and she always got it. I'd be left questioning everything if we missed out on this opportunity or if the sellers rejected our offer. My mind flashed to the morning when Birdie announced she was pregnant. A small part of me was excited, but another part of me worried about our future. Here we were in this tiny apartment—I wanted that house more than ever now that we were about to become a family of three.

When I was flying, all my worries just zoomed past me. I felt free. When we were in college, Birdie used to tease me that I was her Peter Pan and she was Wendy. I'd fly around the world in search of something greater, not realizing the greatest things I had were right in front of me. Maybe, sometimes, I was afraid of growing up. And whenever Birdie and I got into a heated discussion, I'd immediately head to the airport and fly. I would circle around for hours until I couldn't fly any longer. "Who's the real bird now?" she would joke. Her name might be Birdie, but I was the one with the wings. I was the one running off and into the sky. Freedom felt like it did now when I was in the air. But I wouldn't change a thing. I'd give up flying if it meant I'd never lose Birdie.

The Cessna felt like my lucky dragon, ready to take me all the way. Up in the sky, I knew I was truly flying when the cotton-cloud Earth lay below me. That morning, the sun painted the runway, and as I approached my faithful bird, the scent of aviation fuel filled the air. The familiar hum of the engine greeted me like an old friend. This plane wasn't just a machine, it was a partner, always ready for the next adventure. Birdie wasn't keen on airplanes, but now and then she'd get a burst of excitement and join me above the clouds.

The first time I ever brought Birdie up in the plane, we encountered a bit of turbulence. As the aircraft jolted and swayed, I couldn't help but feel a rush of excitement. Birdie, on the other hand, was not thrilled. When we finally touched down, she was furious, and she called me crazy. It dawned on me then that she couldn't quite grasp the unique thrill I found in those moments, the exhilarating dance with the skies. In an attempt to bridge the gap between our perspectives, I began to share more about the world above the clouds. I described the breathtaking views, the feeling of weightlessness, and the sheer freedom that came with soaring through the air. Yet, no matter how vividly I painted the experience, Birdie remained skeptical, unable to fathom the allure of defying gravity.

To deepen her understanding, I decided to plan a special flight, one that would showcase the beauty of the skies in a way she couldn't ignore. As we ascended into the heavens, I pointed out the mesmerizing landscapes below, the sun setting on the horizon, and the city lights beginning to twinkle like stars. I wanted her to see not just the turbulence, but the magic that unfolded amidst the clouds. After that magical flight, Birdie wasn't one hundred percent convinced that flying was as amazing as I believed, but she wasn't scared of it either. She was open to the idea that we could support each other and it didn't always mean we had to love what the other person loved.

She could find the beauty in the thing I loved—flying. But she also wasn't rushing to be my copilot. This I understood. That was the thing about love. When you love someone, you don't always see eye to eye. You don't always agree with what they like or don't like. But you learn to accept them for who they are. You learn to love the differences. Because the differences are what make us unique. Birdie and I understood each other, and that was enough for me.

As the wheels of the Cessna touched the smooth surface of the tarmac, a sense of relief and accomplishment washed over me. The thrill of flying over the vast expanse of the sky was now replaced by a feeling of contentment as I taxied the plane towards the hangar. The hum of the engines gradually softened as I made my way back to the shelter of the hangar, where I could finally unwind and reflect on my morning. I was walking back through the office when I ran into a familiar face. Dutton, one of the groomsmen at our wedding, was walking in. It had been quite some time since we saw each other. Last I'd heard, he was overseas in Japan.

"Dutton, buddy. How is everything?" I asked as we approached each other.

"Roger Scott. It's been a while."

"Indeed, it has been. How was Japan? Are you back for good?"

"It was incredible. I miss it already. But I am back in the states for good now. Actually, Joan and I are expecting our first baby."

Joan and Dutton got married a couple of years before Birdie and me. I didn't know Dutton at the time, but he'd shared the details when we were in the Air Force together and Joan was a guest at our wedding.

"Congratulations! Oh, I am so happy for you and Joan! Birdie will be thrilled to hear the news."

"Thank you. That means a lot. We're very excited but also nervous." There was a pause before Dutton spoke again. "So, how's married life been?"

"It's been amazing. Just when you think you know all there is to know about a person, you get married and suddenly you really know them."

Dutton chuckled. "I hear you. Marriage is a special thing."

"It is. And I love Birdie; we're good together."

I'm not sure what prompted me to say that. It was as if I was trying to convince myself and the world that Birdie and I belonged together. We were married, but still some days were harder than others.

"Indeed, you are. Are you still in that apartment?"

"We are. We'd love a house soon, but only time will

tell."

Part of me wanted to tell Dutton about the house we'd found that we had put an offer in, and that Birdie was pregnant too. But I decided to keep that part to myself. Maybe I thought if I said something, it would jinx it all somehow. I was not superstitious, but I just wanted to keep the house as our thing. Plus, how incredible of a moment it would be if we did get the house and we could truly celebrate and share the news with the people we love.

Dutton and I chatted for a bit longer before he headed for a flight. That was the thing about us pilots—we hated being on the ground for too long. The skies were always calling our names. As we said our goodbyes, I congratulated him one more time and said that Joan would most likely hear from Birdie soon, as she would be excited to hear the news.

"Enjoy your flight, Dutton. And tell Joan we're thrilled for you both. We should plan a dinner soon for the four of us. I'm sure Birdie would love to see Joan again."

"That would be great. I'll inform Joan and we can have the ladies plan it out. I know how much they love dinner parties."

I laughed at Dutton's remarks. Birdie was a natural when it came to dinner parties and she and Joan would have a field day planning it together.

Walking back to my vehicle, Dutton's words still echoed in my mind. I wanted Birdie and me to start our own family, and not getting the house would have felt like a huge setback. But I had to stay positive, for her sake. She had mentioned many times how much she wanted a family, and we both agreed we needed a house before thinking about raising children. Yet there we were—still in an apartment, with a baby on the way.

When I arrived back at the apartment, Birdie was still at work. I noticed a letter in our mailbox, addressed to me. Inside the apartment, I hung up my jacket, grabbed a beer from the fridge and sat down on the sofa. I stared at the letter for what seemed like the longest minutes of my life. I couldn't imagine who would write me, especially only me. Most days, the only things we received in the mail were bills and the occasional invitations addressed to both of us. I set my beer down on the table and picked up the envelope opener. I sliced open the letter and braced myself. A small part of me thought it was from the realtor. That maybe she didn't have it in her to reject us by phone or maybe it was from the realtor, but to congratulate us and get the paperwork signed right away. My hands shook. I unfolded the paper and began to read.

Dear Officer Scott,

We trust this letter finds you in good health and high spirits. We are thrilled to extend a formal invitation for you to join our esteemed team at BeyondBorders Aviation for a long-term assignment that promises to be a significant milestone in your aviation career.

After careful consideration and evaluation of your exceptional skills, experience, and dedication to the field, we are pleased to offer you the opportunity to pilot some of the most advanced aircraft in our fleet. Your proficiency and passion for aviation have not gone unnoticed, and we believe that your expertise will be a valuable asset to our team. The nature of this assignment is both challenging and rewarding. You will be stationed in various countries for extended periods, allowing you to not only command cutting-edge aircraft but also immerse yourself in diverse cultures and environments. From the bustling metropolises of Asia to the historic charm of European cities, each destination will offer a unique set of challenges and opportunities that we are confident you will navigate with skill and enthusiasm.

In addition to the technical aspects of the job, we are excited to share that your name was put forward by Wing Commander Fred Montgomery, a distinguished leader in the Air Force. Wing Commander Montgomery has personally recognized your exceptional talents and believes in your potential to excel in this international endeavor. This endorsement adds another layer of confidence in your ability to contribute significantly to BeyondBorders Aviation.

We believe that your adaptability, cultural awareness, and interpersonal skills will contribute to fostering positive relationships with international counterparts and passengers alike. This assignment is more than a job; it is an opportunity for personal and professional growth on a global scale. We understand that such a commitment requires careful consideration. Therefore, we invite you to contact our human resources department to discuss any questions or concerns you may have. We are committed to providing you with the necessary support and resources to ensure a smooth transition into this exciting phase of your career.

Please signify your acceptance of this invitation by September 20th, and we look forward to welcoming you to the BeyondBorders Aviation family.

Safe travels and best regards,
Samuel Dixon
Chief Pilot
BeyondBorders Aviation

I read the letter over a few more times before folding it up again and placing it back into its envelope. I took another sip of my beer, contemplating what I'd just read. I'd enjoyed my time in the Air Force, and it had allowed me the freedom to fly. But I never in a million years expected Fred Montgomery to be providing any sort of recommendation for me. If anyone, I expected him to recommend Dutton, who had a higher ranking than me. Dutton was a Flight Lieutenant before being promoted to Squadron Leader. That was mainly the reason he was in Japan.

I couldn't help but wonder if Wing Commander Montgomery had originally recommended Dutton. Perhaps Dutton declined the offer and was the one to recommend me. So many questions began circulating in my mind. I wasn't sure what to think. This was a once-in-a-lifetime opportunity. Was I supposed to just throw it all away? Anytime I was uncertain of something, I would grab a pen and paper and write a pros and cons list. It often helped in what seemed like stressful moments. So, I got up off the sofa and grabbed a piece of paper and pen from the desk where Birdie spent most of her time writing. I wrote pros at the top of the page on the left side, and cons and on the righthand side.

Pros:

• Global experience: opportunity to fly in various countries, experiencing diverse cultures and environments.

• Advanced aircraft: access to some of the most advanced and cutting-edge aircraft, enhancing professional skills.

• Career growth: potential for career advancement within a renowned international airline.

• Recommendation: endorsement from Wing Commander Fred Montgomery, indicating trust and confidence in my abilities.

• Networking: an opportunity to build a global network within the aviation industry.

Cons:

• Extended deployments: being deployed to various countries for extended periods may pose challenges in terms of personal life and stability.

• Cultural adaptation: adapting to different cultures and languages might be demanding and require significant adjustment.

• Uncertainty: the nature of the job involves frequent

relocations, leading to uncertainties in long-term planning.

•Family considerations: impact on my marriage with Birdie due to the nature of the assignment.

As I stared at the page, I wondered if I was making a huge mistake either way. If I accepted the job, I'd be uprooting both our lives. And what would that mean about our dream home and the family we were trying to plan for? But if I said no, would I be losing out on one of the biggest and best opportunities? This would be a major shift in my career, and I could not take that lightly. I could spend hours, days, weeks, analyzing my pros and cons lists, but it wouldn't make a difference. I needed to make a decision now. I needed to talk to Birdie.

Just as I was thinking about what I must do, the phone rang. I jumped up to answer it.

"Scott residence. Who is speaking?" I asked.

"Hello, Mr. Scott. This is Fiona Taylor, the realtor from the Green Grove Estate. Hope you're doing well. I've got an update for you. Is Mrs. Scott there, too?"

"Hello, Mrs. Taylor, it's wonderful to hear from you. Unfortunately, Birdie is still at work. Thanks for calling. We've been eagerly waiting to hear about the house. What's the news?" I responded.

"That's too bad. I was really hoping to catch both you and the Mrs. Please be sure to relay this to her. Well, I appreciate your patience and it was so lovely to meet you and Birdie the other day."

There was a pause on the other side of the line, and I

waited for her to continue, as I could tell she had more to say.

Fiona picked up again. "Unfortunately, I've got some tough news. The sellers went through all the offers, and despite liking yours for Green Grove Estate, they've decided to go with another couple."

Now it was my turn to pause, as I needed to recollect on my thoughts. It seemed the day wasn't over in flipping our life upside down.

"Are you still there, Mr. Scott?" Fiona asked.

"Oh yes. I'm sorry about that. Well, that's disappointing. Any idea why they chose the other offer?"

"It's a bit of a bummer, I know. The other folks came in with an offer considerably higher than the asking price. Money talks, and it seems that played a big role in the seller's decision."

"Well, shoot. We really had our hearts set on that place. Anything we could have done differently?" I asked.

"Roger, you and Birdie both made a solid offer. Sometimes, though, these decisions come down to the dollars and cents. The market's competitive, especially lately."

I could hear the sympathy in her voice. She seemed like a nice lady and I understood she was just doing her job. There was only so much one person could do and it wasn't like she could force the sellers to accept our offer. I couldn't help but wonder if this was a sign. Perhaps we weren't meant to get the house because I was meant to accept the job with BeyondBorders Aviation.

"Thanks for letting us know, Fiona. What's our next move? Should we start looking at other homes?" I wasn't quite ready to look at other homes, especially if I decided to accept the job offer. But I didn't want it to seem like we weren't looking to move, especially if this job didn't pan out, as Birdie and I would still want a home of our own. It was best to keep quiet about the potential job and keep in touch with Fiona.

"Absolutely. I get it's a tough spot, but we can bounce back. Let's talk about what you and Birdie are looking for in a new place, and we'll keep the search going."

"Thanks, Fiona. I'll need to speak with Birdie and relay the news. I know she'll be crushed, as she loved the house, as did I. But we'll need to think it over and then catch up with you. We really appreciate your help."

"No problem at all. You and Birdie take all the time you need, and when you're ready, we'll get back to finding that perfect home for you."

"Thank you, Fiona. I hope you have a wonderful evening."

"You, too. Goodbye."

I hung up the phone just when Birdie walked through the door. She had a peculiar look on her face and I could tell something was wrong, or that she just needed to talk. It was perfect timing because boy did I have a lot to share with her. Where to start? Did I tell her about my morning with flying and seeing Dutton and the news about Joan being pregnant? Did I tell her about the unexpected job offer? Or did I start with the bad news of us not getting the house? All I knew was that we needed to talk, and I knew the perfect place.

43
BIRDIE

Entering our apartment, relief washed over me. I hung my purse on the hook near the door and placed my coat on the rack. Roger stood there, and I knew exactly what I had to do. The urge to blurt out my job promotion surged through me, confident he would be proud and happy. He would want me to accept it, I was sure of it. Roger always said he could fly anywhere, that he'd follow me wherever I went. Maybe our next adventure could be in London?

Not because I didn't love it; I did. But for the first time in a long time, I was genuinely happy with where my life was heading, and I knew Roger would want me to pursue my dreams, just as he did after graduation. We had always been each other's rock, complementing each other throughout our relationship. I wanted him to be happy, and I knew he would want the same for me.

This could work. We could have a new life in London. We had always said we wanted to travel the world. Why not start now?

The anticipation of such a significant milestone shimmered in the air. I couldn't contain my excitement any longer. But Roger had a strange look on his face. I couldn't quite pinpoint whether he was happy or sad; perhaps it was a bit of both.

"I need to tell you something," Roger finally said, his voice carrying a weight that made me pause. "But let's get out of here. There's a café down the street; let's go there and talk."

Confusion tugged at me. Why not just tell me now? Still, I nodded. "Alright, let's go."

The aroma of freshly brewed coffee greeted us as we settled into a cozy corner of our favorite café. The warm, dimly lit ambiance felt comforting, a stark contrast to the weight of the conversation hanging between us.

"How was your day?" I asked, attempting to lighten the mood.

Roger's brow furrowed before softening a bit. "It was quite unusual. Truth is, I have a lot to catch you up on."

"Oh." My expression shifted immediately. This was it. The news he couldn't share at home.

"It's nothing bad, but we have a lot to talk about. I don't know how else to say this, so I'm just going to be blunt."

I leaned forward slightly, anticipation mixed with a hint

of apprehension. "Go on."

"Fiona called," Roger began, his voice steady yet filled with a hint of disappointment. "We didn't get the house. It seems the sellers care more about dollars than they do about a lovely family moving in."

"Oh, Rog, I'm so sorry," I replied softly, reaching across the table to touch his hand. "I know how much you loved that house, and I did too. But we both knew it was a long shot. It was a beautiful home, and I'm sure whoever lives in it will have wonderful memories."

"You're right," he sighed, a small smile tugging at his lips. "It's just I know how much you were looking forward to starting a family, maybe even getting a dog. And now it all feels like that is gone."

"It's not gone, Roger," I reassured him gently. "We're just being redirected. We'll find another home. And really, I'm in no rush to have children or even a dog. I know I may bring it up from time to time, but this is our life and our timeline. There's no rulebook on how soon a married couple should buy a house and start a family. And if there is, then we missed it."

Roger chuckled softly. "You, my dear, are right. So what now?"

I took a deep breath, steeling myself to share my own news. "There are some other things I need to tell you too."

Roger's eyes met mine, curiosity mingled with concern. "Oh? What might that be?"

"Well, some good news is I ran into Dutton while I was leaving the airport," Roger continued, his voice lifting with a hint of excitement. "He said Joan is pregnant. Isn't that great?"

"Oh, that is wonderful news," I replied with genuine happiness. "I am so happy for them."

"Indeed, it is," Roger nodded. "Dutton said Joan would love to get together with you soon. We discussed the four of us getting together for dinner."

"That would be marvelous," I agreed warmly. "I will ring Joan."

"She would like that."

He paused, his expression shifting once more as he prepared to share something more personal. "And there's one other thing I need to tell you."

This time, I could see it in his eyes, a weightier silence settling between us. Whatever Roger was about to reveal would undoubtedly affect us both deeply, and I braced myself for the impact.

I had to have faith in our relationship. Roger and I were soulmates, and I would do anything to ensure nothing tore us apart. I knew Roger would not have us risk everything just to walk away.

That was not what marriage was about. You did not give up on the ones you loved. You did not walk away because it got hard or life changed. You often had to make sacrifices, but that didn't mean you also gave up on everything that made you *you*. I had to believe our love was deeper than that. I had to know we would be okay no matter what decision we made. Our fate was always in God's hands. But why did it feel like one of us was losing?

Part of me wanted to ask Roger to defer for at least a

year. I didn't know if that was possible. But I thought if he came to London with me for a year or two, then he could leave and take the job with the airline. Or perhaps the airline job would still work with his base in London. We talked until it seemed as if we had run out of words and ideas. Neither of us knew how to move forward, but we had to make a decision fast.

Roger couldn't keep the pilot chief of BeyondBorders Aviation waiting. And I certainly couldn't put off discussing my answer with the editor-in-chief.

The next morning, Roger was sitting in his armchair, drinking his coffee and reading the comic section. I walked over to the sofa and sat down.

"Good morning, my sweet bird," he said.

"Morning, darling. Did you sleep well?" The truth was, neither of us was sleeping well. It could be the pressure we were both under.

"Better than the previous night," he answered. "And what about you? Have you made your decision?"

"Oh, Roger, don't do that. Do not put this all on me. It's not just my life that is about to change. We are in this together."

"I'm sorry. I didn't mean to upset you. I guess I just assumed you would have it figured out."

"That's not how this marriage works, Roger. We got married to be partners, and to make decisions together. Whatever path we choose, we will choose together. You hear me?" I was furious. We had exhausted all our options.

I wanted to tell Roger I would leave next month for London, and I didn't know how long I'd be there. I also wanted to say that if he wanted this marriage to work, he would be happy for me and accept my decision. And that he would join me in London. I wanted so badly to say that to him, but my heart was breaking. I couldn't risk our marriage for an advancement in my career.

Women didn't choose careers over their husbands. That was how I was raised. My mother lived and breathed being a mother. She was a capable, brave, and smart woman, but she wasn't a career woman. I wanted to be more than just a housewife. I wanted it all. I wanted a husband, I wanted kids, I wanted the house, and I wanted the job. But was I really capable of having all of that?

"I'm sorry, Bird. I didn't mean to come across as insensitive. I want you to have it all. And I know what you're thinking." He was smirking.

I stayed silent and waited for him to speak. He got up from the armchair and sat next to me on the sofa. I knew then he was serious. This was the moment we would make a decision that would affect the rest of our lives.

"I want you to be happy. When I'm with you, Bird, I am so happy. I never want anything to come between us. But if I'm being honest with myself and with you, I want that airline job. And I want you to have that senior editor job. I think we both know what we need to do."

Roger was right. We couldn't prolong the inevitable. I had to follow my heart and say yes to the job in London, and he had to follow his wings and take the pilot job. But the burning question still lingered in both our minds—

what would become of us?

44
ROGER
YEARS: 1953-1954

Birdie accepted the job in London and packed up her belongings to head there a month later. I took on a pilot position with BeyondBorders Aviation. Fortunately, I was able to fly out to London with Birdie, and we spent two beautiful weeks exploring the city together. As my next assignment approached, the days flew by. My career whisked me across the globe, leaving us separated by oceans and time zones.

I returned to London in July 1954, just as our daughter, Daisie, was being born. I spent a few precious weeks with them before my career pulled me back into the cockpit. Despite the miles between us, our bond remained steadfast, maintained through late-night phone calls and heartfelt letters. I did my best to visit Birdie and Daisie whenever possible, but as time passed, our connection felt increasingly fragile, like delicate ink on cardstock, vulnerable to the passage of time.

I never anticipated that what I thought would be brief separations would stretch into months. When I accepted the BeyondBorders Aviation position, I was consumed by my ambition, oblivious to the toll it would take on our relationship. How could I refuse such an opportunity, knowing it was my lifelong dream?

The fear of regret gnawed at me, knowing I might resent Birdie for living out her dreams while mine remained unfulfilled. Yet, I couldn't bring myself to voice these insecurities. She deserved to pursue her passion just as much as I did mine.

Since childhood, the allure of flight had captivated me, tracing back to a vivid memory of a day at the fair with my mother and brother. But the memory that set everything in motion was the day my father took me up in the plane with him. I was his copilot for the day. Obtaining my pilot's license was a pinnacle of achievement, second only to the day I married Birdie. But amidst the exhilaration of soaring through the skies, there lingered an unspoken unease. In the vast expanse above, the unimaginable could transpire at any moment.

The plane's engines roared as it soared through the clouds, and I couldn't help but feel a sense of comfort knowing that this massive metal bird would bring me back to my Birdie. We kept in touch regularly, sharing every detail about our lives. Her letters were always filled with vivid descriptions of her time spent exploring the nooks and crannies of London. She would wander around the city, discovering hidden treasures like charming cafes, quaint bakeries, and cozy bookstores. However, it was the antique shops that truly captivated her. Each store had a distinct story to tell, and Birdie was a master storyteller who could draw inspiration from even the most trivial objects. I always marveled at Birdie's ability to weave a tale. She would describe in exquisite detail the sights, sounds, and smells of the places she visited, and I could almost picture myself there with her. Her letters were a source of inspiration and joy, and I cherished every word she wrote. Sometimes, when Birdie asked me about my life, I would reply with a dismissive, "Oh, I'm just a pilot." But she would never let me get away with it. In her sternest tone, she would say, "Roger Lee Scott," using my full name to emphasize her point. She knew that being a pilot was more than just a job; it was a passion that required skill, dedication, and bravery. She reminded me I was more than just a pilot. I was a hero who had the power to transport people to their loved ones, reunite families, and create unforgettable memories.

Her words always struck a chord with me, and I knew that I owed it to myself to acknowledge my worth and be proud of who I was. Being a pilot wasn't just a job to me, it was a profound responsibility. The trust placed in me by the passengers and crew was immense, and I held it with the utmost reverence. I never demanded more from my team than I was willing to give myself, and I expected nothing but the best from us all. Every decision we made and every action we took was infused with a dedication that went beyond the ordinary, reflecting our commitment to excellence in everything we did. And what we offered in return was a sense of security and assurance that was truly invaluable. It was not just about flying a plane, but about being a guardian of the skies. We were ready to navigate any challenge and face any obstacle without hesitation. It was a level of commitment and leadership that I believed defined our profession.

Sitting in my hotel room, I received an unexpected knock on the door. After a moment's hesitation, I rose from the bed and approached, opening it to find a woman dressed in a maid's uniform. Her name tag read Sylvia. Later, I learned her last name was Delgado.

"Good evening, Captain Scott," she greeted me.

"Hello," I replied, eyeing her curiously. "How can I help you?"

"I'm just bringing by some fresh towels, and this note was left at the front desk for you," she said, handing me a piece of paper along with the towels.

"Thank you," I said, taking the items. As I moved to close the door, she lingered.

"Is there something else I can assist you with?" I asked politely.

"Well, I couldn't help but notice you're often here alone," she said with a suggestive smile. "Being a pilot, I assume you travel quite a bit. If you ever need some company, I'm available."

I furrowed my brow, feeling uncomfortable with her

implication. "I appreciate the offer, but I prefer my solitude. Have a good evening."

Before I could close the door, she interjected, her foot preventing its closure. As she leaned closer, her breath carried a faint scent of bubble gum.

"I don't think you understand," she murmured, beginning to unbutton her dress. "No one wants to be lonely."

Alarm bells rang in my mind as her intentions became clear. Stepping back, I firmly held the door halfway.

"I understand perfectly," I replied, my tone firm. "And I'm not interested. I have a wife, and I intend to remain faithful to her."

Her cheeks flushed with surprise. "Oh, a wife? I didn't realize."

"It's not exactly advertised," I retorted, my patience waning.

She hesitated, but still lingered in the doorway.

My agitation grew. "Is there a reason you're still here?" I asked tersely.

"If I've overstepped, I apologize," she said, her tone still suggestive. "But what she doesn't know won't hurt her, right?"

I felt a surge of anger at her audacity. "How dare you question the sanctity of my marriage! Leave immediately, or I'll speak to your supervisor."

I slammed the door shut before she could respond, seething with frustration. As her muttering faded, I couldn't shake the rush of emotions her proposition had stirred within me. It was a stark reminder of how much I missed Birdie and how precious our marriage truly was.

As I settled onto my bed, eagerly unfolding the note that had arrived. Penned by Samuel Dixon, Chief Pilot of BeyondBorders Aviation, it bore welcoming words addressed to me as Officer Scott.

Officer Scott,

Welcome once more to BeyondBorders. It has been a pleasure collaborating with you. You are adapting well to the various locales across the globe. Tomorrow, you'll be winging your way to Spain for a brief stay, followed by Paris, France. Knowing your wife resides in London, we extend an invitation for her to join you on a flight from London to Paris. Here's to hoping she can steal away and share in your time in Paris.

Au revoir,

Chief Pilot Dixon

A thrill surged through me as I absorbed the news. A mere two-hour flight separated London from Paris, and the possibility of a weekend rendezvous with my wife seemed nothing short of magical. Without delay, I reached for the telephone, punching in Birdie's number.

"Hello, this is Birdie."

"Bird, it's Roger. Darling, I have the most wonderful news!" My excitement bubbled over as I dialed her number.

"Oh, Roger, hearing your voice is a delight. You've been on my mind all day. How are you?" Her warmth washed over me.

"Not to burst forth prematurely, but Chief Pilot Samuel Dixon just messaged me. They're dispatching me to Paris in a few days. I'm flying to Spain tomorrow, and then Paris. They've generously offered to fly you out too. It's just a two-hour flight. Please, say yes!" I pleaded, my heart racing.

"Darling, that's absolutely thrilling! I'd love to rendezvous with you in Paris."

"Then it's settled. I'll inform the team, and they'll provide you with all the necessary details. I can hardly wait to see you, Birdie. I've missed you dearly!"

"I've missed you too! It's been too long."

After exchanging declarations of love and bidding each other goodnight, I replaced the receiver and swiftly penned a reply to Samuel. Despite the tumultuous evening, the prospect of flying off to reunite with Birdie filled me with joy. Although I briefly considered divulging the incident with the maid, I decided against it. Our conversation had been too sweet and too pure, and I couldn't bear to taint it. There would be ample time for such discussions in the days to come.

45
BIRDIE

The anticipation of a weekend getaway in Paris with Roger fueled my excitement. Yet, as I pushed the stroller with Daisie cradled inside through the cobblestone streets, a gnawing ache settled in my chest. Distance, I realized, was an insidious force, capable of weaving its tendrils through even the strongest bonds. Still, amidst the bustling crowds and iconic landmarks, I found solace in the belief that our souls remained intertwined, regardless of the miles between us.

Working at the publishing house in London was a dream realized, but guilt often gnawed at me for being continents away from Roger. His calls from new cities and countries were lifelines, but there were moments when our connection faltered, lost in the vast expanse of the miles between us. Doubts crept in like shadows, testing the strength of our fledgling marriage.

Roger, with his irrepressible spirit and boundless energy, was my Peter Pan, whisking me away on adventures I had never dared to imagine. Yet, as I watched him flit from one place to another, I couldn't shake the feeling of being tethered to the ground, longing to spread my wings and join him in his escapades. But my dreams were rooted in the cobblestones of London, where I found fulfillment in pursuing my career as an editor. In the clash between love and ambition, I grappled with the weight of my choices, knowing that each step forward brought me closer to my aspirations, yet farther from the arms of the man I loved.

And so, amidst the enchanting streets of Paris, I found myself torn between the pull of two worlds, yearning for a way to bridge the chasm that stretched between them.

As I sat in my office working late, I couldn't help but wonder what my beloved Roger was doing at that moment. I pictured him in his hotel room, cozy and comfortable, lost in a book or perhaps out exploring the city with his fellow pilots and flight attendants. Despite the negative stereotypes associated with pilots, I had complete trust in Roger. I knew he would never do anything to jeopardize our relationship. However, being miles apart from each other often led to doubts creeping into my mind. Did Roger ever question my loyalty to him? I had faith in his trust in me, but it was sometimes hard to be sure. The mere thought of losing Roger was enough to bring tears to my eyes. It felt like a giant hand was squeezing my heart, reminding me of what we had given up and what we might ultimately lose.

But then I would receive a letter from Roger or a phone call, and any doubt would flutter away like leaves in the wind. His words carried the warmth of his affection, reminding me that he loved me beyond measure. It was in those moments, whether it was a simple letter or a brief phone call, that I was reassured of our bond.

When Roger called to share the news about Paris, I bubbled with excitement, like a child on Christmas morning. The mere mention of the word Paris had always been enough to set my heart aflutter, but knowing that Roger and I would finally have the chance to explore the City of Love together filled me with indescribable joy.

Our conversations about Paris had always been filled with dreams and aspirations. We had spoken of strolling along the Seine, picnicking beneath the Eiffel Tower, and getting lost in the labyrinthine of the streets of Montmartre. Each time we talked about it, the anticipation grew, like a flame steadily consuming kindling until it burst into a brilliant blaze. But now, with the reality of our trip sinking in, the excitement was almost palpable. I could already imagine the way the city would come alive around us, its streets bustling with energy and its landmarks steeped in history and romance. And to experience it all with Roger by my side, sharing in every moment of wonder and discovery, would be a dream come true.

I counted down the days until our departure, each one bringing us closer to our adventure in the City of Love. And with every passing moment, my heart swelled with gratitude for the love and companionship that Roger brought into my life. Paris might be the destination, but I cherished the journey with him above all else.

As we prepared for our trip, I couldn't help but feel a sense of exhilaration mixed with anticipation. The world might be vast and unpredictable, but as long as I had Roger by my side, I knew every step we took together would be filled with love, laughter, and unforgettable memories.

The late afternoon sun cast a warm glow on the quiet street as I strolled toward the quaint antique shop at the corner. The sign above the entrance creaked in the gentle breeze, inviting me to step into a world of forgotten treasures. Inside, a small bell above the door jingled, and the air became a tapestry of musty scents—aged books, polished wood, and lingering traces of memories long past. My fingers traced the spines of dusty leatherbound books as I walked along the narrow aisles, the creaking wooden floor adding a rhythmic touch to the vintage ambiance. A weathered cardboard box on the counter housed sepia-toned memories waiting to be rediscovered with a sign declaring, "Photos: 25 cents each."

Amid the scattered images, one photograph stood out: a black and white snapshot from the 1930s. A radiant, laughing bride in a tea-length dress stood beside her groom on the porch of their first house, captured in the frame. The palpable love in the photograph evoked an inexplicable familiarity, drawing me into the magnetic force of their connection. In that moment, surrounded by forgotten tales, my senses became heightened. These photographs were more than mere snapshots; they were portals to a bygone era, each one carrying a piece of a compelling love story.

Leaving the antique shop, the images lingered in my mind, reshaping the contours of my day. Envisioning the rotary dial phone awaiting me at home, its metallic ring echoing through the cozy living room, I felt a newfound purpose. Later that evening, reflecting on the comforting embrace of the shop's coziness and the fading traces of our conversation, I marveled at the serendipity that had led me there. The antique shop had become a sensory-rich portal, not just to love stories but to countless narratives resonating through the ages—stories of love and resilience surpassing the constraints of time.

With Roger on the line, I shared a tale—a cobweb-covered book revealing a romance torn apart by fate centuries ago. The images conjured transported me to another era, envisioning us in the 1500s, where our love resonated despite challenges. As I continued, emotions surged—a confirmation that the love glimpsed in those antique shop photographs was indeed enduring, transcending centuries and continents. Roger listened intently as I spoke, reflecting on the profound connection we shared. I sat down, reflecting on my day. In the ambient glow of the antique shop, surrounded by relics of the past and promises of the future, I embraced the certainty that, across all eras and circumstances, our love would persevere—an enduring light echoing through the corridors of history and intertwining our destinies across the ages.

46
ROGER

Against the backdrop of metal birds, wings stretched and gaining the speed needed to become airborne, the airport served as a contemporary gateway for engineers and travelers alike. I was on my way to Paris to see Birdie and Daisie. As a seasoned pilot, I knew the gears of the aircraft intimately, like the back of my hand.

Every time I turned on the intercom, I made a conscious effort to engage with the passengers, greeting them with either a warm "good evening" or a cordial "good afternoon," depending on the time zone.

Some passengers were bright-eyed and bushy-tailed, excited about their journey, while others fought to keep their eyes open after an early start. I exuded an air of confidence and authority as I strode through the busy airport terminal. My navy-blue uniform, adorned with golden stripes, was immaculately pressed, and my cap sat precisely atop my head. I moved like a well-oiled machine, efficiently weaving through the throngs of harried travelers with ease, carrying my small, black luggage bag gracefully.

Despite the chaos around me, my eyes remained fixed on my destination, and my gait steady and purposeful. The din of the airport faded into the background as I focused on my task. With a curt nod to the gate attendant, I took my place in line, ready to board my aircraft and soar into the heavens once more. Sitting in the dimly lit airport lounge, awaiting my boarding call, I mentally ran through my preflight checklist. It was a routine I'd performed countless times, yet each time brought a surge of adrenaline as I prepared for another journey into the clouds.

Before we hit the skies, my crew and I executed our preflight routine with precision to guarantee a smooth flight. We conducted a thorough inspection of the aircraft, checking every inch for dents or damage and ensuring we had ample fuel for the journey ahead. Next, we carefully reviewed the flight plan, confirming its accuracy and making adjustments as necessary. Weather conditions were monitored closely to anticipate any challenges that might arise during the flight. Inside the cockpit, we checked each system meticulously to ensure optimal functionality. Our goal was to achieve peak performance before takeoff, ensuring our passengers could relax and enjoy a safe and comfortable flight experience. Amidst the mechanical precision of our preflight routine, my thoughts inevitably turned to Birdie. It had been too long since I'd seen her and Daisie, and the anticipation of our reunion in Paris coursed through my veins. Memories of her phone call recounting the discovery of an antique shop and our shared nostalgia flooded my mind.

Our love, like the timeless treasure she described, was a testament to enduring beauty. Yet, beneath the surface of our seemingly idyllic relationship lay fears and doubts. Birdie's voice, tinged with apprehension, betrayed her silent worries about the state of our marriage. I grappled with uncertainties, pondering the resentments that lingered between us as we pursued our individual dreams. The temptation to confide in Birdie, to lay bare all my insecurities and fears, weighed heavily on my mind. But the words eluded me, swallowed by uncertainty. As I settled into the cockpit, bound for the City of Lights and the promise of reunion, I resolved to keep my silence—for now at least. But the letters I had written, filled with the raw honesty of my emotions, remained tucked away—a silent testament to the complexities of love and the sacrifices we made to preserve its fragile beauty.

It seemed that life was always one step ahead for Birdie and me. We struggled to make any real plans for ourselves. As I touched down in Paris and saw Daisie cradled in Birdie's arms, my heart raced and my eyes welled up. So much time had passed between us, and the distance felt almost unbearable. I was determined to make up for every missed moment. t was one thing to endure a long-distance marriage with Birdie, but being away from my newborn daughter as a new father was an entirely different challenge.

The pressure was overwhelming. I couldn't bear the thought of Daisie growing up thinking I didn't want to be present in her life. I wanted to show her that despite my frequent absences, my thoughts and love were always with her and her mother.

After taking some time off from BeyondBorders Aviation, Birdie, Daisie, and I relocated to New York. We found a lovely home where we could settle down. I took a position with EagleSky Airlines, allowing me to operate out of JFK and be closer to my family.

In the months that followed, Birdie and I received joyful news—we were going to expand our family. In 1955, we welcomed another daughter, Georgia "Gigi" Scott into the world, completing our little family.

47
GIGI
TWENTY YEARS LATER
LOCATION: CALIFORNIA
TOWN: LAKESHORE RIDGE
YEAR: 1970

Love crashed into my life like a beautiful storm, consuming me entirely and leaving me powerless to resist its alluring pull. Before I knew it, my heart belonged to him completely.

TWO WEEKS BEFORE

I sat on the old creaky attic floors, letters scattered about. Each letter tore apart the one belief in love I had.

Is it all for nothing? I thought. As I sifted through the crinkled pages of letters written by my parents, each word felt like a dagger piercing the sanctuary of my soul. The ink on the paper whispered what I imagined to be tales of betrayal, shattered promises, and a love once pure now tainted by deceit. How could something so beautiful morph into a labyrinth of lies? Doubt crept in like a thief in the night, stealing away the remnants of my faith in love.

But amidst the chaos of my thoughts, there lingered a flicker of hope—a stubborn ember refusing to be extinguished. Perhaps love wasn't solely defined by the scars it left behind, but by the strength found in the healing process. Maybe, just maybe, their letters were not a testament to love's failure, but rather a testament to its endurance. And as I gathered the fragments of my shattered beliefs, I realized that love, true love, wasn't about avoiding storms but learning to dance in the rain.

My eyes began to water, unsure if it was from the dust surrounding me or the sheer shock of the letters I discovered. All my life, I had believed in my parents' whirlwind romance, only to have these letters spill their secrets like cereal from a tipped box. As I picked up each letter, their faint fragrance wafted through the dusty air of the attic, mingling with the musty scent of old wood and forgotten memories. The paper, weathered by time and touched by countless hands, carried a delicate blend of dried ink, aged parchment, and the faint hint of my mother's familiar perfume along with my father's cigars. With each inhale, it was as if I were transported back to the 50s; a simpler time, where love was an untarnished promise whispered between two souls. Yet, beneath the surface of sweetness lingered a subtle bitterness, like the aftertaste of regret. It was the scent of secrets kept hidden between the lines, of truths left unspoken, and of hearts breaking silently in the dead of night. And as I held those letters close, breathing in their bittersweet essence, I couldn't help but wonder if the fragrance of love was always destined to be tainted by the passage of time.

I stared down at the letter in my hand. It was my father's writing. I knew that much. He spoke of being away from my mother, of being in hotel rooms, and the temptations of those around him. I contemplated if I should even be reading them, but I was here. I had to know what all this meant.

My dearest Birdie,

As I sit here in my hotel room, I yearn for the comfort of your presence. Today, an unexpected event occurred. There was a knock at the door, and to my surprise, a maid delivered a letter that had been left for me at the front desk. As she handed me the letter, I noticed a subtle shift in her demeanor—a suggestive gleam in her eye that made me uneasy. Before I could react, she began to make advances towards me, her intentions clear. Her boldness took me aback, and I quickly explained that I am a married man, hoping to dissuade her. However, she persisted, her words dripping with temptation, until I firmly declined her advances. She left with a lingering glance, making it known that if I were to change my mind, she would be waiting. It was a troubling encounter, one that I feel compelled to share with you, my dear Birdie. Please know that my heart belongs to you and you alone. I long for the day we are in London together and can put this unfortunate incident behind us.

With all my love,
Roger

My fingers brushed against the worn edges of another letter, my breath catching in my throat. I recognized the familiar slant of my mother's handwriting, a pang of nostalgia washing over me as I realized the weight of what lay before me. These words weren't just written in any time— they were penned during the early days of Daisie's life, a time that should have been filled with joy and new beginnings. But instead of happiness, there was doubt, fear, and a sense of distance that seeped into every word. I wondered if the strain of having a newborn, of juggling sleepless nights, endless responsibilities, and the long-distance between, had driven a wedge between them. How could they speak of devotion while harboring such secrets during what should have been the happiest time of their lives?

With trembling hands, I sank to the floor, the wooden beams creaking softly above me. I crossed my legs beneath me, leaning against the rough wall. In the dim light filtering through the cobweb-covered windows, the attic seemed to shrink around me, cocooning me in a world of secrets long forgotten.

My heart quickened as I opened the next letter, anticipation mingling with apprehension. Each word felt like a revelation, a glimpse into my parents' hidden world. I could almost hear their voices echoing in the silence, the faint rustle of paper evoking memories of evenings spent curled up by the fire, listening to their stories. Lost in my thoughts, my gaze flickered across the page, my mind racing with questions and emotions. With each sentence, I felt myself drawn deeper into the tangled web of my family's history, a journey through the shadows of the past. And yet, amid the uncertainty, there was a sense of liberation, of finally uncovering the truths that had long eluded me. For better or for worse, the letters held the key to unlocking the mysteries of my parents' lives, and I was determined to unravel them, one word at a time.

My darling Roger,

As I sit here in London, surrounded by the bustling streets and the ever-present hum of life in this city, my thoughts drift to you, thousands of miles away in the sky, navigating through clouds and time zones. It's been too long since we've had a chance to sit down and talk, to share our dreams and fears like we used to. I miss you more than words can express. Your absence is a constant ache in my heart. Lately, it feels like we've been drifting apart, pulled in different directions by the demands of our respective careers. Your job as a pilot takes you to far-off places, while I'm here in London, buried in the world of books while juggling life as a new mother. And now, with the prospect of meeting up in Paris, I find myself torn between the excitement of seeing you again and the fear of what this distance is doing to us. I love what I do here, Roger. The work, the people, the city itself—it's become my home in every sense of the word. But with each passing day, I can't shake the nagging doubt that our marriage is suffering because of our geographical separation. Will we drift further apart with each mile that separates us? Can our love withstand the challenges of distance and time? These questions haunt me.

They keep me awake at night, wondering if we'll ever find our way back to each other again.

I remember those early days in London, just the three of us—Daisie so small and fragile, and me, overwhelmed by the quiet hours when you were gone. The city felt strangely hollow without you. Every park bench and corner we once explored together seemed to echo with memories of a life that felt far away. But in the stillness of those moments, I found a strength I didn't know I had. Raising Daisie alone in this bustling city hasn't been easy, but the thought of your return, of us being a family again, kept me going.

And amidst all the uncertainty and doubt, one thing remains clear: my love for you burns brighter than ever. No matter where this journey takes us, know that you will always have my heart, now and forever. I hope to share these thoughts with you in person soon, my love.

Love always,
Birdie

One by one, I opened a few more letters. My eyes darted across the pages, tears welling in my eyes. My mother seemed to have doubts, and my father, he loved too much. I was beginning to understand it was better to have the upper hand, better to be the one they loved more than to be the one that loves more. Was loving someone just a game? I traced my fingers over the letters as if the memories would step right through the page and into my arms, and in a way, with their words, they did. I was starting to understand my parents while simultaneously feeling more confused than ever.

How was that even possible? I held the letters to my

face as if the ink would carry their heartbeat, taking in the aroma that lingered from their touch. Dust mites danced in the dim light filtering through the small attic window, casting eerie shadows on the walls lined with forgotten trinkets and old cardboard boxes. I had been here for hours when I heard a noise downstairs. Someone was home—I clutched the dusty old letters so tightly that my knuckles turned white, my breath coming in short, shallow gasps.

I tiptoed across the cluttered space, wondering who it might be. It had to be my parents, or it was Daisie; either way, I couldn't let them know I was up here. Daisie wouldn't understand. She'd brush it off. Once I'd overheard our parents arguing about my mother having to go back to London for a few days. I shared this with Daisie, not understanding the significance of London. Daisie looked me dead in the eyes and said, "Come on, peach, let's not dwell on ancient history. It's none of our business." If it was my mother, how would I explain to her what I'd found? And if it was my father, there was that slight fear that he never actually gave my mother his letter. Maybe he didn't have an affair, but what if he hadn't told her everything? Wasn't that just as bad? I needed to get out of here. I swept up the letters and shoved them into my bag before hurrying down the stairs. I heard my name being called out—it was my father.

"Hi, little peach, you're home early from school," he said, a knowing twinkle dancing in his eyes as he took in my disheveled appearance, as if he could read the turmoil swirling within me.

"Oh, it seems late to me," I replied.

His smile faltered slightly at my response, and he crossed the room to where I stood, concern etched into the lines of his face. "Is everything alright, sweetheart?" His voice was gentle, a stark contrast to the tension coiling in my chest.

I shifted uncomfortably under his gaze, as the weight of my secrets threatened to spill forth. "Yeah, just had a lot on my mind today," I replied, forcing a smile that felt as fragile as glass.

His brows furrowed in worry, and he reached out to squeeze my shoulder reassuringly. "You know you can talk to me about anything, right? Whatever it is, we'll figure it out together."

The lump in my throat grew, choking back the words I longed to say. How could I burden him with the truth when it threatened to tear our family apart? "Thanks, Dad," I managed, swallowing past the lump. "I'll, uh, I'll go start my schoolwork."

As I turned to leave, his hand tightened on my shoulder, halting my retreat. "Hey," he said softly, his voice tinged with an unspoken plea. "I love you, kiddo. Remember that."

Tears pricked at the corners of my eyes, a mixture of guilt and longing twisting in my chest. "I love you too, Dad," I whispered, before slipping out of his grasp and fleeing to the solitude of my room.

The weight of what I believed were secrets pressed down on me like a leaden cloak. I knew, even as I longed to release them, that some truths—whether real or imagined—were better left unsaid.

48
BEN
TWO WEEKS EARLIER

Have you ever experienced a profound and inexplicable connection with someone? That's precisely how I felt the initial time I sat next to her during class. Her name was Gigi Scott.

I swear I'd carve our names in the tree next to my house, but I was too afraid she'd notice. The last thing I wanted was for Gigi to think I was a weirdo.

Gigi's bouncy blonde curls cascaded down her shoulders, and her striking blue eyes sparkled in the light. Every time her lips curved into a smile, it felt like the sun was shining its brightest, and when she spoke, it was as if I was listening to the most enchanting melody in the world. Perhaps it was only me, but I could not help but feel drawn to her.

During today's class, I caught Gigi smiling at me and she kindly inquired about my weekend. I responded by mentioning my yard work and skateboarding excursion. In return, I asked about her weekend, and she said she'd spent it with friends. However, little did she know, all weekend long, I hadn't ceased thinking about her. Gigi's intelligence, charm, and kindness had the power to brighten even the gloomiest of days. I was almost certain that her heart was made of pure gold. But I was apprehensive about confessing my feelings to her. What if she didn't reciprocate those same emotions? What if she laughed at me, and all the memories of her beauty and kindness were forever tarnished?

While at school, I happened upon her outside with her friends. She was with her closest confidantes, positioned by a towering tree. They were engaged in conversation, and then, as if on cue, their conversation was overtaken by a cascade of laughter. Of all the sounds I had ever heard, her laughter was the most exquisite. It was as if her laughter had the ability to elevate the soul, uplifting all those within its reach. Her smile and laughter were so contagious that it was impossible not to be swept up in the moment. It was a truly remarkable experience that will forever be etched in my memory.

Sometimes I saw her riding her bike in the neighborhood, her blonde hair blowing underneath her helmet. She always waved but kept on going through the greenbelt, and in and out of the tracks. Her best friend, Martha, was often by her side, and Martha made me nervous—not because she disliked me, but because she wielded significant influence as Gigi's closest confidante. Best friends always had your back and often had strong opinions about potential partners. Maybe it was something akin to girl code, or perhaps it was about not dating the same guy. I had no romantic interest in Martha, nor had we ever dated. Despite my crush on Gigi, I knew winning Martha's approval was crucial. If she liked me, maybe it would pave the way for something more with Gigi.

I saw Gigi drive by today; well, it was her mother who drove by with her in the backseat. Gigi stuck her head out the window and called my name.

"Hi Ben!" she waved.

As I stood outside my house, a vehicle zoomed past me, and I glimpsed Gigi waving at me. Despite not being able to voice my thoughts, that simple wave meant the world to me. It was amazing how such a small gesture could hold so much significance. I found myself replaying that moment in my mind, holding onto it like a lifeline. Days went by, and one day during class, Gigi turned and asked for a pencil. As I gazed into her clear blue eyes, I was overcome with a rush of emotions. Her eyes resembled a perfect spring sky, and her smile was as warm as the gentle sun. In her presence, I felt like I was on top of the world, and I couldn't help but compare her to the sun, while I was the moon, orbiting around her.

"Hey Ben, may I borrow a pencil?" Gigi asked.

"Absolutely!" I handed her the pencil I had in my hand and leaned into my backpack to grab myself another one.

"Did you study for this week's exam?" she asked.

I want to say I couldn't stop studying her face, but she

would probably think that was cheesy.

"Definitely. I'm so going to ace this!" I responded.

"Confident. I like it!" replied Gigi.

"Did you study?" I asked.

"Duh! English is my middle name, and I am gonna ace this quiz too!" she responded confidently.

"Let's make a bet!" I said.

"OK, Benjamin. What's it gonna be?"

"How about, if I get a higher grade than you, then you have to feed my pet snake for a week?"

"And if I get a higher grade than you," she said, "well, we both know I'm going to."

"Not so fast, Scott. What happens if you do?" I asked.

"Well, if I get a higher grade than you, then you have to clean our pool for a week," said Gigi.

"It's a deal!" I stuck out my hand to shake on it.

"Deal!" She grabbed my hand and shook it.

After class, when the final bell rang to leave for the day, she looked over at me and said, "It's on, Sutton! I hope you have gloves to prevent your hands from pruning after you have to clean the pool for a week!"

"Please, Gigi! You really think you can beat me?" I scoffed.

"I know for a fact that I can!" Gigi responded.

"Good luck, little lady!" I lifted my hand to my forehead in a salute. She giggled, and we went our separate ways.

"Bye, Ben!" she waved.

"Adios, Gigi!" I responded.

We walked in separate directions, but my mind was still

on Gigi. I was so going to win the bet, but part of me wanted to keep it going, you know, finding a way to keep a connection with her. I know I shouldn't overthink things, but I had had a crush on her for a while, and I wish she would give me some sign that she felt the same way.

49
GIGI

Ben was convinced that he had something on me, but I was not worried. I knew I would win our bet, and it would be my pleasure to watch him clean our pool for a week. And maybe he'd fall in love with me after that. The challenge was initially a silly one, but the more I thought about Ben Sutton, the more I found myself intrigued by him.

However, I had to stay focused on acing our upcoming English exam and not let his flirting distract me. I had no intention of feeding his pet snake, which I found gross.

When I arrived home from school, I immediately sat down at the table and started studying. I meticulously laid out all my notebooks and highlighters and grabbed a soda from the fridge. I was determined to ace the exam, and I could feel the adrenaline pumping through my veins. I was so engrossed in my studies that I barely noticed my mother walk in.

"Hi, Gigi. How was school today?" my mother asked.

"Fine," I replied.

"Are you doing your homework?"

"No. I am studying for our English exam on Friday."

"Oh, good for you. If you need someone to quiz you, I'd be happy to," my mother replied cheerfully.

"Thanks, Mom. But I really need to focus."

My mother walked over and kissed me on the forehead. "Alright, sweetie. Well, if you need me, I'll be over here." She walked away and went about her business.

As I continued studying, my mother started preparing dinner. "It's so lovely seeing my two favorite girls, but where's my third favorite?"

My father, who had just arrived home, came into the room looking for my sister, Daisie. She walked in a few moments later, covered in dirt. Daisie's name may have sounded like a delicate flower, but she was anything but that. She was brave, unafraid of taking risks, and never hesitated to stand up to people she disagreed with. She was passionate about sports and played softball as a pitcher. My father and Daisie often bonded over sports, spending hours watching games and discussing them. In contrast, my mother and I preferred shopping as our preferred recreational activity.

The sun was setting over the mountain, and the kitchen was filled with a sense of warmth and comfort as we sat down for dinner. We gathered around the sturdy wooden table, its surface adorned with a colorful tablecloth. The warm glow of a lamp illuminated the room, casting a soft light over our faces as we enjoyed our dinner. I looked around the room at their smiling faces. The clinking of silverware and the gentle murmur of conversation filled the air as Daisie passed a steaming dish of food to my father—dishes being shared back and forth. The tantalizing aroma of the meal wafted through the room, making my mouth water in anticipation.

We savored every bite, enjoying the flavors and textures of the food as we chatted and laughed happily together. It was moments like these that made me grateful for a family. It also made me wonder what it would be like someday to have a family of my own.

I knew I was too young to think about that now, but I hoped someday my family would be gathering around a table and enjoying a delicious meal. After the last morsel of food was savored and the conversation had died down, my father and mother rose from their seats. Daisie and I followed suit and began to clear the table. We worked in unison, like a well-oiled machine, with each of us taking on a specific task. I picked up the dishes and utensils and passed them to my father, who deftly scraped the leftover food into a bin. My mother began wiping the table clean of any crumbs and spills while Daisie started gathering the empty glasses and cups.

The clinking of dishes and silverware rang through the room as we worked, each sound a testament to our collective effort. The dishes were then passed to the sink, where they were rinsed with hot water before being stacked neatly on the counter to be washed. The sound of the water running and the clatter of dishes being washed and dried filled the air as we worked tirelessly to clean the kitchen.

After the dishes were dry, each piece was carefully placed back in its designated spot in the cabinets and drawers. The table and chairs were wiped down and pushed back into place. With the kitchen now spotless, we each exchanged a satisfied smile, knowing our teamwork had paid off. We were now ready for a fresh start in the morning, and I was prepared to get back to studying. The evening had come to a close, and I retired to my bedroom to hit the books before turning in for the night. I needed to get a restful sleep as the upcoming exam was fast approaching. I felt a sense of anticipation; it was not the exam that I was looking forward to, but the prospect of another day seeing Ben.

As I lay on my bed, staring at the ceiling, my thoughts drifted to Ben. I wondered what he was doing at that moment. Was he working hard to prepare for the exam, or was he thinking about me as I was thinking about him? Before I could ponder this any further, a wave of fatigue washed over me. I knew it was time to retire for the night, so I carefully placed my English book and notes back on my desk and snuggled up under my blankets. As I drifted off to sleep, I hoped I would dream of Ben and find the courage to express my feelings to him in my dream.

50
BEN

When my alarm clock went off and the sun shined through my window, exhaustion flooded over me. I had been up half the night studying. Part of me considered letting Gigi win so I could spend more time with her, even if it meant cleaning her pool. But what kind of person would I be to fail an exam because of a girl I had a crush on? And what would Gigi think of me if she ever found out? I knew I needed to win Gigi's heart the right way, and that also meant playing the long game.

When thinking about the pros and cons of our bet, I realized that if Gigi lost, she would have to care for my pet snake, which would mean ample time for us to hang out. So, I would win either way. I'd get to spend time with Gigi, no matter what.

As I got dressed for school, I ran down the stairs and

poured myself a bowl of Wheaties, added a perfect ratio of milk, and sat down at the table. I was enjoying my bowl of cereal when my mother walked in.

"Good morning, Benjamin. Did you sleep alright?"

I swallowed before answering. "I think I got a decent amount."

"I saw your light on, and it was almost midnight. Why were you up so late?"

"I was studying for this English exam on Friday. I really need to ace it."

"Well, I'm very proud of you for working so hard, but don't burn yourself out. A growing young man needs rest."

"I understand. I'll do my best to get a good night's rest sooner."

"That's my boy." She patted my hand before getting up from the table and walking over to the coffeepot.

Not long after, my brothers Joe and Dash and my sister Rosie came downstairs. Joe was in eighth grade, Dash was in sixth, and Rosie was in third. My mother was juggling our three different schools. We lived right next to the elementary school so Rosie could walk or ride her bike to school. She always met up with her friend Joan, and they rode their bikes. Joe and Dash were at the same middle school; sometimes, my mother would drive us, and she'd drop off Joe and Dash before taking me to the high school. Most days, I would take the bus, and the same with Joe and Dash. Our mother worked and sometimes she wasn't able to always take us. Our father traveled for business often, which made me the man of the house most of the time. I didn't mind, though; I loved my mother, and I'd always be there to protect her. And I was happy to look out for my siblings as well. But some days, I just wanted to be a kid.

As I finished my breakfast and watched my siblings trickle into the kitchen, I felt a sense of responsibility settle on my shoulders once again. Being the oldest among them meant being a role model, a protector, and sometimes even a second parent. It wasn't always easy, but seeing them grow and thrive made it all worth it.

After bidding my family goodbye, I made my way to school by catching the bus, the weight of my upcoming exam heavy on my mind. The hallways were abuzz with students rushing to their classes, their backpacks slung over their shoulders, and conversations blending into a cacophony of teenage energy.

Arriving at my locker, I exchanged greetings with friends and classmates, yet my mind remained fixated on the impending exam and the irresistible allure of winning the bet.

"Hey, Ben," Gigi greeted as I settled into my seat. Not only were we in the same English class, but we also shared a science class where she was my lab partner. Now, faced with the final test—would Gigi and I have chemistry beyond the lab?

I stowed my backpack beneath my seat and braced myself for the day ahead. "Hi, Gigi. Ready to take care of Burt the snake?" I teased.

She rolled her eyes. "Oh, Sutton, your hands are going to be as wrinkled as raisins after a week of cleaning my pool, because I'm definitely going to win this bet."

"You seem pretty confident for someone about to lose," I retorted, unable to resist a jab.

Gigi feigned offense. "Oh, Benjamin, do you really have so little faith in me? I'm offended," she teased, placing a hand over her heart.

"Give it a rest, Gigi. I'm going to ace this exam so thoroughly, you'll question if English is even your first language."

Gigi countered with a smirk. "Nice try, Ben. But before you judge my English skills, consider this: my mother worked for a publishing company for years, lived in London, and is an author. So, think again."

Her quick wit always impressed me. With each banter, I found myself falling deeper for her, though she remained oblivious. I replayed the earlier conversation in my mind as I worked side by side with her. What had started as a playful teasing about my pet snake, Burt, had taken an unexpected turn. In a moment of unguarded honesty, I'd let the word "charming" slip into the mix, aimed at her.

The word had hung between us for a beat longer than I wanted to admit, and though Gigi's response had been lighthearted, I'd spent the rest of the exchange scrambling to recover my footing. Did she notice? Did she think it was just another joke? Or worse, had she read too much into it?

Now, seated next to her in class, I found myself hyperaware of everything she did. The way her pen tapped lightly against the edge of the desk, the way her hair slipped over her shoulder as she leaned forward. It was maddening and, at the same time, something I couldn't quite bring myself to stop.

The dissected frog lay on the tray before me, but my focus kept slipping, drawn instead to Gigi's quick, confident movements. She had an effortless way of turning even the most mundane task into something captivating. I forced myself to adjust the scalpel in my hand, pretending to scrutinize the anatomy chart in front of me, though I'd already memorized it.

Out of the corner of my eye, I caught her smirk, the way her lips curved like she was holding back some clever remark. It hit me then, how her teasing always seemed to draw out the best and the worst in me. My fingers tightened around the scalpel, the familiar thrill of our rivalry sparking in my chest.

The bell rang, jarring me out of my thoughts. Gigi's voice reached me through the din of chairs scraping and backpacks zipping, her tone light but edged with that unspoken challenge that always kept me on my toes. I responded without hesitation, matching her energy, though my heart thudded with something far less controlled. She laughed, quick and bright, and it felt like she had tugged a thread I hadn't realized I'd been holding so tightly. She tossed her hair over her shoulder and turned to leave, her words lingering in the space between us.

I stood there, watching her go, the noise of the classroom receding into the background. My stomach churned, equal parts adrenaline and something else I couldn't name. Did she know what she was doing to me? The way she could disarm me with just a glance or a laugh?

Clutching my bag, I followed the rest of the students out of the room, my steps heavy with the realization that I'd let another moment slip by. But this wasn't just about missing a chance to one-up her in our playful battle. It was about the weight she carried in my thoughts, the way she lingered long after she was gone.

I berated myself as I headed to my next class, the embarrassment of my earlier slipup gnawing at me. Surely, Gigi must think I'm strange. I could almost hear her and Martha laughing in the bathroom, the whole school finding out by tomorrow thanks to Martha's big mouth. It had been a disaster.

As the final bell rang, signaling the end of classes, I decided I would study harder than ever before. This was not just for the sake of winning a bet, but for my future. Gigi was undoubtedly a motivating factor, but I refused to let her define my worth or determine my success. With determination fueling my steps, I headed home, ready to face the challenges that lay ahead. As I walked through the door, greeted by the familiar sights and sounds of family, I knew that no matter what obstacles came my way I had the love and support of those who mattered most.

51
GIGI
DAYS BEFORE FINDING THE LETTERS IN THE ATTIC

Settling into my seat beside Ben in the crowded science classroom, I felt the air buzz with the anticipation of the impending English exam. "I'm going to win," I declared with a playful grin, nudging Ben's elbow.

He chuckled, his confidence unwavering. "You wish. I'll be acing that test."

I shot him a playful glare. "We'll see about that," I countered, a competitive spark igniting within me.

The teacher's voice interrupted our banter, signaling the start of the day's lesson. My stomach churned as I realized what awaited us: frog dissection. I couldn't help but feel a pang of sympathy for the poor amphibian lying motionless on the lab table.

A TIMELESS TAPESTRY

Despite my reluctance, I persuaded Ben to join me in the task. His hesitation was palpable, but he relented, albeit reluctantly. As he tentatively made the first incision, I observed his expression, noting the mixture of apprehension and curiosity that flickered across his face. Working together, the initial discomfort seemed to fade, replaced by a strange sense of fascination. Ben's hands moved with newfound confidence, his curiosity overcoming his initial reluctance. Meanwhile, I struggled to mask my unease, my thoughts lingering on the fragility of life and the ethical implications of our actions. Amidst the dissection, a sense of camaraderie emerged between us, bonding us in the shared experience of exploration and discovery. Despite my reservations, I couldn't deny the thrill of uncovering the intricacies of the frog's anatomy alongside Ben.

The class seemed to fly by, the hum of anticipation for the upcoming experiment mingling with the soft shuffling of papers and whispered conversations. Before we knew it, the final bell signaling the next class rang, snapping us out of our reverie. "Well done, Benjamin," I remarked with a smile as I gathered my books, my gaze lingering on him for a moment longer than necessary.

As I got up out of my seat and pushed my chair in, he flashed me a grin. "Your turn next time, Gigi," he quipped, his voice playful.

Chuckling, I retorted, "Uh, I don't think so." With a casual toss of my hair, I added, "Our next class involves experimenting with beakers. I can't wait to concoct some magic in a jar."

Ben's eyes lit up with mischief as he leaned in closer.

"Ah, in that case, I suppose you'll be encountering Burt, my resident amphibian," he said, a smirk playing on his lips.

I rolled my eyes, though a small smile tugged at the corners of my mouth. "Not this again, Ben. I'm going to win this bet, you know," I said, my tone confident.

"Never, Gigi. I won't give up," he declared, his eyes locking with mine.

With a laugh, I teased, "Ah, the classic tale of the determined hero."

"It's not a story, and I'm not a hero," Ben replied, his voice softening as he met my gaze. He continued by noting he's just a guy who made a bet with a charming girl. Heat rushed to my cheeks as I realized the depth of his words. Did he really call me charming? My heart fluttered at the thought.

As I hastily gathered my things, a whirlwind of emotions churned within me. "Well, Ben, this was fun, but I've got some studying to do," I said, trying to mask the turmoil in my voice. "And you should, too, if you're serious about winning."

Hurrying out of the lab, I couldn't shake the lingering warmth of Ben's words. I was acting like one of those little school girls with a massive crush, but this felt different. Ben was different. The air crackled with anticipation, leaving me wondering—did he feel the same?

I Martha and I boarded the bus, the day's events simmering in my mind. I debated sharing the happenings of the science lab with Ben, wary of Martha's tendency to spread information. Martha, with her voluminous hair and boundless enthusiasm, was my best friend, but I knew some secrets needed to be kept close.

"Did you have to dissect a frog today?" Martha chirped, her curiosity palpable.

"Yes. It was so gross. My lab partner handled it while I took notes," I replied cautiously.

"Oh, who's your partner?" Martha asked, her interest piqued.

"Ben," I said quickly, hoping to steer the conversation away from potentially sensitive details.

"Nancy and I flipped a coin for it. You're lucky yours is a boy," Martha remarked, unwittingly setting the stage for gossip.

I forced a smile, masking my discomfort. "Yeah, convenient, I guess."

"Speaking of lab partners, Josie told Mallory, who heard from Diane, that Margaret has a crush on Ben," Martha spilled, oblivious to my unease. "Can you believe it?"

Suppressing a sigh, I interjected, trying to steer away from the topic. "I doubt it. Margaret's usually into jocks, isn't she?"

"She's in her skater boy phase now, apparently," Martha continued eagerly, delving deeper into the rumor mill.

As Martha prattled on, I tuned out, my thoughts drifting to my impending English exam. When the bus finally halted, relief flooded me. Exiting the bus, Martha invited me over for a snack, but I declined, citing the need to study. "I'll see you tomorrow," I said, eager to escape the vortex of gossip.

At home, I settled into my studies until a knock interrupted. It was Dad offering a reprieve from my solitude with a pizza dinner.

"Hey there, Georgia peach." He always called me that. It was endearing.

"Hi, Dad," I said without taking my eyes off my notes.

"Say, kiddo, Mom's working late tonight, and Daisie is out with some softball friends. Why don't we go out for some pizza?"

"That sounds like a plan. Pepperoni with olives, please," I requested, seizing the opportunity for a break.

"Sure thing. It'll just be us two, so why not?" Dad suggested, offering a welcome change of scenery. "We can eat at the pizza shop."

Over dinner, he shared tales of his travels, igniting a spark of wanderlust within me. As he recounted his adventures, I realized the world held boundless possibilities awaiting exploration beyond the confines of gossip-filled bus rides and teenage drama.

As we settled into the cozy booth at the pizza shop, the aroma of freshly baked dough enveloped us, mingling with the chatter of other diners. Dad leaned back, a contented smile playing on his lips.

"This brings back memories," he mused, glancing around the familiar surroundings. "Your mom and I used to come here all the time before you came along."

I nodded, a pang of nostalgia tugging at my heartstrings. "I wish I could remember those times."

Dad chuckled, a twinkle in his eye. "You and your sister were just little tykes then, but we made some unforgettable memories together."

Taking a sip of soda, I savored the fizzy sweetness before mustering the courage to broach a topic weighing heavily on my mind. "Dad, do you ever regret choosing a career that keeps you away from home so often?"

His expression softened, a hint of wistfulness flickering in his gaze. "Sometimes, kiddo. But flying isn't just a job to me, it's a passion. And every time I return home, I appreciate our time together even more."

I nodded, understanding dawning upon me. "I guess it's about finding balance, right?"

"Exactly," Dad affirmed, his smile warm and reassuring. "Life's a journey, Gigi. We each have our paths to follow, but it's the people we meet along the way that make it worthwhile."

Our conversation ebbed and flowed, spanning topics from favorite travel destinations to dreams of the future. With each passing moment, I felt closer to Dad, a newfound sense of connection blossoming between us.

As we polished off the last slice of pizza, he glanced at his watch, a hint of reluctance in his gaze. "I should get us back home. Your mom will be wondering where we've disappeared to."

Reluctantly leaving the cozy confines of the pizza shop, I realized that our evening together had been more than just a break from studying. It had been a reminder of the importance of cherishing moments with loved ones, no matter how fleeting.

As we stepped outside into the cool evening air, I

linked arms with Dad, a newfound sense of gratitude warming my heart. Though our paths diverged in the vast expanse of life, I knew our bond would always remain unbreakable, anchoring me amidst the tumultuous seas of adolescence.

52
BEN
DAY OF EXAM

It was Friday morning, and exam day was upon us. I was awash with nerves. My eyes burned from reading more than one person probably should. But I was ready. In fact, I was so ready I just knew I was going to ace this exam.

"Good morning, my loving family!" I said cheerfully as I came downstairs.

Rosie was sitting in front of the TV with a tray in front of her and a bowl of cereal. Joe and Dash were both at the counter fighting over who would get the last banana. And my dearest mother was once again pouring herself a cup of coffee.

"Good morning, darling," my mother said.

"Good morning, Ben," Rosie chimed in, not taking her

eyes off the television. Cartoons were a real hit in this family, especially for Rosie.

"Boys, boys, will you stop fighting over that banana!" my mother yelled for Joe and Dash to stop.

I snatched the banana from both their hands and immediately unpeeled it and took a bite.

"Problem solved," I said with a mouthful.

"Not fair!" Joe and Dash said at the same time.

"Well, life isn't always fair, is it?" I remarked.

"MOM! Ben took our banana!" they both yelled.

"Boys, I'm right here so you don't have to yell. And honestly, the way you two were fighting over that banana it serves you right."

I loved it when my mother sided with me. I was the eldest, after all. Rosie was their little princess, and I was the favorite son. Joe and Dash were two peas-in-a-pod.

"Is today your English exam?" my mother asked.

"It is. I'm so pumped!" I poured myself a bowl of cheerios and sat down at the table where I finished my banana.

My mother set down a cup of orange juice in front of me. Vitamin C is good for you, she always said. "I know you will do just great. Don't be so hard on yourself."

"Mother, I appreciate the support, but I have a lot riding on this. I need to ace this test."

"As if you haven't aced all your other tests," Dash snickered.

"Dash, if you studied half as hard as your brother Ben does, perhaps you wouldn't have to take summer school, hmm?" my mother retorted.

"Not fair. I work hard," Dash complained.

"Yeah right, dude. The only thing you work hard at is staring out the window," Joe joked.

Dash smacked Joe over the head and the two began to go at it again before Mom separated them.

"Dash and Joe, get to school now."

"But Mom, what about Ben?"

"What about him?"

Joe and Dash got up from the table, crossing their arms.

"Fine. But if you find your snake down the drain one day, don't come running to me," Dash remarked.

I almost choked as he said the words. "How dare you! You wouldn't hurt Burt."

"Watch me!" Dash said angrily.

"Mom! You can't let Dash get away with this."

"Ben, honey, it's fine. I'll keep an eye on Burt."

"How can you do that when you're not always here and neither is Dad?"

I was angry. Burt was my special pet. In some ways, he was my best friend. I knew I couldn't trust Dash around Burt. "I'm taking Burt to school with me; he'll be safer there."

"No, you are not. Benjamin, you leave that snake here. And Dash, you apologize to your brother immediately."

"Yeah dude, you don't mess with the guy's snake," Joe chimed in.

"I'm sorry, Ben. Burt the snake will be unharmed," said Dash.

"Now, boys, get to school. You don't want to be late,"

my mother said.

Joe and Dash rushed to the bus stop, and I decided to walk Rosie to school today. I had a few more minutes before my bus arrived. After dropping Rosie off, I made my way to the bus stop. There, I saw Gigi standing waiting for the bus. I waved at her and she waved back. I kept thinking about the exam. I was certain I would win the bet, but I knew Gigi wasn't the type to back down from anything. She would make sure she won. I tried to tell myself that winning didn't matter, but who was I kidding? I wanted to rub it in her face so badly. I wanted to show her I was smart because being smart meant I might have a chance with Gigi. She was always the brightest kid in class and for once, I just wanted to prove I could be at her level—or above it. I walked over to where Gigi was standing, her nose in her books. A nerd, but a cute nerd, I thought. She was always reading something.

"Hey, Gigi," I greeted.

Without looking up from her book, she replied, "Oh, hey there, Ben."

"Ready to admit defeat?" I challenged.

"Oh, Benny Benjamin Ben, do you honestly think I would ever admit to something that isn't true?" she jested.

I hated it when I was called Benny or Benjamin. Only my mother used Benjamin, but she was the only one that got a pass. I was seething. Not because Gigi made me angry, but because she had the audacity to assume she was better than me. I liked Gigi, but I was not about to lose to the girl I liked, either.

"Since when did you become so cocky?" I hissed.

"Who got you all bent out of shape, Benjamin Sutton?" Martha chimed in, walking up to Gigi and me.

"Oh, leave the boy alone," Gigi muttered.

"What? I'm just having a little fun. Besides, it's important that a best friend always has the other friend's back," Martha claimed.

"I think that's my cue to stand over there." I pointed to a spot far enough away from Martha and Gigi.

"Don't be so gloomy, Ben," Martha shouted after me.

I'd woken up in such a great mood today, but then Martha had to step in and spoil it. It was frustrating how she meddled in everyone's business. Suddenly, my heart started to race, not because of my feelings for Gigi, but because of Martha's meddling words. She claimed to be Gigi's best friend, yet I couldn't help but feel she didn't truly have Gigi's best interests at heart. If Gigi ever deviated slightly from expectations, I'm certain Martha would be the first to turn on her.

Martha seemed to fancy herself as some kind of queen bee. As these thoughts swirled in my mind, a James Taylor song reverberates, "You've Got a Friend," a reminder of genuine, steadfast support. I'd like Gigi to see me as that kind of friend, someone she can always count on, unlike Martha.

I keep pondering their friendship. I knew that if there was ever a chance for something more between Gigi and me, I'd need to find a way to at least coexist with Martha. But it truly was hard to imagine counting on Martha for anything real or supportive. At last, the bus pulled up, and we all boarded. Upon arriving at school, a knot of anxiety tightened in my stomach. History was my first class of the day, followed by P.E. Soon, lunch rolled around, and I spent the time studying for English. After lunch, I had auto shop and math class. I found myself rocking back and forth on a plastic chair that felt increasingly small under me. It used to fit perfectly, but not anymore. My gaze flickered toward the small window at the front of the classroom before hastily returning to the door. Somehow, the ordinary sight of it was difficult to ensure, though I couldn't understand why.

I found myself daydreaming about English class, where I'd be sitting next to Gigi amid rows of desks laden with papers and pencils. In just two hours, everything would come to a head. Distracted and restless, I struggled to concentrate on the math equations before me. All I wanted was for English class to arrive so I could face whatever awaited me. Swallowing down the bile that threatened to rise, I consciously relaxed my clenched hand. When the school bell shattered the quiet, I nearly bit my tongue. Rising from my seat, I barely noticed the faint echo of voices in the air as I placed my fingers on the cool metal of the door handle, ready to step out.

The exam loomed, and my nerves crackled with electric anticipation. My body reacted as though facing down a charging gorilla, not just a page of English exam questions. Yet, in the serene classroom environment, I maintained confidence in my ability to master the content. The tasks—matching words with definitions, defining similes, and analyzing characters—were genuinely intriguing. Despite feeling as prepared as if I were bracing for a grueling marathon rather than a brief sit-down, I remained seated on that stark plastic chair, battling the urge to flee. Winning a bet depended on my ability to stay and face the exam head-on. However, with my mind in full panic mode, grasping the necessary details became a Herculean task.

Once everyone had turned in their exam, the teacher congratulated the class. I wasn't sure what she was congratulating us on, since she had ordered the exam in the first place. But again, maybe I should be thanking her. If we didn't have this exam, there wouldn't be a bet between Gigi and me.

The bell rang, and I was ready to go home. I needed to get out of this classroom immediately. As I packed up my belongings and grabbed my backpack, I heard Gigi's voice.

"How did you do, Ben?"

"I aced that, baby!" I said confidently.

"Well done. But I'm not taking care of your snake."

"A deal is a deal, Gigi. You should know better. Besides, Burt is more human than you think."

"No reptile is human, Ben. That's why there's a difference."

"Say what you want, but Burt is a kind snake and you would be lucky to care for him."

Sticking her nose in the air, she said, "Well, Ben, I guess we'll find out next week. But I suggest you get yourself some pool gloves because no one likes prune hands."

"You are so sure of yourself, Gigi Scott," I proclaimed.

"Why wouldn't I be?" she asked.

"I just think a little mystery is a good thing."

"And you think you're being oh-so-mysterious," Gigi remarked.

"Well, I hate to toot my own horn, but yes. I've been fairly subtle about winning this bet compared to you."

"And what would you want me to do, Ben? Pretend like I think you're going to beat me?"

"No, I didn't say that. I just think sometimes you get a little too cocky. It's unattractive." Oh no. Why did I say that? Gigi was beautiful, sweet, and kind and I had just unleased the harshest word I could muster. Today was supposed to be my day to shine, like I was on a roll, or even butter sliding off a hot roll. Now, I felt more like burnt toast. I tried to smooth things over, but I wasn't sure it helped.

Gigi said nothing. She just looked at me with her big blue eyes, now icier than ever. Had I just provoked an ice queen? Maybe it was time I stopped talking.

"Have a nice day, Ben," she said coldly.

I'd really messed up. Why was I acting like such a jerk today? Perhaps I was too caught up in studying, trying to win that silly bet, and struggling to hide how much I liked Gigi. Ultimately, I'd ended up being mean to her for absolutely no reason. She must think the world of me now—*not*.

53
GIGI

Today was a weird day. In the morning, Ben and Martha almost had a fight. I wasn't sure why Martha felt the need to insert herself into everything in my life, especially into the conversation I was having with Ben. But she was my best friend, so what was I supposed to do?

While waiting for the bus before school, Ben approached me. What I thought would be silly banter about who would ace the exam turned into him storming off and Martha being a bane in my existence once again. I probably shouldn't say that about my best friend, but some days she really got on my nerves.

Maybe it was because we'd known each other for so long that she was practically like a sister to me. I couldn't imagine this strange and beautiful world without her in it but I also wished sometimes she'd take a chill-pill.

The exam was easier than I anticipated and I was glad when it was over with. However, the strangest thing happened afterwards. I don't know what got into Ben, but he was kind of rude to me. He basically said my cockiness was unattractive. I'm not cocky. But why should I suppress my academic knowledge to make him feel better? I didn't have it in me to argue with him, and I just walked away. There was no point getting into an argument over something so silly. Besides, isn't the best reaction no reaction?

I was so excited to get home and relax for the weekend. Fridays have always been my favorite day, and Sunday, because my dad would go to this little bakery down the street and get the most delicious donuts. Sometimes, I would wake up early and walk to the bakery with him. Mine would have pink frosting and sprinkles and his would be a bear claw. We'd sit on the bench outside, enjoying our donuts. He'd tell me stories about him and Mom in the good old days when they lived in NYC. He used to tell me about the café just down the street from their apartment, where the aroma of freshly baked goods would drift through the early morning air. I cherished his stories from their younger days. Their whirlwind romance felt like something lifted directly from the pages of a fairytale.

Perhaps their love story was why I'd always kept guys at a safe distance. I was only in high school, but it seemed like everyone had a boyfriend or was dating. But me? I'd never really had a boyfriend. I'd been on a few dates, and this boy, Dexter, in middle school, told everyone I was his girlfriend, but that was all in name. We never went on a real date, and I shied away from even holding hands. I'd always been more focused on my schoolwork, spending time with Martha, or family. It never seemed like a priority. Now I was a sophomore in high school and doubted if I would ever meet someone who liked me for me. The more I thought about it, the sillier it seemed. Was it really so terrible to have never had a boyfriend? There was still a lifetime ahead for me to meet someone special. Maybe after I graduated, I'd move away, and that's when I'd meet him. I was bound for Millikin University, like my parents before me, and maybe that was where I'll find my own love story, like something out of an Audrey Hepburn film, maybe "Roman Holiday" or "Breakfast at Tiffany's"? My mind raced with possibilities about who my soulmate might be.

As soon as I got home from school, I headed directly to my room and collapsed onto my bed, gazing up at the ceiling. With a heavy sigh, louder than I intended, thoughts of Ben crept into my mind. He had acted so strangely today. Lost in the shadows dancing across my ceiling, I hardly noticed my mother walk in.

"Hi, sweetie, how was your exam?" my mother inquired.

Startled, I sat up abruptly from the bed, perhaps a little too fast, as the room began to spin. I closed my eyes and took a deep breath, steadying myself until the dizzy spell passed.

"It was good. I have a pretty good feeling I aced it," I chirped brightly.

She walked over to the bed and sat down next to me,

gently brushing away a strand of hair that had fallen across my face and tucking it behind my ear. Her fingertips lightly grazed my cheek. I closed my eyes and leaned into her warm palm, a comforting reminder of those nights when I was younger and couldn't sleep. She would sing softly to me, her fingers brushing my cheek until I drifted off. I sometimes missed those simple moments of childhood.

"I knew you could do it. I'm so proud of you, honey, and I know your father is equally proud," she exclaimed earnestly.

"Thank you, Mom. Making you and Dad proud has always been my goal."

"Why don't we, us girls, go out to dinner tonight and celebrate?" she suggested.

"What are we celebrating?" I asked, curious.

"Do we ever need a reason to celebrate?" she winked at me, then stood up from my bed.

"I guess not. But what about Dad and Daisie?"

"Daisie is out with Travis, and your father had to leave for a business trip," she explained.

I couldn't hide my disappointment; this was the first I'd heard of Dad's trip. Why hadn't he told me?

"Don't look so sad, kiddo. We'll have a great time," she assured me.

"Absolutely. I'll freshen up and then we can head out," I agreed, my spirits lifting.

"Sounds lovely. Any ideas on where we should go?" she asked. But before I could respond, she added, "How about that Italian restaurant by the water, Riva Bella Trattoria?" she suggested.

"That sounds fab," I replied, already looking forward to the evening.

We arrived at the restaurant and were seated on the patio, which offered a stunning view of the town's tranquil lake. The setting sun cast a warm, golden reflection on the water, painting a breathtaking backdrop. In that moment, I couldn't imagine calling any place other than Lakeshore Ridge home. A cool breeze made me glad I had brought my cardigan. As the waiter approached with water and a basket of fresh bread, we unfolded our menus, eager to explore the evening's possibilities.

"Welcome to Riva Bella Trattoria. How is your evening going?" the waiter asked with a smile.

"It's lovely, thank you," my mother responded warmly.

"May I start you off with some drinks and appetizers?" he continued.

"I'll have a glass of Malbec, thank you," my mother decided, then glanced at me.

I nodded to the waiter. "I'll take a Diet Coke, please. Thank you."

"Certainly. And will you ladies have any appetizers to start off with?" he inquired.

My mother opted for a Caesar salad as her appetizer and looked towards me, asking, "And sweetie, would you like one as well?"

"That would be grand, thank you," I replied.

The waiter nodded, jotting down our choices before departing. Left alone again, we delved back into our menus. I found myself torn between the pillowy gnocchi and my usual favorite, the aromatic tortellini in pesto sauce. The rich scents of fresh basil and garlic mingled with the savory allure of perfectly cooked pasta made choosing a delightful challenge. As the waiter returned promptly with our drinks and the starter salads. I had already delved into the breadbasket, liberally buttering a roll and taking a hearty bite, perhaps more than I could comfortably chew. Hastily, I reached for my water, taking a gulp just as my mother concluded her order. With the waiter's attention on me, I seized the opportunity to choose the ravioli, treating myself to something I seldom ate but deeply enjoyed. As the waiter nodded and retreated to relay our orders to the kitchen, my mother and I settled into the serene ambiance, enjoying our private moment by the lake.

"It's quite beautiful here," my mother proclaimed.

"Indeed, it is. I don't think I could ever tire from this view," I said, staring off into the distance of the lakeside.

"Did I ever tell you about the time your father proposed and where?" my mother asked, speaking freely.

"I'm not sure ..." I allowed my words to falter, but was eager to hear more.

"It was magical. We were apartment hunting that day in the city. We had seen dozens of places, but none really hit home until the last apartment. I wanted it so badly, and I could tell your father did too, but neither one of us was willing to show it for fear we'd get our hopes up."

My mother continued her story, her voice growing warm as she mentioned the place where it unfolded, Blue

Haven Pond, and I could hear the significance of the name as she spoke it. There was a wistful expression on her face that told me of the cherished memories she made at that pond with my father.

"And there he got down on one knee and asked me to be his wife. It was such a grand gesture, my heart was beating out of my chest. I would have said yes a million times over." She beamed as she recounted the story.

I listened, a soft smile playing at the corners of my lips as I absorbed the weight of my mother's words. It was almost as if I could see the scene unfolding before me—the nervous excitement in my dad's eyes, the shimmering water of the pond in the backdrop, and the joyous surprise etching my mother's youthful face. The story wasn't just a recounting of events but a treasured family legend, etched deep into the constitution of our lives. I felt a surge of gratitude and a twinge of longing, wishing I could have witnessed that magical moment for myself. It might sound silly, given that I wasn't even born at the time, and far from being a thought in my parents' minds. Yet hearing my mother recount the tale filled my heart with a warmth I hadn't known was possible.

"Mom, it truly sounds so magical hearing you recount yours and dad's story," I said, my face alight with emotion. It was magical.

"Darling, your day will come too. And when you meet that special someone, everything will brighten," my mother replied, her words of wisdom echoing warmly in my ears.

"I'm looking forward to that day," I said warmly.

Before we knew it, our meals arrived, and I was eager to dive into the ravioli. After savoring every bite of our dinner, Mom and I decided to extend the evening with a visit to the nearby ice cream shop located in the same plaza. We took a little stroll around while enjoying our ice creams. The story of my mother and father was still ringing in my mind. Their relationship was perfect, like it was straight out of a classic love story film. I wondered if that would ever happen to me. It didn't take long before I started thinking about how I clearly lacked in the boyfriend department. I couldn't help but think about Daisie and Travis. They had been dating since the freshman year of high school, and now Daisie was a senior.

"Mom, what do you think will happen with Daisie and Travis at the end of the year?"

"What do you mean?"

"Well, Daisie's going to Columbia University and Travis is going to Yale. Do you really think they can do a long-distance relationship?"

"Oh, sweetie, your sister is young and has so much life ahead of her. While I adore Travis, there's no telling where they'll end up in the long run."

"So, you're saying they're going to break up?" I posed.

"I'm not sure what they'll do. But that will be a decision made by your sister and Travis."

"I know. Of course, it is."

"But?" she asked.

"Well, I've never had a boyfriend or even been in love. What if you meet your soulmate, but fate has other plans?"

"Oh, Georgia, you're too young to be worrying about

that."

"Daisie isn't that much older than me, but she has Travis."

"Yes, but they aren't you," she replied. "Why all the sudden questions?" she pressed.

I sighed, "I just don't want to miss out on what it feels like to love and to lose someone."

"Gigi, you have plenty of time to date many boys, break a few hearts, maybe get your own heart broken, before settling down," she replied, "I think you need to have a little faith that everything will work out."

"But you met Dad and fell in love."

"And we were in college, dear. I was much like you in high school. I dated, but it was nothing serious until I met your father."

"And lived happily ever after—yes, your life is a fairytale."

We reached a nearby bench, and I plopped down, letting out a big sigh. My mother sat down next to me, allowing silence to fill the air.

"I love your father dearly, but to compare us to a fairytale isn't accurate. This is real life and relationships have their ups and downs. You will learn this someday."

"I guess …"

She wrapped her arm around me and gave a tight squeeze. The familiar scent of lavender and honey from her perfume enveloped me, bringing a smile to my face as she hugged me even tighter.

"What kind of ups and downs did you and Dad have?" I asked, my curiosity getting the better of me.

With a dismissive flick of her hand, as though swatting away a fly, she replied, "Nothing we couldn't work out."

Before I could dig deeper, she sprang up from the bench. "It's getting late; we should head home," she said, her tone suggesting urgency.

Most likely, Daisie was already home. Although my mother had left a note for her, she seemed eager to return. I didn't press the matter. We had enjoyed such a lovely evening, and I wasn't about to spoil it by being petulant. Yet, as we walked, a cloud of unanswered questions followed silently behind us. Was my parents' love story not such a love story after all?

54
BEN

I slung my backpack onto the bedroom floor and dashed into the bathroom to douse my face with water. I had eagerly anticipated today, but somehow, I managed to ruin everything. Thoughts of whether Gigi was upset with me swirled in my mind. I knew I shouldn't care, yet I couldn't help it.

Returning to my room, I approached Burt's cage. He lay curled up inside, a quiet solace in the chaos of my emotions. Gently, I tapped on the glass, startling him. He slowly uncoiled and slid toward the glass, flicking his tongue inquisitively.

At that moment, Burt was exactly the company I needed: silent, undemanding, and a peaceful presence amid the storm. I pressed my face closer to the glass, looking Burt in the eyes. "You always have my back, right,

Burt?" I asked aloud. He flicked his tongue a few times as if to confirm that, yes, he was indeed my steadfast companion. Feeling the need to clear my head, I laced up my running shoes and decided on an afternoon run. Just as I was about to step out, my mother halted me with a question.

"And where do you think you're going?" she inquired, one eyebrow raised.

"Out for a run. I'll be back in an hour," I replied, reaching for the door handle, but she stepped in front of me.

"Your English exam was today. How did it go?"

"It was fine," I shrugged, trying to keep it casual.

"Benjamin?" She gave me a pleading look.

"It went great, actually. I'm pretty sure I aced it," I said with more enthusiasm than I felt.

"That's my boy. I'm so proud of you," she beamed, her face lighting up with a proud smile.

Just as she was about to probe further, Rosie called out to her from the kitchen. She glanced back at me before heading off, "Be safe and enjoy your run, Benjamin. But don't be late for dinner, understood?"

"Yes, Mother," I nodded, finally stepping outside, grateful for the escape into the crisp air.

My feet pounded the pavement, and a surge of energy coursed through me, reminiscent of a racehorse bolting out of the gates on opening day. The rhythm of my running shoes hitting the ground, combined with the brisk wind slicing past my face, created a sense of freedom and release. The air held a crisp stillness that sent shivers down my spine, heightening my senses and grounding me in the moment. With each stride, the day's frustrations—a jumbled mess of anger and disappointment—dissolved into the ether. It felt like the open road, or in my case, the greenbelt, had a magical ability to absorb my woes and replace them with a sense of purity and possibility. My breath synced with my steps, creating a meditative cadence that cleared my mind and sharpened my focus.

The path ahead stretched invitingly, lined with the early blooms of spring and the occasional flutter of wildlife. The rhythmic rustling of leaves and the distant calls of birds formed a natural chorus, playing a soundtrack to my escape. Here, amidst the tranquility of nature, I wasn't just running away from the chaos of the day; I was running toward peace, toward clarity.

The sun began its descent, casting a golden glow over the landscape, and the beauty of the world around me seemed amplified. Each beam of light filtering through the trees painted the path in warm hues, encouraging me forward, promising new beginnings, and affirming the simple yet profound joy of being completely free at this moment—just me and the endless path ahead. I hurried home, keen not to break my promise of being on time for dinner. My mother's expectations dwelled in my mind with every step. As I rounded the corner, a familiar car passed by. It was Gigi's. Recognizing the vehicle I had seen countless times before, a flutter of nervousness touched my heart. Her mother was driving, and Gigi was in the passenger seat. They noticed me; her mother waved, and Gigi rolled down the window.

"Hi, Ben!" Gigi called out, her voice carrying a warmth

that immediately eased my worries.

"Hi, Gigi!" I shouted back, waving vigorously as their car disappeared around the bend. The headlights faded into the growing dusk, and a laugh escaped me. The absurdity of the day's earlier tensions melted away. She wasn't mad, or if she had been, she wasn't anymore. It felt as though a heavy weight had been lifted off my chest.

With newfound energy, I sprinted the last few blocks home. Bursting through the door, I was panting and flushed with exertion, arriving just as dinner was about to start. Inside, the familiar scene of home wrapped around me. My siblings were setting the last of the plates, and my mother was bustling around the kitchen.

"Ben, is that you?" her voice floated from the kitchen.

"It is," I replied, still catching my breath.

"Good. Go wash up and meet us at the table," she instructed.

"Yes, ma'am."

I quickly washed my hands and face, scrubbing away the sweat of my run. After changing into clean clothes, I returned to the kitchen, where my siblings, Dash and Joe, were already seated. Rosie ambled over with a glass of milk, setting it carefully next to her plate.

"Need any help with anything else?" I asked my mother as I took my place.

She shook her head, then paused, "Actually, yes. Could you fill the rest of the glasses with water?"

I nodded, taking the pitcher and filling each glass. The normalcy of the task and the evening routine grounded me, and a smile found its way to my face. Dinner was going to be good tonight.

After dinner, I insisted on cleaning the table. After all, my siblings set it, and my mother cooked dinner for us all. As I stood at the sink, scrubbing the plates and throwing away any leftovers into the garbage, I couldn't help but wonder where Dad was again this evening. He has missed a lot of dinners lately, especially during the week. Mother didn't like to talk about it, but I could sense she didn't like it when he was gone so much. Late nights at the office, he was sometimes traveling for work.

I knew my parents loved each other, but how could they stand to be apart for so long? I didn't have it in me to ask too many questions, and anytime I did, my mother would get very defensive. She'd ramble on about how my father was doing what was best for this family in order to put food on the table. My mother worked, too, but less than him. Some days, she worked at the local library, and other days, she was a receptionist for a dental office. I was proud of my dad, but that didn't mean I didn't miss him. It affected Dash and Joe more so. Rosie was too young to really understand the gravity of it all. She was always so eager to give him a big hug every time he was home. She'd clasp her little fingers around his ankles and hold on for dear life. Our dad would stumble around the house, mocking her and pretending he had a creature attached to him. She giggled and squeezed tighter.

I remembered the days when Joe and I would each grab onto one leg and watch our father try to move—having two of us hanging on made it feel as if his feet were stuck to cement. When Dash was born, I took on the big brother role and allowed Dash and Joe to grasp onto his legs. No matter how late he was at work or how long he was traveling for, the moment he got home, he enjoyed every minute of us holding on to him. This is why I couldn't find it in me to question my mother. Because I knew deep down my father was working hard to provide for us, to give us a life we could be proud of, and I couldn't fault him for that.

After finishing the dishes, I trudged toward my bedroom. The fatigue from a long school day seemed to wait for the precise moment when I stopped moving to pounce, enveloping me like a thick, suffocating blanket. As I crossed the threshold, the familiar comfort of my room offered a slight reprieve. Almost tripping over my backpack, I let out a long, weary sigh. The sound seemed unnaturally loud in the quiet of the evening, echoing slightly against the walls, a reminder of the day's relentless pace. I was finally done with my English exam, and it was the weekend. I collapsed onto my bed, the mattress embracing my tired body. Above me, the ceiling fan whirred gently, the soft hum and the cool breeze it created feeling almost therapeutic. Closing my eyes, I took a moment to breathe, letting the stress of quizzes, presentations, and endless notes dissolve in the tranquility of my own space.

But rest was a luxury I couldn't indulge in for long. My mind, as relentless as ever, started replaying my conversation with Gigi. Just as anxiety began to tighten its grip, I recalled her cheerful wave from the car window earlier today. That simple gesture brought a fleeting smile to my lips. With a reluctant groan, I sat up and stretched out my hand toward the nightstand. My fingers closed around the well-worn spine of "The Grapes of Wrath" by John Steinbeck. Holding the book, a solid reminder of the resilience and endurance within its pages, offered a strange comfort as I prepared to dive into another challenging narrative.

As I opened the book, its familiar weight in my hands anchored me. The trials of the Joad family, etched in Steinbeck's gritty prose, mirrored the sense of endurance that I was trying to foster in myself. Each page turned like a reflection of my daily struggles; though admittedly less dire, they were no less real to me. The hardships faced by the Joads and their resilience in the face of unyielding adversity stirred something within me. It was a reminder of the strength required to face my challenges: the grueling academic expectations, the social dynamics at school, and even my conversation with Gigi—each a battle in its own right. Steinbeck's depiction of hope and solidarity in the midst of despair encouraged me not just to endure but to find meaning in the struggle. As Tom Joad's words resonated with a profound sense of justice and human dignity, I felt a renewed sense of purpose. I realized that, like the Joads, I was not merely subject to the whims of fate but could shape my response to the adversities I faced.

Reading further, I let the undercurrents of social critique in Steinbeck's narrative seep into my thoughts. Perhaps there was a lesson here in empathy and advocacy, not just for fictional characters in a novel, but in my interactions with friends like Gigi. Like Ma Joad, I could strive to be a pillar of support and kindness in my world. I gently set the book back on my nightstand and pulled my notebook from my backpack, ready to jot down my thoughts for the upcoming essay on "The Grapes of Wrath." As I scribbled, my eyelids grew heavier with each word, the fatigue of the day finally claiming its toll. Reluctantly, I closed my notebook, its pages filled with reflections and analyses, and placed it neatly on my desk.

Standing up, I stretched out the kinks from hours of sitting and made my way to the bathroom to brush my teeth. The routine motions were soothing, a quiet end to a bustling day. Back in my room, I switched off the light, the soft darkness enveloping me as I slid under the covers. "Goodnight, Burt," I whispered. Comforted by the stillness, I closed my eyes, and sleep overtook me almost immediately, a peaceful respite from the whirlwind of thoughts and obligations. Tomorrow was a new day, and I was ready to make it a great one.

55
GIGI

Sunday morning appeared faster than I anticipated it to. Saturday felt like such a blur, but here I was on Sunday morning, up early and riding my bike to the donut shop. I had my basket latched to the front and decided to pick up some baked goods.

My dad was still away on business—flying around the world, more like flying other people around the world. I knew I should be happy for him since he was doing what he loved, but sometimes, I really hated that his profession was a pilot. He came and went, and there were times when I just wanted him here, on the ground.

I sped through the streets, and as I passed by Ben's house, I noticed he was out front. I decided to stop by and say hello.

"Good morning, Benjamin," I yelled over the lawn

mower.

He looked up from cutting the grass and noticed me. I rode my bike over, and he turned the lawn mower off before walking over.

"Hey there, Gigi. How's your morning going?"

"It's fine. Just on my way to the donut shop."

"Oh, nice. You going to bring me back a donut, I surmise?"

"Depends. Are you ready to forfeit the bet?"

"Not a chance, Georgia Scott." I had said his full name, so it was only fair that he did the same to me. Though I couldn't help but wince at the name Georgia coming from his lips.

There was a pebble on the ground, and I shifted to kick it. Suddenly, a wave of nervousness hit me. Why was I so nervous around Ben?

"Is it Sunday mow day for you?" I teased.

"Yeah, my dad is coming back tomorrow, so I wanted to make sure the yard looked good."

"That's very kind of you. Where is your dad away on business?" I asked.

"I'm not sure, actually. I think he's in North Carolina this time, but sometimes he's out of the country."

"I see. Does he ever bring back neat stuff for you and your siblings?"

"Sometimes. Mainly for Rosie, she's his little princess."

I chuckled at his remarks, unsure of what else to say. Normally, I was a total chatterbox, but with Ben, sometimes it felt as if my throat was closing up. Not in a bad way, but I was afraid of saying the wrong thing, so I found myself not saying anything at all. He probably thought I was the weirdest girl in school. Although, I didn't know he was too fond of Martha—which was fair. She wasn't always nice to him. One of these days, he was going to get back at her, and she wouldn't like it. But maybe she'd deserve it. Did it make me a terrible friend that I would condone it? Maybe, maybe not. I shrugged to myself.

"Isn't your dad off being Superman and flying around the world?" Ben remarked.

"Yeah, I guess he is like Superman."

Ben and I chatted for a bit more before we said our goodbyes. I continued toward the donut shop, and Ben continued his yard work. It was a beautiful Sunday morning. Birds were chirping, and the sun was out. It was the start of a beautiful week.

Monday morning, I couldn't contain my excitement as I asked my mom for a ride to school, eager to start the day early. Despite her late start, she agreed, and as we rounded the corner, I spotted Ben heading toward the bus stop.

"Mom, slow down!" I urged, catching sight of Ben.

Without hesitation, she slowed and pulled in front of Ben's house. "Hi, Mrs. Scott," Ben greeted as he approached the car.

"Hello, Ben," my mom replied, exchanging pleasantries.

"Ben, would you like a ride to school?" I offered, trying to avoid my mother's gaze.

"Thank you, that's very kind," Ben accepted, sliding into the backseat.

As we drove, Ben, sitting quietly in the back, engaged in conversation with my mother. I jumped in awkwardly, contributing to the small talk.

Having Ben in the car made me reflect on the stark differences between him and my dad. Ben was a realist, focused, and polite, while my dad was impulsive yet kindhearted.

When we reached the school, my mom dropped us off at the front. "Thank you for the ride, Mrs. Godwin," Ben expressed his gratitude.

"You're welcome, Ben. And call me Birdie," Mom insisted, prompting a polite refusal from Ben.

"May I continue to call you Mrs. Godwin?" Ben asked respectfully.

My mom chuckled, waving goodbye as she drove off. "Of course, Ben."

"Bye, Mom," I waved back, ready to start the day with Ben by my side.

As I walked into school, the hustle and bustle of the morning set in. I caught up with friends, discussed our plans for the day, and tried to shake off the lingering excitement from seeing Ben. Classes went by in a blur of notes and teachers' voices, each passing minute bringing me closer to the moment I'd been looking forward to all day.

I spent lunch with my friends, trying to stay engaged in conversation despite my mind wandering to the English class I was about to enter. It felt like the whole day was a countdown to that final bell. The anticipation built up as the day dragged on, with each period feeling longer than the last. Finally, the school day came to an end, and I made my way to English class. I saw Ben already sitting at his desk, with a seat open right next to him. I sat down in the empty seat as more students began to pile in. The room was dimly lit, with the last rays of the sun streaming in through the dusty windows. My heart was pounding with anticipation.

"Hi, Ben," I replied, my voice betraying a slight tremor that I couldn't quite conceal.

"Are you ready to see who wins our bet?" he teased, his tone filled with curiosity and apprehension.

"As ready as I'll ever be."

We sat among other students, the air thick with tension as we awaited the distribution of our grades. I could feel the eyes of my classmates, especially Ben's, on me as we all waited for our fate to be revealed.

When the teacher finally began to distribute the graded papers, my hands shook with nervousness. As I scanned the page for my grade, my eyes widened in surprise and relief. Despite my fears, I managed to earn a decent score. The feeling of elation and satisfaction that washed over me was indescribable, and I couldn't help but smile as I thought about all the hard work that had gone into achieving this grade.

I stole a sideways glance, hoping to read the verdict written on Ben's face when he received his grade. Ben's expression was unreadable, his features composed and pokerfaced as he reviewed his exam results.

I maintained my composure outwardly, but inside, I was screaming, 'What did you get?' Yet, I remained silent and patient, waiting for Ben to break the tense silence.

As I watched him stare at his exam for what felt like an eternity, my mind raced with uncertainty. Was his prolonged contemplation a sign of good news or bad? It was clear he was playing with my nerves. The longer he hesitated, the more my imagination ran wild. Suddenly, I envisioned a week ahead spent caring for his pet snake—a bizarre consequence that seemed increasingly likely with each passing moment. The seconds dragged on as Ben continued to scrutinize his exam paper, oblivious to the turmoil he was causing me. My palms grew clammy, and my heart pounded against my ribs, each beat echoing my escalating apprehension.

I glanced around the room, seeking any distraction from the overwhelming suspense. The faint sound of shuffling papers and whispers only amplified my unease.

Finally, Ben looked up, his expression inscrutable. "I got…" he began, his voice trailing off for a moment that felt like an eternity.

I held my breath, waiting for his next words to determine the outcome of my week. Would it be filled with textbooks or a slithering reptile?

56
BEN

I watched as Gigi received her paper, she was smiling. Before I could ask her what she had gotten, the teacher reached my desk and handed me my paper. My hands trembled slightly as I flipped through my exam, each mark and comment scrutinized under my focused gaze. A mixture of anticipation and dread churned in my stomach, unsure of what the next few moments would reveal.

My mind raced with self-doubt and hope, a whirlwind of emotions threatening to overwhelm me. What if I had yet to do as well as I'd hoped? What if all those late-night study sessions hadn't paid off?

With each passing second, I felt the weight of expectation bearing down on me. My thoughts were a jumble of anxiety and cautious optimism, battling for dominance. Finally, I reached the last page and a sense of relief washed over me. Despite the challenges and uncertainties, I knew I had given my all. Whatever the outcome, I was ready to face it with acceptance.

I turned to Gigi, attempting to maintain my best poker face. As she looked at me expectantly, I finally revealed, "I got an 89%…"

Pausing for a moment, I gathered the courage to ask about her score, hoping to win our bet. But as soon as I saw her expression, I knew I had lost. Gigi was never one to conceal her emotions well, and her face told me everything before she spoke a word. I felt a sinking feeling in my stomach; I had lost the bet, and a week of cleaning her pool awaited me. The prospect of spending a week with Gigi should have excited me, but instead, dread settled in. What had I gotten myself into? Gigi tucked a strand of her hair behind her ear, her hands trembling with anticipation. With a deep breath, she flipped her exam face up and stared at the page for a split second before answering. "I got a 96%," she said confidently, her eyes sparkling with joy and relief.

It was a moment of triumph, one that we both knew signaled her victory. Throughout the week, Gigi had walked around the classroom with an air of confidence, boasting about winning. But now that she had emerged victorious, her expression seemed more subdued than expected. The excitement of the moment had given way to a sense of calm and satisfaction, and a quiet smile of contentment played on her lips. After class, we walked together to the bus stop, the weight of our exam results lingering in the air. While waiting for the bus, I decided to acknowledge the outcome of our bet.

"Well done, Gigi. You won our bet," I said, trying to sound gracious despite my disappointment.

"Thank you," Gigi replied softly, her tone somewhat subdued.

I noticed a hint of uncertainty in her response as if she wasn't entirely comfortable with the outcome. Sensing her hesitation, I broke the tension with a touch of humor.

"Looks like I'll be your pool boy for the week," I chuckled, trying to lighten the mood.

Gigi managed a small smile, but her eyes betrayed a flicker of guilt. I wondered what was going through her mind as we boarded the bus, leaving behind the weight of our exam grades.

When I burst through the front door, changing into my running clothes provided a brief distraction from the whirlwind of thoughts in my mind. I laced up my shoes with a sense of urgency, eager to escape into the rhythmic cadence of my evening run. As I hit the pavement, the cool evening air filled my lungs, clearing my head but failing to dispel the lingering confusion over Gigi's demeanor. A B+ was nothing to sneeze at, yet the memory of her hollow gaze haunted me.

On the bus ride home, Gigi sat beside Martha, who prattled on without pause, her voice blending into the background noise of the bus engine. Gigi, however, stared out the window as if searching for answers in the passing scenery. Martha's obliviousness was almost comical, unaware that her friend was a world away. When our stop arrived, Gigi bolted off the bus like a sprinter at the starting line. I wanted to catch up, to ask what was wrong, but she disappeared into the dusk before I could even take a step.

Walking the familiar route home, my thoughts were consumed by Gigi's troubled expression. The weight of concern settled on my shoulders like a heavy backpack. I hoped she was okay, but her distant demeanor had left me uneasy. The sun was casting long shadows across the quiet neighborhood as I hit my stride on the familiar path. Each step beat the pavement like a drum, a physical release for the pent-up emotions swirling in my mind. Thoughts of Gigi tugged at the corners of my consciousness like a persistent whisper. What was bothering her? Why did she seem so distant today despite her academic success? My pace quickened with the urgency of unanswered questions.

The cool breeze brushed against my face, offering a welcome respite from the day's lingering heat. Yet, it did little to soothe the knot of concern in my chest. I replayed the scene on the bus. There was vulnerability in her gaze. Was it something I said or didn't say? Had I missed a sign that she needed someone to reach out? My mind was ablaze with a flurry of possibilities, and my racing thoughts reverberated in the thud of my footsteps.

57
GIGI
THE WEEK OF FINDING THE LETTERS IN THE ATTIC

I should have been elated. I had won the bet against Ben, and he was going to be cleaning our pool for the next week. But as I sat on the bus, staring out the window, my thoughts were elsewhere—locked away in the attic, with the letters that had unraveled everything I thought I knew.

I couldn't shake the memory of that day. The bus rumbled beneath me, but in my mind, I was back in the attic, surrounded by relics of my parents' past. The sunlight filtering through the dusty windows had cast a surreal glow on the scene, as if the room itself knew the weight of what I was about to uncover. Those letters—they were just words on paper, yet they carried the power to redefine my entire existence.

How could something so simple—a few sheets of aged paper—contain such a devastating truth? I remembered the way my hands trembled as I unfolded the first letter, my breath catching in my throat. Each word had chipped away at my belief in their love, like a sculptor slowly eroding a masterpiece. By the time I'd finished, the image of my parents' perfect romance had crumbled into dust. It wasn't just the discovery that haunted me—it was the aftermath. The way I had to pretend nothing had changed when my father found me later, his eyes searching mine for a hint of what I was hiding. The weight of those letters pressed down on me like a leaden cloak, even now, as I tried to make sense of it all.

As I sat there, trying to process everything, a stray thought crossed my mind—Daisie was born around the time these letters were written. It was strange to think that while my parents were navigating these difficult moments, they were also welcoming her into the world. I wondered if they ever looked at her and saw both a reminder of their struggles and a symbol of hope. But that was just it—Daisie had always seemed untouched by the complexities that now weighed on me. Maybe that was why she was so quick to dismiss any talk of the past, always urging me to leave things alone. I realized then that whatever had happened back then, it had shaped us all in ways we might never fully understand.

The bus jolted, pulling me back to the present. I glanced around at the other students, laughing and chatting, their lives blissfully uncomplicated. They didn't know what it was like to have your entire world turned upside down by a few scribbled words. They didn't know the burden of secrets, the kind that made you question everything you thought you knew. The bus pulled into my stop, and I knew I couldn't keep running from this. The letters had revealed a side of my parents I had never known—a side that scared me because it was so human, so flawed. I had always seen them as larger than life, their love a beacon of hope in a world full of broken promises. But now, I realized they were just like everyone else, stumbling through life, making mistakes, and hiding the mess behind closed doors.

I stepped off the bus, my mind still churning. I had to confront these feelings, these doubts that gnawed at me. The letters were a window into a past I had never been privy to, and now that I'd seen it, I couldn't unsee it. But maybe, just maybe, there was something to learn from it all. Maybe love wasn't about perfection but about surviving the imperfections together.

As I walked home, I knew I couldn't talk to anyone about this—not yet. I wasn't ready to share the burden, to let anyone else into this tangled web of emotions. But I also knew that I couldn't ignore it forever. The letters had opened a door, and whether I liked it or not, I had to walk through it. The questions swirled in my mind. How much of what I'd believed about love was a lie? Was it better to be the one who loved more or the one who was loved? And what did it mean for my own future, my own relationships? Could I ever trust in love the way I had before?

I reached the front door and paused, taking a deep breath. This was just the beginning. The letters were only the first step in unraveling a truth that had been hidden for too long. But now that it was out in the open, there was no going back. I had to face whatever came next, even if it meant tearing down the illusions I had built my life around. With a sigh, I pushed open the door and stepped inside. The house was quiet, the stillness heavy with unspoken words. I knew I had to deal with this, but for now, I just needed a moment to breathe.

DAYS BEFORE THE EXAM

The familiar aroma of melted cheese and tomato sauce enveloped us as we stepped into the pizza parlor, the place my father and I frequented like clockwork. We made our way to our cherished booth tucked in the corner; its worn vinyl seats held countless memories of family outings.

My father settled across from me, his eyes twinkling with interest. "How's school going, peach? That big English exam coming up?"

I nodded, trying to muster enthusiasm despite my mind on the letters from the trove. "Yeah, it's tomorrow. Been hitting the books pretty hard."

He chuckled, reaching for a menu. "You'll do great, peach. Remember, it's just one test. Don't let it stress you out too much."

I couldn't help but smile at his reassuring words. "Thanks, Dad. I'll try not to let it get to me. Besides, Ben and I made a bet that if I get a better grade, he'll have to clean our pool for a week!"

"Is that so? And what happens if he gets a better grade than you?"

"Well, that won't happen. But if it does, I have to feed his pet snake. So you better pray for me to get a better grade."

"You don't need my prayers, kiddo. I believe in you."

"Thanks, Dad."

We ordered our usual: a large pizza with pepperoni, olives, and extra cheese. We settled into a comfortable conversation, my mind letting go of what I found in the attic for just a moment. He asked about my favorite subjects, sharing anecdotes from his school days that never failed to make me laugh.

Amidst the lively chatter and the sounds of sizzling pizzas from the kitchen, I felt a sense of calm wash over me. His presence was like an anchor, grounding me in the midst of academic turmoil.

While we savored our slices and shared stories, it became clear that it wasn't just the pizza I loved about this place; it was the cherished moments spent with him. Pulling into the driveway, he turned off the engine but remained seated, his expression contemplative. A mix of curiosity and concern etched on his face, like he was carefully treading delicate ground, caught my attention.

"Dad..." I started, but he beat me to it.

"Peach, I know you were in the attic. Would you like to share what you were looking for up there?" His tone was gentle, inviting honesty.

I swallowed hard, feeling the weight of his gaze. "I...I was trying to find some old memorabilia from when you and Mom were younger."

His eyebrows arched slightly. "Is that all?"

"Yeah, pretty much. What else would be up there?" I replied, attempting nonchalance.

He studied me for a moment, his eyes crinkling at the corners with a hint of amusement. "So, what interesting things did you stumble upon?"

I hesitated, then mentioned the items I had discovered: a mix of Mom's writings, Dad's football and pilot memorabilia, and Mom's cheerleading uniform.

He chuckled softly, a nostalgic glint in his eyes. "Ah, those were good times."

"Yeah, I bet," I said, relieved that he seemed more amused than upset. "I'm sorry I didn't ask before going up there. I didn't think it would be a big deal."

He shook his head reassuringly. "You're not in trouble, peach. Just next time, give us a heads-up. We wouldn't want any ladder mishaps up there."

I nodded earnestly, "Got it. I hadn't even thought about that." I lied. I knew it was a possibility, but I kept an eye on the ladder and my ears open for anyone in the house.

Dad's smile softened. "Well, dinner was nice. And hey, anytime you want to know more about our Millikin days or my Air Force days, ask."

"Thanks, Dad," I said, feeling a rush of gratitude. "This was fun, and…I appreciate everything."

He reached over to squeeze my shoulder before getting out of the car. "Anytime, kiddo."

58
GIGI

Two days ago, I had dinner with my dad, pretending everything I found in the attic was normal. For a brief moment during dinner, I began to forget about the letters. I thought I was reading it all wrong. But now that I've had time to let it all sink in, I'm not sure I can let it go.

My father was leaving for another flight and would be gone for a couple of days. Daisie was hardly ever around. Too busy with her boyfriend or softball team. My mother was always there for me. Could I trust her to tell her what I found? My mind was playing endless tricks on me and spinning like a record player, with the only song belting out the words displayed in each letter.

It was finally the weekend, and I had aced my English exam but now the looming feeling of my parents' whole relationship being a lie still festered. I wanted to tell someone, anybody who would listen. I couldn't say a word to Martha. Not if I wanted my family's secrets to be the talk of the town. I couldn't tell Daisie; she'd tell me I was overreacting and worrying about nothing. My parents seemed so in love and happy. How could I break the news to them? I could tell Ben... No. I couldn't do that.

My mother was gone to the grocery store, and Daisie was out—in fact, Daisie was never home. Maybe now would be a good time to go over to Martha's, to take my mind off all of this.

Stepping into the kitchen, I reached for the telephone and dialed Ben's number with a satisfying click of the rotary dial. As I waited, the cord stretched just enough for me to perch on a nearby stool. The phone rang, each tone resonating through the receiver, while I absentmindedly twirled the cord around my fingers, feeling a rush of anticipation building within me.

"Sutton residence, may I ask who's calling?" Mrs. Sutton's voice greeted me through the receiver.

"Hello, Mrs. Sutton, this is Gigi Scott. Is Ben home?"

"Hi, Gigi. Ben is out at the moment, but I can take a message for when he gets home."

"Oh, okay. Will you tell him I called?"

"Certainly. I will relay the message."

"Thank you, Mrs. Sutton. Have a wonderful day."

"Thank you. You too."

"Goodbye," I said before hanging up.

I heard a click on the other end, indicating she had hung up the phone. I remained there with the phone pressed against my ear, half expecting Ben to respond magically. After a few minutes, I reluctantly hung up the phone back on its cradle.

Stepping outside, I made my way over to our pool and sat down, letting my feet dangle into the cool water. I imagined Ben on the other side, meticulously cleaning leaves from the pool. In my mind's eye, I pictured myself lounging nearby with an iced tea, tuning the radio in hopes of hearing my favorite song. We would share a laugh about something trivial, and I'd play it cool as if nothing mattered. Ah, the whims of imagination.

I looked up at the sky as a plane passed over, and I thought about my father. How many places he had traveled to and the people he's met. I thought about the letter about Paris. My parents made their love story seem like magic. As if the world was always against them but they always persevered. We all have secrets, even our parents do. I just never thought their relationship would have so many secrets. I wondered if there were more. Ones that were never once written down. My mother always seemed perfectly content with my father always hopping on a plane and leaving us, even if it was only for a few days. And my father never seemed to mind how much my mother loved to work. They certainly weren't traditional, but when they were together, you could see the love between them. I grew up with stars in my eyes because their love seemed so perfect. All this time, I compared my fantasy of love with theirs, and now I don't even know what is real and what isn't.

I opted to retreat to the front porch; the open air

seemed more inviting than the solitude within the house. Seated on the porch, the weathered steps bore witness to years of shared laughter and intimate conversations. The California sun, now dipping below the rooftops, bathed the suburban landscape in a soothing golden glow. It was the distant sounds of children playing and bicycles passing by that provided a gentle backdrop to the tumult of thoughts swirling in my mind.

Life unfolds in a series of unpredictable moments, each laden with its significance. It's within these fleeting instances that the potency of words becomes apparent. Uttering the right words at the right time can wield profound influence over someone's destiny. Yet, the weight of this realization often leads us to second-guess every syllable that escapes our lips, fearing that one misstep could alter everything. However, I've come to recognize that there's a fear even more formidable than misspeaking—it's the dread of allowing those pivotal moments to slip through our fingers, shrouded in silence. The remorse of remaining mute can prove to be an unbearable burden.

Ben's bicycle clattered down the tranquil street before he parked it by the curb and joined me on the porch. His familiar grin welcomed me, dissipating the anxious flutter in my chest.

"Hey, Gigi! My mom mentioned you called home. I was at the skatepark. What's on your mind?" Ben inquired, his voice resonating with the warmth of a summer evening.

Returning his smile, I cherished the simplicity of our bond. "Hey, Ben. I've been contemplating a lot lately, you know?"

"About what?" Ben leaned casually against the porch railing, genuine curiosity gleaming in his eyes.

"About life, about moments, and about seizing them before they slip away," I responded, my gaze trailing to the waning sunlight.

Ben's brow furrowed slightly, sensing the depth beneath my words. "Is everything alright?"

Summoning courage, I traced patterns on the aged wood beneath my fingertips. "Yeah, everything's okay. It's just... I've been holding back, afraid of saying too much or too little. But what if silence is the gravest mistake of all?"

Ben listened attentively, his empathetic gaze urging me onward.

"I suppose what I'm trying to convey is that life affords no room for regrets. I don't want to look back and rue the words left unsaid when the opportunity presented itself," I confessed, vulnerability mingling with resolve in my voice.

Ben nodded understandingly, his reassuring presence a balm to my unease. "Gigi, you can always count on me. I'm here for you, through thick and thin."

A wave of relief washed over me as I met his gaze with gratitude. "Thanks, Ben. I needed to unload that weight. Let's pledge not to let these moments elude us, alright?"

"Absolutely, Gigi. We won't," Ben affirmed, a silent pact forming between us as we watched the sun's descent, its radiant hues painting the sky with a farewell embrace. Amidst the tranquility of the porch amidst the suburban symphony, our connection transcended the unspoken words of the past.

I wasn't quite ready to disclose the letters I unearthed to Ben. I feared it might unsettle him. The revelations about my parents' relationship cast doubt on everything I thought I knew about their love. Though their affection for each other and me was undeniable, their narrative had been spun into a fairy tale. Part of me yearned to confront them about the letters, but what purpose would it serve? It was evidently a cherished secret they intended to keep. For so long, I believed my father was the one making sacrifices. In truth, it was my mother who bore the weight of the greatest sacrifice of all.

59
BEN

Time is a fascinating concept. I used to think of time as a stream of passing cars on the road, but now I see it as both the vehicle and the very path it travels on. Each moment isn't just a fleeting vehicle moving forward; it's also the road that defines its journey. In this understanding, time isn't merely passing by; it's the essence of the journey itself, shaping and being shaped by the moments along its course.

As I sat on Gigi's porch with her, listening to her speak, I wasn't sure what she was trying to convey. It seemed like she wanted to share something significant with me but then changed her mind. None of it made sense to me, but in that moment, it felt like we were back on track.

Neither of us dared to mention the exam or the bet we made. Honestly, I didn't mind. Making the bet with Gigi made us both act out of character. She was overly confident in her ability to beat me, and although she did win in the end, it brought out a side of me that I didn't like. I was unfairly rude to Gigi. Standing up from beside Gigi, I gazed out across the sky. It was ablaze with the vivid hues of a setting sun, resembling an expansive ocean of flickering flames. Waves of crimson, gold, and amber rolled across the horizon, painting the heavens in a fiery tapestry that mirrored the dance of flames on a vast, celestial sea.

"Leaving already, Ben?" she remarked.

"Yeah, I better get home for supper."

She nodded and moved to stand beside me.

"This was nice, Ben."

"Yeah, it was. We should do it again sometime."

"I'd like that." A smile graced Gigi's lips.

I hopped on my bike, thoughts of Gigi swirling in my mind. This may be my chance to ask her on a proper date. With determination surging through me, I abruptly turned my bike around and pedaled back towards Gigi's place, silently hoping she was still outside. As I rounded the corner, relief washed over me—there she was, still on the porch steps.

Gigi immediately stood up as she noticed me dismounting my bike and running up to her porch.

"Ben, did you forget something?" she asked.

"In fact, I did. Gigi, will you go on a date with me?"

Silence fell between us, and my heart raced as I awaited her response. Then, her features softened, and a smile illuminated her face.

"I would love to, Benjamin," she replied, playfully tapping my shoulder.

I couldn't help but grin. "Perfect," I managed to say, though I knew I needed to plan something special. "How about tomorrow at noon? I'll pick you up."

"Perfect," she echoed.

"I'll see you tomorrow at noon, Gigi."

I turned around, exhilaration coursing through me as I sprinted back to my bike. But before I could ride off again, Gigi's voice stopped me.

"Wait! Ben, what are we doing?" she asked.

"It's a surprise!" I yelled.

"Well, can you at least let me know what to wear?"

"Anything you wear will be perfect!" I replied with a smile, hopping onto my bike and riding off.

The few minutes from Gigi's house to mine were a whirlwind of emotions. I had done it. I finally mustered the courage to ask Gigi out. Now, as I pedaled home, the reality sank in: I needed to plan the perfect date. The problem was that I needed to learn more about dating. Gigi was no ordinary girl. She was special, and I wanted our first date to be amazing. Neither of us had our driver's licenses, which complicated things. How could I take her on a proper date without the ability to drive? I would turn sixteen in less than three months, and I had been diligently studying for my driver's test. But even if I had my license now, my parents wouldn't allow me to drive anyone, let alone take Gigi out on a date.

As these thoughts raced through my mind, I began brainstorming alternative ideas for our date. A picnic by the lake or a bike ride through the park? I was determined to make this a memorable experience for Gigi, regardless of my limited resources.

60
GIGI
DATE: SEPTEMBER 1970

In the heat of the moment, everything can change. And sometimes you have to forget about how you're feeling and consider what it is you deserve. So, I decided to push aside my parents' letters and the million little question marks hanging over my head. I deserved to have some fun, and that meant going on my first date with Ben.

Despite the butterflies swirling in my stomach, I knew it was time to take a chance, to step out of my comfort zone. The anticipation of our upcoming date was both nerve-wracking and exhilarating, a welcome distraction from the weight of my worries. Maybe this was exactly what I needed: a chance to escape and embrace the unknown.

I stood in front of my mirror, admiring my outfit. My

look for tonight was a blend of retro charm and effortless cool, perfect for whatever adventure Ben had planned. I wore a high-waisted denim skirt, slightly faded with a row of buttons down the front, paired with a fitted, striped turtleneck top in vibrant shades of mustard and rust. Over my shoulders, I draped a soft, knitted cardigan, its earthy tones complementing the autumn hues of my outfit. On my feet, I slipped into a pair of classic platform shoes, adding just the right amount of height and a touch of vintage flair. Accessories were simple yet stylish: a couple of woven friendship bracelets on one wrist and a pendant necklace with a peace sign dangling from my neck. My hair, styled with loose waves and adorned with a fabric headband, completed the look. I smiled, feeling confident and ready for a fun date ahead, filled with the promise of teenage adventures and carefree moments.

Just then, the doorbell rang. Suddenly, I felt as if my stomach was doing backflips while my heart was doing cartwheels—if that was even possible. Ben was here. I turned to grab my purse before heading to the door. My mother answered it before I could, standing in the atrium with Ben, engaged in conversation. I took a deep breath, smoothing down my skirt one last time, and approached them with a smile. Ben's eyes lit up as he saw me, a grin spreading across his face.

"Hey, Gigi, you look amazing," he said warmly, causing a delightful blush to rise on my cheeks.

"Hi, Ben," I replied, trying to keep my cool. "Thanks! Ready to go?" Ben nodded eagerly. "Definitely."

I said goodbye to my mother as Ben and I walked out

the front door. "What's the plan, Ben?" I asked, eager for the day ahead. Ben grinned, adjusting his bike helmet. "Well, I thought we'd start with a ride through the park. Then maybe grab some burgers at that new joint downtown. After that, who knows? We'll go wherever the day takes us."

I nodded, liking the sound of spontaneity. "Sounds great! Let's go."

With a sense of excitement in the air, we mounted our bikes and pedaled off into the afternoon, ready for an unforgettable date filled with laughter, adventure, and the magic of being young in the '70s.

The cool evening air tousled my hair as we rode through the park. Ben's laughter echoed joyfully in the open space, contagious and bright. He pointed out interesting shapes in the clouds, transforming them into imaginary creatures with a childlike wonder that made me smile.

Pedaling along, Ben shared his latest idea for a short film—a whimsical tale set in our small town, infused with nostalgic charm and unexpected twists. His eyes gleamed with excitement as he described the scenes, each one painted with vivid detail and imaginative flair. Moments like these made me realize how much I admired Ben. His creative energy was infectious, breathing life into ordinary moments and turning them into something extraordinary. My crush on Ben wasn't just about his laughter or kindness; it was about the way he saw the world as a stage waiting to be filled with wonder and magic. We ended up at the lake shore, setting our bikes down and walking over to where the water lapped against the sand. The rhythmic sound of the waves matched the fluttering of my heart. Each wave seemed to echo the anticipation building inside me, rising and falling in sync with my emotions.

Ben picked up a stone and skipped it across the water. I couldn't help but notice how effortlessly he seemed to connect with the natural beauty around us. His laughter mingled with the gentle breeze, creating a harmonious melody that soothed my racing heart. I glanced at Ben, his eyes reflecting the shimmering water, and felt a warmth spread through me like the sun beaming down on us. This moment by the lake shore was more than just a date; it was a glimpse into a world where every heartbeat resonated with the ebb and flow of life's simple joys.

"Hey Ben, can I ask you something?"

"Sure, shoot," he replied. I shifted my gaze towards Ben, my curiosity piqued. "I'm curious," I began, meeting his eyes, "what's it like growing up in California? You've been here your whole life, right?" Ben nodded thoughtfully, the smooth skip of his stone across the water matching his contemplative expression. "Yeah, born and raised. It's pretty chill, I guess. Lots of sunshine, beaches, and stuff. Why do you ask?" "I moved here when I was seven, but sometimes I still feel like I don't quite fit in, you know?"

As boats glided by in the distance and ducks paddled nearby, the scene felt serene. "I get that," Ben nodded in agreement, his eyes scanning the tranquil waters. "California can have its vibe. What's been feeling off for you?"

"I'm not sure. It's like everyone here has these long

histories, and I'm still playing catch up." "You have Martha and the other girls, though."

"Yeah, but it's not the same. Martha and I...well, we're just different," I admitted, my voice trailing off as I hesitated to divulge more. She was my best friend, but we were opposite. Still it wasn't right of me to be talking about her behind her back. Ben didn't press about Martha. Instead, he skipped another stone across the water. "What's the best part about growing up here?" I asked, changing the subject. "Hmm..that's a tough one. Probably the outdoor lifestyle. Skateboarding, surfing after school, hiking on weekends...there's always something fun to do." "That does sound pretty awesome."

"You'll find your groove. And remember, being from New York originally makes you more interesting around here," he said, winking playfully.

"Haha, thanks, Ben. I needed that."

Ben picked up another stone, his fingers deftly caressing its surface before launching it into a perfect skip.

"Wow, Ben, you're really good at skipping rocks! How did you learn to do that?" I asked, admiring his skill.

"Thanks, Gigi! I've been doing this since I was a kid. My father showed me and my brothers one summer down here at the lake. It's a good way to pass the time.

I felt a lump in my throat, briefly wondering if Ben regretted our date. This was my first date, and I didn't know what to say or how to act. I quickly shook off the negative thoughts and refocused on the conversation.

"Sounds like a fun childhood. I wish I had a talent like that. I always end up splashing more than skipping."

"It's all about finding the right rocks. Here, let me show you," he said, handing me a smooth, flat rock.

"Try holding it like this and then flick your wrist gently. Like this."

I attempted to mimic Ben's technique but ended up plopping the rock into the water.

"Oops! I need more practice."

After a failed attempt, I laughed, feeling a bit embarrassed. But Ben was sweet.

"No worries. It's all about having fun."

"This lake is breathtaking. Back in New York, we had parks and rivers, but this lake…it's like a whole new world. And being here with you makes it even better."

"I'm glad you're enjoying it. I'm curious, Gigi, what was it like growing up in New York?"

"Busy, noisy, full of character. Moving here was like stepping into a whole new world."

"Yeah, I can imagine. California's got a different vibe, more laidback. But I bet you brought some of that New York energy with you," he teased.

"Maybe a little. It's just…" I was momentarily speechless. I was nervous and just wanted to say the right thing. Ben didn't seem to notice.

"So, what do you think of this spot?"

"It's beautiful. The calm water, the fresh air…it's a world away…" I let my words falter.

"Exactly. Sometimes, you need a break from it all."

"You know what? I'm feeling inspired. Mind if I give rock skipping another shot?" I asked, reaching for another rock before Ben found the right one.

"Not at all! Here, take this one. Remember, it's all in the wrist."

I took the rock from Ben and gave it a try, sending it skimming gracefully across the water.

"I did it!" I exclaimed, joyfully leaping up and down with excitement.

"Nice one! Looks like you owe me ice cream now."

"First burgers, then ice cream," I noted.

"Fair enough."

We walked back over to our bikes, both smiling at each other. The sun illuminated the lake, igniting a spark of enthusiasm within me for burgers and a sweet treat to cap off the date.

61
BEN

We chose a table on the patio and opened our menus. The waitress came over and placed two cups of iced cold water down, she asked if there were any drinks she could get us started with. Gigi ordered a diet cocoa cola, and I got myself a root beer. I was tempted to order a Shirley Temple, but I was nervous she'd think I was weird for ordering such a girly drink.

"Everything looks so good!" Gigi exclaimed, her eyes scanning the menu.

"I know what I'm getting!" I grinned, leaning forward eagerly.

"And what's that, Benjamin?" Gigi lowered her menu, her gaze fixed on me.

"A burger and chili fries." I couldn't help but lick my lips, my mouth watering at the thought.

"Ah. Well, I want a cheeseburger with all the fixings and just regular fries," Gigi decided.

"Cool beans," I responded casually, my excitement evident.

The waitress arrived at our table carrying our drinks and ready to take the rest of our order. She set down the two frosty glasses of cola with beads of condensation running down the sides. Gigi thanked her and then turned back to me, her eyes sparkling with excitement.

"So, Ben, what have you been up to lately?" she asked, her voice warm and inviting.

I stirred my drink with the straw, considering her question. "Oh, you know, the usual. School, skatepark, chores, and trying to survive my little brother's latest pranks." I chuckled, recalling the antics of my mischievous siblings.

Gigi laughed, her smile lighting up her whole face. "Sounds like quite the adventure. I've been buried under assignments myself. Finals are just around the corner."

We chatted about our classes, swapping stories about challenging teachers. As Gigi spoke, her gestures were animated, her hands punctuating her words.

The scent of sizzling burgers wafted from the kitchen, mingling with the lively chatter around us. Inside, a jukebox in the corner played a familiar tune from the '50s, carrying outside and adding to the nostalgic atmosphere.

"Oh, I love this song," Gigi exclaimed with a bright smile. "My parents used to play it for me and Daisie all the time when we were growing up."

Buddy Holly's classic tune, "That'll Be The Day," filled the air, eliciting a nostalgic spark in Gigi's eyes. Without hesitation, she began to sing along, her voice sweet and confident as she effortlessly recited every word. As Gigi sang, her face lit up with fond memories. I watched, captivated by her infectious energy and the way the music seemed to transport her back in time. Even out on the patio, I could feel the diner's ambiance shift, blending the retro décor with Gigi's animated performance.

Joining in, I tapped my fingers lightly on the table, caught up in the infectious rhythm. The familiar melody brought back my childhood reminiscences, bridging a connection between us.

When the song ended, Gigi grinned at me, her eyes sparkling. "Sorry, I couldn't resist."

"There's no need to apologize," I replied, genuinely touched by her enthusiasm. "You have a great voice."

Gigi's cheeks flushed slightly, and she thanked me before taking a sip of her drink.

The song lingered in the background, creating a comfortable backdrop for our conversation. At that moment, we shared a piece of our past through music, and I felt a deeper connection forming between us, a connection that went beyond casual acquaintance.

Our meals arrived, and we each dug into our burgers. As I took a bite, Gigi sneaked one of my chili fries. I didn't mind sharing with her. After dinner, we strolled to the nearby ice cream shop, conveniently close enough to walk our bikes and secure them outside. Upon entering, we were greeted by a delightful blend of sweet and creamy aromas that filled the air. The moment we stepped inside, a wave of sugary scents enveloped us, instantly sparking a craving for something cold and delicious. The air was redolent with the aroma of freshly made waffle cones and the rich, enticing fragrances of various ice cream flavors.

"What's your favorite flavor?" I asked Gigi.

"Hmm.. it's between mint chocolate chip or chocolate. What about you?" Gigi inquired.

"Hands down Rocky Road," I declared.

"There are so many great flavors. It's hard to choose."

Gigi chose mint chocolate chip, while I opted for Rocky Road. After getting our ice cream cones, we headed outside to sit at a nearby bench. Despite the time, the sun was shining brightly, casting a warm glow over the neighborhood. As we savored each creamy bite, the sweet aroma of waffle cones filled the air, accompanied by the sounds of children playing nearby. It was a perfect afternoon to indulge in something sweet.

We were having such a grand time; I wanted to ask about the bet but didn't want to ruin our date.

"This has been fun, Ben," Gigi remarked with a smile.

"It has been. I'm glad you said yes," I replied warmly.

"Me too." She smiled before taking a lick of her ice cream.

"Gigi, I have a question, and I hope I don't ruin things..." I spoke hesitantly.

"What's your question?"

"Are we still on for our bet? Because if so, then I owe you a week of cleaning your pool. You did win after all..."

"You have a point, Ben. Do you want the bet to still be on?"

"I am a man of my word, Gigi Scott. You won, so it's

only fair that I keep my end of the bargain."

"That seems fair. Well then, starting Monday after school, you can report to duty at my house to clean our pool."

"You got it, Gigi."

Once we finished our ice cream, we got back on our bikes and headed home. Stopping at Gigi's place, I walked her up to the door.

"Thanks again for a lovely time," Gigi said.

"The pleasure is all mine. Let's do this again sometime," I replied.

"I would like that."

Before I could say anything further, Gigi leaned in and kissed me on the cheek.

"Bye, Ben."

"Bye, Gigi." I walked back to my bike and watched as she entered her house and disappeared behind the door.

I rode home with the biggest smile on my face. I just had my first date with Gigi Scott. I stood up from my bike, pumping my fist in the air, only to sit back down quickly in embarrassment, scanning the neighborhood in case anyone saw me. The coast was clear.

62
GIGI

My date with Ben went better than I could have imagined. felt like a girl spinning in a brand-new dress. When I got home, my mother was sitting on the couch with a book in her hand and a glass of wine.

"Hi, sweetie; how was your date with Ben?"

"How did you know it was a date?" I stammered.

I walked over to the couch and sat down next to her.

"Because a mother knows. Besides, you spent all day getting ready, and Ben has never come to 'pick you up' before. I knew something was different."

"I see…"

"Well, how was it?" she asked again.

"It was good. He's… he's a gentleman."

"You like him?"

"I do." I couldn't help but smile at the thought of Ben.

"I'm going to tell you something that my mother once told me. It's okay to be open and to give someone a chance, but don't fall so fast that you lose your head and your heart at the same time."

"What does that mean?" I asked.

"Well, the way I interpreted it is that you're young, and first crushes can feel like a lot. Give Ben a chance, but don't close the door on any other opportunities that come your way."

"Mother, I'm fifteen. I don't know what the future holds for me."

"No, you don't. But your future is bright. I like Ben, but you're my daughter, and I love you more."

"I know you do. And I love you too. Besides, it's just a crush, and it was one date. It's not like I'm rushing to get married."

"Give it time. Ben could be the one or the one is out there and you just haven't met him yet."

"Thanks, Mom." I wrapped my arms around her, holding on tightly as if afraid she might slip away.

Something in the way she hugged me back stirred memories of the letters I had found. A sinking pit settled in my stomach. Was this the moment to share what I had discovered?

"Sweetie, is everything okay?" Her voice held a note of concern, sensing the shift in my demeanor.

I swallowed hard. "Mother, I need to tell you something, but I'm not sure how you'll react."

"Okay…" Her tone was cautious, bracing herself for my news, which I probably made out to be worse than it actually was.

"A few days ago, I was in the attic and stumbled upon a trove of letters between you and Dad—some exchanged, some unsent, and what seemed like journal entries."

"I see…what were you doing in the attic?" She asked, her voice gentle yet probing.

"I don't know, really. I was just at home and felt the urge to explore. I had no idea what I would uncover…"

"You shouldn't go snooping around, but I understand your curiosity about the letters."

"So you know about them? About dad's letters…" My words trailed off, uncertain.

"Well…" She paused, choosing her next words carefully. "Georgia, do you still have these letters, or are they still in the attic?"

"I have them in my room." Guilt etched across my face.

"I'd like to see them," Birdie said, rising from the couch and gesturing towards my room. I led the way, feeling her eyes on my back as we walked.

In my room, she sat on the edge of my bed, her gaze fixed on the letters. I watched as she stared at them, her expression a mix of nostalgia and apprehension, as if each letter held a flood of memories she had long kept hidden. We sat together in a heavy silence. My heart hammered against my ribs, frantic like a caged bird. Each time I attempted to speak, the words caught in my throat, leaving me speechless. I was at a loss for what to say.

I observed her closely as she flipped through the pages, absorbing every word. Occasionally, she would murmur a thoughtful "hmm," a confirming "yep," or an intrigued "oh…" Her reactions varied. Nodding her head, tilting it to the side, or sometimes shaking it back and forth. It wasn't easy to decipher her emotions. Was she upset by the letters, or was she delving deep into her memories? And if it was memories, were they pleasant recollections or moments she wished to erase?

63
BIRDIE

Memories of Roger and me together reignite a powerful flame, evoking feelings of magic and legend. Before our move to California, while packing up the house, I stumbled upon a small box hidden in the garage. Initially, I assumed it contained Roger's old pilot notes, but as I flipped through, I saw my name written within.

A gnawing feeling twisted in my gut. I clutched my chest, willing my heart to slow its pounding. The words leaped off the pages, leaving me reeling. Why hadn't Roger told me about Sylvia? I would have understood. I trusted him, but his silence after all these years shattered that trust. How could I trust him now?

The mind blurs the boundaries of time, reliving painful memories as if they were happening now. Once we confront and gain new perspectives on these experiences, it's crucial to focus on happier moments. By doing so, we can process and release the pain, choosing true healing and self-love, ultimately setting ourselves free. Sitting in Georgia's bedroom, holding the letters in my hands, a rush of memories transported me back to our New York garage as if I were there again.

"Mom, are you okay?" Gigi's voice interrupted my reverie.

Shaking off my thoughts, I replied, "Yes, darling. I'm fine."

I turned to face her, reaching out to gently brush her cheek. A tear slipped from her eye, and I fought to maintain my composure, not wanting to break down in front of her.

"Mom…" Gigi said again.

"I've seen these letters from your father. It was a long time ago, and honestly, I had forgotten all about them."

"Oh, mother, I'm so sorry. I didn't mean to reopen old wounds."

"Nonsense, dear. You couldn't have known."

"When did you find out?" Gigi asked.

"It was right before we moved to California. You and Daisie were playing in the backyard, and your father and I were finishing packing up the house. I stumbled upon the box in the garage."

"Oh…" Gigi's voice trailed off.

Taking a deep breath, I continued. "Gigi, that was a long time ago. Your father and I love each other, and everything we've shared with you and Daisie is true."

"But those letters…Dad had an emotional affair."

Shaking my head gently, I responded, "No, Gigi, you're mistaken. He didn't. Sylvia was a maid at one of the hotels and your father never returned to that hotel or had any contact with her. He planned to tell me the truth, but life got busy, and the letter was forgotten."

"And you believe him?"

"I do, Gigi. Your father loves us. Please trust me when I say he is a good man."

Gigi regarded me with a mixture of concern and uncertainty. "But, Mom, how can you be so sure?"

I sighed softly, grappling with the weight of my convictions. "Because I know your father, Gigi. Despite any misunderstandings or past mistakes, our love has endured. People make choices they regret, but it doesn't define who they are."

She nodded slowly, absorbing my words. "I want to believe you, Mom. It's just that it's hard to ignore after finding those letters."

"I understand, sweetheart," I said, my voice gentle yet resolute. "It's natural to have doubts, especially when faced with unexpected revelations. But trust is built on more than just words. It's built on a lifetime of shared moments and unwavering support."

Gigi's eyes glistened with unspoken questions. "What are we going to do now? Should we confront Dad about this? Does Daisie know?"

I paused, considering the implications. "No, Gigi. This is a private matter between your father and me. I believe in our ability to navigate this together, with love and understanding."

She nodded again, albeit reluctantly. "Okay, mom."

Leaning forward, I enveloped her in a comforting embrace. "Remember, Gigi, our family is built on love and forgiveness. We'll get through this, I promise."

As we sat there, mother and daughter, a sense of unity washed over us. Despite the storm of emotions stirred by the discovery of those letters, a newfound resolve took root within me. I would confront the shadows of the past with courage and grace, guided by the enduring strength of our family bond.

64
GIGI

The days that followed haunted me. I couldn't shake the images of those letters. Part of me wanted to believe my mom's reassurance that she trusted Dad and that there was a reasonable explanation. But another part of me felt a growing urge to confront him, to confront them both together. Why did Mom discourage me from doing so? Was she protecting him, or was there more to this secrecy than she let on?

The idea of covert secrets gnawed at me. What good could come from hiding the truth? I believe in open honesty, except when the truth might cause unnecessary harm. This principle applied to all covert operations, whether they were romantic or otherwise.

I needed answers. The tension in our home was palpable, like a thick fog enveloping us all. Birdie seemed preoccupied, her smiles forced, her eyes distant. Roger, oblivious to the storm brewing within me, carried on as usual, unaware of the turmoil simmering beneath the surface.

One evening, unable to contain my turmoil any longer, I approached Birdie tentatively. "Mom, I need to understand," I began, my voice trembling slightly. "Why don't you want me to confront Dad about the letters?"

She looked at me with a mixture of sadness and resolve. "Gigi, there are things between your father and me that are best left to us to handle. I promise you, we will work through this."

"But, Mom," I pressed. Frustration is building within me. "How can we move forward if we don't address what's happened?"

Mom sighed, her gaze softening. "Sweetheart, trust me when I say that love is not always straightforward. Sometimes, it requires forgiveness and understanding."

Her words offered little comfort, leaving me feeling even more adrift in a sea of uncertainty. I wanted to believe in my parents' love, but doubts continued to gnaw at my heart. The days stretched on, and I grappled with conflicting emotions—loyalty to my family, the desire for transparency, and the overwhelming need for clarity. The clandestine nature of the situation weighed on me like a heavy burden, leaving me questioning the very foundation of trust upon which our family was built.

I needed to get out of the house, away from the lingering tension that seemed to suffocate me. Riding my bike over to Ben's house felt like a welcome escape. Ever since our first date a few weeks ago, we have been spending more and more time together. I suppose it's safe to call him my boyfriend—well, at least that's what I've been calling him in my mind. I pedaled along the familiar route to Ben's, my thoughts racing. What exactly defines a boyfriend-girlfriend relationship? Does he have to ask me to be his girlfriend formally, or do I start referring to him as such? Maybe titles aren't even necessary. We may be two people enjoying each other's company. The uncertainty of it all made me feel both exhilarated and anxious.

When I arrived at Ben's house, a wave of relief washed over me. His place always had a calming effect on me. I leaned my bike against the fence and walked up to the front door, my heart fluttering with a mix of anticipation and nervousness.

Ben greeted me with a warm smile as he opened the door. "Hey, Gigi! So glad you're here."

"Hi, Ben," I replied, trying to push aside the whirlwind of emotions swirling inside me.

As we settled into his comfortable living room, I found myself yearning to confide in him about the turmoil I was experiencing at home. Ben's easygoing demeanor always put me at ease.

"You seem a bit off today," Ben observed, his eyes filled with concern.

I hesitated, unsure of where to begin. "It's just... things at home have been complicated lately."

Ben nodded understandingly. "Do you want to talk about it?"

Taking a deep breath, I opened up to him about the discovery of the letters and the ensuing doubts that plagued my mind. "I don't know what to believe anymore, Ben. I want to trust my parents, but…"

He listened attentively, his presence a reassuring anchor amidst my inner turmoil. "Sometimes, things aren't as clearcut as we'd like them to be," Ben offered gently. "But you'll figure it out, Gigi. Just give yourself time."

His words brought a sense of solace, reminding me that I wasn't alone in navigating the complexities of relationships and trust. Sitting beside Ben, I realized that even amidst uncertainty, moments like these with him offered a sense of stability and comfort that I desperately needed.

Ben stood up from the couch, "Do you want to go get ice cream, Gigi?"

"Now?" I asked.

"Sure. Why not? Ice cream always puts me in a good mood."

I chuckled at the way he said, "Ice cream." He drew out the words with childlike glee, his eyes widening as if he were a kid being offered candy.

"Alright, let's do it," I said. I was grabbing my jacket from the coat rack.

Ben's face lit up with a grin. "Great! There's that new place down the street. They have all sorts of crazy flavors."

As we walked out the door, a light breeze danced across our skin, prompting me to put on my jacket. Leaving my bike propped up by the side fence, we started walking through the neighborhood toward the ice cream shop down the road. It wasn't too far of a walk. Ben started talking about his favorite ice cream flavors, animatedly describing each one with infectious enthusiasm.

"So, what's your favorite?" he asked, glancing at me.

"You already know the answer. Remember our first date?" I winked at him.

"Ah, yes. A tie between mint chocolate chip or was it cookie dough?" he said.

I smiled at the memory of countless summers going to another local shop and getting ice cream with my dad. We'd always savor the flavors. Something inside me made me want to turn back around and talk to Roger. I had to know what he and Mom were thinking.

"Close. It's chocolate, though. But honestly, all flavors are too good to pass up."

He nodded approvingly. "I'm more of a rocky road kind of guy, but maybe I'll try something different this time."

We reached the ice cream shop, its bright neon sign flickering invitingly. The sweet aroma of freshly made waffle cones filled the air as we stepped inside. The shop was cozy, with a retro vibe and an impressive array of ice cream tubs displayed behind the glass counter.

"Welcome! What can I get for you two?" the cheerful attendant asked.

Ben looked at me, "Ladies first."

I scanned the colorful selection, my eyes landing on a new flavor that piqued my curiosity. "I'll have a scoop of

Raspberry Ripple, please. And on a cone would be fine. Thank you."

"Ooh, adventurous choice," Ben said, stepping up to order. "I'll take a scoop of Rocky Road and a scoop of peanut butter fudge."

We found a small table by the window and settled in, savoring our ice cream.

"This was a good idea," I said between bites. "Thanks for dragging me out."

Ben shrugged modestly. "Anytime, Gigi. It's nice to take a break and enjoy the little things, you know?"

I nodded, realizing how true that was. We continued chatting and laughing, the worries of the day melting away with each spoonful of ice cream.

When we got back to Ben's house, the sun was already setting. Before hopping on my bike and riding home, I kissed Ben goodbye. I could taste the remnants of the peanut butter fudge on his lips. How could a kiss make every bad feeling melt away, just like our ice creams? I lingered for a moment, unable to leave just yet. Something was pulling me towards Ben. I wanted to stay longer.

Ben smiled, sensing my hesitation. "You know," he said softly, "you don't have to go just yet. We could watch the sunset together."

I looked into his eyes, feeling the warmth of his offer. "I'd like that," I replied, in a near-silent tone.

He took my hand and led me inside the house and up the stairs. There was a ledge just outside the office window, and we climbed out the window and onto the roof.

We sat down, and Ben wrapped an arm around my shoulders, pulling me close.

"Sometimes," he said, his voice tender, "the best moments are the unexpected ones, like together. I'm glad we did this."

"Me too," I murmured, resting my head against his chest. Watching the sunset, I felt an overwhelming sense of peace and contentment. This was exactly where I wanted to be.

65
BIRDIE
DATE: JANUARY 1971

The house was quiet. Daisie was out with Travis while Gigi was off, most likely with Ben. She didn't say where she was going, only to storm out of the house. I know I should be furious with her. I'm her mother and deserve to know where my kids are at all times. But how could I blame her? She was upset, and rightfully so. Roger would be home any minute now, and it was the perfect time for us to have a conversation.

I sighed, glancing at the clock on the wall. Each tick seemed to echo through the empty house, amplifying my anxiety. Roger and I hadn't had a proper conversation in weeks. He was gone on work trips, and when he was home, it felt like we were just two strangers sharing the same space.

Tonight was going to be different. Tonight, I needed to talk to him about everything: Gigi's recent outburst, the letters, and most importantly, the unspoken tension that had settled between us like a heavy fog. I walked into the kitchen and began preparing some tea, the familiar motions calming my nerves slightly. The kettle whistled, and I poured the steaming water into two cups, placing them on the table. The sound of Roger's car pulling into the driveway made my heart skip a beat. I inhaled deeply, trying to steady myself. This conversation needed to happen, and it needed to happen now.

The front door creaked open, and Roger stepped inside. His face was weary but softening as he saw me. "Hi," he said, his voice gentle.

"Hi," I replied, offering a small smile. "I made us some tea."

He nodded, hanging up his jacket in the front coat closet. "Thanks. That sounds good."

We sat down at the table, the silence between us filled with the sounds of the house settling for the night. I wrapped my hands around the warm cup, searching for the right words.

"Roger, we need to talk," I began, my voice trembling slightly.

He looked up, his eyes meeting mine with a mixture of concern and curiosity. "I know," he said softly. "I've been meaning to talk too."

I took a deep breath, feeling a surge of relief. We could work through this. "It's about the girls. And us. Well, mostly about Gigi. Things have been…interesting lately."

He nodded, taking a sip of his tea. "I've noticed. I'm sorry I've been so absent. Work has been…"

"It's not just work," I interrupted gently. "It's everything. Gigi's been so angry, and I don't know how to reach her. She was in the attic recently and found a trove of letters between the both of us…" My words trailed off. I was grasping for the easiest way to tell him.

His eyes softened, and he reached across the table to take my hand. "I know. I caught Gigi the day she was coming from the attic. However, I didn't know about the letters. This explains why she's been a bit cold towards me as well."

Tears welled up in my eyes, and I squeezed his hand. "We need to be a team again. For them and us."

He nodded, his grip on my hand tightening. "We will be. We'll figure it out together."

"Roger, Gigi thinks you had an emotional affair. I tried to tell her that's not what happened, but she seems inclined to think otherwise. We need to show we have a united front. That our love is stronger than anything that happened in the past. But you flying off to god-knows-where every week isn't doing us any favors."

"And what do you propose I do, Birdie? Quit?" I could hear the anger in his voice, but he remained steady as if he were choking down the heat from within.

"Absolutely not, Roger. But we do need to show Gigi, and Daisie, that love can conquer all. We need a family day."

He nodded. "I would like that very much."

"What if we planned a little trip? School is ending soon,

and it'll be summer. Let's get away, just the four of us."

"Sounds perfect to me." He squeezed my hand again before leaning in for a kiss.

At that moment, the house didn't feel quite so empty. There was still a long road ahead, but for the first time in a while, I felt hopeful. We had a lot to talk about and a lot to work through, but at least we were doing it together. And that was a start.

The next morning, I made a big breakfast and asked for Gigi and Daisie to stay as we had some family matters to discuss. Daisie seemed unphased by the request, while Gigi seemed concerned. I assured her it was all going to be alright. We sat down at the table, passing around a hot plate of pancakes, bacon, eggs, and fruit. I had made a fresh pot of coffee and freshly squeezed orange juice.

"What's the occasion?" Daisie said with a mouthful of eggs.

"Swallow your meal first before speaking, darling," I prompted.

I watched as Gigi took a sip of her orange juice. "Yeah, I want to know too."

"Well, your mother and I have some things to share with you both," Roger said.

"You're not getting a divorce, are you?" Gigi blurted out.

"Excuse you?" Daisie yelled at her sister. "What is the matter with you?"

"No, that is not happening," I said sternly.

"Why on earth would you say that?" Daisie asked Gigi.

"I don't feel comfortable answering that," Gigi responded.

"Can't back up your stupid reasoning," Daisie said angrily.

Gigi stuck her tongue out at Daisie, "I don't have to answer you."

"You're such a brat and a drama queen," Daisie said as she rolled her eyes.

Gigi's eyes started to water, "Am not!"

"See, you're such a baby, too. About to cry."

"That's enough girls!" Roger addressed them both. "Now, your mother and I do have something important to discuss. And I ask you both to be on your best behavior. Understood?"

"Yes, father," Daisie mumbled.

"Sure." Said Gigi.

We began discussing the letters that Gigi had found, carefully explaining their contents to Daisie. She sat quietly, her eyes focused and attentive, unlike Gigi, who had a fiery temperament and quick tongue—traits she undoubtedly inherited from me. Daisie was always more levelheaded, a quality she got from her father.

"Daisie," I began, trying to gauge her feelings. "What do you think about all this?"

She took a moment before answering, her voice steady. "I understand why Gigi is upset, mom. But we need to figure out a way to handle this without tearing each other apart."

Her words were wise beyond her years, and I felt a

surge of pride. "You're right. We need to stay united and communicate better. This affects all of us."

Daisie nodded, a determined look in her eyes. "What happens now?"

A pang of anxiety washed over me. My conversation with Roger last night felt as if we had just started to bridge the gap between us, and now this morning added another layer of complexity. But we needed to face this as a family.

"I have something to say," Gigi spoke up. Her voice trembling slightly.

"What is it, peach?" Roger responded gently. Concern etched on his face.

"Why write letters and then never give them to each other?" Gigi asked, her eyes darting between us.

"We did exchange them eventually," I explained. My heart aches at the memory. "But over time, we forgot about them. When you found the letters, Gigi, all those old feelings came flooding back. It was like reopening a chapter of our lives we had left behind."

Gigi's gaze shifted to Roger, and there was a hint of accusation in her eyes. "Why didn't you tell Mom about Sylvia right away?"

Roger sighed, running a hand through his hair. "I guess I was afraid of making a mountain out of molehill. We were so young, and we both wanted our marriage to be perfect. We thought keeping the bad to ourselves would help, but it was a mistake—a lesson we both had to learn the hard way. I'm not proud of myself for not telling your mother right away. But I didn't do anything wrong, and your mother knows that."

I nodded in agreement, reaching out to squeeze Roger's hand. "It was a different time, Gigi. We were trying to protect each other, but in the end, honesty is what matters most."

Gigi's eyes softened, and she nodded slowly, absorbing our words. "I understand. It's just…hard to process all of this."

"I know it is, sweetheart," I said, my voice gentle. "But we're here, and we're talking about it. That's what matters now."

Roger leaned in, his expression earnest. "We love you both, Gigi and Daisie. We made mistakes, but we're learning from them. And we want to be better for each other and you girls."

Gigi took a deep breath, her tension easing slightly. "I want us to be better too. I just needed to hear it from you."

"We'll get through this together," I assured her, feeling a glimmer of hope. "As a family."

Gigi nodded, a small smile playing on her lips. "Okay. Let's do that."

Gazing around the beautifully set dining room table, with the morning sun streaming through the window, I felt a surge of emotion taking in the sight of my family gathered together. Roger, who had been away on business, was finally back with us, and the joy of knowing he was planning to take a much-needed break was palpable. Daisie and Gigi, who had been at odds this morning, had set aside their differences and embraced each other, their apologies bringing a sense of peace to the room. In that poignant moment, I felt the warmth of our rekindled bond, and I couldn't help but hope that this newfound closeness would endure. Only time would reveal the full extent of our reinvigorated family dynamic.

66
ROGER

I made a promise to Birdie when we said I do. I made a promise to her when we passed on the home I found in New York in order for both of us to chase our dreams. I committed to Birdie when we were in Paris. I made her a promise when we had Daisie and Gigi. I made her a promise when we packed up all our belongings and moved across the country to California.

And now I sit here at the dining room table, making yet another promise. Every promise I've ever made, I intend to keep. And I will do so with my last breath.

I charge ahead with unwavering determination to fulfill my promises, mindful of the delicate balance set by nature's design. Should I stumble, I pledge to mend my wounds and press forward at the earliest opportunity, like a resilient phoenix rising from the ashes.

"This morning was something else, wasn't it?" Birdie sits down in the sofa chair across from me.

I look up from the newspaper, making eye contact. "Indeed it was."

"Roger, I meant it when I said we need to have a united front, especially with the girls getting older."

"I know."

"Do you?"

I folded the newspaper gently in my lap and shifted my body so I was looking directly at her. "Birdie, I know the importance of presenting a united front, especially as our daughters mature. I promise to stand by your side and ensure that we navigate the challenges ahead together, with understanding and solidarity."

Birdie smiled, her eyes reflecting gratitude and relief. "Thank you, Roger," she said softly. She reached across the space between us to place her hand over mine. "Knowing that we're in this together means everything to me."

"I know, Birdie. And I love you."

"I love you too."

When you marry young, every moment feels like an adventure. I can vividly recall the day I first laid eyes on Birdie. The excitement of our dates, the heartaches of our separations, and the fierce determination to fight for our love were each memory is a thread intricately woven into the fabric of our shared journey. As Birdie and I continue to grow together, new challenges inevitably arise. The discovery of our old letters by Gigi was one such unexpected hurdle, but I was relieved when it was resolved swiftly.

With Gigi's sixteenth birthday approaching, Birdie and I felt compelled to plan something truly special for her. We knew we needed Daisie's help, so while Gigi was out with Ben, the three of us gathered to start brainstorming.

"Alright, team, we have a mission. Gigi's Sweet 16 is just around the corner, and we need to make it unforgettable. Birdie, any ideas on where to start?" I said.

"Well, it's the seventies! We should embrace the era. How about a disco theme? We could transform the backyard into a dance floor, complete with a glitter ball," Birdie suggested.

"Oh, that's a great idea, mom! Gigi loves dancing. Plus, we could have a DJ play all her favorite records. But we need more than just music. What about decorations?" said Daisie.

"We can get some neon lights and rent a fog machine to make it feel like a real disco. And what about food? We need some snacks that teens will love."

"We can make it a bit fancy with a fondue set up, cheese, and chocolate. Everyone loves dipping things! And we could also have some classic snacks like pigs in a blanket." Birdie mentioned.

"For drinks, we could do nonalcoholic cocktails. I can make some recipes I saw in a magazine. Virgin pina coladas and Shirley Temples would be fun." Daisie's excitement grew the more she shared her ideas.

"Sounds groovy. Now, about the guest list. We need

to make sure all her friends are there. Daisie, you're in charge of that. Make sure to invite Ben, too."

"Got it, Dad," Daisie replied. "I'll ask her friends at school tomorrow. But we need to keep this a total surprise. Gigi's always been good at figuring things out."

"We can send out the invites discreetly. Maybe we should say it's for a different event and then surprise everyone when they arrive," Birdie suggested.

"That's clever. And what about a gift? We need something really special for her sixteenth birthday."

"How about a locket? Gigi loves jewelry, and a locket with a photo of all of us inside would be perfect." Daisie remarked.

"I love that idea, Daisie. It's personal and something she can keep forever. Roger, can you handle getting the locket?"

"Consider it done. I'll find the perfect one. Alright, team, we have a plan. Let's make this the best Sweet 16 ever for Gigi!"

Daisie was grinning, "She's going to be so surprised! I can't wait to see the look on her face."

"Okay, let's get to work. We don't have much time, and we want everything to be perfect."

67
BEN
DATE: APRIL 1971

Gigi's sixteenth birthday was coming up. Daisie invited me to a surprise party. Having to keep a secret from Gigi was a lot harder than I thought.

We had been spending a lot of time together, neither one of us making a statement about what we were. I considered Gigi to be my girlfriend, but what if she didn't want to be locked down by a title? I knew it was time for me to say something. Should I formally ask her on her birthday? No. I could make her a cake with writing on it. No. I was shaking my head. I don't know how to bake, let alone write anything on a cake. And I definitely can't afford to buy one. I was still shaking these thoughts from my mind. Nothing quite jumped out at me.

While I was out with Gigi, I couldn't help but feel a

knot in my stomach. Should I tell her how I feel on her birthday, or would that overshadow her special day? I hoped she couldn't see through what I was thinking at this very moment. There may be a way to do both. The more I thought about it, the more I realized I needed advice. I could ask Daisie discreetly. She always seemed to know what Gigi would appreciate. She was her sister, after all.

I knew Gigi was going to be at Martha's house, and that was the perfect moment for me to go over and talk to Daisie. I rang the doorbell, and Daisie came to the door.

"Hi, Ben! Gigi isn't home right now, but I can tell her you stopped by."

Just when she was about to shut the door, I placed my foot down to stop her. "Hey, Daisie, I'm actually here to see you. Do you have a moment?"

She pulled the door back open a bit and gestured for me to come inside. Once inside the foyer, we sat down on the nearby bench.

"Sure, Ben. What's up?"

"I've been thinking about Gigi's birthday and, well, about telling her how I feel. I want it to be special, but I don't want to mess it up or take away from her day."

"I get it. Gigi's been waiting for you to say something, you know? Why not write her a letter? It's personal, and she can keep it. You can give it to her after the party so it doesn't take the spotlight away."

"A letter, huh? That sounds like a great idea. Thanks, Daisie. I'll do that."

With a plan in mind, I felt more at ease. Now, all I had to do was write the perfect letter and help make sure Gigi's

Sweet 16 was everything she dreamed of.

* * *

It was the day of the birthday party, and I had spent the entire week crafting the perfect letter for her. In my focus on the letter, I had completely forgotten to get an actual gift. Panicking, I decided on flowers and headed out to my mom's garden. She wouldn't mind—I hoped. I cut a red rose, a yellow rose, and a few of the peonies she was growing. Then, I hopped on my bike and rode through the neighborhood, gathering a few more flowers from other yards. I knew it wasn't the kindest thing to do, but I had to make sure Gigi got the best. Besides, who would miss a few flowers?

When I got home, I went into my mother's sewing room and cut off a long piece of pink ribbon with white polka dots. I rubber-banded the flowers together in a bouquet and tied the ribbon around them. Just then, my mother walked into the kitchen.

"Those are lovely flowers. Who are they for?"

I cleared my throat. "Uh, they're for Gigi. It's her birthday."

"Gigi Scott down the street? You've been spending a lot of time with that girl."

"She's nice," I said, not knowing what else to say.

"Well, I think she will love those flowers."

"Thanks, mom."

I turned to walk out of the room to get ready for the party. Just as I reached the stairs, I heard my mother's voice.

"Oh, and Benjamin, the next time you want to take some of my roses and ribbon, all you have to do is ask."

Busted. I slowly turned on my heel to face her as she stood in the hallway with her hands on her hips.

"Yes, mother. I'm sorry."

"It's alright. But please don't take things from me or anyone else again. Understood?"

"Understood."

I turned and ran up the stairs as fast as I could. I set the flowers down next to the lettering before hopping in the shower.

The party had a disco theme. After my shower, I stood in front of my closet, contemplating what to wear. The disco then called for something special, something that would make an impression. I rummaged through my clothes until I found the perfect outfit.

First, I pulled out a pair of flared jeans. They were light blue and hugged my legs until they flared out dramatically at the bottom, almost covering my shoes. I slipped them on, the fabric soft but snug, fitting just right. Next, I grabbed a bold, patterned shirt. It was bright orange with swirling white and yellow designs, reminiscent of a lava lamp. The fabric was silky and cool against my skin. I left the top few buttons undone, knowing I looked the quintessential 70s vibe. I found an old leather belt with a large, round buckle and threaded it through the loops of my jeans. The belt added just the right touch of retro flair, the buckle gleaming under the bedroom light.

On my feet, I wore platform shoes. Not my typical getup but I had to look the part. These added a few inches to my height and had a funky, multicolored design that matched the psychedelic patterns of my shirt. The soles were thick and solid, making each step feel significant. I completed the look with a pair of aviator sunglasses. The tinted lenses gave everything a warm, golden hue and made me feel like a true disco star.

I took one last look in the mirror, smoothing down my hair. I didn't have time to style it into a perfect do, but the natural waves would have to do. If Gigi didn't fall in love with me tonight—maybe she never will. I grabbed the bouquet and the letter, taking a deep breath before heading downstairs.

As I descended, I heard my mother call out, "Looking groovy, Ben!" I couldn't help but smile. I felt ready to impress Gigi, and I hoped she would love both the flowers and the effort I had put into my outfit.

With one last look in the mirror by the front door, I headed out, ready for a night of disco and celebration.

68
```
GIGI
DATE: APRIL 1971
```

Birthdays serve as a special and meaningful celebration, symbolizing the passage of another year in which we are granted 365 days to spread job, kindness, and positivity to make the world a more delightful and enriched place for all individuals.

It was my birthday! I immediately threw the covers off, jumped out of bed, and ran to my mirror to take a good look at myself. I was finally sixteen! This was the moment I had been waiting for. And to top it all off, I passed my driver's test. I was officially a full-fledged licensed driver, ready to conquer the world or at least attempt to conquer it before my curfew.

With a wide grin plastered on my face, I dashed down the hallway, practically tripping over my excitement. As I reached the kitchen, my family greeted me with cheers and hugs, their smiles mirroring my own. The table was adorned with balloons, confetti, and a towering pancake with candles spelling out "Sweet 16." After blowing out the candles and making my birthday wishes, I couldn't wait to hop into the car and hit the open road. To top this ever-so-sweet 16, Grandma "Grams" Sutton gave me her old car. She couldn't drive as well and decided it was time to pass it on to me under one condition: I had to share it with Daisie. Which was only fair, or so I had to believe it was fair. But today was my day, so Daisie had to let me have my moment. But first, there was the traditional birthday breakfast I had with my family. Each moment was a gift, like a treasure waiting to be discovered. I looked around the table, filling up with so much love.

Finally, it was time to embark on my first solo drive as a licensed driver. With the car keys in hand, adrenaline coursing through my veins, and Daisie in the passenger seat, I pulled out of the driveway and onto the road ahead. The wind tousled our hair as we cruised down familiar streets, feeling a newfound sense of freedom and independence. As we merged onto Pacific Coast Highway, the salty breeze swept through the open windows, instantly invigorating our senses. With one hand confidently steering the wheel, I let the other dance playfully in the wind, feeling the rush of freedom coursing through my veins. Daisie cranked up the radio, and the infectious beat of "Waterloo" by ABBA filled the car, prompting spontaneous laughter before we enthusiastically joined in, singing along at the top of our lungs.

"Pull over here!" Daisie motioned to the side of the road, which had white sandy beaches sprinkled below.

I did as she said and pulled over before shutting off the engine. We both took in the air, the sun beating down on us. Daisie got out first and walked over to the edge of the cliff. I followed suit. Both of us stared out into the vastness of the ocean.

"I don't understand how anyone could hate California," I said, the admiration for our home state evident in my voice.

"I can," Daisie replied cryptically, her expression hinting at deeper thoughts. "But I also can't imagine myself leaving."

"What do you mean you can?" I pressed. I am eager for insight into her enigmatic statement.

Daisie hesitated for a moment, her gaze shifting before she responded, "Another time."

"Oh, come on, Daisie. You can't just say that and then expect me not to ask questions."

"Well, if you really want to know..." her voice trailed off, uncertainty flickering in her eyes.

"I do," I affirmed, sensing there was more to her reluctance than met the eye.

"California has its flaws, as do many other places in this world," Daisie began cautiously. "But those flaws can push people to their limits. I can see why some people might want a fresh start."

"I see. And you aren't going to elaborate on these so-called flaws?" I prodded gently, noting the change in her demeanor.

Daisie turned to look at me, a fleeting regret flashing across her features.

"Gigi, it's your birthday. I want to talk about something other than the flaws of our state. I'm sorry I brought it up."

"It's okay, Daisie. Consider it wiped from today's conversation." I reassured her, sensing her discomfort. I respected her boundaries, and understanding reticence hinted at underlying concerns about California, ones that mirrored my own growing doubts.

"Look, there's a path over here. Shall we head down to the beach?" Daisie pointed out, clearly desperate to change the subject.

"Let's!" I agreed.

I followed Daisie as we made our way down the steps and onto the beach. The sand was thick and hot when it touched our bare feet. Feeling the heat underneath, we both ran as fast as we could in search of cooler sand. As we got closer to the water, both of us laughed uncontrollably.

"Oh, Gigi, you should see yourself run." Daisie bubbled with laughter, making fun of the way I ran through the hot sand.

"Well, you should put a mirror to yourself, too."

"Fair enough. But really, why was that sand so intense?"

"Sun, I suppose." I shrugged.

"Let's dip our toes in the water."

"Race you!" I screamed as I bolted for the water.

"Hey, wait for me!" Daisie called out, following behind

me.

My feet touched the cold salt water, and I felt an immediate rush of relief. The waves continued to crash up against my ankles. As Daisie and I frolicked in the water, splashing each other and laughing. This had to be the most special birthday. Time snuck away from us—it had to be nearly noon and so we decided it was time to head back into town. Daisie wouldn't share any details, just that she had something special planned and that we needed to get ready.

We headed back to the car and continued through PCH before making it back onto the city streets. Every neighborhood looked so different in the driver's seat. I was always a passenger, but something about being the driver made it seem like another town.

I pulled into the driveway and headed into the house.

"Hey, Daisie," I said before heading to the bathroom to shower.

"Yeah, Georgia."

"Thanks for today. It was really special."

"Yeah, it was, wasn't it?" She smiled before heading into her room.

"Well, I'm going to shower and get ready. Any idea what I should wear?"

"Hurry up, I need to shower too. And your outfit is already picked out and on your bed FYI." Daisie winked at me before shutting her bedroom door.

I quickly took a shower, excitement building as I rushed back to my room. On my bed lay an outfit that perfectly captured the disco essence of the 70s. There was a shimmering silver halter top covered in sequins that caught the light and sparkled with every movement. Paired with it were high-waisted bellbottom pants in a matching silver fabric, flaring dramatically at the ankles. A wide, glittery belt cinched at the waist completes the ensemble. To top it all off, I found platform shoes that added at least three inches to my height. Alongside the outfit, there was a pair of large hoop earrings and a chunky, metallic bracelet, adding to the retro vibe.

A note from Daisie lay on top of the clothes, reading, 'Get ready to shine, Dancing Queen!' I couldn't help but smile, feeling a rush of anticipation for what awaited me.

69
GIGI

Daisie placed a blindfold over my eyes, her fingers brushing my temples as she adjusted it snugly. She carefully guided me down the hallway, her hand warm and reassuring in mine. Just moments ago, she had knocked on my door with an excited grin, asking if I was ready. When I said yes, she told me to wait, promising to return shortly. The anticipation made each second stretch into eternity, and soon enough, she was back.

"Put this on," she said, pressing a soft handkerchief into my palm.

I held it up, eyeing both her and the handkerchief curiously.

"Go on, Gigi!" she urged, her eyes twinkling with mischief.

With a reluctant shrug, I placed it over my eyes. She

deftly tied it behind my head, the fabric smooth and cool against my skin.

"How am I supposed to see where I'm walking?" I asked, my voice tinged with apprehension.

"I'll guide you. Do you trust me?" she replied, her tone gentle but firm.

"Do I have any other choice?" I teased back.

Daisie laughed, the sound light and infectious. "Nope. You do not. Now come on, birthday girl."

She took my hand again, her grip reassuring. I followed her lead, and the world around me was reduced to darkness. My other senses heightened: Daisie's light floral perfume, the faint creak of the floorboards beneath our feet, and the muffled hum of distant voices. My fingers itched to lift the blindfold, curiosity burning inside me.

"No peeking, Gigi," Daisie said. Her voice was laced with knowing amusement.

"Fine!" I grumbled. Surrendering to the mystery.

Suddenly, we halted, and I stumbled slightly, my foot catching on the edge of a rug.

"Can I take this thing off now?" I asked. My impatience bubbled over.

"Not yet. Hang tight."

She told me not to move, and I heard her opening the back slider door. *If she's going to push me in the pool after I get all ready, I'll be so mad...*

Just then, she tugged at my blindfold, and as it slipped away, my eyes took a moment to adjust to the sudden burst of light. When they finally focused, I was met with a scene that left me utterly speechless. The backyard was filled with the familiar faces of all my friends and family, their smiles wide and eyes twinkling with excitement. The air buzzed with a contagious energy, and then, all at once, they erupted in the loudest "SURPRISE!" I had never heard. For a split second, my mind couldn't quite process the sight before me. My heart raced, pounding against my chest like a drum. I stood frozen, mouth agape, as a wave of joy and disbelief washed over me. Surprised was an understatement; I was utterly astonished, overwhelmed by the sheer magnitude of the moment.

Friends came to give me hugs and wish me a happy birthday, and I felt enveloped in a warm cocoon of love. The backyard was a kaleidoscope of colors and lights, buzzing with laughter and the faint strains of disco music. The patio had been transformed into a makeshift dance floor, complete with a sparkling mirrorball twirling under the patio cover, casting a myriad of reflections that danced across the crowd.

Just then, I saw my parents making their way towards me, their faces lit up with pride and joy.

"Mom, Dad—I can't believe you put this all together!" I exclaimed, stretching out my arms to embrace them both.

"We couldn't have done it without Daisie," Birdie replied, her eyes twinkling with affection.

"Happy Birthday, peach," Roger said, his voice warm and tender.

"Thanks, Dad. This is really something…"

"We're so glad you like it, sweetie. Happy Sweet 16." Birdie pulled me in for another hug, her embrace tight and filled with love.

When I pulled away from her hug, I noticed Ben lingering at the edge of the crowd, his eyes catching mine. My heart skipped a beat.

"Hey there, birthday girl," Ben said as he approached, his smile bright and genuine.

"Thanks, Ben. I'm glad you could make it." My voice wavered slightly, butterflies swirling in my stomach.

"Yeah, this is really neat. Quite the shebang," he said, glancing around appreciatively at the decorations and the disco ball.

"It is," I agreed. I suddenly felt nervous. My palms felt clammy, and I resisted the urge to fidget.

"There are for you," he said, presenting me with a bouquet of the most beautiful flowers I had ever seen. Their vibrant colors stood out against the backdrop of the yard.

"Wow, Ben. These are stunning. Thank you so much." I took the bouquet, inhaling the sweet fragrance.

"You're welcome. I believe the birthday girl deserves something as beautiful as she is."

Blushing, I stammered, "Oh, Ben, you're so sweet." Impulsively, I leaned in to kiss him on the cheek, only to realize with a start that my red lipstick had left a mark.

"Oh, I'm so sorry," I said, hurriedly turning to retrieve a napkin. I handed it to him, my cheeks burning.

"I don't mind," Ben replied, taking the napkin and gently rubbing at his cheek. He grinned. "Are you trying to brand me, Gigi?"

"So what if I am?" I teased back, a playful smile tugging at my lips.

Before Ben could respond, Martha came barging up, her eyes sparkling with mischief. "Get a room, you two!"

"Hi there, Martha," Ben said, his tone lighthearted.

"Benjamin," Martha snarked, rolling her eyes but smiling all the same.

Ben smirked, not missing a beat. "Jealous, Martha? I can get you a bouquet, too, if you're feeling left out."

Martha crossed her arms, pretending to be offended. "As if, Ben. You'd have to do a lot more than that to impress me."

He laughed a carefree sound that made my heart flutter. "It's a good thing I'm not trying, then."

I couldn't help but chuckle at their banter. "You two are impossible."

Martha winked at me. "Just keeping him on his toes, Gigi."

Ben shook his head, feigning exasperation. "Well, as much fun as this is, I think the birthday girl deserves a dance. What do you say, Gigi?"

My breath caught in my throat. "A dance? I—sure, I'd love to."

Ben extended his hand, and I placed mine in his, feeling a spark of excitement. He led me to the makeshift dance floor, the mirrorball casting shimmering patterns over everyone. The music changed to a slow romantic tune, and Ben pulled me close, his hand warm on my waist. We swayed to the music, 'Helplessly Hoping' by Crosby, Stills & Nash playing softly in the background. Its harmonies wrapped around us like a warm embrace, creating a moment of perfect serenity. I looked up into his eyes, feeling a mixture of nervousness and happiness fluttering in my chest. "You're a good dancer," I said softly.

He grinned. "I have my moments. And you're not so bad yourself."

We danced in comfortable silence for a moment, the world around us fading away. Just then, Daisie's voice rang out from the sidelines, "Alright, lovebirds, don't hog the dance floor!"

Ben chuckled but didn't let go. "I think Daisie's the one who's jealous now."

I laughed, feeling lighter than air. "Maybe so."

The song ended, and Ben gave me a twirl before dipping me gently. As he pulled me back up, our faces were inches apart, and for a moment, everything else disappeared.

"Happy sweet 16, Gigi," he whispered.

"Thank you, Ben," I replied, my heart pounding.

Just as the song ended, we began to pull away. The unmistakable melody of "Dancing Queen" by ABBA echoed through the speakers. The familiar tune brought a new surge of energy to the party.

Out of nowhere, Daisie rushed onto the dance floor, her eyes sparkling with excitement. "This one's for you, birthday girl!" she giggled, grabbing my hands and pulling me away from Ben. She started to sing along, her voice blending with the music, and pointed at me as she belted out, "Only 16!" changing the lyrics because it was my sweet sixteen. I couldn't help but laugh, feeling a wave of joy wash over me. I really was having the time of my life. Daisie's enthusiasm was infectious, and soon, we were both dancing and singing along to the iconic chorus. The crowd around us cheered and clapped, creating a lively, celebratory atmosphere.

"Come on, everyone!" Daisie called out, encouraging our friends and family to join us on the dance floor. The disco ball cast shimmering lights over us as people soon filled the patio, dancing and singing.

Ben stood at the edge of the dance floor, watching with an amused smile. He gave me a playful wink, and I felt my heart skip a beat. But at that moment, surrounded by the people I loved and the music that filled the night air, I felt truly happy and carefree.

As the song reached its crescendo, Daisie twirled me around, and we both dissolved into fits of laughter. "Happy sweet 16, sister!" she shouted over the music, pulling me into a tight hug.

"Thank you, Daisie," I said, hugging her back just as fiercely. "This is the best birthday ever."

As "Dancing Queen" ended, I took a deep breath, thinking I could finally catch my breath. But then, "You're so Vain" blared through the speakers, and my heart raced with excitement. I squealed with delight, turning to Ben with a mischievous grin, wiggling my hips, and pointing at him in time with the beat.

"Come on, Ben!" I motioned for him to join me, but he just stood there, shaking his head with a smile. Not taking no for an answer, I ran over and grabbed his hands, pulling him onto the dance floor.

We laughed as we danced, our movements carefree

and joyful. The night we flowed with a soundtrack of timeless hits—everything from The Eagles to Van Morrison to Fleetwood Mac and plenty of ABBA. Each song captured a moment, etching it into my memory. Ben and I spun and twirled, our laughing mingling with the music. The disco ball cast a dazzling array of colors over us, creating a magical, almost surreal atmosphere. Now and then, I would catch his eye, and we would share a smile that made my heart race.

As the night wore on, the backyard became a blur of happy faces, vibrant lights, and unforgettable melodies. It felt like a dream, one that I never wanted to end. We danced until our feet ached and our faces hurt from smiling, the music carrying us through the night.

70
BEN

The night was winding down, and most of the partygoers were making their way home. I lingered, wanting to be the last one. This would be my chance to give Gigi my letter. I spotted Gigi sitting by the pool, and her bellbottoms rolled up as she dangled her feet in the water. The faint shimmer of the pool lights reflected off the water, casting gentle ripples of light on her face.

"Was tonight everything you could dream of?" I asked as I walked up and sat down next to her.

She turned towards me, her eyes sparkling with the remnants of the night's joy. "It was so magical, Ben. Thanks for coming."

"I wouldn't have missed it for anything." I took this moment to reach for her hand. She didn't pull away, which I took as a good sign.

We sat there in comfortable silence. I gently played with the rings on her fingers, spinning them around. Her skin was soft, her delicate fingers resting trustingly in my hand.

We sat there in comfortable silence. The cool night air enveloped us, and the gentle lapping of the pool water created a soothing backdrop. The remaining party sounds faded into the distance, leaving just the two of us in our little bubble of tranquility.

"Gigi," I began, speaking in a near whisper. "There's something I've been meaning to tell you." I could feel my heart pounding, the letter in my pocket suddenly feeling heavy with the weight of unspoken words.

She gazed at me, her eyes full of curiosity and something else—anticipation, perhaps. "What is it, Ben?"

I took a deep breath, summoning all my courage. "I wrote you a letter," I said, reaching into my pocket and pulling out the neatly folded envelope. "I've been carrying it around, waiting for the right moment to give it to you."

Her eyes widened with surprise, and she took the envelope from my hand, her fingers brushing mine and sending a shiver up my spine. "A letter? For me?"

"Yes," I said, nodding. "It's…well, it's everything I've been wanting to say but didn't know how."

She smiled softly, her eyes never leaving mine. "Can I read it now?"

I hesitated for a moment, then nodded. "Sure."

Gigi unfolded the letter carefully, her eyes scanning the words I had poured my heart into. As she read, I watched her face for any sign of her thoughts, my own emotions a whirlwind of hope and fear.

When she finished, she looked up at me, her eyes shimmering with unshed tears. "Ben, I...I don't know what to say. This is the sweetest thing anyone has ever done for me."

I reached out, gently cupping her face in my hand. "You don't have to say anything, Gigi. I just needed you to know how I feel."

She leaned into my touch, closing her eyes briefly as if savoring the moment. "I feel the same way, Ben," she whispered, her voice thick with emotion. "I was just too scared to admit it."

A wave of relief washed over me, and I pulled her into a tender embrace. We stayed like that for what felt like an eternity, wrapped in each other's warmth and the promise of something beautiful.

The distant sound of a car engine brought us back to reality, and we reluctantly pulled apart. Gigi looked at me, a smile playing on her lips. "Let's not let this night end just yet. Besides, it's my birthday," she said, her voice filled with newfound determination.

I smiled back, feeling a surge of happiness. "What do you have in mind?"

She stood up, pulling me to my feed. "How about one last dance?" she suggested, glancing at the makeshift dance floor that was now deserted.

"I'd love that," I replied, taking her hand as we walked over to the patio.

Gigi found the portable radio and tuned it to a slow, romantic song. As the music filled the air, we wrapped our arms around each other and swayed gently to the rhythm, the world fading away once more. Under the starry sky, we danced together, the night stretching on with endless possibilities. And in that moment, surrounded by the remnants of the party and the promise of tomorrow, I knew that this was just the beginning of our story.

In Gigi's presence, I experienced a profound sense of connection, as if our very souls were entwining and reaching out to one another. It was on Gigi's birthday that I mustered the courage to ask her to be my girlfriend, pouring my heart into a letter that expressed my feelings in countless ways. Her response, though simple, spoke volumes to me. With Gigi Scott officially by my side, I felt an overwhelming desire to proclaim our love to the world from the highest mountains to the rooftops of every building. I longed to share with the entire town that Gigi was mine, and I was hers.

71
GIGI

In the face of emotional turmoil, a woman exercises restraint, carefully considering her responses instead of succumbing to impulsive reactions. Her presence exudes serenity and compassion, bringing a sense of peace to even the most trying circumstances.

Like a steadfast mast in a storm, she remains unshaken, demonstrating unparalleled strength and resilience reminiscent of the most revered historical figures. Romance is a complex and deeply personal experience that cannot be acquired through material means. True emotions go beyond physical objects, creating a connection that is intangible and profound. It is a depth of feeling that exceeds any material offering, encompassing a range of emotions and experiences unique to each individual.

Upon reading Ben's letter, it was as if a jigsaw puzzle

suddenly had fallen into place. Each word was carefully chosen, resonating deeply and revealing his heart and intentions. In his heartfelt prose, Ben officially asked me to be his girlfriend. My heart swelled with joy, and I knew without hesitation that the only right answer was yes. I've come to realize that romance is found in simple, unexpected gestures: a delicate flower carefully plucked from our garden, its petals soft and fragrant; an impromptu kiss that steals my breath away; a lingering, warm second hug before parting. These moments encapsulate the essence of romance, the profound connection I feel whenever I'm near Ben.

As I held the letter close, I could almost feel his presence, the tenderness of his words wrapping around me like a warm embrace. At that moment, I understood that true romance is not grandiose or ostentatious but rather a collection of small, meaningful acts that speak directly to the heart. That night, I lay on my bed, rereading Ben's letter.

Dear Gigi,

I've been wanting to find the right words to say to you for a while now, and I hope this letter does justice to the feelings I've been carrying in my heart. From the moment I met you, there was something different about you, something that drew me in and made me want to get to know you better. Your smile lights up the room, and your laughter is like music to my ears. But it's not just your outward beauty that captivates me, it's the kindness and warmth you show to everyone you meet, the way you make people feel valued and appreciated.

I've spent countless hours thinking about you, wondering if you feel the same way about me. And now, as I write this letter, I realize that I can't keep these feelings to myself any longer. Gigi, I care about you more than words can express. You've become such an important part of my life, and I can't imagine it without you. I want to be there for you, to support you, and to encourage you in everything you do. I want to laugh with you, cry with you, and share all of life's ups and downs. So, with all of that being said, I have a question for you, one that I've been working up the courage to ask. Gigi, will you be my girlfriend? I understand if you need time to think about it, but I hope with all my heart that you'll say yes.

No matter what your answer is, please know that I cherish our friendship more than anything, and I'll always be here for you, no matter what.

With all my love,
Ben

Reading Ben's heartfelt words, I felt a rush of emotions flood through me. Each line resonated deeply within me, touching the very core of my being. I could feel the sincerity in every word, the depth of Ben's feelings shining through the ink on the page. As I lay on my bed, bathed in the soft glow of my bedside lamp, I traced my fingers over the familiar handwriting, committing each word to memory. Ben's letter spoke directly to my heart, capturing the essence of our connection in a way that left me breathless.

Tears welled up in my eyes as I read and reread the

letter, each pass through its contents bringing a fresh wave of emotion. I felt overwhelmed by the love and affection pouring out of his words, grateful for the depth of our bond.

72
BEN
DATE: MAY 1971

With each passing day, the last remnants of spring faded away, a triumphant announcement echoed through the skies: Summer had finally unfurled its vibrant banners. The sun, once a shy visitor, now stood proudly at the helm, casting its golden tendrils across the land, enveloping everything it touched in a warm embrace. It was a season ripe with promise, beckoning us to step out of our winter cocoons and into the world of endless possibilities.

My anticipation for the upcoming summer knew no bounds, especially as I anticipated the moments I would share with Gigi, my cherished companion. We had meticulously crafted plans that spanned the spectrum of summer delights. From lazy days at the beach to spontaneous explorations of quaint towns, from winding hikes along nature trails to blissful afternoons by the pool. Each adventure promised to be a chapter in our shared story of summer bliss.

On the day of our planned beach excursion, I eagerly embarked on the journey, my heart aflutter with excitement. With the hum of the engines as my companion, I navigated the familiar streets, only a couple blocks down to Gigi's. Parking the car with a sense of purpose, I made my way to the entrance, my footsteps echoing in anticipation of the reunion that awaited. While I stood before the door, a symphony of emotions played within me, each note a chord of excitement, nervousness, and affection. With a composed demeanor, I reached out to ring the bell, feeling the weight of the moment settle upon my shoulders. Hands clasped behind my back, I awaited her arrival with bated breath, every passing second stretching out into eternity.

The sound of approaching footsteps heralded her presence, each step a rhythmic melody that danced upon the air. And then, like a vision materializing from the depths of my longing, there she stood, Gigi, radiant and resplendent, her smile a beacon of warmth that illuminated the space between us. In an instant, she crossed the threshold and into my awaiting embrace, the familiarity of her touch a balm to my soul.

"Ben!" Her voice was like a melody crafted specifically for my ears, ringing through the air and infusing the moment with an ethereal charm. I savored the way she uttered my name, each syllable carrying the weight of our shared history.

With our hands intertwined, we made our way to the car, each step a testament to the day that lay before us. As I opened the passenger door, a spontaneous impulse seized me, drawing her closer until our lips met in a tender embrace. In that fleeting moment, amidst the backdrop of a sun-kissed driveway, time seemed to stand still, encapsulating a universe of emotions within the gentle caress of our lips. It was a kiss born of longing and desire, a silent proclamation.

We arrived at Point Dume, a picturesque haven nestled along the coastline of Malibu. As I eased the car off the road and brought it to a gentle halt, the allure of the beach beckoned us forth with its siren song. But before I could even reach for the door handle, Gigi, ever the embodiment of boundless energy, leaped from the car with a vitality that left footprints etched into the soft sand, a testament to her impulsive spirit.

"Come on, Ben!" Her buoyant voice carried on the salty breeze as she waved me forward, her enthusiasm infectious and irresistible.

With a fond smile playing on my lips, I gathered the remaining accouterments of our beach adventure—the meticulously stacked beach towels and the picnic basket lovingly prepared by my mother—and followed in her wake.

Catching up to Gigi, I found her in the midst of spreading out a blanket, the vibrant colors contrasting beautifully against the sun-kissed sand. Positioned with meticulous precision, it offered us the perfect vantage point—neither too close to the lapping waves nor too distant from their rhythmic embrace, striking a delicate balance between proximity and safety.

Gigi, ever the purveyor of simple pleasures, reached for the cooler with anticipation, her fingers deftly plucking a succulent grape from its confines. With a delighted hum, she savored each bite, the sweetness of the fruit mingling with the salty tang of the sea air in a symphony of flavors.

"Mmmm, delicious!" her voice, a melodic chorus of satisfaction, filled the air as she reached for another grape, her enjoyment palpable in every movement.

Caught in the spell of her joy, I found myself momentarily captivated by the sight before me—the way the sunlight danced in her hair, the laughter that bubbled forth from her lips, and the sheer exuberance that radiated from her being. As I stood on the sun-drenched beach, I was engulfed by a fleeting moment that filled me with an overwhelming sense of gratitude. It was a profound feeling sparked by the simple yet meaningful moments we had shared.

"Let's go down to the water, shall we?" I asked, my voice low and inviting as I looked at Gigi with an impish grin.

"Alright," she exclaimed, her eyes shimmering with delight as she sprang up from the blanket, her laughter echoing through the afternoon air like a joyous celebration.

I reached out my hand, feeling a rush of warmth when her fingers mingled with mine. Together, we made our way down to the water, the sand cool and soft beneath our feet. The sun hung high in the sky, painting the world in a palette of blues and greens.

As we reached the water's edge, the gentle waves lapped at our toes, sending a shiver up our spines. Gigi giggled and squeezed my hand, her eyes meeting mine with a mischievous glint.

"It's so refreshing," she remarked, dipping her toes into the cool water.

"Refreshing, huh? I can think of something even more refreshing," I teased, winking at her.

Her laughter was music to my ears. "Oh really? And what's that?" she asked, playing along.

"Maybe a little splash fight?" I suggested, already scooping up water in my hands.

Gigi's eyes lit up. "You're on!" she exclaimed, retaliating with her handful of water.

And so it began, our playful battle against the waves. Laughter filled the air as we chased each other along the shoreline, the cool water providing relief from the summer heat. Gigi was quick and agile, ducking and dodging my attempts to soak her. But eventually, I managed to catch her, wrapping my arms around her waist and pulling her close. We were breathless from laughter, our faces inches apart as we caught our breath.

"I think I win this round," I declared, a smirk playing on my lips.

Gigi raised an eyebrow, a mischievous glint in her eyes. "Oh, is that so? I guess you'll have to claim your prize then," she said, leaning in closer.

Before I knew it, our lips met in a sweet, lingering kiss, sealing our playful afternoon. The sun was shining down on us, and the waves whispered secrets to the shore. I wanted more than anything for this summer with Gigi to be unforgettable.

73
GIGI

That's the funny thing about plans. When you try to plan something out—God laughs. I thought Ben and I would have the summer to ourselves. I finally had a boyfriend, someone I could go on dates with. This summer was going to be marvelous.

When I got home from the beach, my parents and Daisie were waiting. My heart stopped. I thought something terrible happened, and in a way, it did. That day, I learned that my personal summer plans were turning into my parents' summer plans. I know most girls would dream of a summer like this, but I wanted my summer with Ben.

"Gigi, honey, we have some news to share," Roger said as he gestured to the nearby chair.

I walked over slowly. "Gee Gigi, how was the beach? Oh, did you and Ben have a lovely time? I'm sure you're excited for the summer?" I mocked.

Birdie sighed. "Gigi, we aren't trying to ruin your summer."

"Okay." I sat down and folded my arms. Ready to listen.

"Girls, your mother and I want to start doing more things as a family. So this summer we'll be traveling to Europe. You'll get the chance to experience life abroad."

"Really? I'm so excited!" Daisie practically leaped out of her chair.

Part of me wanted to be equally excited, but it also meant my summer plans with Ben were coming to a screeching halt.

I wanted to run out of the house, get a getaway car, and run to Ben at that moment.

"What do you think, peach?" Roger looked.

"Oh well, that sounds great, I suppose."

"Gigi, we are having a European summer! Get excited!" Daisie latched onto my shoulders, shaking my whole body back and forth.

"Sweetie, I know Ben is your first boyfriend. But you will have plenty of time to spend with him. This isn't the end." Birdie reached out to place her hand over mine.

I pulled away swiftly before jumping out of the chair.

"I need air." I walked out of the room and out the front door.

My heart was racing. Why wasn't I excited? Everyone dreams about a European summer, and here I was, getting the opportunity, and yet all I could think about was Ben.

I started to walk. I was still determining where I was

heading, but I knew I needed to move. Suddenly, I heard a voice behind me.

"Gigi, wait!" I turned to see Daisie chasing after me.

She caught up to me, and we walked in silence for a bit.

"Gigi, do you want to talk about it?" Daisie asked.

"Not really."

"Okay."

I let out a deep breath. "It's just not fair, you know? I'm finally old enough to drive, I have this amazing boyfriend and I was really looking forward to doing my own thing this summer."

"Gigi, I hate to break it to you. But there's more to life than driving aimlessly and spending your days with the cute boy down the street."

I rolled my eyes at her comment. "You don't understand, Daisie."

"I think I do. I've been in your shoes, Georgia. Remember when Travis and I first started dating, and Mom and Dad planned that two-week-long road trip?"

I chuckled, remembering that summer. "Oh wow, I forgot about that."

Nodding, Daisie laced her arm over my shoulder. "Look, Gigi. I get it's not the summer you wanted, but imagine the places we get to see. We truly get to broaden our horizons. And who knows, maybe we'll each meet a cute European man." She winked at me.

"Am I missing something? Did you and Travis break up?"

"No. Absolutely not." Daisie was giggling. "But that

doesn't mean we can't flirt a little while in Europe. We're young, Gigi. We can't be tethered to someone just yet."

I shrugged. "I guess."

"Look, Gigi. This trip is happening whether you are excited about it or not. But don't you think it would be better to get excited?"

"Yeah. You're right."

"See, listen to your older sis. She's brilliant, you know?" Daisie laughed at her comment.

"Yeah. Yeah. She's not so bad."

"Say we go back home and tell Mom and Dad the news?"

"Let them sweat just a little bit longer."

"Gigi Scott, you are bad!" Daisie shoved me a little before we both burst into laughter.

Daisie and I took a stroll around the block before heading home. When I got inside, I apologized for storming out. I decided to be excited about Europe. What sixteen-year-old gets to spend an entire summer galivanting around Europe?

The next day, Mom, Daisie, and I went to the local mall in search of some summer outfits. I found a travel journal and decided to document the summer so I could share it with Ben when I got back. It had slots for polaroids.

When we pulled into the driveway, I saw Ben waiting for me.

"Hey, Ben!" I ran over to hug him.

As Mom and Daisie went into the house, I pulled myself closer to Ben and kissed him. In this moment of our kiss, our chemistry becomes an ever-bright flame.

"Do you want to go for a drive?" Ben asked.

I nodded before walking over to the passenger side, where Ben opened the doorknob, and I got inside.

We drove through the town streets, the sun setting in the distance. We pulled off to the side of the road. In front of us, we could see Catalina Island fading into the clouds and the ocean below us.

"Ben, there's something I need to tell you."

"What is it?"

"Well, you know how we had those summer plans… turns out my parents had other plans."

"What do you mean, Gigi?"

"We're going on a family vacation. I'll be gone most of the summer."

"I see. Where are you going?"

"Europe. All over. From Greece, Italy, Spain, Paris, and London. I'm not quite sure where else, but I won't be back until two weeks before school starts."

"Oh." I could see the hurt paint across his face, but he kept his composure.

"I'm excited for you, Gigi. Europe sounds like a great opportunity."

"Really, Ben? You think so."

"I do."

"Then tell me this: are you actually excited for me or just trying to be positive?"

After finding my parents' letters, I didn't want Ben and me to have any secrets or possible resentment. I wanted him to be able to speak freely with me, and if I didn't ask for that now, I could possibly end up in a relationship where we hide our true feelings for fear of hurting the other.

"Since you asked, I am excited for you. But I was really looking forward to this summer with you. And that's a hard pill to swallow, knowing we won't have that."

"I know. I was devastated when I found out. But the more I think about it, the more it'll be a good opportunity.

"It is a really great opportunity. We're young, Gigi; you have to make the most of the life you're given."

"So you're not mad?"

"Of course not. Am I bummed, sure. But there's plenty of time for us to spend summers together. I don't know what the future holds, but we should make the most of it.

"Yeah. You're right."

Ben dropped me off that night. We spent most of the time talking about Europe. How I planned to send him a postcard from every country I visit.

"I'm going to miss you this summer, Gigi." Ben's arms were wrapped around my waist, and he was leaning against his car.

"I'll miss you more, Benjamin."

He laughed before kissing me softly. "When do you leave?"

"A week from today."

"That's soon."

"It is. But we can spend what little time I have together."

"I'd like that very much."

"Good!" I sealed the moment with a kiss, feeling the

anticipation of summer and the sweetness of our impending reunion after my European adventure.

He escorted me to the door, bidding goodnight with another kiss. This wasn't a cinematic embrace but one filled with passion, a raw display of primal desire that resonated deeply.

"Goodnight, Gigi." He whispered.

"Night, Ben," I replied, lingering by the doorway, watching him depart. As he moved away from the house, a question lingered in my mind: What exactly was I diving into?

74
BEN

What I thought would become the best summer quickly turned. The only excitement I felt was rushing to the mailbox in hopes of a postcard from Gigi. I was happy for her to be traveling the world, but why did it have to be this summer, of all summers? Gigi was finally my girlfriend, and I was looking forward to an endless summer with her.

Now, I anticipated what our relationship would look like when she got back. Will Europe change her? I shook the thought from my mind. It wasn't fair of me to rain on her parade, even if it was all in my head.

With the summer sun blazing overhead, I resolved that it would be a season of new experiences for me. Venturing down to the local restaurant, I mustered the courage to ask for a job. Despite the modest pay and sparse hours, I saw it as an opportunity to earn some extra cash and fill my summer days with purpose. Starting as a busboy, I threw myself into the role with determination, swiftly learning the ins and outs of the job, clearing tables with precision, and greeting customers with a warm smile. My dedication didn't go unnoticed, and before long, I found myself offered the position of a waiter. It was a moment of pride for me, knowing that my hard work had paid off in the form of a promotion. Donning my apron and carrying trays laden with food, I relished the newfound responsibility and the chance to interact more directly with diners.

One person I couldn't wait to share my news with was Gigi. Even though she was thousands of miles away in a European town, I felt her presence with me as I penned each letter. Her updates on her whereabouts served as milestones for me, giving me something to look forward to amidst the hustle and bustle of my job. Doubt crept in at times, unsure if she'd receive my letters in time, but I pressed on, jotting down every detail of my summer escapades to share with her upon her return. As the days turned into weeks and then months, I found myself counting down the days, secretly marking off each passing day on the calendar.

When I wasn't working, I would take Joe, Dash, and Rosie to the beach or the Santa Monica Pier amusement park. Rosie always wanted to ride the Ferris wheel at least six times. After a couple of times on the Ferris Wheel, Dash and Joe would run off to the arcade. We'd have hot dogs, popcorn, and funnel cakes. Sometimes, we'd see Martha and other kids from school at the beach or the local ice cream shop. Most of the time, we kept our distance from each other. But now and then, she would get under my skin with her snarky comments. I was beginning to despise her. I was wondering how I would ever tell Gigi that I wasn't a fan of her best friend. I can't quite put my finger on it, but there's always been this uneasy tension between Martha and me, even though she's Gigi's best friend. Whenever we're together, there's this underlying discomfort that hangs in the air.

So, when I decided to bring Rosie along to the summer concert at the local park, I was hoping to avoid running into Martha. When Rosie begged for a popsicle, we waited in line, just as my heart sank at the sight of Martha and some other girls from school. I silently prayed that she wouldn't notice me, but of course, she did.

"Benjamin!" I see you have a life outside of spending all your time with Gigi. Martha called out, her tone dripping with sarcasm. I forced a smile, trying to hide the discomfort that churned in the pit of my stomach.

"Martha," I said, my voice firm, "I'm not sure why you feel the need to make snide remarks every time we cross paths. But let me make one thing clear. I have a life outside of Gigi, just as you have one outside of being her friend. And while I may not have your knack for drawing attention, I'm secure enough in who I am not to need constant validation from others."

Her eyes widened in surprise, clearly caught off guard by my directness. But I pressed on, determined to assert myself.

"I brought Rosie here tonight because she wanted to

enjoy the concert, not to be subjected to your unnecessary comments. So, if you can't treat me with the same respect you expect from others, then it's time we reassess our interactions.

With that, I turned away, refusing to let Martha's rudeness ruin the evening for Rosie or myself. Martha exuded an aura of malice, her inner turmoil manifesting as sharp claws. It was evident that she harbored a deep fear of revealing her true self, a contradiction both simple and complex. I find it difficult to comprehend why Gigi would choose to be best friends with someone like Martha. This will always remain a mystery to me.

75
GIGI
DATE: JUNE 1971

When you're in Europe, the experience is truly transformative. The diverse cultures, centuries of history, and breathtaking scenery all combine to shift your perspective on life completely. Take it from me: standing in the heart of Europe feels like stepping into a storybook where every cobblestone street and towering cathedral whispers tales of the past.

Right now, I find myself wanting the enchanting streets of Paris, where the air is perfumed with the aroma of freshly baked croissants and the sound of accordion music fills the air. Each corner turned reveals a new facet of this vibrant city. From the majestic Sacré-Cœur Basilica perched atop Montmartre to the quaint cafés tucked away in hidden alleyways.

But Paris was just the beginning of our family adventure. The next stop was Italy. The mere thought of indulging in authentic pasta and gelato has me practically drooling. And then there's the art. Oh, the art! I can't wait to lose myself in the masterpieces of Michelangelo and Leonardo da Vinci, to feel the weight of history pressing down on me as I stand before the ruins of ancient Rome. From there, who knows where the road will take us? Greece beckons with its sun-drenched islands and ancient ruins that seem to echo with the voices of gods and heroes. It's there, amidst the whitewashed buildings and azure waters of Santorini, I find myself drawn to a quaint seaside café, its tables adorned with vibrant bougainvillea and overlooking the shimmering Aegean Sea. As I sip on a glass of refreshing lemonade and watch all the boats in the harbor, I can't help but feel a sense of serenity wash over me.

And it's at that moment that I notice him—a Greek youth with an easy smile and a twinkle in his eye. I imagine striking up a conversation and sharing stories of our travels, and our laughs echo across the cobblestone streets. It's then that I realize this is the magic of Europe. The chance encounters and unexpected connections. I'm only sixteen once; what's the harm in making new friends, handsome friends, that is, while in Greece? It's not like we'll ever see each other again.

"Gigi, what are you looking at?" Daisie breaks me from my daydream.

"Oh, nothing."

"Are you dreaming about Ben?"

Clearing my throat, I replied nervously, "Uhm, sure.

Yes. Of course. Who else?"

It's then that she draws a line between my eyes and the young man across the way.

"Ah, I see."

"What, Daisie?"

"Nothing.." she pauses. "So, are you going to go talk to him?"

"What? Absolutely not."

"Why not, Gigi?"

"Because…because I have a boyfriend."

"Gigi, it's just talking. Live a little."

"I don't know.."

"What's that saying.. when in Greece.."

"I think it's 'when in Rome, do as the Romans do.'" I replied.

Rolling her eyes. "Well, we're in Greece, so um, go do what the Greeks do." She ushered me to go over to him.

Before I had enough courage, he was already gone.

The next day, it was a sunny afternoon as I strolled through the town square of a quaint Greek village. I couldn't help but notice the man from the café. I overheard someone call out his name. Deacon. His effortless charm and devil-may-care attitude drew me in like a moth to a flame.

"Hey there, sunshine," Deacon called out, flashing me a cocky grin as he expertly juggled a trio of oranges. "Impressive, huh?"

I chuckled, shaking my head in amusement. "Not bad, but I've seen better," I teased, a playful glint in my eye.

"Oh, really? Care to show me?" Deacon retorted, tossing one of the oranges my way with a wink.

Caught off guard, I fumbled with the fruit, nearly dropping it before regaining my composure. "Smooth move," I quipped. A grin tugged at the corners of my lips. "But I'll have you know, I'm a quick learner."

And so, under the watchful gaze of amused onlookers, Deacon and I engaged in a playful competition, each trying to outdo the other with our juggling skills. As the oranges flew through the air, so too did the banter between us, a playful dance of wit and charm.

Hours passed in the blink of an eye as we roamed the sun-drenched streets together, our laughter mingling with the sound of music drifting from nearby cafes. And though our time together was fleeting, there was an unspoken understanding between us, a silent acknowledgment of the connection that had blossomed between two souls on a warm summer day in Greece. When the sun descended into the sky, casting a golden glow over the village square, I found myself lingering by Deacon's side, reluctant to say goodbye. "Same time tomorrow?" he asked with a hopeful smile, his eyes holding a hint of something more.

I hesitated for a moment, torn between the desire to stay and the knowledge that my vacation was drawing to a close. "I wish I could," I replied softly, my voice tinged with regret. "But my family and I are leaving soon."

There was a flicker of disappointment in Deacon's eyes before he masked it with a charming grin. "Well, then, let's make the most of the time we have left," he said, taking my hand in his and leading me towards the nearest café.

As we disappeared into the fading light of the evening, I couldn't shake the feeling that I had just embarked on the most thrilling adventure of my life—a whirlwind romance with a charming stranger in a faraway land.

I got back to the meeting spot that Daisie and I promised to meet. We told our parents we wanted some sisterly bonding time to explore alone. Little did they know that Daisie had met someone she wanted to adventure off with, and well, I had my eye on Deacon and was hoping to run into him.

"So, how was it with the adorable Greek god?" Daisie teased.

"Stop it!" giggling, I replied. "But it was amazing."

"Did you two kiss?" she asked.

"No!" my cheeks were burning red.

"But I wanted to," I replied.

"I see.." Daisie responded.

"Is that bad? I didn't act upon it."

"Well, if you ask me, there's no such thing as bad thoughts. As you said, you didn't do anything."

"Daisie…" I drown out her name.

"Oh, come on, Gigi. You're sixteen. You're not getting married, and Ben's a new boy, but that's just it—he's a boy. Are you really telling me that you've already met your soulmate?"

"I don't know. Maybe." I shrugged.

"We're not Mom and Dad, you know that, right?"

"Yeah. But I really like Ben."

"That's fine. But don't put all your eggs in one basket."

"Okay. I won't."

"So how was it with Deacon?" she asked again.

"So much fun!"

We both giggled the rest of the way back to the hotel. She shared about her day, and I shared about running into a Deacon in the village. How we caught each other's eyes, and the rest was history. I went to bed that night, wondering if I had crossed a line. Was spending an entire day with Deacon a form of cheating? I cared for Ben, but Daisie was right; I was only sixteen. Why did I have to get a boyfriend just before my Europe vacation? I fell asleep with some thoughts dancing in my mind.

76
BEN
DATE: LATE AUGUST 1971

As the warmth of summer began to fade, my anticipation for Gigi's return reached new heights. After her enchanting European vacation, she is set to arrive back this week, and I am absolutely bursting with excitement to listen to every detail of her extraordinary trip.

I still remember the day she left, her eyes sparkling with a mix of nervousness and thrill. I imagined she'd have the same glint in her eyes as she boarded the plane. Each postcard she sent was like a small treasure, offering glimpses of her adventures.

The Eiffel Tower lit up against the Parisian night sky, the serene canals of Venice reflecting centuries of history, the vibrant markets of Barcelona bursting with colors and life, and the ancient ruins of Athens standing proudly against the blue Greek sky. Each card was a piece of her experience, but I craved the full story, her voice bringing the scenes to life. On some nights, I'd go for a run around the neighborhood; I'd imagine Gigi strolling through ancient ruins, tasting exotic foods, and meeting fascinating people. Her laughter, her awe, and her curiosity must have been contagious, enchanting everyone she met along the way.

Now, as I run through these familiar streets, the lingering warmth of summer in the air, my mind is filled with questions. What were her favorite moments? Did she find inspiration for her art in the frescoes of Florence, the mosaics of Istanbul, or the whitewashed buildings and the azure waters of Santorini? My anticipation grows with each passing day, fueled by the countless possibilities of her tales. But one question lingered. Did she miss me as much as I missed her? Looking at the calendar, counting down the days, I could hardly contain my excitement. Gigi's return signified more than just the end of her trip; it marked the beginning of a new chapter for us both. We'd be starting our junior year together as boyfriend and girlfriend. Her stories would weave into the fabric of our lives, enriching our daily routines and sparking dreams.

Parking my car in front of Gigi's, the house felt different, as if it were holding its breath, waiting for her laughter to fill the rooms again. Finally, I see their familiar vehicle turn down the street, my heart racing. It turns into the driveway, and I hear the engine shut off. Gigi gets out, her smile lighting up her face. She waves enthusiastically, and in that moment, everything feels right again. We run towards each other, the months of separation melting away as I wrap my arms around her. Her warmth, her scent, her presence—it's as if she never left.

"Tell me everything," I whisper, pulling back to look at her face.

"Oh, you won't believe half of it," she laughs, her eyes twinkling with the promise of stories to come.

"Do you want to go for a drive?" I ask.

She looks back and I wave to Birdie, Roger, and Daisie. "Welcome home!" I yell.

"Thanks, Ben!" they say in unison.

"Gigi, don't forget to grab your suitcase!" Roger calls.

"Okay, Dad!" Gigi looks back at me. "I'd love to. Let me bring my suitcase in. Okay?"

I nodded. "Let me help you!" I ran over to assist with her bags. As we carried her belongings into the house and set them down in her bedroom, I looked around the room. If I'm being honest, I've never really set foot in her room before. I noticed the stacks of books, which didn't surprise me. And her guitar was in the corner.

"Shall we go?" she asks.

"Yes. Of course."

We walk out of her room and onto the cemented sidewalk.

"I was thinking we could take a walk instead." She prompts.

"Yeah, of course. It's just great to see you."

"It's—it's great to see you too, Ben." Her smile is bright, but there's a hint of something else in her eyes.

A TIMELESS TAPESTRY

The morning air is filled with her animated chatter and my eager questions. I realize how much I've missed this—missed her. We walk through the familiar streets, and her stories flow effortlessly.

"You should have seen the Acropolis, Ben. It's like standing in the middle of history," she says, her eyes lighting up. "And the sunsets in Santorini? Absolutely breathtaking."

I listen intently, hanging on to every word. "It all sounds amazing, Gigi. What was your favorite part?"

She pauses, considering. "Honestly, Greece. The culture, the people. It felt like a second home."

As we turn down a quieter street, I can sense a shift in her mood. She grows more introspective, her words slower, less buoyant. We find a bench and sit down. Gigi grows silent, staring at the ground.

"Hey," I nudge her gently, "everything okay?"

She hesitates, biting her lip. "Yeah, it's just... being back, it's a lot to take in." Her eyes dart away, and I can tell there's more to it.

I wait, giving her space to open up. Finally, she speaks, her voice softer. "While I was in Greece, I met someone."

My heart skips a beat, but I keep my tone even. "Oh?"

"His name is Deacon. Daisie and I met him while out one of the days." She glances at me, gauging my reaction. "Nothing happened, really. We just...connected. Talked a lot. He was easy to talk to, you know?"

I nod. Trying to understand. "And that's bothering you?"

Gigi takes a deep breath. "Not exactly. It's just... it

made me think about my dad's letter."

I furrow my brow, confused. "What do you mean?"

"My dad wrote about what happened with Sylvia. Then to know my parents split up at one point, before they were married. My dad wrote about feeling stuck, about not following his heart and making choices that left him feeling empty." Her voice wavers. "I've been wondering if I'm in the same position."

I reach out, covering her hand in mine. "Gigi, you're one of the most passionate people I know. You follow your heart in everything you do."

She looks at me, eyes filled with uncertainty. "But what if I'm not? We're only sixteen, Ben. What if I'm drifting, missing something important?"

The weight of her words hangs between us. I want to say the right thing to ease her worries, but I know this is something she needs to figure out herself.

"Maybe 'Deacon' was a wakeup call," she continues, her gaze distant. "A reminder to be true to myself."

I squeeze her hand, offering silent support. "I would be lying if I said I'm not disappointed. Just feels like a big decision after one vacation."

She tries to hide her emotions with a faint smile. "I know. I need time to sort through it all."

"I can give you time, Gigi. But don't take too much time."

"Thanks, Ben. Let's spend the next couple of weeks apart. You know what they say, distance makes the heart grow fonder."

Gigi and I had plenty of distance, and instead of her

heart growing fonder, it grew apart. But I didn't have it in me to make her feel any worse, so I nodded in understanding.

77
GIGI

I told myself I was making the right decision. Ben and I had the rest of our lives to figure things out. If two people are meant to be, they will find their way to each other. I had to believe that much. I had to believe that distance was just an illusion.

If Ben and I's souls were truly woven as one, then it wouldn't matter how much time passed. We would always be with each other. Now, as I lie in my room, visions of my time in Greece play out vividly in my mind, particularly of the day I met Deacon. What was in the Greek water?

FLASHBACK TO EUROPEAN VACATION

A TIMELESS TAPESTRY

It was a blistering sultry afternoon when I first met Deacon, standing by the harbor in Santorini. The sun shimmered on the cerulean waves, while the air carried the scent of salt and blooming bougainvillea. Deacon was sketching the scene, his intense gaze capturing every detail. There was something magnetic about him, a riddle of calm and energy that drew me in. Our meeting was brief, just a single day, but it felt like an eternity compressed into hours. We talked about everything and nothing, sharing stories and dreams under the Greek sun. His laughter resounded as an outflow of merriment, reverberating across the sunlit expanse of the afternoon, his insights profound. He had a way of making me feel seen, truly seen, in a way I hadn't felt before. I remember the exact moment things changed for me. We were sitting on a rocky outcrop, witnessing the sun slowly descending. Deacon turned to me, his eyes reflecting the fiery sky, and asked, "What do you really want, Gigi? Out of life, out of love?" His Greek accent was so strong, adding an exotic flair to his words.

His question caught me off guard. It wasn't something I had ever contemplated. I had always been content with the path I was on, especially now with Ben by my side. Maybe it was the waves crashing below and the future stretching out before me, but I felt a yearning for something more, something undefined.

"Honestly, I don't know," I confessed. The words surprised even me. "I've never really thought about it."

Deacon smiled, a knowing, almost wistful smile. "That's the beauty of it, you know? Not knowing. It means you're open to all the possibilities.

As the night grew darker, we shared more about our lives before I had to meet Daisie. Deacon was like a mirror, reflecting my uncertainties and dreams. He was a paradox, a mystery I wanted to unravel.

★ ★ ★

DATE: LATE AUGUST – EARLY SEPTEMBER

Now, back home, Deacon's words flashed in my mind. In my dreams, I envision myself skillfully picking locks, surrendering my life to the untamed wilderness or the relentless force of the ocean, and colliding with him under the night sky. He is a riddle wrapped in a mystery. Visions haunt me—am I tainted or consumed by madness? Or perhaps, simply enlightened? My mind is a maelstrom, and I cannot rid myself of the sensation that a profound transformation has taken place within me. Ben was the first boy I ever truly crushed on. Our relationship felt safe and predictable. But at sixteen, I wonder if I'm making a mistake jumping into something so serious. I'm about to be a junior in high school, and before I know it, I'll be graduating.

What if I don't want to belong to just one person? What if I want to experience dating other guys, to see what else is out there? What if I want to be single, to figure out who I am on my own? These thoughts are terrifying yet exhilarating. They made me question everything I thought I knew about love and life. Ben is wonderful, and our connection is undeniable, but is it enough to keep me grounded? Or do I need to spread my wings, explore, make mistakes, and learn from them?

With summer nights growing shorter and school looming on the horizon, a sense of urgency crept in. I had to make a choice, but for now, I wasn't ready to decide. Holding on to the belief that if Ben and I were truly meant to be, we'd find our way back to each other, no matter where life took us, was all I could do.

For now, I'll cherish the memories of Greece and the questions Deacon stirred within me. I'll embrace the uncertainty and anomaly of my feelings and trust that, in time, the answers will come.

78
GIGI
ONE YEAR LATER
YEAR: 1972

You know, age and time are such curious concepts. They feel like they should be measurable, but in reality, they slip through our fingers like sand.

A year has passed, and I'm now a Senior in High School. It feels like I blinked, and suddenly, the world had moved on, pulling me along. Yet, part of me remains anchored in the past.

I often revisit memories from when I was 15—discovering hidden letters in the attic, talking with my mother, and going on my first date with Ben. It all seemed to blur together: my sixteenth birthday, getting my license, and our time together. A kaleidoscope of moments urges me to hold on, but I wonder if I should let go entirely. What if I wanted to erase the past and start fresh?

I broke things off with Ben in September 1971, right as Junior year began. The crisp autumn air mirrored the chill between us. By January 1972, however, winter had thawed our hearts enough to reconnect. We stayed together for the rest of the year, but summer's arrival brought more heat than harmony. Our relationship was marked by arguments and threats to end things, each fight leaving us both drained. By August 1972, Ben had decided he'd had enough. Our relationship ended for good, leaving me with a mix of relief and sadness.

In the aftermath of our breakup, we tried to cling to the idea that our story wasn't truly over. We told ourselves it was just a pause, and that when we were older and wiser, we might find our way back to each other. It was a comforting thought, wrapped in the hope that we could both change and somehow remain the same. As the weeks passed, we navigated a delicate balance, our interactions tinged with unspoken emotions and lingering looks. We continued to meet occasionally, sharing coffee or walking through the park, hoping to rekindle our connection. Each encounter was a bittersweet reminder of what we once had and what we had lost. We shared forced laughs and heavy silences.

One summer evening before our senior year, we made a pact. Sitting on the hill overlooking the town where we'd spent countless sunsets, Ben turned to me, his eyes full of earnest longing.

"Let's promise," he said, "that no matter where life takes us, we'll find each other again. When we're older, if we're still not over each other, we'll come back to this spot."

I nodded, swallowing hard. "Deal," I whispered, sealing the promise with a pinky swear, just like we did as kids. It was a childish gesture, but it felt right. We spent hours talking about our dreams and fears, imagining a future where we might still be a part of each other's lives.

Senior year spared us the awkwardness of shared classes. To keep busy, I took a job at the local newspaper, hoping to follow in my mother's footsteps. But everything changed the day my father took me flying.

Soaring above the town, the earth below seemed to shrink. The horizon stretched endlessly, a tapestry of blue and white. Breaking through the clouds, everything else faded away. The sun glinted off the wings, and a profound sense of freedom washed over me. I finally understood why my dad preferred the sky to the ground. Up there, above the worries and constraints of life below, I realized I wanted to be a pilot. Determined, I spent every free moment at the airstrip. I quit my newspaper job to work as a receptionist at the local airport. On days I wasn't working, my father became my guide. His patience was unwavering as he taught me the intricacies of flying—how to read the weather, navigate by instruments, and maintain the aircraft. Each lesson was a step closer to my dream. The first time I took the controls alone, my heart raced with a mix of fear and exhilaration. The plane responded to my touch, lifting gracefully into the sky. I practiced tirelessly, mastering takeoffs and landings, learning to handle turbulence, and executing maneuvers with precision. You could say, I really was my father's daughter.

One crisp autumn morning, almost a year after Ben and I had parted ways, I stood at the airfield, ready for my solo flight exam. My father, pride and encouragement in his eyes, stood beside me.

"You've got this, peach," he said, clapping a reassuring hand on my shoulder.

I nodded, taking a deep breath before climbing into the cockpit. Just days before, I had graduated from high school and received my acceptance letter to Millikin. I had dreamed of this moment, but now, I was unsure about college.

Shaking those thoughts away, I focused solely on the flight. Taxiing to the runway, a calm sense of purpose washed over me. My father's voice crackled in my headset.

"November Two-Five-Tango, you are cleared for take-off."

With a smooth push of the throttle, the plane roared to life. The wheels left the ground, and I was airborne. The world below transformed into a panorama of colors and shapes. I executed the flight plan flawlessly, each maneuver a testament to my hours of practice and my father's guidance.

When I touched down, my father's approving voice came through the headset.

"Congratulations, Gigi. You've earned your pilot's license."

Stepping out of the plane, I was enveloped in his proud embrace. "Just like your old man," he said, his voice thick with emotion.

I grinned, feeling a deep sense of accomplishment. Flying had become more than a hobby; it was a part of who I was. As we walked back to the hangar, the setting sun behind us, I knew this was just the beginning of my journey. The sky was no longer the limit—it was my home.

Reflecting on senior year, I remember how Ben's and my paths diverged. His passion for music became his focus. I recall how he transformed a corner of his bedroom into a makeshift studio, with a reel-to-reel tape recorder, microphones, and vinyl records scattered about. His dedication was evident as he spent hours writing lyrics, composing melodies, and experimenting with sounds. Ben's music became a fixture in our high school, his songs echoing through the halls. When we said our goodbyes, I wondered what the future held for us. I decided to attend Millikin, but after one semester, I realized college wasn't for me. I dropped out and set off to travel the world. Mom wasn't thrilled, but Dad was encouraging. After many discussions, my parents finally supported my decision.

Starting this chapter of exploration, the world revealed its wonders in unexpected ways. From Tokyo's bustling streets to Bali's serene beaches, each destination left an indelible mark on my soul. Along the way, I met a diverse array of people, forming fleeting connections and deep bonds that transcended language and culture. We navigated new terrains, shared laughter and tears, and created lasting memories. Despite the exhilaration of exploration, I sometimes felt homesick and doubted my path. Yet, each day revealed a resilience within me, a courage to embrace the unknown and thrive amidst change.

A TIMELESS TAPESTRY

Music, whether from Parisian street performers or Rio's drum circles, became my constant companion, offering comfort and inspiration. Throughout my travels, I carried Ben's songs with me, a reminder of where I came from and the dreams that drove me forward.

79
BEN
FIVE YEARS LATER
YEAR: 1977

In the quiet moments of reflection, I often revisited the memories of Ben and me—the whispered promises and shared dreams that once seemed destined to bloom forever. But as life so frequently does, it wove its intricate tapestry of twists and turns, leaving us both adrift in the currents of its unpredictability.

The pact we forged, sealed with youthful fervor and the tender innocence of first love, lingered like a silent sentinel in the chambers of my heart. Despite the glistening allure of fame and the siren call of success, a part of me remained tethered to that solemn vow, a flickering ember amidst the blaze of my burgeoning music career.

And oh, how the world unfolded before me like a

grand symphony, each note a testament to the serendipitous dance of fate. From the dimly lit stages of intimate clubs to the hallowed arenas where legends roamed, I traversed continents and crossed oceans, my guitar strumming the soundtrack to my odyssey. Opening for icons like Fleetwood Mac, The Carpenters, Foghat, and Tom Petty felt like stepping into the pantheon of gods, their music a sacred hymn that reverberated through the ages. Yet, amidst the adulation of adoring fans and the glittering accolades that adorned my path, there lingered a quiet longing—a wistful whisper of what could have been.

I traveled the globe, each city calling my name. I met souls of myriad shades; their stories etched in the lines of their laughter and the depths of their eyes. And yes, there were women, their beauty like a tempestuous storm that threatened to engulf me in its seductive embrace. Among the transient allure of each encounter, I yearned for a connection that transcended the ephemeral confines of lust and desire. In the quiet hours before dawn, when the world slumbered beneath a blanket of stars, I found myself haunted by the ghost of what could have been—the phantom touch of a love that once burned bright.

As I stood upon the precipice of my dreams, with the world at my feet and the future unfurling like a tapestry woven from stardust, I knew that every twist and turn had led me to this moment. And though the road ahead remained veiled in mystery, I embraced it with the fierce determination of one who understands that destiny is not a destination but a journey—a journey that I wasn't about to give up on. The tour had been relentless, each city blending into the next, leaving me craving solitude amidst the chaos. Greece was a welcomed respite, a chance to breathe and reflect.

As I wandered through the narrow streets of Athens, memories of Gigi flooded my mind. She was my high school sweetheart, the girl I thought I'd spend forever with. But life had a funny way of unraveling even the best-laid plans. Our love story had ended in Greece, a bitter twist of fate that still haunted me.

I remembered the summer Gigi left, her laughter pulsating through the empty hallways of my heart. She had been so full of life, her eyes fizzy with wanderlust as she embarked on her European adventure. I promised to wait for her, to hold onto our love until she returned. But time had a way of slipping through our fingers, and by the time Gigi came back, we were different people. Senior year brought with it a newfound sense of independence, of dreams diverging like paths in the woods. Our love had withered under the weight of growing up, leaving behind a hollow ache where once there had been passion.

Now, at 23, I found myself adrift in a sea of regrets. The pact we had made seemed like a cruel joke, a childish fantasy that had no place in the harsh light of reality. Yet, despite my best efforts to move on, Gigi lingered like a ghost, haunting the corners of my mind.

Lost in thought, I stumbled upon a quaint café tucked away in a quiet corner of the city. There, sitting at a table bathed in golden sunlight, was Gigi. My heart skipped a beat as I watched her, the familiar curve of her smile sending a jolt of recognition coursing through my veins. She was just as I remembered her, her blonde hair catching the light as she turned the pages of a book. For a moment, time stood still as I drank in the sight of her, the ache in my chest threatening to consume me.

Then, as if sensing my presence, Gigi looked up, and our eyes met across the crowded square. For a heartbeat, we were frozen in time—two souls bound by a love that had never truly died. Without a word, I crossed the distance between us, my heart pounding in my chest. As I stood before her, I realized that despite the passage of time and the pain of our past, there was still a flicker of hope burning bright between us.

"Gigi," I whispered, my voice barely a breath against the backdrop of the bustling city. "It's been too long."

Beneath the golden hues of the setting sun, which painted the sky and cast a warm glow over the ancient ruins of Greece, I found myself immersed in a moment of deep realization. The tranquil beauty of the starlit sky above us had whispered promises of enduring love and connection. In that very moment, amidst the timeless presence of history and nature, the unyielding bond between us became clear. No matter where life's unpredictable journey led, we were destined to find our way back to each other. Among the remnants of shattered aspirations, we unearthed and rekindled the love that had quietly smoldered within us.

80
```
    GIGI
 YEAR: 1977
PLACE: GREECE
```

"Benjamin," I said, looking up from my book to find myself face-to-face with him. Of all the places in the world, after all these years, here we both were in Greece at the same time. If this isn't fate, I don't know what is.

I blinked, almost believing it was an illusion. Suddenly, every part of me flashed back to the day I broke Ben's heart. Was he the love of my life that I lost? We were just kids back then. I thought it was better to be safe than to be starry-eyed.

Ben believed what we had was forever, but for me, it was only temporary. I knew I needed to explore the world. If we are destined to be together, we will reunite. Did this signify that we were meant to be?

Ben walked over and pulled out a nearby chair. I closed my book to get a better look at him. He was older, more of a man and yet he had changed little at all. Every good thing I ever learned was on the other side of a curious wandering. And now I was curious about Ben. What brought him to Greece? His eyes, once golden like honey, had deepened to the smoldering hue of embers, carrying a quiet intensity. His dark brown locks, now kissed by the sun, had lightened to a rich, tawny shade reminiscent of autumn leaves. I let my eyes trace his face as if drawing an invisible portrait. His jawline was chiseled like marble; his lips were sculpted with the precision of an artist's hand. My gaze traveled down to his broad shoulders, strong and steady like the pillars of an ancient temple. In high school he had been a charming sketch; now, he was a masterpiece.

I gave him a onceover, unable to help biting my bottom lip.

"Hey, Gigi," he said, sitting down across from me. "Long time."

"It—it has been quite long."

"Well, you look good," he said nonchalantly, though his eyes betrayed a hint of something deeper.

"Thanks, you too. Greece suits you," I replied, trying to keep my voice steady.

He smiled faintly, his eyes lingering on mine. "Of all the places in the world, funny how we're both here. What brings you back to Greece?"

"A bit of a soul-searching trip. I needed a break from everything back home. You?"

"I'm on tour. But I guess you could say I'm doing some soul-searching too," he said, his voice softening.

There was a moment of silence, heavy with unspoken words.

"Do you want to go for a walk?" He asked abruptly.

"Oh, um…" I paused, trying to think how to reply.

"It's okay if you need to be somewhere. I just thought…" he didn't finish his sentence.

Smiling, I replied, "You know what, I'd love it."

"Great."

Walking along the cobblestones, we chatted about life and where each of us had been all these years. I shared about Millikin—how I dropped out to travel, and how I'd been gallivanting all over the world before settling in Greece. Having been here for a year, I couldn't imagine living anywhere else.

"Do you ever think about those days?" I asked, in a near inaudible voice.

"Sometimes," he admitted. "More than I'd like to, maybe. We were just kids back then, trying to figure out life."

"Yeah," I nodded. "I was so scared of getting hurt, and I didn't realize I was hurting you."

He looked down for a moment, then back at me. "We both made mistakes. But it's in the past now."

"I've missed you, Ben. I didn't realize how much until I saw you again."

"I've missed you too, Gigi," he said, a smile touching his lips. "This is our chance to get things right."

"Maybe it is," I said, feeling a spark of hope flicker inside me.

"I'm having a show tonight at one of the local pubs. I would love for you to come," he said.

"I would love to, Ben."

There was something in the way he looked at me as if an unspoken vow just took place.

Later in the evening, I stood outside the pub, the warm glow of its lights spilling onto the cobblestone street. The sounds of laughter and clinking glasses mingled with the distant hum of the sea. A sign above the door read, "The Siren's Call," its letters curling like waves.

Inside, the air was thick with the scent of salt and ale. Wooden beams crisscrossed the ceiling, adorned with nautical trinkets and fairy lights that twinkled like stars. The place was packed, a lively crowd filling the space with chatter and anticipation. I had dressed to impress, wearing a flowing emerald-green dress that hugged my curves in all the right places. My hair was loosely curled, cascading over my shoulders, and I wore a touch of makeup to highlight my eyes. I felt a mix of excitement and nervousness flutter in my chest as I made my way through the crowd. The stage was set at the far end of the pub, modest but elevated, adorned with soft lighting that cast a warm glow. Ben stood there, tuning his guitar, his bandmates adjusting their instruments around him. He looked up, and our eyes locked.

At that moment, the world seemed to slow. His gaze was intense, filled with a mixture of surprise and something deeper, something that echoed the memories we shared. I felt a rush of emotions—nostalgia, longing, and a flicker of hope. His lips curved into a smile that sent a shiver down my spine. He strummed the first chord, and rich and soulful music enveloped the room. The crowd's chatter faded, replaced by the rhythm and melody. Ben's voice was smooth and resonant, carrying the weight of every word. It felt as though he was singing just for me, each note weaving a thread between our past and present.

I found a spot near the stage, my heart pounding in sync with the music. The atmosphere was electric, the energy of the audience pulsing around me. People swayed and tapped their feet, lost in the rhythm. With the song drawing to a close, Ben's eyes met mine once more. His gaze held a promise, a silent understanding that together was only the beginning. He gave a slight nod, and I responded with a smile, experiencing a certainty I hadn't felt in years.

In that crowded pub, amidst the music and warmth of the night, it felt as though everything had aligned perfectly. For the first time in a long time, I allowed myself to believe in the magic of second chances.

81
BEN

I noticed Gigi right away. She stood out in the crowd, her green dress lighting up the room. I can sense her beauty in my heart because it's woven from threads of love. The pub was buzzing with life, a sea of faces and voices blending in a chaotic symphony. Yet, the moment she walked in, everything else faded into the background.

Her dress hugged her curves, making her look like she belonged on a canvas in a gallery rather than amidst the clinking glasses and revelry. Her blonde curls tumbled loosely over her shoulders, catching the light with every step she took. But it wasn't just her appearance that drew me in; it was the way she carried herself.

There was grace to her movements, a quiet confidence that had grown over the years. She was no longer the girl I once knew, she was a woman who had come into her own. As she made her way through the crowd, our eyes met, and a rush of emotions hit me like a wave—sentimentally, yearning, and a spark of something new and hopeful. I strummed the first chord, my fingers moving almost automatically over the strings as my mind stayed fixed on her. Gigi's presence filled the room, her beauty not just in her physical appearance but in the way she made me feel. She was like a melody that had been playing in the back of my mind, familiar yet fresh, resonating the notes of our shared past. Her beauty was in the way she looked at me, her eyes filled with impulses we both left unspoken. As I sang, I couldn't help but direct the lyrics to her, each word carrying a piece of my heart. The crowd seemed to dissolve, leaving just the two of us in a world of music and memories. The connection between us was palpable, an invisible thread pulling us closer together.

When the song ended, I glanced her way again, catching the subtle smile on her lips. It was a smile that promised second chances and new beginnings. I nodded slightly, acknowledging the unspoken understanding between us. At that moment, under the soft lights of the pub, surrounded by the warmth of the night, I realized just how much I had missed her. Gigi wasn't just a part of my past; she was hope for the future.

Stepping out of the pub, my eyes scanned the area and settled on Gigi, standing alone. Guitar case in hand, I walked purposefully toward her, the weight of the instrument offering a comforting presence as I drew closer.

"You sound really great," Gigi extolled.

"Thank you! I'm glad you came." I replied, feeling a

rush of warmth at her praise.

"Me too." She beamed, her eyes sparkling with genuine joy.

"Are you feeling hungry?" I blurted out, unable to contain my curiosity.

Gigi, with a playful giggle, responded, "Yes, I am indeed quite hungry."

"I know the perfect place," I remarked.

"Well then, lead the way." She said, falling into step beside me with a smile that lit up the evening. With each step, the weight of the past seemed to lift.

Walking through the winding streets of Athens, the city seemed to come alive with the remnants of our shared past. Five years had passed since we last saw each other, five years since we parted ways as teenagers burdened by the weight of the world. We met in 1970, two fifteen-year-olds navigating the tumultuous waters of adolescence. Our love burned bright and fierce, a flame that consumed us both as we embarked on a journey of discovery together. But as the senior year approached, the realities of life began to pull us apart. Dreams clashed, ambitions diverged, and we found ourselves standing at a crossroads with no clear path forward.

My mind recalled the day we made the painful decision to end our relationship, to let go of the love that had defined us for so long. It was a decision born out of necessity, out of the harsh reality of growing up. And yet, despite the passage of time, despite the distance that separated us, the bond we shared remained unbroken. It was a bond forged in the fires of youth, a bond that had stood the test of time.

Now, at 23, we found ourselves standing on the precipice of possibility once again. The years had been kind to us, shaping us into the people we were meant to be.

82
GIGI

The first time Ben shook my father's hand, I watched intently. His grip was firm but not overbearing, and he looked him straight in the eyes. That handshake held a thousand unspoken words, a silent promise of respect and sincerity. My father, a man of few words and many judgments, nodded in approval.

I fell a little more in love with Ben that day—not because of the handshake itself but because of the way he respected the things that mattered to me. Maybe it meant more because of how young we were. As if respect was a thing to be taught, which meant that if Ben was able to respect my father at such a young age, then that reflected back on the way his parents raised him. And I loved his parents for that—for creating a man able to show respect, which seemed rare these days.

I loved the way he walked with his hands in his pockets, a casual confidence that seemed so effortless. It was in the small, everyday moments that I found myself most captivated by Ben. The way he navigated the world with a quiet assurance, never hurried, always present. When we walked side by side, his hands tucked away, I felt a sense of peace. It was as if everything in the world slowed down, and there was only us, moving in harmony.

Being here in Greece and running into Ben, I recalled all the feelings I felt at sixteen and now seeing him at twenty-three. My mind remembered it all. His kisses. Oh, how I loved his kisses. They were spontaneous, like the sudden burst of summer rain. Sometimes, they came in the middle of a conversation when I was in the midst of saying something important or completely trivial. His lips interrupted me, rude and sweet, and for a moment, words became unnecessary. Those interruptions were filled with an urgency, a need to connect that transcended whatever mundane thing I was talking about.

As we sat inside that restaurant, I could hardly make sense of his words because all I could think about was the way things used to be.

"You know, it used to annoy me, the way you'd cut me off mid-sentence," I blurted out.

"What do you mean, Gigi?" he asked, a curious glint reflecting in his amber eyes.

"I was raised to believe in the importance of finishing thoughts, of being heard. But with you, I've learned that some interruptions are worth the disruption. They remind me that life isn't about neat endings or perfectly completed conversations. It's messy and beautiful, and sometimes the best moments are the ones that don't follow the script." I carried on as if Ben could instantly read my mind.

When he didn't say anything more, when he just sat there, hanging on every word I said, I decided to continue talking.

"I remember one evening, sophomore year. We were sitting on the porch, the sun setting in a blaze of orange and pink. I was talking about my day, recounting every little detail, when you leaned in and kissed me. It was unexpected, sudden. For a heartbeat, I was stunned into silence. And then, I kissed you back, forgetting whatever trivial thing I was saying. In that kiss, I felt understood, loved, and cherished."

Ben's interruptions taught me to embrace the present and to find joy in the unexpected. They were a testament to his passion, his unfiltered love.

"Every time you kissed me mid-sentence, I was reminded that love doesn't always wait for the perfect moment. It crashes into our lives unapologetically, demanding to be felt and experienced in all its raw intensity."

I finally stopped talking and just took in the moment. These seemingly insignificant moments were the threads that wove the tapestry of our lives together.

"Ben—" I began to say before pausing. "I've learned it's the small things that hold the greatest meaning. Your handshake, the walk, the kiss; they are fragments of our story, each one a piece of the love we share. And I wouldn't trade them for anything in the world."

Ben was born of pure love, a protector, a friend to all, and a loving and kind man. How could I not fall for him? I wondered if I had never broken up with him, would we have made it? Would we have gotten married and had babies of our own? I didn't know. I didn't have the answer to that. There was an invisible string tied to this vessel, and a part of me would forever be his.

We left the restaurant and wandered through the streets, taking in the beauty of Greece.

"My father would tell me, 'Roll with the punches, peach.' Life can be like a complicated puzzle, full of surprises and unexpected turns," I said.

Ben smiled. "Your dad is a wise man. Did he give you that advice often?"

"All the time. Especially when things didn't go as planned, he had this way of making the chaos seem manageable." I paused. "I guess that's why your interruptions don't bother me anymore. They remind me of his words."

Ben chuckled. "I never thought I'd be compared to your father's wisdom. But I like it." He took my hand in his without hesitation—I didn't stop him. "You know, life with you felt like the perfect kind of chaos. Here we are in the same place at the same time, and I wouldn't have it any other way."

I squeezed his hand. "Neither would I. I love this unpredictability."

Nodding, Ben said, "Exactly. I've been meaning to ask you." Looking into my eyes, he continued, "Where do we go from here?"

I didn't know, but I felt like life was giving us another

chance, and this time, I didn't want to lose Ben.

"I'm not going anywhere, Ben. I'm here, and I won't hide how I feel. So if you want me, then tell me."

A smirk painted his face. "Come on tour with me!"

My eyes widened, and without thinking, I pulled him in for a kiss. Our lips met with a fervent hunger, years of longing, and missed moments culminating in this instant. My fingers threaded through Ben's hair, pulling him closer as if afraid he might vanish. He responded with equal intensity, his hands sliding around my waist, anchoring me to him. He broke the kiss for a breathless second, his eyes dark with desire. Without a word, he guided me into the shadowed embrace of the alleyway. The dim light cast a soft glow on our entwined figures, making the moment feel almost dreamlike. With a gentle push, Ben pressed me against the cool, rough wall. The contrast between the hard surface and his warm touch sent a shiver down my spine. His lips found mine again, more insistent this time, exploring, claiming. Each kiss was a promise, a reminder of the love we'd kept burning despite the distance.

Our surroundings faded away, the world narrowing down to just the two of us. My senses were overwhelmed by the taste of him, the scent of his skin, the feel of his hands roaming my back. The kiss deepened, becoming a dance of tongues and breaths, each movement a testament to the passion we'd held back for too long.

Ben pulled away slightly, just enough to rest his forehead against mine, his breath ragged and heavy.

He whispered, "I've missed you so much, Gigi."

"Me too, Ben. More than you know," I said breathlessly.

He captured my lips again, the kiss softer now, filled with tenderness. It spoke of promises and new beginnings, of the adventures that were awaiting us. In this alleyway, with the world around us forgotten, I rediscovered Ben, our love burning brighter than ever. Finally, we pulled away, eyes locked, breaths mingling in the narrow space between us.

Smiling, Ben asked again. "So, is that a yes?"

"Absolutely. I wouldn't miss it for the world," I said, grinning.

Our hands remained intertwined as we stepped out of the alleyway, ready to face whatever came next together.

83
BEN

Being loved is a sensation to cherish, but if you have never felt the real thing before, it can be terrifying. The unfamiliarity of it all is both thrilling and daunting, much like stepping onto an uncharted path. The ground beneath you feels different; the air carries a new fragrance, and the rhythm of your heart seems to dance to a new melody.

Love, true love, transforms you in ways you never imagined. It elevates you and makes you soar if it's genuine.

Knowing that Gigi loved me was an unparalleled joy. Our day in Greece marked a turning point, a moment that forever altered the course of our relationship. Rekindling our love breathed new life into us, lifting us to heights we hadn't dared to dream of. When Gigi agreed to join me on tour, I had no inkling of what the decision would mean for us. Her willingness to follow me made it clear that I needed to give our relationship the chance it deserved.

One unforgettable day, we found ourselves in London. I had just finished a show the moment I stepped off the stage and rushed to Gigi's side. As we strolled back to our hotel, she turned to me and asked how I knew music was my calling. I explained that music has a unique way of resonating with my mind, teaching it to flow and find peace. Each note, each changing tone, felt like a gentle massage for my brain, an invitation to slow down and be truly present. It was as if the patient, introspective part of me was being coaxed out, content in its quiet contemplation. The indigenous people of North America, known as Native Americans, held the belief that natural elements such as light, wind, and nature had their distinct ways of communicating with individuals. However, it was the emotive and transformative power of music that enabled me to establish a profound and introspective connection with my inner self.

On our final day of the tour in London, we boarded the plane heading back to California. I watched Gigi whisper to herself while gazing out the window. "So long, London," she murmured, her voice tinged with nostalgia and a hint of sadness. The city had been a pivotal chapter in our lives, and as we took off, I couldn't help but wonder what this meant for us once we were back in our hometown.

84
GIGI

As the plane ascended, the sprawling lights of London faded into the distance, a glimmering reminder of all we were leaving behind. My forehead rested gently against the cool glass, and I traced a finger along the window, as if I could capture the city's essence in my touch.

Each evening, I'd watched Ben pour his soul into every note, his face illuminated by stage lights, the sweat glistening on his brow as he locked eyes with me in the crowd. I could still hear the echoes of our late-night talks, his laughter blending with the hum of the city, his voice soft and reassuring in the dim light of our hotel room.

I remembered the way his eyes, deep and searching, would find mine after each show, as if the entire world had vanished, leaving only us in that moment. London had wrapped itself around us like an old friend, the cobblestone streets and historic architecture mirroring the new foundation we were building. Leaving it behind was like closing the pages of a beloved book—not knowing if we'd ever find that same magic again. Ben was asleep in the seat next to me. I looked over to see his eyelids fluttering gently, his face softened by sleep. I wondered if he was dreaming of me, if the city we left behind still danced in his dreams like it did in mine. I couldn't resist reaching out to brush a stray curl from his forehead, feeling the warmth of his skin beneath my fingertips. His hand rested on the armrest between us, and I intertwined my fingers with his, careful not to wake him. The sensation of his touch even in sleep, sent a comforting warmth through me, grounding me in the moment.

Gazing out the window once more, my mind drifted back to our time in London. I recalled the night we wandered along the riverbank, the cool breeze ruffling our hair, and the way Ben's hand tightened around mine as if he was afraid to let go. The city had been alive with its own rhythm, syncing with the beating of our hearts. We'd found something special there—something that felt like it had been waiting for us all along. But now, as the plane carried us away from the city that had rekindled our love, I couldn't help but feel a pang of sadness. London had become more than just a backdrop; it was a part of us, woven into the fabric of our relationship. Leaving it behind felt like leaving a piece of our story, and I wasn't sure if we could recapture that magic back home.

Still, as I looked over at Ben, his face relaxed and

peaceful, I knew that whatever came next, we would face it together. And that, more than anything, was enough to keep me grounded, even as we soared above the clouds.

We landed at LAX, stepping into a world where the sleek, futuristic curves of the terminal welcomed us with open arms. The air was alive with the hustle of travelers, their luggage clattering over the tiled floors, while flight attendants in bright uniforms glided by with perfectly coiffed hair. The smell of cigarette smoke mingled with the scent of coffee brewing at the corner café, a sign of the times.

Outside, the iconic arches of the Theme Building reached towards the sky, casting their shadows over a sea of brightly colored taxis and gleaming chrome.

The walls around us were adorned with vibrant, geometric patterns, and the hum of conversation was punctuated by the distant click of payphones as travelers made their calls. As we made our way through the terminal, the soft sounds of smooth jazz floated through the air, blending with the steady rhythm of footsteps, signaling that we were back in California. As we stepped outside into the warm California sun, a mix of anticipation and unease settled in my chest. Looking around, I couldn't help but think of the summer of 1971 when my family took our trip to Europe. I remembered the look on Ben's face when I told him I was leaving. We were so young and so unsure of what the future held. California hadn't changed much, but we had—marked by the places we'd been and the love we'd rekindled.

Daisie was picking us up at the airport. As we waited for her vehicle to emerge, an older gentleman in a crisp suit and fedora tipped his hat at us as we passed, a nod to the timeless charm of Los Angeles, where the past always seemed just a step behind the present.

I breathed in the warm breeze as it kissed my skin, carrying with it the familiar scent of salt and smog that always seemed to cling to the Los Angeles air. The palm trees swayed gently in the distance, a reminder that we were finally home.

Just then, a bright yellow VW van with flowers painted on the sides pulled up to the curb, its engine rumbling like an old friend. The sliding door creaked open, and Daisie leaned out, her wide smile as welcoming as the California sun. She wore oversized sunglasses, and her hair was a wild halo of curls. The van, with its worn leather seats and faded curtains, was as much a symbol of the 70s as anything else around us. As Ben and I climbed in, I couldn't help but feel a surge of warmth—this was our California, a place where the past and present collided in the most beautiful of ways.

85
BEN

Daisie and Gigi had dropped me off at my house, and as the van pulled away, I stood for a moment, taking in the familiar sight of the place I once called home. The front yard looked the same, with the roses my mother had tended still in full bloom. Yet, there was something different in the air—perhaps a sense of anticipation for the changes that had occurred while I was away.

I pushed open the front door, a smile forming as I called out, "Guess who's home? Your favorite son!" Mt voice echoed through the hallway, and almost immediately, I heard the sound of footsteps rushing toward me.

My mother appeared first, emerging from the kitchen with a look of pure surprise on her face. "Ben!" she exclaimed, wiping her hands on her apron before wrapping me in a warm hug. The comforting scent of her cooking clung to her, evoking nostalgia.

On the nearby sofa, my father sat with a newspaper in hand, his reading glasses perched on the bridge of his nose. He looked up, his stern expression softening into a smile as he set the paper aside. "Welcome home, son," he said, standing up to join the embrace.

From the backyard, I heard the lively sounds of laughter and play. Moments later, Joe and Dash burst through the back door, followed closely by Rosie, their energy filling the room. Joe, about to enter his senior year, and Dash, a junior, had significantly matured since I last saw them. Rosie wasn't so little anymore; she was on the brink of starting high school. Her eyes lit up when she saw me, and she rushed forward to throw her arms around me. "Ben! I missed you so much!" she squealed, her voice still carrying that youthful enthusiasm.

I was eager to share the news of my time abroad and the tour I had been on. My letter to my mother from Greece mentioned running into Gigi. However, I hadn't revealed that we were back together, and I now envisioned our future. While we gathered in the living room, the late afternoon sun streamed through the windows, and I began recounting my adventures. Each word carried the excitement and hope that had been building inside me. This homecoming was more than just a return to those who were dearest to me.

We sat around the dining room table, and as I spoke, their faces reflected a mix of joy, curiosity, and anticipation. My mother's eyes were wide with excitement as she listened, her hands resting on her lap as if to steady the whirlwind of emotions. "You've been to Greece, Ben," she began, recalling my letter. "It must have been amazing. But tell us, how did Gigi fit into all this?"

My father, seated on the edge of his chair, leaned forward. His expression was a blend of pride and disbelief. "Yes, Ben. You mentioned her in your letter. What's the story?" he asked, his tone serious but inviting.

Dash, who had always been the louder one, couldn't contain his enthusiasm. "Yeah, and did you get to try all the local food? I bet it was incredible!" he said, his excitement palpable.

Joe, always a bit quieter, nodded with a smile. "And what about the rest of your tour? Did you have any other memorable experiences?"

Rosie, perched on the arm of the sofa with her eyes sparkling with curiosity, piped up, "Did you get any groovy souvenirs? And what about Gigi? Are you two…?"

Her question trailed off, but the hopeful look on her face said everything. I couldn't help but smile, feeling a surge of warmth at their genuine interest and affection.

"Well, Greece was breathtaking," I began, my voice steadying. "The ancient ruins and beautiful islands were incredible. But the real highlight was running into Gigi there. It was such an unexpected yet perfect coincidence."

My mother's eyes widened even more. "Gigi Scott? The same Gigi from before?" she asked, her voice filled with both surprise and hope.

"Yes, the very same," I confirmed. "We reconnected, and it was like no time had passed at all. We talked, spent time together, and by the end of the tour, I realized how much I wanted to be with her."

Dash leaned in, his curiosity piqued. "So, what's next? Are you going to ask her to marry you?"

I nodded, feeling a sense of anticipation. "Yes, that's the plan. I'm going to ask Gigi to marry me. But first, I want to ask her father, Roger, for his blessing."

My father's face softened with understanding. "That's a big step, son. Are you ready for that?"

"I am," I said with conviction. "I want to do it right, and I know how much it would mean to both Gigi and her father."

Rosie's eyes lit up with excitement. "And will you be bringing Gigi here? I haven't seen her in ages!"

The room buzzed with lively conversation and questions as we caught up. My stories from the tour, filled with unexpected adventures and new experiences, were met with bursts of laughter and exclamations of surprise. The warmth of their presence and the joy of reconnecting made me feel more certain than ever that returning home was the right choice. When we finally started to eat, the table was laden with all of my favorite dishes—comfort food that spoke of home and family. The conversation flowed easily, punctuated by bursts of laughter and the clinking of utensils. Each moment and shared story felt like a thread connecting us all, weaving us closer together.

As I glanced around the table, surrounded by the people who meant the most to me, I realized that this homecoming was more than just a return to where I started; it was a reunion with the people who had always stood by me. Their love and enthusiasm made me feel that whatever lay ahead, I would be ready to face it with their support guiding me every step of the way.

With the passing years, Gigi and I's relationship grew stronger. This newfound love encapsulated each of us. It was then I knew the only proper way to move forward in our relationship was to ask for Gigi's hand in marriage. One day, I went to the local airport where Roger was working. He had retired as a pilot but still spent his time at the airport. Once a pilot, always a pilot, and no one could remove him from being around airplanes.

He had his own office. I knocked lightly, my heart pounding. I heard Roger's voice inviting me in, and I stepped into the warm, book-filled room. On one shelf was a toy airplane, one Roger built years ago. Another shined of memorabilia of his time in the Air Force. A black-and-white photo of him standing in front of the first plane he had ever flown. There were a few photos on his desk—one of him and Birdie's wedding day, one of him and Daisie at a baseball game, and another of him and Gigi in front of an airplane. I remembered that day; it was the day Gigi got her pilot's license.

"Ben, it's good to see you. Have a seat." Roger said, smiling.

I sat down, trying to steady my nerves. "Mr. Scott, I love Gigi with all my heart. I want to spend my life making her happy. I'm here to ask for your blessing to marry her."

Roger's eyes softened, and he smiled. "Ben, I remember the day I asked Birdie's father the same question. It's clear you love Gigi deeply and have shown her respect and kindness. You have my blessing. Take care of her."

Relief washed over me. "Thank you, sir. I promise to cherish her always."

Roger stood and extended his hand. I shook it firmly. "Welcome to the family, Ben."

"Thank you, Mr. Scott. It's an honor."

Roger patted me on the back. "Take good care of her. She's one of a kind."

"I will, sir. I promise."

I left his office feeling a whirlwind of emotions. Relief washed over me first, like a weight lifting off my shoulders. Gratitude followed, swelling in my chest for the trust Roger had placed in me. A sense of accomplishment mingled with a profound love for Gigi, knowing I had taken this significant step toward our future together. My heart was light, and my steps were buoyant as I walked away, already envisioning the life we could build.

86
ROGER

I sat in my study, the soft glow of the lamp casting shadows across the room. I looked at the framed family photos displayed on my desk, each capturing a precious moment. My eyes lingered on a photo of Birdie taken on our wedding day. The memory of that day brought a smile to my face, but it was another day, years earlier, that filled my mind. It was the day I had asked Birdie's father for her hand in marriage.

Now, there was a knock on my door, bringing me back to the present. Ben entered, looking nervous but determined. My heart went out to him; I knew exactly how Ben felt. I asked him to take a seat, remembering the moment I stood in Birdie's backyard with her father.

He sat down, taking a deep breath before speaking. The words spilled out like tea. I felt a wave of déjà vu—

Ben's earnest expression and heartfelt words mirrored mine years ago. I could see the love and sincerity in his eyes, just as Birdie's father must have seen in mine. I gave Ben my blessing just as Birdie's father gave me. Relief washed over Ben's face, and he thanked me, making the same promise I once made. We stood, and I extended my hand to his. Ben shook it firmly, gratitude evident in his eyes.

"Welcome to the family, Ben," I said.

As Ben left my office, I sat back down, my heart full. I felt a deep sense of fulfillment, knowing that the love I had for Birdie was now being mirrored in the next generation. It was a full-circle moment, a beautiful continuation of the love story that had begun all those years ago.

Birdie and I's love story was a tumultuous journey filled with highs and lows. There were fleeting moments where we sought to paint ourselves perfect, but eventually, the harsh realities of life crashed down on us like a relentless wave onto the shore, forcing us to confront the imperfections in our love.

When Ben got down on one knee and proposed to Gigi, she immediately came to my office. There we were in the same spots where, just weeks prior, Ben was standing, asking for my permission.

"Peach, what are you doing here?"

"Dad, I need to ask you something."

"Go ahead," I encouraged her to speak freely.

"I'm going to marry Ben. I love him…"

"I see. Well, Ben is a good man."

"He is."

"So what's on your mind, peach? Because you certainly didn't come here just to tell me something I already know."

"Dad, how did you know that mom was the one?"

"Simple. It was in the way she looked at me, her eyes sparkling with a mixture of adoration and mischief. It was in the softness of her touch, the way her hand fit perfectly in mine as if they were always meant to be intertwined…" I continued to tell her that it was in the way Birdie's laughter bellowed through the room, contagious and joyful, filling every corner with warmth. It was in the late-night conversations we shared where time seemed to stand still as we talked about our hopes, dreams, and fears.

I paused, remembering every little detail of why I fell in love with Birdie and how I knew she was the one for me. "Gigi, it was in the way she stood by me during the toughest moments of my life. Her unwavering support gave me strength."

"It was the way her presence filled your heart with a sense of completeness that you had never known before?" Gigi asked.

I nodded. "Love. It was pure and unconditional, a force that swept me off my feet and changed my life forever."

Gigi absorbed the words I shared with her, taking them in with thoughtful consideration.

"Georgia, what's really on your mind?"

"What do you mean, Dad?"

"I know you didn't just come here to ask how I knew your mother was the one."

She didn't say anything. I watched her eyes land on the photo of Birdie and me on our wedding day.

"Gigi, when you encounter the person you believe is your soulmate, the universe will reveal the true cost of your deepest desires."

I shared that authentic love takes work and effort. You will be confronted with the sacrifices and challenges required to attain what you truly seek. This process operates on the principle of honesty. Those who are unwilling to endure the trials of waiting or struggle may never find their true soulmate. Genuine love demands personal sacrifice and perseverance. You may find yourself waiting for your soulmate, and your paths may converge or diverge over months or even years.

"Like they diverged between Ben and I?" she asked.

"Something like that. But those who are willing to endure the emotional pain and hardship will come to understand the true nature of love and experience the profound blessing of genuine love." I reminded her.

I got up from my desk and walked around to lean against it. Gigi remained seated, looking intently at the portraits on my desk.

"Peach, I have to ask you: is your love truly worth the effort? The choice is yours."

Gigi's gaze shifted from the portraits to me, a soft smile playing on the corners of her lips. She took a moment to gather her thoughts before responding.

"Dad," she began, her voice steady but filled with ardor, "love is never easy, but it's always worth it. It's worth the late-night conversations and the compromise. It's worth the laughter and the tears. It's worth the moments of doubt because it's in those moments that you learn and grow together. Love isn't just a feeling; it's a choice we make every day to be there for each other, to support and uplift one another. And yes, Dad, my love for Ben is worth every effort because he makes me a better person, and together, we're stronger."

Her words hung in the air, a witness to the depth of her feelings.

"I think you have your answer then, peach. Be happy. That's all I've ever wanted for you and Daisie."

Gigi rose from her chair, her movements graceful yet filled with a quiet strength. Without uttering a single word, she enfolded me in a warm clutch. I returned the embrace, feeling the comfort of her presence against my chest, a bittersweet reminder of how quickly time passes. My darling daughters were growing up before my eyes. Daisie had already sealed her fate in marriage, and now it was Gigi's turn. As I held her close, a wave of poignancy washed over me, mingled with a sense of pride.

Gigi and I had always shared a special bond, like two peas in a pod. She possessed a fierce bullheadedness, inherited perhaps from Birdie, but beneath that determination lay a heart as tender and loving as my own. She was a tornado of chaos and wild joy, a force of nature that filled our lives with laughter and light. As I held her in my arms,

I couldn't help but feel an overwhelming sense of gratitude for the privilege of being her father. Gigi was more than just my daughter; she was my confidante, my ally, my source of endless joy. And as I prepared to give her away to the man she loved, I knew deep in my heart that she was ready for this new era of her life.

87
BEN

Five years had slipped by since our last days in California, and the passage of time had only deepened my sense of regret. The memory of that fateful day when I had let Gigi walk away at eighteen still stung. I often wondered, with a heavy heart, whether I could have fought harder for her, for us. We had been so young, so full of dreams and uncertainties.

But Gigi had reassured me with her calm and forgiving voice that it had been no one's fault. We were exactly where we were meant to be now, she had said. I had needed to learn to let go of the past to embrace the present and what we had together.

Returning to California had felt like stepping into a time capsule where everything seemed to have paused just for us. The warmth of Gigi's family had enveloped me like a familiar embrace, their acceptance as genuine as it was immediate. It had been as if the years apart were mere whispers in the wind, and we were effortlessly reunited. That fall of 1977, Daisie and Travis had gotten married. Their wedding had been a celebration that shimmered with magic and possibility. The backyard of her parents' home had been transformed into an enchanting venue, with fairy lights draped among the trees and floral arrangements adding vibrant splashes of color to the lush greenery. The air had been filled with the soft hum of conversations and the gentle strains of a string quartet.

As I had sat in one of the elegantly set chairs, my eyes had been drawn to Gigi walking down the aisle. The sunlight had filtered through the canopy of trees, casting a golden glow around her. Her gown had flowed gracefully with each step, and she had moved with a serene elegance that had taken my breath away. In that moment, I had imagined what it would have been like if she were walking toward me, envisioning a future where we might have been the ones exchanging vows. Gigi had embodied everything I had ever dreamed of in a life partner. The sight of her in that idyllic setting had been a touching reminder of the future we had once dreamed of and the life we had yet to build together. It had been as though the universe had conjured this moment just for me—a bittersweet reflection on what might have been and a poignant reminder of the love that had still lingered in my heart.

But as life often does, it had its own plans. Reflecting

on the years that had passed, each had brought its own set of challenges and changes. The fleeting moments of our youth had slowly given way to the realities of adulthood. Yet, as if guided by fate itself, I had found myself entering a new chapter of my life—one that had led Gigi and me back together. Our connection had remained strong, and our mutual longing for something more had finally brought us to this moment.

In the summer of 1980, standing on the precipice of our future together, Gigi and I had decided to take the leap. The day of our wedding had dawned bright and clear, a perfect reflection of the joy and anticipation we had felt.

The ceremony had been held at our local church, a place filled with cherished memories and a comforting sense of home. Gigi had looked radiant in a delicate lace gown that had seemed to shimmer with every movement. The air had been filled with the scent of fresh blossoms and the soft strains of a violin, creating a serene and intimate atmosphere. As she had walked down the aisle toward me, my heart had raced with the same excitement and wonder I had felt all those years ago.

As we had sealed our vows with a kiss, surrounded by friends and family, it had been clear that the journey had been worth every twist and turn. The love that had lingered had been a testament to the enduring power and beauty of finding one's way back to where it all began.

88
GIGI

Each morning, my thoughts gently drifted back to the day I first met Ben, a day that felt both distant and intimately close. I often wished I could fast-forward past the chapter where we parted ways—because, ultimately, the present was what mattered most. Ben was now my husband, and that was what truly counted.

When we returned from our grand adventures around the world, it felt as though every piece of our lives had effortlessly fallen into place. Reconnecting with our families was a joyous reunion; the laughter and shared memories felt like a warm embrace.

We celebrated Daisie and Travis's wedding with hearts brimming with happiness, and a year later, we marveled at the arrival of their beautiful baby boy. Soon, their family grew even sweeter with the birth of a little girl. Ben and I had chosen a summer wedding, and the memory of that day remained vividly etched in my mind. I could still see the fragrant blooms that adorned the church aisles, their vibrant colors and delicate scents blending with the golden rays of the summer sun. As I glided down the aisle with my father by my side, I recalled his whimsical idea of turning the moment into something extraordinary. He had envisioned a playful twist: setting up chairs along the tarmac, transforming the aisle into a grand flight down the runway.

I vividly remembered the day he first proposed this unconventional idea. My mother's voice had cut through the room with firm resolve.

"Roger, no daughter of mine is flying down an aisle. She is getting married right here on the ground," she declared, her tone brooking no argument.

Though I had no intention of boarding a plane for my wedding procession, I admired my father's creativity and, more importantly, his deep passion for flying. It was part of what made him so uniquely himself. In the end, I walked down the grand church aisle in my mother's shimmering lace dress, feeling the weight of tradition and the warmth of love in every step. The ceremony itself was a beautiful testament to our love, the air around us shimmering with joy. As the final vows were exchanged and the ceremony concluded, the celebration continued in a uniquely touching way.

After heartfelt farewells from our dear guests—Daisie, Travis, my parents, Ben's parents, and siblings—we were guided to Camarillo Airport. There, to our delightful surprise, my father had orchestrated a charming spectacle. A majestic plane stood ready, its side proudly emblazoned with "Just Married" in bright letters. From the ground, our loved ones watched with beaming smiles as Ben and I ascended into the sky, embarking on our journey together. The scene felt like a perfect blend of our dreams and cherished traditions, a soaring beginning to our shared adventure.

Ben and I celebrated two years of marriage before we welcomed our first child, a boy, into our lives. Our family grew steadily from that moment on. We had found a charming home in a picturesque neighborhood, just a few towns away from our parents, eager to create a family of our own and watch our children grow.

The memory of announcing my pregnancy is as clear as day. My heart raced with excitement as I dialed my mother's number, my hands trembling slightly. When I finally heard her voice, I could barely contain my joy. As I shared the news, her response was immediate and filled with emotion. Her voice cracked with happy tears, and I could almost picture the tears of joy streaming down her face. It felt as though she was born to be a grandmother, her joy and love palpable in every word. Over the years, she and my father had become the doting grandparents we had always hoped for. Their dedication was evident in the way they lovingly cared for our children, as well as Daisie and Travis's.

I watched with a warm heart as my parents showered

our children with the same love and attention they had always given Daisie and Travis's kids. Their affection created a growing circle of love that seemed to expand with each passing year.

Growing up came with its own set of challenges, but watching our parents age presented a different kind of difficulty. As Ben and I grew older, so did our parents. Their once lively energy began to wane, replaced by the inevitable signs of aging. The vibrant spark that had always been a part of them gradually dimmed, and their movements became slower, their voices softer. It was a somber reminder of the passage of time and the bittersweet reality of watching the people who had once been our pillars of strength become more fragile. As Ben and I faced the inevitable changes in our parents, we also found ourselves navigating the challenges of our own lives and responsibilities. The weight of their aging and the responsibilities of our growing family began to intersect, shaping our journey in unexpected ways.

With each passing year, life seemed to unfold new chapters—some filled with joy, others with trials. As we confronted these changes, it became clear that our own story was about to take another significant turn. The strength and love that had defined our family and sustained us through so much would now guide us through the evolving challenges that lay ahead. And so, as we embraced the future with a mix of anticipation and trepidation, we prepared ourselves for the next chapter of our lives—a chapter that would bring new beginnings, unforeseen obstacles, and the continual evolution of our family's story.

89
BIRDIE
TEN YEARS LATER
YEAR: 1990

Sitting at my vanity, as the soft morning light filtered through the lace curtains, my thoughts drifted back to Gigi's wedding day. It was one of those moments in life that stays with you, the kind you revisit often, each time uncovering a new layer of emotion. Even now, years later, the memories of that day were as vivid as ever, etched into my heart like a delicate engraving.

I remember preparing for the ceremony, my hands steady but my heart fluttering with a mixture of joy and bittersweet nostalgia. As I brushed my hair, the rhythmic strokes of the brush seemed to echo the rhythm of my thoughts, each stroke bringing forth a new memory.

The scent of lavender, so familiar, lingered in the air,

just as it had that day. I could almost feel the weight of my own wedding dress in my hands, the cool silk smooth against my skin, as I recalled the morning of my wedding so many years before. My mind conjured up an image of my mother, her face glowing with pride and love as she watched me prepare to walk down the aisle. Her eyes, so full of warmth, held a depth of emotion I hadn't fully understood until I found myself in her shoes, watching my daughters take that same monumental step. I hadn't known then just how powerful that look was, how it was a mix of pride, love, and the bittersweet realization that your child is stepping into a new chapter of life.

When Daisie married Travis, the day was filled with the simple joys she had always cherished. We held the wedding in our backyard, beneath the old oak tree that had seen so many of our family's milestones. The laughter of our guests danced on the breeze, mingling with the gentle rustling of leaves, filling the air with a melody of happiness that seemed to ripple across the garden. Daisie's smile, radiant and full of love, was all I needed to see to know that she had found her perfect match. Travis was a good man, kind and devoted, and I couldn't have asked for more for my daughter. But when it came time for Gigi to marry Ben, there was something different in the air. It wasn't that I loved Gigi more than Daisie—not at all—but watching your youngest get married brings with it a certain poignancy, a realization that time is moving on, no matter how much you wish it would slow down. It felt like the closing of a chapter in our family's story, a gentle reminder that the years were slipping by.

A TIMELESS TAPESTRY

Gigi and Ben chose to marry in our local church here in California, where Roger and I had settled after so many years in New York. The church wasn't grand, but it had a warmth and familiarity that made it feel like home. I remember the way the sunlight streamed through the stained-glass windows, casting a kaleidoscope of colors onto the floor. It wasn't the same church where Roger and I had exchanged our vows all those years ago, but there was a comfort in knowing that Gigi and Ben were creating their own memories, just as we had done.

As I watched Roger walk Gigi down the aisle that day, a swell of pride filled my heart, so strong it brought tears to my eyes. The way he looked at her, his eyes shining with the love only a father can have for his daughter, was a sight I would never forget.

Gigi, with her lace veil trailing behind her, looked every bit the radiant bride. And Ben, standing at the altar, his eyes fixed on her with a look of pure devotion, made my heart swell with happiness. Once they reached the end of the aisle, a memory of my own wedding day flashed before me.

Reflecting on Gigi's wedding day now, I can see how much that moment meant to all of us. It wasn't just about the wedding itself—it was about the love, the family, the years we had spent together leading up to that day. Watching Gigi and Ben exchange their vows, seeing the way they looked at each other with such tenderness and understanding, I knew they were going to have a beautiful life together. And as a mother, there was no greater gift than knowing your children are loved.

Taking a deep breath, I dabbed at the corners of my eyes, remembering how full of emotion that day had been—joy, pride, a touch of nostalgia—but above all, it had been filled with love. The love of family, of lifelong partners, and of the memories we had created together. That day would always hold a special place in my heart, a day when everything felt right in the world.

* * *

TWENTY-SEVEN YEARS LATER
YEAR: 2017

Time had a way of slipping by unnoticed, each day blending into the next until the years had woven themselves into a rich tapestry of experiences and memories. Now, as I sat in the living room of the home that Roger and I had built together, surrounded by the artifacts of a life well-lived, I found myself reflecting on how quickly things had changed. I was eighty-seven, and Roger was eighty-nine.

The house was quieter now, filled with echoes of laughter and conversations that had once been a constant. Gigi, Ben, Daisie, and Travis had built their own lives, and as I looked at the family photos that adorned the walls, I saw the progression of time etched in their smiles and the way their faces had matured. The youthful exuberance of their wedding days had given way to a deep, abiding love.

Gigi often spoke of the lessons she had learned and the growth she had experienced since those early days. And

A TIMELESS TAPESTRY

Ben, always the steady rock beside her, had become a father himself, bringing a new generation into the family journey. I'm in awe at the young adults they have become and feel a sense of gratitude for the moments we've all shared together. The passage of time had its own rhythm, one that I now understood with greater clarity. The years had been kind to us, allowing us to build a legacy. And as I sit here, reminiscing about the past, I find comfort in knowing that the love Roger and I nurtured and the lessons we learned continue to shape the future.

90
ROGER

Watching Daisie and Gigi grow had been like unfolding a cherished photograph, each frame revealing new layers of joy and pride. I remembered Daisie, once a timid teenager, stepping onto the stage for her school play. Her face, a mix of anxiety and determination, had been illuminated by the spotlight, casting her in a warm, golden glow as she delivered her lines.

Gigi, with her ever-curious eyes, had approached each new challenge with an infectious excitement that turned everyday moments into small adventures. Now, as I sat on the porch, the scent of freshly cut grass blending with the aroma of Sunday morning donuts from the local shop, my heart swelled with a different kind of pride.

The backyard had been alive with the sounds of our grandchildren's laughter, their voices mingling with the chirping of birds. Birdie, her apron dusted with flour, had patiently guided them through baking, her every gesture reflecting a lifetime of love and tradition. Family camping trips had become a cherished ritual, the crackling campfire and the scent of pine trees framing stories told beneath a starlit sky. Fishing trips had offered a quieter, reflective contrast, with the early morning stillness broken only by the gentle tug on the line as the next generation learned the art of patience and the thrill of the catch.

These moments, rich and fleeting, had been the heart of grandparenthood, captured in the vibrant scenes of family traditions and the profound simplicity of shared experiences.

Birdie had come into my life like a blessing from above. When I first met her, I could never have imagined that she would not only become the love of my life but also effortlessly care for our adoring daughters. If someone had told me back then that all of this would happen, I wouldn't have known what to say—I'm not even sure I would have believed them.

Every now and then, memories sprinkled in, and some days I wasn't sure if they were real or not. But then I'd bring it up to Birdie, and she'd smile at me—in her smile, I knew it was real. It was a story I'd told her many times.

I liked to sit out on the back porch in my favorite chair, looking out at the mountaintops. As I took a deep breath and closed my eyes, I thought about the first time Birdie had walked into my life. We hadn't met yet, but I knew who she was, always feeling that she was someone I had to know. Visions of crisp autumn days came to mind—the kind where the air was laced with the scent of fallen leaves and the sky stretched out in a brilliant expanse of blue.

Sometimes in my dreams, I stood at the edge of the park, back on Millikin's campus, just watching the world move around me. And that's when she appeared—Birdie. She was a vision of warmth and grace, her auburn hair catching the sunlight like a flame. Birdie would look at me with those kind, knowing eyes, and something would shift inside of me. I might never be able to put it into words—how do you describe the moment when you begin to believe in fate? But there she was; Birdie was always there. We didn't know it back then, but all those little moments had allowed something to grow between us.

I sat on the old, creaking porch, bathed in the warm glow of the setting sun, allowing myself to get lost in a sea of memories from those early days. The recollections of the crisp autumn days spent at Millikin's campus washed over me, and I felt an immense sense of gratitude for the serendipitous twist of fate that had brought Birdie into my life. I couldn't help but appreciate the significant role she had played in shaping my life. Her presence, like a blazing sunburst amidst the ordinary, had set in motion a beautiful chain of events that had led us to where we were now. Our love, like a sturdy oak tree, had weathered the passing of countless seasons, each one leaving its mark and adding a new layer to the fabric of our shared history. It stood as a testament to the enduring nature of love, inspiring hope for the future.

The vivid memories of our early years together had been etched into the very core of my being—strolling hand in hand through fields bathed in golden light, sharing dreams under vast, starlit skies, and fashioning a home resonant with the joyful melodies of laughter and love. These memories, like precious gems, had added unique beauty to our shared history.

As I gazed out at the imposing mountains and the glassy pond that held echoes of our past, I realized that these moments were not just memories but the very essence of our extraordinary journey together. The pond, with its tranquil waters and the faint whispers of days long gone, felt like a sacred sanctuary where the essence of our shared history hung in the air, blending seamlessly with the promise of new beginnings. It was a place where the past and present intertwined, serving as a poignant reminder of the timeless nature of our love.

With the first signs of spring starting to emerge, a renewed sense of hope and revival welled up within me. The world around us was awakening, bursting back to life, much like our love had done over time. The ever-changing seasons mirrored the incredible journey we had embarked on together—a testament to the unwavering resilience and exquisite beauty of a love that had blossomed from those early, uncertain moments into something enduring and profoundly beautiful.

Taking a deep, nourishing breath, I welcomed the tranquility of the moment, fully comprehending that Birdie and I's love was not simply a part of our past but a living, breathing force that would continue to shape our lives in the years to come.

Rising from the time-worn bench, I cast my eyes over the familiar landscape, feeling a profound sense of peace. I knew that our story was far from over—it was, in many ways, just beginning anew.

91
GIGI
YEAR: 2020

What my parents shared was nothing short of legendary. My mother was my father's soulmate, the love of his life. Together, they forged a bond that transcended time and space, creating a kingdom built on the pillars of love, kindness, strength, and an unfaltering belief in each other. Their love story was the hallmark of fairytales, the kind that poets wrote about and dreamers yearned for.

As their daughter, I always felt blessed to witness the depth of their love. It was a love that weathered storms and soared to the highest peaks, a love that inspired and uplifted everyone in its presence.

I Daisie and I were privileged to be part of their world, to bask in the warmth of their affection, and to learn from their example. Their love was a pharos of hope in a world filled with qualms and darkness. It reminded me that true love knows no bounds and has the power to conquer even the greatest obstacles. As I stood on the threshold of my own trek into love, I couldn't help but feel a surge of emotions at the thought of following in their footsteps and experiencing a love as acute and enduring as theirs.

The weight of time pressed down on me like a heavy burden, reminding me that life is unpredictable and often unfair. I had always taken comfort in the illusion that time would be on our side, and I wouldn't have to say goodbye until I was ready. But as I stood in the backyard, watching my father sitting in his wheelchair, so frail and vulnerable, I realized how fleeting and fragile life truly is.

"Dad," I called out softly, my voice barely above a whisper as I approached him.

He didn't respond, his gaze fixed on the distant mountains, lost in a world I couldn't reach.

"He can't hear you, Georgia," Birdie's voice broke the silence, her words a painful reminder of the harsh reality we were living in. He was still alive, but it felt like everything else around him was slipping away, as if the world had turned gray and his light was slowly dimming.

It began with the cruel whispers of early dementia, stealing pieces of his memory, and soon the harsh reality of cancer invaded, casting a shadow over our lives. I felt a lump form in my throat, choking back the tears threatening to spill over. It was a cruel twist of fate to see the man who had always been my pillar of strength reduced to a mere shadow of his former self. In that moment, time stood still, and all I could do was hold on to the memories of better days, praying that somehow, some way, we could find the strength to weather this storm together.

***

YEAR: 2021

Doctors said he had six months to live, but we were bless with a year. That extra time felt like a precious gift, a series of stolen moments we cherished deeply. Each day, we gathered around him, sharing stories, laughter, and tears, trying to hold on to every second. Despite the heartache, those twelve months were filled with love and connection, creating memories that would sustain us long after he was gone.

I remember mornings spent sitting by his side, the sunlight filtering through the curtains as we talked about everything and nothing. Some days, he remembered it all, and other days, it was like he was grasping for the past. His voice, though weaker, still carried the warmth and wisdom I had always known. We laughed at old family stories, reminiscing about the adventures we had shared and the lessons he had taught me. He would smile, a twinkle in his eye, as if savoring each memory along with me. Afternoons were for quiet reflection. I would wheel him out to the backyard where he could see the mountains he loved so much. We would sit in silence, the gentle rustling of leaves and the distant chirping of birds creating a serene picture. Sometimes, I would read to him from his favorite books. Even when his eyes would close, I knew he was listening, absorbing every word.

Evenings were the hardest. As the sun's glow diminished, a sense of melancholy would settle in. Birdie, Daisie, Travis, Ben, and I would gather around, sharing a meal and trying to keep the atmosphere light. But the reality of our situation was never far from our minds. We would hold hands, drawing strength from one another, our unity deepening with each passing day.

One of the most poignant moments came on a cool autumn evening. I found Roger staring at an old photo album, his fingers tracing the edges of the pictures. He looked up at me, his eyes filled with a mixture of sadness and contentment.

"Peach," he said softly, "I want you to remember something. Life is full of uncertainties, but love is the one constant. Hold on to it, cherish it, and let it guide you."

Those words became my anchor. As the year progressed, I saw the toll his illness took on him, but I also saw the incredible strength he possessed. He faced each day with a grace and courage that inspired all of us.

The final days were a blur of emotions. We knew the end was near, yet we tried to remain strong for him and each other. When the time finally came, we were by his side, holding his hand, whispering our love and gratitude. His passing was peaceful, a gentle release from the pain he had endured. At first, a sense of anger consumed me—the stages of grief can really take a toll, and I was angry that he had got cancer. It wasn't fair. Bless Ben's heart for being there for me as I went through the roller coaster of emotions. One day, I was talking to Daisie, who seemed to be handling things better than me.

"I don't understand why good people get cancer," I said angrily.

"I don't either, Gigi."

"Why did he have to die? I wasn't ready," I said.

"None of us were. That's the part about death no one can prepare you for. But think of it this way: God reached out his hand to welcome Dad home."

Daisie was way more levelheaded than me. She always had been. I allowed my emotions to swallow me whole sometimes.

"I guess he lived a good life," I replied.

"He did, Gigi. He really did," Daisie said.

When he passed, he was ninety-one. In the weeks that followed, the house felt emptier, but the memories of that final year lingered like a comforting embrace. We had been given the gift of time, and in that time, we had reaffirmed the man he was to us all. Roger's legacy lived on in our hearts, a testament to the power of love.

As we came to terms with the passing of a cherished individual, we found ourselves standing at the crossroads where sorrow and joy intersected. We grieved the palpable absence that reverberated through our lives, yet we also found ourselves compelled to honor and exalt the impact they had left behind. Each reflection on their lifetime of accomplishments, their embodiment of virtue, and their contributions to humanity served as a poignant reminder of the legacy they had woven. It was during these times we were acutely attuned to the sanctity of existence, fostering a deepened appreciation for the preciousness inherent in every breath and heartbeat.

While reflecting on that year, I realized how it had shaped me. It taught me the importance of savoring every moment, expressing love openly, and finding strength in the face of adversity. My father's wisdom and love would forever be my guiding light, a source of comfort and inspiration as I navigated the world without him.

92
```
ROGER
YEARS: 2020-2021
```

There comes a time in every man's life when the days stretch out behind him like a long shadow, and he begins to see the end of the road ahead. For me, that moment came on a crisp autumn afternoon, sitting in the doctor's office with Birdie by my side. The words "dementia" and "cancer" hung heavy in the air, cutting through the silence like a knife. It felt surreal, as if I were watching someone else's life unfold. But this was my reality, and the road ahead suddenly seemed much shorter.

After leaving the office that day, Birdie clung to my arm, her grip tighter than usual. I could feel her fear, her unspoken dread of what was to come. She didn't need to say anything; we had always been able to communicate without words. The thought of leaving her behind, of not being there to protect her, was more terrifying than any diagnosis.

The days that followed were a blur of emotions. I tried to stay strong, for Birdie, for the girls but there were moments when the weight of it all threatened to crush me. I would find myself staring at my reflection, trying to recognize the man I had been—strong, capable, full of life. But the man looking back at me seemed like a stranger, worn down by time and the knowledge of what lay ahead. It wasn't long before the memory lapses began. At first, they were small, almost unnoticeable—forgetting where I put my keys, struggling to recall a word. But as time went on, the gaps in my memory grew wider, and I began to lose pieces of myself. The fear of what was happening gnawed at me, but I tried to hide it, not wanting to burden Birdie any more than she already was. But she saw through me, like she always did, and her eyes would fill with a sadness that tore at my heart.

Even as my mind began to betray me, there was one thing I never forgot: the love I had for Birdie. It was as if that love was woven into the very fabric of my being, something that could never be taken away, no matter how much I faded. I would wake up in the middle of the night, my mind lost in a fog and reach out for her, needing to feel her warmth, to reassure myself that she was still there. She always was, her presence grounding me in a world that was slowly slipping away. I found solace in the moments we spent together, sitting quietly on the porch or walking hand in hand through the garden.

Even when the words wouldn't come, the silence between us was filled with a deep understanding, a connection that went beyond memory or time. She would look at me with those beautiful eyes, and I would see the girl I fell in love with all those years ago, the one who had captured my heart and never let go. There were days when the fog lifted, and I felt like myself again. On those days, I would hold Birdie close, trying to imprint every detail of her face, her voice, her laughter into my mind, as if by doing so, I could keep those memories safe from the darkness that was slowly encroaching. I would tell her stories from our youth, reminiscing about the adventures we had shared, the love we had built together. Her laughter was like music to my ears, a melody that anchored me to the present, to her.

But the good days were becoming fewer, and the bad ones were harder to bear. The pain from the cancer was a constant reminder of what was coming, and I could see the toll it was taking on Birdie. She tried to hide it, But I knew her too well.

I wanted to comfort her, to tell her that everything would be alright but I couldn't bring myself to lie to her. We both knew that the end was near, and that knowledge was like a shadow hanging over us. With the passing of weeks into months, I began to accept what was happening. It wasn't easy, but I found a strange peace in the knowledge that my time was running out. I had lived a good life, a full life, and I had been blessed with a love that few people ever find. That love was my anchor, my constant, even as everything else slipped away. There was one moment, late at night, when I found myself sitting alone in the dark, my mind clearer than it had been in weeks. I thought about Birdie, about the life we had built together and I felt an overwhelming sense of gratitude. I had been given more time than I deserved, more love than I could have ever hoped for. And even as my body and mind began to fail me, that love remained, a beacon in the darkness.

I knew that soon, I would be leaving Birdie and the girls behind, and the thought filled me with a deep sorrow. But I also knew that they would be alright. Birdie was strong, stronger than she realized, and she had the girls by her side. They would grieve, but they would also find a way to move forward, to continue living and loving, just as we had taught them.

In those final days, as the world around me began to fade, I held on to the love I had for Birdie, drawing strength from it. It was the last thing I had left, the one thing that even dementia and cancer couldn't take from me.

And in that love, I found peace. Knowing that it would continue to guide me, even as I slipped away.

The day I finally let go, I wasn't afraid. Birdie was by my side, holding my hand, her touch a reminder of the life we had shared. I closed my eyes, letting the memories wash over me—our first kiss, the birth of our daughters, the quiet moments of joy that had filled our days. And as the darkness closed in, I felt her love wrap around me, carrying me gently into the unknown.

93
GIGI
DATE: AUTUMN 2021

The backyard felt different now, quieter somehow. The mountains that once held the warmth of shared memories with my father now seemed distant as if the landscape itself had shifted in his absence. Standing there in my red dress—the color my father always said suited me best—I couldn't help but reflect on how much had changed since those final days with him.

Red had been his favorite, a color he often associated with strength and passion. Wearing it now felt like a small tribute to him, a way to keep his spirit close as I navigated life without him.

Time had a way of softening the edges of grief, turning sharp pain into a dull ache that lingered in the background of everyday life. It had been months since my father passed, and while the world had moved on, I found myself still grappling with the void he left behind. But this was different from the raw grief I felt immediately after his passing. Now, it was a quiet, contemplative sorrow—a recognition of the empty spaces he used to fill.

The days of mourning had given way to a kind of acceptance, though not without difficulty. I had returned to my routines, found joy in small moments, and even laughed again. Yet, there was an undeniable shift within me. My father's absence was a constant, a shadow that followed me, a reminder of the impermanence of life. Flying had once been our shared escape, the skies offering a freedom that grounded us in a way nothing else could. My father had taught me to fly, and those moments in the cockpit, with the world spread out beneath us, were some of my most cherished memories. Now, whenever I took to the skies, it was bittersweet—his presence felt so vividly beside me, yet painfully absent at the same time. The open-air that once brought exhilaration now carried a sense of loss, a reminder that while I could soar to great heights, I could never truly escape the gravity of his absence.

As I stood in the backyard, I realized that this place, which once brought so much comfort, now carried a different weight. The memories we had made here were no longer a source of pain but of quiet reflection. The stories he had told, the wisdom he had imparted—they remained with me, deeply rooted in my soul. But I no longer sought solace in the past. Instead, I found myself looking forward, contemplating how to honor his legacy as I moved into the future. I thought back to 1977, a time when life felt full of promise, and the future stretched out like an open road. Ben and I were just twenty-three, returning to California after years of exploring the world on our own terms. My father was still in the prime of his life, a man of strength and certainty who had always been my anchor. Back then, I couldn't have imagined a day when he wouldn't be there, guiding me with his steady hand.

Ben and I were young, in love, and eager to build a life together. I remember how we would sit with my father on the porch, discussing our dreams and plans for the future. He would listen intently, offering advice when asked, but always encouraging us to follow our own path.

His love for my mother was evident in everything he did. They were partners in every sense of the word. It was the kind of love story that shaped my understanding of what a marriage should be. My mind flashes back to 1980, just a year after we returned, Ben and I were married. I was twenty-five, full of hope and excitement for the life we were about to create. My father was there, beaming with pride as he walked me down the aisle. It was a perfect day, surrounded by family and friends, with the man who had been my first hero giving me away to the man who would become my partner for life.

We had three children: two boys, Wesley and Grant, and a girl, Autumn—named because Fall was my father's favorite season. Our home was a place of love and laughter, and my parents were an integral part of that. They were the doting grandparents, always there to support us, to share in our triumphs, and to help us through the tough times. As the years went by, our family grew. Daisie and Travis had children of their own—a girl, Paige, and a boy, Tyler—adding another layer of love to our lives. My father reveled in his role as a grandfather, as did my mother in her role as a grandmother—passing on their wisdom and values to the next generation.

But time, as it always does, moved forward. My father, once so strong and full of life, began to age. It wasn't until his late 80s that we received the news no one ever wants to hear—a diagnosis that would change everything. Daisie was sixty-seven, and I was sixty-six when he passed. Our father left behind a legacy that would forever be a part of who we were.

Now, as I stood in this backyard, the place where so many memories were made, I felt the weight of those years. The laughter of our children, the sound of my father's voice, and the warmth of his embrace—were all still here. Ben understood the depth of my loss, having loved my father as much as I did. Together, we faced the challenges of life, just as my parents had done before us. And now, as grandparents ourselves, we found joy in watching our grandchildren grow, knowing that a part of my father lived on in them. In many ways, my father's spirit had never left us. It was in the way Ben and I navigated our marriage, in the lessons we taught our children, and in the love we shared with our grandchildren.

I took one more look at the backyard before walking back inside. I knew that the best way to honor my father was to live my life with the same passion and dedication that he had shown every day—to cherish the moments, love deeply, and always look forward, even when the past seemed to call me back. My father's journey had ended, but mine was still unfolding. And I knew, without a doubt, that he would be with me every step of the way.

94
BIRDIE
DATE: AUTUMN 2021

Roger Scott was not merely a name on a page; he embodied an unstoppable energy, a fire that radiated warmth and light, igniting joy in everyone around him, and he was the love of my life.

Our meeting in college marked the beginning of an enthralling journey, as his profound passion for airplanes and his inexhaustible enthusiasm for life captivated me. Roger's unique perspective on the world combined with his intellect and mischief infused each day with an irresistible sense of adventure.

Old age, once a distant whisper on an unseen path, had arrived as steadily as each footfall carries one forward. My hair, now a flowing tapestry of silver, reflected every shade from the glimmer of newly minted coins to the muted gray of weathered slate, marking this passage. Sometimes, closing my eyes, I would listen to the resonance of my voice still tinged with the quick humor and joy of bygone days. In those moments, I envisioned Roger and me as kids again, his mischievous grin lighting up his face as he spun some tall tale or irreverent joke. He was like that, always full of life and wonder.

When we met in college, a serendipitous encounter that felt like destiny, his eyes had sparkled with a blend of intellect and kindness that drew me in from the moment we first spoke. I recall it was autumn, and the campus was alive with the vibrant hues of falling leaves. We spent hours discussing books, dreams, and our visions of the future, often losing track of time in the golden glow of the setting sun. Our courtship was a dance of discovery, filled with late-night study sessions, stolen kisses under the stars, and endless conversations that made the world feel simultaneously vast and intimate. Roger had a unique way of making the ordinary seem extraordinary. He listened with an intensity that made me feel like the most important person in the world, his presence a balm to my soul.

Our wedding day was a simple yet profound celebration of our love. Surrounded by close friends and family, we vowed to walk through life together. I still remember the way Roger looked at me as I walked down the aisle, his eyes brimming with a love so deep it seemed to encompass the entire universe. That look promised a lifetime of shared joys and challenges, a promise we kept through all the years that followed.

We built a life rich with love and laughter, raising two

beautiful daughters, Daisie and Gigi. They were the light of our lives, each day a new adventure with them. Roger's career as a pilot flourished, and I stood by his side, our dreams intertwined. We traveled the world, explored new horizons, and created memories that would last a lifetime.

As the years passed, our love only deepened, a steady flame that warmed us through every storm. We faced the trials of life together, and our bond grew stronger with each challenge we overcame. Roger's diagnosis of cancer was a cruel twist of fate, a stark reminder of the fragility of life.

Aging was inevitable, but I had always believed we would grow old together, hand in hand, until the very end. In his final year, we made the most of every moment.

Despite the shadow of his illness, we found joy in the small things like a shared cup of tea, a walk in the garden, and the comfort of each other's presence. Roger's spirit never waned; he remained the same vibrant soul I had fallen in love with all those years ago.

One autumn evening, as we sat in the garden watching the sunset, he took my hand in his, his grip still strong despite his frailty.

"Birdie," his voice a gentle whisper, "our love story is the greatest tale I've ever written."

Tears filled my eyes as I looked at him, the man who had been my everything. "It's been a beautiful story, Roger," I replied, my heart full of both sorrow and gratitude.

Roger passed away on a crisp winter morning, the first rays of sunlight breaking through the clouds. His passing left an emptiness in my heart, a void that would never be filled. But as I sat by the window, looking out at the garden he had loved so much, I felt his presence in every rustle of the leaves, every whisper of the wind. Our journey together had ended, but the legacy of our love would live on. Roger Scott was the love of my life, and he always would be. The memories of our time together, the laughter, the tears, the quiet moments of connection, would remain etched in my heart forever.

Reflecting on the years we had shared, I felt a profound sense of gratitude. Life had been a journey, and though it had its share of sorrows, it had been beautiful because we had walked it together. Roger's love had been my guiding light, and as I faced the future without him, I knew that light would continue to shine, illuminating the path ahead.

In the twilight of my years, I often found myself drifting back to the beginning, to that autumn day on the college campus where it all started. The echoes of our laughter, the warmth of his embrace, the shared dreams and whispered promises—they were all there, woven into the fabric of my being. Roger Scott had been my partner, my confidante, my greatest love. And though he was no longer by my side, his presence was a constant in my heart, a testament to a love that was truly eternal.

★ ★ ★

DATE: EARLY SPRING 2022

A couple of months after Roger passed, I decided to fly back to New York. Gigi came with me. I took her to our old stomping grounds. We drove past the house that Roger and I had almost bought before we decided to chase our dreams.

"That is some house," Gigi remarked.

"It was," I said, remembering the day Roger came home beaming. We rushed to look at the house and even put in an offer. We thought it would be our forever home, but life had other plans, which turned out to be the best thing to happen to us.

"Mom?" Gigi pulled me from my thoughts.

"Yes, dear," I replied.

"I know it may not seem like it right now, but I think it will get easier."

"I know, Gigi. And you're right. It doesn't seem like it right now."

"Thank you for giving Daisie and me the greatest gift," she said.

"And what's that, Gigi?"

"You and Dad…your love."

Tears welled in my eyes. "Oh, Gigi. Thank you for that." I pulled her closer, and we lingered in a hug. "If you don't mind, Gigi, I'd like to make one last stop today."

"I don't mind. Tell me where you would like to go?" she asked.

"Blue Haven Pond."

It didn't take long to get to the pond. Somehow, it looked the same, but different in so many ways. I got out and walked along the familiar path. Each tree stood like a figurine, a vibrant reflection of Roger's memories, their branches cradling the laughter we shared and the moments that shaped our lives together. My mind flashed back to many moons ago when Roger got down on one knee to propose. We were just kids back then.

I sat down on the weathered wooden bench overlooking the pond, my fingers absentmindedly tracing the patterns etched into its surface. As the last rays of the sun faded, bathing the landscape in hues of gold and crimson and reflecting on the tranquil water, the air was filled with the gentle rustling of leaves and the distant chirping of crickets, weaving a melodic tapestry that seemed to encapsulate the essence of the moment. I couldn't help but think about the statement that pulsated in my mind: *It was a great love, one for the ages.* The words held weight, carrying the bittersweet melody of a love that had weathered storms and stood the test of time. My heart swelled with a mix of emotions, memories flooding my thoughts like a cherished photo album.

My gaze drifted towards the horizon, where the last rays of sunlight reflected on the rippling water. I recalled the defining moments of our journey. Our vows were exchanged under a canopy of cherry blossoms, the challenges we faced hand in hand, and the quiet, tender moments spoke louder than any grand gesture. It was sometimes challenging. Life had a way of throwing curveballs, testing our commitment and resilience. Yet, through it all, our love remained steady. My heart skipped a beat as I remembered the whispered promises, the shared dreams, and the simple joy of waking up each day beside my soulmate.

A TIMELESS TAPESTRY

The passage of time had etched lines on our faces, but it had also deepened the connection between Roger and me. We had grown together. There were moments of doubt, of fear, but in the end, our love had prevailed, stronger and more profound.

I sat on the bench reading the letter Roger left for me after he passed. I must have been there for an hour before the stars emerged in the velvety sky. I closed my eyes, savoring the serenity of the moment. I felt the soft breeze against my face, carrying with it the essence of our shared history. It was a great love, one for the ages, a love that had stood tall against the sands of time, a testament to the enduring power of two hearts intertwined.

I smiled, my heart filled with gratitude for the journey Roger and I had walked together. In that quiet moment by the pond, I knew that our love was a story written in the stars, a tale whispered by the wind—*a timeless tapestry*.

ROGER'S LETTER

My Dearest Birdie,

If you're reading this, it means my time on this earth has come to an end. It's hard to find the words, knowing I won't be there to see your face as you read them. But there's one thing I need you to know—something that's been true every day for over seventy years: I have loved you with all my heart, and I always will.

Do you remember the day we met back in 1950, at Millikin University? You might remember the first time we truly met was at your Sorority house, but I remember you sitting under a big oak tree, your nose buried in a book, and I thought to myself, "That's the girl I'm going to spend my life with." You had this spark in your eyes, this quiet grace that drew me in from the moment I saw you. From our first date, I was hooked. We talked about everything—our dreams, our fears, the world we wanted to create together—and I knew, even then, that my life would never be the same.

Our college years were some of the bests of my life, filled with late-night study sessions, long walks around campus, and that unforgettable spring formal where you wore that blue dress, the one that made you look like a movie star. I was the luckiest man in the world when you agreed to be my girl. And as the years went by, that feeling never faded. We built a beautiful life together, Birdie. We got married, had Daisie and Gigi, and filled our home with love, laughter, and a few too many books. I loved you through every moment—through the milestones and the mundane, the highs and the lows. I loved you in every dance in our living room, in every road trip across the country, in every cup of coffee shared on the porch as the sun came up. As we grew older, I watched with awe as you navigated life's changes with the same grace and wisdom that first captivated me. Our hair turned grey, our steps slowed, but my love for you only grew stronger. I cherished every moment we had, knowing that we were living a love story that would last a lifetime.

And now, even though I've left this world, that love remains. Our story isn't over, Birdie. It's just moving to a new chapter. I'll be waiting for you, just as I waited for you under that oak tree all those years ago.

So, my darling Birdie, when you think of me, don't dwell on the sadness. Remember the laughter, the love, the life we shared. Hold on to those memories and know that I am with you in every smile, every tear, and every beat of your heart. Our love is timeless, eternal, and it will carry us through until we meet again.

With all my love, now and forever,
Roger

Thank you for journeying through these pages.

Your voice is part of the story now. Whether you found something that lingered in your mind or a detail that left you wondering, I would love to hear your thoughts.

Please share them in a review on Amazon or wherever you discovered this book.

With endless gratitude for your time and reflection.

ACKNOWLEDGMENTS

As I reflect on the journey of bringing *A Timeless Tapestry* to life, I am filled with gratitude for the many people who have been instrumental in this endeavor. To my beloved parents and grandparents, whose love has shown me what it means to believe in something timeless. The enduring romance between you has taught me that love is not merely a feeling, but a tapestry woven from moments of joy, perseverance, and shared dreams. Your relationships have been a testament to the beauty of commitment and the strength found in the true partnerships.

To my friends, your steadfast support has been my anchor throughout this creative journey. Whether through late-night brainstorming sessions, reading drafts, or simply being there to listen, your encouragement has fueled my passion and kept me moving forward. Your belief in me and my work has been a constant source of motivation, and I am deeply appreciative of your kindness and loyalty.

To my readers, your enthusiasm and connection to my story are the heart of this novel. Your support has not only made this journey possible but has also made every challenge worthwhile. Thank you for welcoming *A Timeless Tapestry* into your lives and for letting its characters and their stories become a part of your own.

With sincere thanks and all my love,

Kristen

ABOUT THE AUTHOR

Kristen is an accomplished author with a background in Journalism and Marketing. Her passion for storytelling and romance shines through in her well-received series, *La Vie En Rose* and its sequel, *City of Roses*. Originally from California, Kristen is captivated by the East Coast's charm, often setting her novels in the bustling streets of New York City. An aspiring traveler, she dreams of visiting Paris, a city that has long inspired her. When she isn't writing novels, Kristen shares her thoughts on fashion, recipes, and travel on her blog, SoCal Charm. With each new book, she continues to explore the intricate dance of love, secrets, and adventure, inviting readers into her vividly imagined worlds.

Kristen loves hearing from readers and connecting with them. If you'd like to stay updated on her latest books or share your favorite moments, you can follow her on social media:

Instagram: @socal_charm
TikTok: @authorkristen

www.ingramcontent.com/pod-product-compliance
Lightning Source LLC
LaVergne TN
LVHW041736060526
838201LV00046B/829